Santiago's Purple Skies
at Morning's Light

Santiago's Purple Skies at Morning's Light

Bernadette Gabay Dyer

First Edition

Hidden Brook Press
www.HiddenBrookPress.com
writers@HiddenBrookPress.com

Santiago's Purple Skies at Morning's Light
by Bernadette Gabay Dyer

Editor – Richard M. Grove
Cover Art – Bernadette Gabay Dyer
Cover Design – Richard M. Grove
Layout and Design – Richard M. Grove

Typeset in Garamond
Printed and bound in Canada
Distributed in USA by Ingram,
          in Canada by Hidden Brook Distribution

Library and Archives Canada Cataloguing in Publication

Title: Santiago's purple skies at morning's light / Bernadette Gabay Dyer.
Names: Dyer, Bernadette, author.
Identifiers: Canadiana (print) 2019018213X
          Canadiana (ebook) 20190182148
          ISBN 9781927725832 (softcover)
          ISBN 9781927725849 (EPUB)
          ISBN 9781927725856 (Kindle)
Subjects: LCGFT: Novels.
Classification: LCC PS8557.Y47 S26 2019 | DDC C813/.54—dc23

This novel
is dedicated to
the memory of my late, dear friends,
Daphne Steadman
and
Eleanor Hillman,
who both were passionate about life,
literacy and literature.

An Introduction to
Santiago's Purple Skies at Morning's Light
by Bernadette Gabay Dyer

When I started writing this novel, my intention was to pay tribute to my children who are half Irish and half Jamaican, and my Irish Friends. As a result of my meticulous research, and attention to detail, my publisher, Richard Grove, of Hidden Brook Press immediately sent me an email to inquire if my story was autobiographical or even a memoir, since the story resonated so well as such. I reassured him that the story was neither of those classifications but was purely a product of my imagination with absolutely no connection to my personal life.

This is exactly why I enjoy the creativity of writing, since it is how an artist can live and breath through their own invented characters, themes and plot. It is the permission we give ourselves, as writers, to suspend our own reality, and enjoy another, as we mold characters and their surroundings, both good and bad.

The story is seen through the eyes of Kathleen, a teenager, whose father as a young Irish-Canadian man, had visited Ireland in search of his ancestry. In his search he happened upon a extraordinary woman in the wild and rustic countryside, in a place he thought might have been an abode of fairies. The tale follows him home to Canada to a tiny village in Northern Ontario called Siddon, where we are given a taste of his isolated existence, far from towns and cities. His home is surrounded by natural uncultivated land where wild flowers bloom, and woodland quickly descended into forests in a wilderness inhabited by animals, both threatening and docile. This is a land where even spirits might dwell and the haunting cry of a wolf is often heard.

Now an older teen, Kathleen, as a result of fatal circumstances that include murder and mayhem, is forced to leave this almost magical and menacing habitat to begin a new life in the hustle bustle of a city, where she is soon to find that predators of a different nature exist among humans.

Without giving away too much of the story, Kathleen soon realizes that she is constantly haunted by memories, voices, and apparitions which tug at her soul. She embraces an opportunity to travel outside of Canada to Jamaica with new found friends. Even though, perhaps subconsciously, attempting to escape the traumas of her past, she finds that encounters with the supernatural are as prevalent while away, as they were at home in Canada. It is almost as though the demons of the past continue to follow her every step, even when visiting Jamaica and staying near the infamous Rose Hall Plantation.

Through dialogue and plot-lines I have tried to make the story feel as real as possible. My goal is to blur reality so it is hard for a reader to surmise what is fiction and what is based on reality. The plantation called Rose Hall and its Great House, in Jamaica are real, so are the stories about the notorious White Witch of Rose Hall, Annie Palmer, who lived there as a slave owner, and whose evil knew no bounds as she tortured and killed dozens of her slaves after her romantic encounters.

We are left to wonder if Santiago, the ghost boy who had lived near Rose Hall, actually existed or if there ever was a house called Santiago House, where Kathleen stayed, or was it all created from the stroke of a pen. Perhaps we will never know where fiction and reality merge.

Table of Contents

Part One

Chapter 1

Kathleen's Story

When my Canadian-born father, Tom Dunkley, was twenty-five, he went to Ireland in search of his ancestry. Nothing prepared him for the emotions that welled up in him when he first viewed that cold inhospitable landscape. The rustic cottages hidden in the undulating land, the stonewalled pastures, the sparse Hazel, Rowan and Hawthorn trees, the bogs and even the shallow tide pools along the dramatic rocky coastline filled him with a sense of awe. So intense was his emotion that he immediately abandoned his ancestry search.

Such a quest would have meant endless hours poring over old wills, deeds and ancient church records and would have left him no time for sightseeing or other personal activities. Instead, he spent his days wandering. He set out each day at dawn exploring. By late afternoon he would often find himself near the sea coast under the shadow of magnificently wild and rugged cliffs.

Father learned to revel in the spectacular isolation. Only on rare occasions did he come in close contact with locals. He never spoke of such encounters and it was as though those meetings were merely incidental to his growing romance with the land. He found and negotiated cheap lodgings on farms and often stayed in cottages that leaned boldly into the weather. He spoke fondly of the green pastures on lush hillsides where sheep, horses and cattle grazed freely. The memory of which, always watered his eye.

I soon realized that Father was a shy man, for it was only the times when we were alone as a family that he found eloquent words to express how he had felt in Ireland. He spoke of the purple skies at morning's light and how he marvelled at the indomitable strength of the sea. In a voice barely above a whisper, he confessed that those waves reminded him of some great restless northern animal in pursuit of prey. With a hand shading one eye, he glanced skyward, as if reminding himself of that time spent abroad silently watching unfamiliar sea birds cut across leaden skies. He said that those birds reminded him of swift arrows or the sudden flight of startled wild loons, terns and even darting hawks. He was reminded also of swooping herons in northern Ontario. How joyful father was in those days, contemplating the duality of his ancestry Irish and Canadian.

Father's home in Canada was situated in a small Northern Ontario mining town called Siddon, a mere blip along a dusty back road. It boasted a church, a tiny library, a general store and a greasy-spoon grill called Eddy's Burgers, all on one street. The other buildings were nondescript retail stores and hardly worth mentioning. The houses were set well back from the main road and away from the old mine shafts and the lone mechanic's garage run by a father and son. The town's proximity to bush-land must have influenced Father's appreciation of nature, for it was there that he first admired its lush tree filled majesty. He spoke of times when the forest floor flourished with soft growing ground cover, though the forest was dense with strong stoic maples and tall majestic pines that stood erect and scraped against the wide Siddon sky.

"Despite how different this landscape is there is something of this land that is lodged in my heart and soul," he declared while tramping along the Irish coast, where cold bracing-winds set his thick blond hair on end and smarted his eyes with its salty fury. He missed Canada, despite being caught in the strange conundrum of wanting to stay right where he was and also, to go home.

One morning, he had set out with the intention of exploring the rocky hillsides where waterfalls and streams gurgled and babbled against wild ferns and grasses. He was amazed that such a rocky landscape sustained vegetation. So engrossed was he with his thoughts that he hardly noticed the hues of grey oranges and magenta that splintered across the dawning sky.

Chapter 2

Storm

When he headed eastward, he climbed up a rocky crag and whistled, softly, unmindful of changes in the atmosphere. It had become windy and the air was bone-chillingly damp. But after a twenty-minute sojourn he came upon a Hawthorn that dominated the landscape.

He skirted the tree and headed away from the usual rolling pasturelands, out to where the land was entirely uncultivated. He had not gone far, when he heard a low whistle. He turned around cautiously, realizing that he might not be alone.

Storm clouds had darkened the horizon and without warning great splashes of rain began to hammer the low foliage and the skies rumbled with dissonant thunder, as lightning split the heavens.

Pulling out his anorak, father quickly headed back towards the lone Hawthorn, as though unmindful that a tree might not be the safest place to shelter in a storm.

When he was within a few feet of the tree, he saw that a woman dressed entirely in black, was pressed up against the tree trunk. She was so still, that at first he thought perhaps she might be a carving and he was quite taken aback when she beckoned. Drawing closer he realized that she was young, perhaps twenty, with a pale rain-slicked luminous face framed in lively red-gold curls.

Father's heart quickened. Had he not read somewhere that a lone Hawthorn could well be the abode of fairies. Stuff and nonsense, he thought to himself, as he took a deep breath and laughed, hesitant no longer.

"Hi ya," the woman called out to him, as she tossed her wet hair disarmingly and extended her pale worker's hand. "Hi I'm Carlita O'Brien," she said, "I'm from a farm just over there on the rise. And who might you be?"

Father said that the lilt in her voice had sounded playful and her dewy complexion was reminiscent of a wild flower; and he assured me that he would not have been surprised to learn that she was fey, for her green eyes seemed full of ancient wisdom.

It must have taken a great deal of effort for my father to set his shyness aside and proceed to become better acquainted. And when he opened his mouth, he surprised himself when words came out at all.

"My name's Tom," He said hesitantly, finding it almost impossible to be coherent, "I'm visiting from Canada."

Carlita met his shy reply with a warm encouraging smile and he, mindful of the pelting rain, went to stand alongside her beneath the tree.

They were silent for the longest while, with only the sound of the wind, the rain and thunder that trembled in the distance and it reminded father of the sounds of the steady whirring and clangor of a well-oiled machine. When Carlita spoke again, father thought her voice was as soft, as a patch of clover, as though being careful not to infringe upon their communion with nature.

"It feels as if I am drawing strength from this old Hawthorn." She whispered, breaking the holy silence that hung between them. "In all the years since I was born, this tree has never been struck by lightning and if you ask me I'd say that some sort of magic must live here. Some folks say that Hawthorns wards off witches" She laughed a low melodic laugh and tossed her ringlets carelessly and alarmed father as she moved closer to him.

"Here Tom, give me your hand," she said gleefully, eyes bright with excitement. "Now, place your palm against the tree. There, that's it, can you feel the vibrations from the rumbling thunder? It's so powerful! Don't try to hide your smile Tom; you're as thrilled, as I am. I know you are. And to think I thought you were one of those stodgy English prospectors I wasn't even going to say a word to you. But I'm glad I did. I whistled at you earlier on, did hear me? There it goes again Tom, the thunder I mean, the vibration is intoxicating."

"You might be right Carlita. It is exciting, but quite dangerous. What if a lightning bolt were to hit that tree; that would be the end, wouldn't it? I'm serious Carlita, stop grinning It's a wicked game and anyway I'm not English, nor am I a prospector."

As they stood and talked companionably, father said he began to feel almost enchanted by her presence.

"I'm beginning to think that it's a pity that I'll be leaving Ireland soon." He said regretfully, as he stared into her luminous face, full of fascination.

There was a shy sad smile on Carlita's lips and father felt that he had found a kindred spirit. He noticed too that Carlita barely could look him in the eye. It was as though the weight of his words was slowly sinking in, not so much about the lightning but about the fact that he would be leaving.

"Will you be going over to England first," she asked? Her small worn hands involuntarily forming fists.

"Not at all," father replied biting his lip, though the thought had crossed his mind, "I'm quite homesick. So I'm heading directly home to Canada."

"Have you been here long?" she asked, as she pulled her sweater more tightly around herself. Seeing her shiver, father immediately removed his anorak and placed it round her shoulders. She was grateful for the warmth and from the look on her gentle face, father realized that in her presence his trancelike romance with the land had come to an end and he longed to hold her.

"I've been here six months already," father said and seeing a hint of disappointment in her eyes he added, "there's still a little time left though, perhaps we could get together again before I go. Agreed?"

"If it suits you, you can see me again," she replied lackadaisically, "But I ought to go now, before they come looking for me."

"Who would come looking for you? Your family, oh, are you married? Would you be the farmer's wife?"

"Oh no, not me I'm only the cook. When the farmer's wife died he took me on. He and the other farm hands would come looking if there's no meal on the table."

"I see."

Father and Carlita spoke long into the cold wet afternoon, for the weather did not let up and no one had come looking for Carlita, who shyly told my father that he was the embodiment of someone she had always wanted to know.

Father confessed over the howling wind that his feelings for her were very much the same. He knew then that he dreaded his impending journey home away from her.

Chapter 3

Home Again

"Come to Canada with me," father urged, with no hesitations. "You'd like it I promise you will and I have a home to offer you."

At first, Carlita did not respond one way or another. But finally, on the day father was to fly back home, at the very last minute, at the airport Carlita finally let her guard down. She threw herself into father's arms, and dissolved into a torrent of tears.

"Don't you ever go forgetting me!" she pleaded.

"As if I ever could," was father's tearful reply.

Some six months later, using the last of his savings, father sent for her. How happy they were to be finally together.

But it did not take long before Carlita found that life in the isolated mining town of Siddon was somewhat foreboding and even lonesome. At first, she had tried to be content with staying indoors in the bungalow, cooking from father's old recipes and rearranging things as if to show that now a woman's hand reigned there.

But the proximity of the untamed forest so close by, soon lured her with its gentle callings as though strange spirits lived in the trees that could entice her with the sweetness of birdsongs, the haunting padding feet of scampering wild deer and occasional sightings of moose moving majestically in the Northern moonlight and quick glimpses of small animals that rustled in the enticing undergrowth. Occasionally, she thought she heard a mournful howl that served to seduce her senses.

She began to disappear from the cottage for long hours at a time, often not returning until late afternoon, with her hair tangled and scented from buttercups, pine sap, moss and calendula flowers. She often brought home wild bouquets she had gathered, to place on the kitchen table, though knowing that some shy blooms would never last through the night.

"My own heart is not unlike those flowers," she would say forlornly, "flourishing and beautiful one moment, then dying in the next."

It saddened father to see her like that. It was as though she were slowly withering away. He watched as over time she grew pale and thin, her eyes sunken and misty with tears. Father felt that he could not forgive himself, for having caused her to miss Ireland.

One cold morning he found her retching at the back of the house. Full of concern, he put his arms around her.

"What's the matter darling?" he said.

"It's nothing. It's nothing," she replied, with a stooped head, "it's all because Canadian food is so unbearably bland, even the milk is tasteless and runny."

Later that same morning while Carlita was away in the forest, father drove all the way to a larger town a few miles away and brought spices, herbs and a butter-chicken meal with rice.

"I love you and thank you," Carlita said when she saw the things he had bought and she came to sit near him at the table, "but Tom I can't eat any of this," she said, "I couldn't keep it down."

"Something's dreadfully wrong with you. Isn't that right, my darling?" Father trembled.

His gut tightened with fear, as he let out the terrible words he had not wanted to ever say. "Do you want to leave me and go back to Ireland?"

"No, no Tom, it's a wee baby," she said; avoiding his eyes, "a wee baby's coming."

Father sprang to his feet and wrapped his arms round her and wept with joy.

"We are having a baby!" he sobbed, again and again.

Chapter 4

Married

Two long months went by before my parent's married. They drove to Kingston, Ontario from Siddon in father's pickup truck, keeping to the highway to avoid unnecessary bumps and jolts associated with back roads.

The sky was filled with birds and fluffy white clouds that looked like sheep scuttling in the breeze, reminding them both of Ireland.

"It's so lovely here," Carlita said, resting her head on the back of her seat, her voice reverential, her cheeks flushed pink. "Sometimes Tom, when I am in the forest I seem in some strange way, to become as one with the wild surroundings. I'm not in the least bit afraid of anything. Sometimes I even have the feeling that my baby is being watched over by nature spirits, animals and the trees"

Glancing over at her, father smiled softly, a worry line etched across his brow. "Nevertheless," he said hesitantly, as his heart hammered against his chest, "One has to be very careful. Many animals are predators. They'll hunt and kill without discrimination. Promise me, you'll always be careful, darling."

Carlita's laughing answer floated on the wind. "I'm never in any real danger my love, don't you worry. You are the wildest animal to have dared to come this close to me."

Father reached out a hand and patted her stomach reassuringly. "I'd like to think so too." he said, "Perhaps for the baby's sake...."

He never finished his sentence, for Carlita leaned more closely against him and the scent of her silken hair awoke a great longing in him. If indeed I were a wild animal, he thought I would indeed have ravished her. "I love you so much," he whispered, barely able to restrain himself, as he lightly kissed the top of her head. "How's our baby today?"

"The baby's fine. It has been kicking like one of those miner's mules or an unruly dairy cow from the farm back home. I can only hope it doesn't have hooves." She laughed and collapsed in fits against father as she squeezed his thigh. "But then again," she continued, her eyes bright with merriment, "it will be half you, and half me. That couldn't be half bad, could it? But come to think of it, yes, I suppose it could, the midwife says I'm almost ready to deliver. She wasn't even sure that I should be travelling."

Father slowed the truck, his face white with fear "You should have told me about that before we left home. Darling, I wouldn't want to risk your health, or the baby's for that matter. We could have married in Siddon, you know, there's a justice of the peace there, he's right next to the mechanic's garage"

"And miss being married in a proper church and getting away for a whole day! Not on your life!" she declared, as she hurriedly kissed his cheek. "The baby's fine," she repeated, "we will be good and married before it comes. Just think, we'll be Mr. and Mrs. Tom Dunkley by the end of the day." She smiled, "A fabulous thought isn't it, and when we have a wee one, we will be three!"

Father's seriousness softened, for seeing her so animated

awoke fresh longing in him. "Just look at you," he said, dabbing back tears, his eyes filled with undisguised delight. With great strength he gripped the wheel, while holding Carlita protectively in the crook of his other arm. Despite their months together, he still felt somewhat shy around her. For the longest while, lost in silence, he pondered what to say until at last the words poured out of him of their own accord "Carlita darling, you're all blossoming and bulging. I can't think of a happier man than me, or a woman more beautiful than you."

They laughed at the slightest thing as mile after mile of wilderness and broad fields, long gone fallow, sped by. The sky was but a blur of colour as they came ever closer to the city.

Gradually, dark forests gave way to cultivation, to reveal habitation. Billboards, painted signs, traffic lights and wooden suburban houses began to clutter the landscape. Compared to the isolation of Siddon, there were crowds everywhere.

"So, you are absolutely sure that the minister knows my situation?" Carlita breathed, for in her state of mind she must have thought that the whole town might condemn her. "Tom my love, you wouldn't be wanting me to have to hide my belly, would you? My frock already makes me look as if I'm carrying cabbages in an apron. You think so too, don't you?"

"Darling I told the minister absolutely everything," father grinned. "It's not like it would be the first time he'd be marrying a couple like us. But if it makes you feel any better, he happens to be an old family friend; he buried my parents years ago. And did I tell you how beautiful you look today?"

"You've told me a dozen times already. But I hardly believe a word, considering this bump of mine. But what's the name of this understanding parson, minister or whatever? You don't really think he'd be nonjudgmental, do you?

"He's a good and honest man, Carlita, his name is Reverend Liam Bannerman; he's been in Ontario for years and years."

"Sounds Irish if you ask me, perhaps he'll give us special blessings and the baby too of course."

"He could be Irish; I remember hearing talk that he was born overseas."

"Well at least we will have somewhat of an Irish wedding. Did you bring the whisky? It's for him you know."

"Yes, I know, that's why I packed it in a box next to the wildflower bouquet you gathered. Everything's in the back of the truck and I haven't forgotten the rings. They're in my breast pocket. We're well prepared but if you're a little tired, we could stop to rest. We just passed a couple of motels."

"Tom, you are a real darling but we both know we don't have much money with us. So shouldn't we save it to celebrate after the service? Indian food perhaps? You know, Tom I've been hankering after a curry. It's not like I couldn't rest right here in the truck. Nothing's going to get in the way of our wedding. There's you, all handsome in that suit, your eyes as gloriously blue as the Irish sky on a good day. I couldn't resist you if I tried, and I'm lucky aren't I?"

Chapter 5

After the Wedding

My parents were married in St. Bartholomew's Chapel, a small Anglican chapel in downtown Kingston. Two strangers were witnesses. It was a short ceremony. In fact, father said it could not have been more than twenty minutes. After signing the documentation, they were toasted with cheap bubbly champagne, as well as the Irish whisky they brought themselves. Their wedding feast was an East Indian buffet lunch in an elegant downtown restaurant near the harbour. They were oblivious to other diners as they held hands, hardly even noticing the arrivals and departures of yachts and boats, and the cheerful tourists gathered on Confederation Park's pier.

Arm in arm they strolled in sheer delirium as the restless Lake Ontario lashed against the shoreline. "This takes me right back darling," Carlita sighed, "those waves. That dark body of water. it's a pity it is not salty. It could almost be Ireland."

"I know, I know," father replied, voice trembling, "Dearest, this is our home now. We are married and you know of course, that what's mine is yours, so even the land, the trees and the lake are yours now." As he spoke, bold white gulls sailed across the broad Kingston skyline as though paying homage to their new life.

It was a wonderful romantic day of love, then there was the

long drive back to Siddon. It was dark by then, with only the lights of their pickup truck to guide them along the deserted highway. Father remembered how menacing the forest seemed that night, and how ominous he thought it was, as owls hooted in the dark trees they sped by. 'Leave us alone,' father sighed.

Hours passed and the wind rose and bellowed and rocked the truck, even as Carlita slept peacefully on her new husband's shoulder. In the moonlit night, father saw wide-eyed deer scamper across the highway and his headlights picked up the sight of a dead coyote at the side of the road. It was perhaps killed by a hunter's gun he surmised. How awfully alone he felt in the silky darkness, as the threatening howl of a wolf close by echoed in the night and set his heart to pounding. The drumming in his ears proved impossible to shut out; for he had no doubt that the dangerous northern beast he had always feared, was by leaps and bounds catching up with him.

Chapter 6

Born

A few months after their wedding I was born in Siddon. Carlita and father would laugh and say "She was lucky not to have been shaken out, by the speed of our pickup truck, that night on the way home from Kingston."

The day I was born, Carlita remembered being in the bush close to the house, as it was her usual morning ritual but then her water broke and a horrendous pain started. If it were not for her sheer determination, she would not have made it back home. Father was home having lunch and by chance glanced out the window and saw her doubled over struggling towards the house. He immediately abandoned his meal and ran to assist her.

"What's happened? Is it time?" he gasped; his ears red, his eager hands unsure. "Call the midwife!" Carlita moaned, before her strong legs gave way. Father gently scooped her up and ran into the house to lay her on their bed. "Call the bloody midwife!" Carlita screamed, her eyes bulging, teeth clenched with fear and pain.

A long thirty minutes went by before the midwife arrived. By then Carlita was almost ready to push. Father was assigned to boil water and to lay down a sheet of plastic under Carlita to protect the bed-sheets. "I love you Carlita," he reassured her over and over, as he gently moved her into place, but Carlita's screams only grew louder. In her distress, she might have perceived father as nothing more than an annoyance and the cause of her pain. Get out!!" She screamed with gusto, "I cannot stand the likes of you near me!" Reverting to Irish brogue she ordered him out of the house. "Holy Mary and Joseph, why the hell can't you, get out of this here house!"

"Best you leave the room Tom." the midwife said, sharply, "Wait outside on the porch. It's the pain that's causing her to say such things. Everyone knows she loves you still."

As soon as the front door slammed and it was evident that father had left the house, the midwife smiled once more and wiped mother's sweaty brow. "Push" she said gently, "The baby's slipping out nicely." Then all brusque and businesslike, she declared: "If you ask me, I'd swear this wasn't your first baby. Some other child must have paved the way for this one to slide out so easily. Correct me if I'm wrong."

"Hush," Carlita panted, perspiration washing her body. "He mustn't hear you say such things. He'd go believing every word he hears."

"The head's showing!" The midwife sighed, as she shook her head at mother's words and clamped her own jaws shut. It was a moment or so before with a gentle tug she pulled, and Carlita pushed the rest of me out. What a terrible wailing arose, father said, for standing outside of the house he was privy to the silences of the forest and then the sudden banshee-like howls inside the house.

"It's a beautiful baby girl" the midwife whispered, hushing us both into silence. Then she slapped my back and snuggled me down at mother's heaving breast in my parent's own warm blankets. "Tom Dunkley, come quick!" The midwife hollered, "Your daughter's born, you're a daddy now, all you need do is cut the cord!"

It was at that exact moment outside the house, that father heard the clear ominous moaning call of a wolf. It sounded close to the house, then there was an answering call. "Leave us be," father hissed at the unseen animals, baring his teeth and tightening his fists. "I will not let you harm a single hair of mine, or my dear family." and without a backward glance he strode boldly into the house.

"Look Tom darling," mother sobbed from their bed, her voice sweet and filled with apologies, as father, suddenly gone shy, slowly entered the birthing room. "She's so beautiful Tom, come sit beside me, have a look. Her eyes are as blue as yours aren't they Tom? And look, her hair is reddish gold like mine."

Father sat beside mother and me, his handsome face transfixed from his many blessings. "She's gorgeous," He said in a husky whisper, barely catching his breath.

"Congratulations to both of you," the midwife said, gathering up her things and wiping away all traces of her recent bustling activity, "what do you plan to call her anyway?"

'We've decided on Kathleen Shannon if it was a girl," mother smiled as she held father's rough hand against the small bundle on her chest, "those names remind us both of Ireland."

Chapter 7

Time Passes

Months and years and more years passed.

It seemed not long before I, Kathleen Dunkley, knew Siddon like the back of my hand. Father loved taking me everywhere in his pickup truck, which always had a large metal work box sitting in the back filled with stuff the town folk wanted him to repair. Every day he tried to empty it, but it would again be filled with more work each day. How I loved those afternoons with him driving from customer to customer. As much as I loved being with father it was mother who took me to the forest in the early mornings to commune with nature. As I grew older I befriended people as well as animals. I was told that when I was small, chipmunks, small deer and other curious wild animals often came up to me without fear, though I barely remember. The thick forest was daunting and mysterious, though I can almost still remember how soft the green moss was underfoot where mother used to set me down to play.

My memories are haunted by a strange unfamiliar voice close by, that always seemed to disappear on my awaking from sleep on that mossy forest floor.

There were photographs on our mantle that followed my life's progress. Usually I was on mother's knee smiling into the camera. My long curly hair the exact shade of hers, and at four years old my eyes were still as blue as father's.

I'm not sure how old I was when mother no longer took me to the forest. She claimed to need more time to herself. Time to energize and contemplate was what she said. Father who adored her, saw the restlessness in her eyes and attributed it to her missing the land where she was born. More and more, he began to bring his odd jobs home, to be with me while she was away, and as a result, he and I grew even closer. We had the most wonderful long conversations at the kitchen table while he fixed old locks and set old blenders to working again, then he would repair lamps and radios and a stack of watches. I cannot forget the determination in his jaws as he bent in deep concentration over each broken thing to set it right to the way that it should be.

By the time I was ten years old I knew more about the insides of things than most children my age. It was at that time that I too noticed for the first time the weary sadness in mother's eyes. "What's wrong Mummy?" I often asked and she would kiss me and squeeze me to her breast. "Nothing's wrong kitten." She always replied, whispering softly in my hair. "There is no cure for missing something." She'd often say with a tear already visible at her eye. "Are you missing your home in Ireland?" I asked a dozen times over, until one day she replied. "Not so much missing the home my love," She said with a sigh, "I miss things I never even had a chance to know better." It was the most she ever said concerning her moodiness, but before I could ask any more questions, she would find excuses to quickly retreat to the solitude of the forest.

Whenever father had to travel to Ottawa to pick up spare parts for broken mechanical things, mother always declined his offers to accompany him. Instead she always chose to remain behind with only the forest for company. Therefore, it was I who ended up going with him on those long journeys, happy as ever to miss a day or two at school. "What's to become of your mother?" Father used to say as we drove along the lonely miles together. He would look weary and spent, and I would feel sad for mother and for him.

One day when I was fifteen I was sent home sick from school. I walked on the dusty back roads rather than taking the local bus, feeling that fresh air would surely clear my stuffy head. No warning was sent home regarding my imminent early arrival.

As I approached our home I stopped in my tracks for I heard loud voices. I was surprised to realize that it was my parents shouting at each other! Something they never did. What could have brought this on I wondered and in my shame I decided to crouch behind a low bush near the half open front door, too embarrassed to alert them to my presence. My heart pounded uncontrollably as though, afraid of whatever I might hear.

"Carlita, tell me honestly, did you ever love me at all?" I heard my father shout, the sound of heartbreak rich in his voice.

"You know I love you Tom," my mother replied harshly, "but there are things you don't know, I'm serious Tom." She sounded almost repentant but it crossed my mind that she might be playing to an audience, though there was no possibility of others overhearing, since the house was isolated from all the others in Siddon.

"What don't I know Carlita?" Father demanded roughly, and I wondered if he had been at the whiskey he always kept in the house. "We've been together almost sixteen years! Tell me just what it is that I've missed?"

"You never knew me Tom. Not in a million years could you know me," mother laughed gutturally. Had she been drinking too I wondered.

"What more is there to know Carlita?" father demanded. I heard his work boots pound threateningly on the wooden floor. "I fell in love with you," he said, sounding calmer, "and I married you as soon as I could, and Carlita if you must know I love you more than ever now."

"Stop it Tom!" mother screamed, "Don't you make me tell you things you won't want to hear."

I squirmed in my cramped position, wanting to get away from the dissonance and yet wanting to stay to hear it out.

"Are you saying you don't love me or never have? What the hell are you saying Carlita?"

"Be quiet Tom!" mother hissed, a harsher edge coming into her tone. "Don't you know by now that love's not everything?"

I couldn't bear to hear what I was hearing, yet I was mesmerized by the sheer awfulness of it, and I leaned even closer towards the door, hardly daring to draw a breath, as tears welled in my eyes.

"Love's everything! Damn it!" father shouted banging his fist on something that clattered dangerously.

I almost jumped out of my skin, when there was a loud crash. and I imagined dozens of glasses shattering into zillions of pieces. I still don't know how I stopped myself from crying out.

"Christ!! Tom, don't you go breaking things!" mother screamed, "I don't like the look of you. I really don't. That's it Tom. I might as well tell you everything, you've brought me to it, you have! Don't look at me like that! You've never been a passionate man! Stop it Tom I see a wild animal in your eyes and you used to be so shy and all! Love me or hate me Tom this is what happened."

The house went suddenly silent, there were no birds

chattering in the trees and no cries or scurrying sounds came from the brooding forest.

"Hear me out Tom." mother pleaded, "There's still time before our Kathleen's due home."

"Say your piece Carlita," father replied sounding resigned to whatever fate she was offering. I almost could see the sadness in his pale blue eyes and I imagined that his blond hair was falling carelessly over his beautiful face, as his strong coarse hands lay limp in his lap and his firm jaw must have gone slack from the interminable waiting.

Chapter 8

The Painful Truth Revealed

"Tom," mother began, "Promise me you won't be interrupting. Hear me out please. Then you can decide for yourself what's best. Agreed?"

There was a long silence and I knew father must have nodded in obedience.

"Tom, when you first saw me under that Hawthorn Tree in Ireland, do you remember that I was dressed all in black? Were you not even a little bit curious as to why darling? Well it might come as a shock to you, but I was in mourning. Every blessed day of my life I went to that desolate place no matter the weather. There's a grave there Tom. It's a place of death, and the living are not welcome there, at least I shouldn't be welcomed. I don't know how many times I wished myself dead in the company of that tree, for that is where I buried my son. Yes, love me or hate me Tom I had a child before I met you. I never intended to tell you about him, but I have suffered enough through all these years. The poor thing's name was Gavin Joseph O'Brian. He never stood a chance Tom, for I aborted him and buried him in a shallow grave in the shadow of that tree. Don't you be judging me though, for surely you must understand the poverty back home It's not all beauty Tom. It really isn't. I was young and needed money and I plied the easiest trade I knew. I don't even know if my Gavin was the farmer's son, or someone else's I wasn't sure if it was someone I met in a pub, or else someone I seduced at the railway station. It could have been a number of men that I will never see again. I was foolish enough to think that it didn't matter if I got pregnant, since I could easily get rid of the baby anyway. There was always someone that one of us girls knew who could do that for us. I had no fears at all but when the grief and the guilt set in from losing my Gavin, there was no forgetting him ever. His hair was coal black as a raven's wing, as were his eyes but it is his skin I can't stop remembering for it was pale as the snow that falls in early winter storms. I wanted to die from loving him and still do.

Then Tom, there was you coming along loving beautiful things like sunsets, plants and flowers and the strength of the wild sea, and even the patchy grass that grew on the rocky land. You were all bursting with love Tom, so much so that when you offered me a new start I didn't know what to make of it. I was afraid at first but then I gave in, thinking it might help me to forget. I grew to love you my dear Tom more than any other thing, I really did. But the worst is to come if you can stand listening. I hardly know how to tell you, but I know I must confess it all to you my poor Tom.

When I first went into the forest behind this house, I was as mesmerized by its beauty as you had been with Ireland. Then that same week in my wandering I came upon a native man amongst the trees, down near the brook. At first we just stared at each other like two startled deer but when he saw that I wasn't afraid of him, we struck up a conversation. He told me that he was twenty-three and that his name was Luke Whitefawn. Yes,

Tom I know that you already know him, so don't you be saying one word, for he told me that his father runs the mechanic garage right here in Siddon. There was something about him that was so untamed that it attracted me dangerously to him, his bronze complexion, his long black hair and his deep-set eyes that bored right into me and his firm rounded biceps and his rock hard hands that were so gentle with forest animals! He knew every single tree by name and every clump of bush and he even knew the very meaning of every kind of wolf's howl. He believes in ancient things like nature spirits and beings that live in trees and in the air, water, fire and other such things, much the same as we do in Ireland. I couldn't stay away from him Tom, even if I tried. He was like a magnet. I was drawn to him and went to see him every day, without your knowledge, and worst of all Tom, when I became pregnant I didn't even know if the baby was yours or his. It was only when our Kathleen was born and I saw for myself that she wasn't dark-skinned or had eyes like his, that I knew she was truly ours."

Father had been sobbing throughout her story and those sobs grew increasingly louder and unbearably heartbreaking by the time she finished. I knew that his dear head must be buried in his hands, for I buried mine in much the same manner as my whole world fell apart.

"I can't bear this," I heard father sob, his voice choked with emotion; while I in my hiding place shared his tears.

"Carlita, our whole life together was nothing but a lie! What was I thinking when I married you! My life might as well be over Carlita, you are talking to a dead man! I couldn't possibly live here in Siddon anymore. You've humiliated me to the core! To imagine that all this time you kept your sordid past from me, and as for Luke Whitefawn he must have laughed and lorded over us both behind our backs! Want to know something Carlita? He's scum! It's not the first time that his father has been disgraced by him. He's a womanizer Carlita! He's known from here to three towns over, where he's fathered a string of unwanted children. He's never stepped up to the plate! Everyone knows! And he's no nature god as you seem to think, he survives by stealing from his own father. Listen now and listen good, don't you even try to come near me again; alive or dead, you are a disease Carlita, that's what you are!

"No, Tom, that's not true. Please forgive my indiscretions I love you I really do. Let me show you."

"Get out of my way!" father cried out, his grief not unlike that of a wounded animal, with all its energy spent. "You've made a mockery of everything I ever believed in."

I heard the sound of his boots, and his chair scraped against the floor, then I heard him running. His boots were like bullets pounding across the kitchen's hard floor. With a huge bang, the front door flew open, the spring must have broken and I shrunk back in terror; forgetting I was already hidden, and father was at the door!

I will never forget his face; it haunts me still for it was a picture of rage and suffering. What if he saw me I thought as I trembled in fear. But I needn't have worried; he never once looked left or right, as he ran down the steps, his legs pumping as though possessed. Then out of the stillness of the day I heard the plaintive cry of a wolf, and I knew without doubt that father heard it too, for he ran even faster towards the long dusty back road that stretched behind, and away from us.

It was nightfall before I crept into the house. I was distraught and shaken after overhearing my parents quarrel. Mother was sitting at the table lost in silence as broken glasses lay strew at her feet. We did not exchange a single word, she was burning a red candle, and tears were dried on her cheek. She had always believed glowing red candles generated lasting love.

How trivial all that seemed, considering the enormity of the quarrel. Then it crossed my mind that she might be burning the candle for her lover Luke Whitefawn, but then again, it might be for the return of my father. Neither of us said anything about the disarray in the kitchen or that there was no supper on the stove.

I threw myself onto my bed, knowing I wouldn't sleep. I cocked my ear for any sound that might prove to be father returning home to us. How I longed to hear words of repentance uttered by mother, but the house was ghostly silent, as though the very life and heartbeat of its bones were dead.

Candle after candle flickered, painting great shadows against the walls, and still mother kept her vigil, not a single word passing her lips nor mine. I didn't know if I should hate or forgive her, or run.

Then in the wee hours of that dreadful morning we heard a hesitant knock at the door. Father's home I thought, my heart near ready to burst. I heard the kitchen chair creak as mother slowly rose from her seat, stopping only to snuff out her magic candle. I heard when the front door yawned opened and my legs were already half way off the bed.

The house became morbidly still. It was not father at the door at all; it was Mrs. Allen the midwife who had delivered me. I heard her profuse apologies for the early hour, and I heard the thump of her shoes as mother let her in. They whispered softly in the darkness of the front room but I could tell that compassion and urgency was being imparted. I climbed from my bed only to hear a long steady animal-like wail coming from mother. I ran barefoot across the cold floors and hugged her around her middle, truly afraid as I buried my head against her. "What's wrong Mama?" I said, already half guessing the worst, but mother could not speak or offer tenderness, for her eyes spilled great tears that drowned out all around her. The midwife hesitantly took hold of my limp hand and whispered so softly I could hardly hear her, "Your father's been found dead, my pet," she said, as I searched her face for answers. Her wrinkled eyelids were curved downwards as though pulled by an invisible unbearable weight. "Your father's dead," she said again, her lips slightly trembling as she carefully phrased each word.

"Are you sure?" I asked, my eyes wide and hoping for a miracle.

"Yes I'm sure he's gone sweetie. An hour or so ago Zack Whitefawn, the good man that he is, told me that your father had passed away. Might have been a heart attack or a stroke but he was found behind the Whitefawn's garage. Sometimes it's even hard for me to understand how the Lord works. Why on earth would a contented man like Tom Dunkley be taken just like that. It's not as though he was sick or anything. I saw him a few days ago and he seemed as right as rain. But poor Zack will have to live with that memory, since he said that it was his good for nothing son Luke who was the one that found him.

Only then did I fully absorb the implications of the news that the midwife bore and my tears for my gentle beloved father flowed unending in that room.

"One of you will have to identify the body" The midwife said. "Not me," mother immediately replied, dabbing at her tears "I couldn't bear it; I know I couldn't, not under these circumstances."

"I'll do it." I said hesitantly, though my heart was already heavy with grief.

"Thank you," Mrs. Allen sighed, "But it is just as well that I should identify him. I've known him longer than any of you. But excuse me Pet, I have to have a quiet word with your mother outside.

I went to sit in my father's chair and I held the arms of that chair so tightly, that one would have thought I was trying to harness him there, though I knew he was well and truly gone, and it was the worst day of my life.

Chapter 9

In the Aftermath

Our home was soon packed with good people who had come to offer condolence and whatever they could bring. There were sandwiches and soup, stews, coffee and bottles of pop. Yet I couldn't help but noticing that a hush fell over conversations, the moment I walked by. Was there something being kept from me. I wondered. It seemed that mother and I were never alone, there was no privacy and no possibility of getting questions answered.

For two long days following father's passing, mother took to mourning, dressed all in black, reminding me that black was the colour she had been wearing when father first saw her, and he was unaware that she was mourning for my brother. And after the quarrel that I heard between them, I had to wonder if she was truly mourning my father.

A proper service was held on the third day of his passing. Father would have marvelled at it, for everyone he had ever serviced, as well as curiosity seekers, all attended. Mother and I were the centre of attention every waking hour. My father, Tom Joseph Dunkley, was buried just outside of Siddon in a desolate cemetery, alongside his parents' graves, on a small hill that obscured the busy highway. I wondered if he might have preferred to be closer to home. Then I remembered his last

32

words to mother, and I thought perhaps it was best that he was laid to rest way out there, with his parents.

It was midmorning, five days after father's untimely passing, that we finally opened our curtains. The house had been in a semi-darkened state, and somehow reflected the torment from the recent tragedy. When sunlight was allowed to finally peep in, it streamed through the windows like a current of life. Dust particles danced in the solemn air, and what a wealth of colours the light picked out, the yellow chairs, the patchwork quilts included, though from outside, there was not a sound, no birdsong, no small animals scurrying, and for a few brief moments tranquillity took precedence over grief in our isolation.

Mother and I, finally left to ourselves, were able to mourn in private in our own fashion. All day I ran my fingers and my nose over father's clothes that still hung in his closet, and it filled my heart with remembering, as mother gently wept and packed away the broken things that he would have no hand in repairing.

Despite our painful loss, mother looked lovelier than ever. One would never have suspected that the truth was, that she was released from heavy burdens she had carried for so long. One morning, on awakening I found that she was already up. There was no breakfast on the table, though she was already dressed and was no longer wearing black. Her pale blue sweater and navy trousers accentuated her every curve. Her long curly hair was let loose from the restricting hairpins she so recently wore. Deep in contemplation, she stood at the front door illuminated by bright sunlight. I saw her wipe away tears, before she pulled the imprisoning door latch, to let herself out.

"I'm going to the forest." she called out, sounding as though such a soirée was the most natural thing in the world.

"Going to see him?" I said boldly, and she seemed momentarily startled, "Who?" she replied, her lips a perfect O.

"Luke." I replied, though all the bravado was knocked out of me by the innocence expressed in her eyes. "Who's to tell who might be there?" she replied, as she quickly pulled the stout door shut behind her.

I watched from the window and saw the direction she took. I waited a moment, then slowly and silently opened the door and followed. For a long while she kept to the old tracks, the ones father and I knew well, then she veered off to where the forest thickened to wilderness. Stopping momentarily, she removed what looked like a bulging canvas bag from an old tree stump, then sat there, as though waiting. Fifteen minutes went by before there was a crackling of twigs and leaves, coming from the opposite direction, and I knew without doubt that someone was approaching. I held my breath and crouched deeper into the thick bush. Then out from the forest's interior came Luke Whitefawn!

He was as handsome as my mother had described, dark, compelling and wild. He looked both weary and forest born, and my fair snowy skinned European mother seemed alien in comparison.

Mother flew to him. I saw their fingers intertwine, as their lips met and I turned my head away in shame. Then I saw Luke carry mother to the mossy forest bed that I remembered from childhood. They spoke in muffled tones, as mother eagerly embraced him, and I couldn't watch anymore

"I've got the whisky," I heard mother say enticingly, "I sneaked it out earlier this morning, as my Kathleen slept."

"Let's party then." Luke laughed, and their laugher echoed in that quiet place. "You've always known exactly what I need Carlita. You're the best!"

It was almost as though wolves were at my heels. I shot up from my hiding place like a bullet and ran uncaring whether Luke Whitefawn or my mother were aware of me. I crashed through the dense forestry, heart pumping as sharp twigs and branches barred my way. I startled small animals, and quarrelsome sounding birds, and I imagined that a whole menagerie was chasing after me. However, nothing stopped me. I headed back to the house unharmed, as though guided by the sound of my father's voice, that came into my ear, sounding calm, loving and supportive.

"Run Kathleen, run," he said softly, "there are some broken things that cannot be fixed."

I clenched my fists and ran even faster.

I waited for three long lonely hours in bed, under the cover of my thick blanket, unable to stop shivering. Anger had made a mess of my head. It wasn't until midafternoon that I heard voices outside, as well as the familiar sound of father's pickup truck starting. For one brief moment I thought it might be my father, and I raced to the front door, only to see Luke Whitefawn with mother outside.

They had obviously been drinking. Luke Whitefawn looked wilder than I remembered, his clothes were disheveled; his hair askew, and the whiskey bottle clenched in his fist, was half empty. He was at the wheel of father's truck, fumbling with the keys, as mother sat stock still beside him. He looked in my direction, and banged the truck door shut. Then he revved the engine, and with a muscled arm and drew my mother closer. Her face was pallid, and her expression distant, as she slumped against her lover, with dried leaves and forest debris lodged in her beautiful hair.

I was never sure if they saw me framed in the bright

doorway or if my presence would have made even a scrap of difference to them.

The truck skidded and zigzagged from its parking spot, before the engine kicked in, and started to purr, as it had done under the gentle hands of my father. I watched with bated breath as the truck picked up speed, and I heard the rubber squeal against the dry soil, as dust flew in all directions.

My hand flew to my mouth as the pickup zoomed forward like a wayward arrow, all the way down the long back road and the sound of their distant laughter echoed as far as the forest.

Chapter 10

Consequences

That evening I was hungry, not having had lunch. I threw together a light supper of scrambled eggs and toast. It was terrifying being alone with thoughts of my father, and his strong belief in spirits, when he himself might well now be one. I was so freaked, I fixated on every shadow cast by our lamp light. I checked behind doors and was reluctant to even go into my own room, choosing instead to keep a watchful eye on the door to my parent's room, expecting at any moment to see the phantom figure of father. "I'm fifteen," I said to myself I shouldn't be such a baby but then I heard a vehicle pull up to the house.

I left my meal on the table, feeling all pumped up to confront my wayward mother. I angrily pulled open the front door and was taken aback to see a police cruiser parked outside in the dark. Oh my gosh, she's got herself thrown in jail, I thought, with an 'I told you so' expression written all over my face.

"Are you Miss Dunkley?" The male officer behind the wheel inquired, staring me straight in the eye. I gulped hard, taken aback by the fact that he knew my name, and I replied cautiously. "Yes.... I'm Kathleen Dunkley." My chin was already trembling.

The other officer, who was female, came out of the cruiser

and stood at the bottom of the steps. "I'm Sgt. Nelligan" she said, her voice steady and her eyes unwavering. "Have a seat here with me Kathleen." She motioned to the bottom step where she sat down. I found myself quickly doing as I was told. "I'm going to have to be the one to bring you this bad news." she said.

"Has my mother been arrested?" I blurted out. "Oh no, she's not arrested, however I regret I have to inform you that there's been a horrific highway accident not too far from town."

The officer's manner was gentle and caring but there was no stopping my trembling. I tried to focus on her words but I was afraid of what I might hear. "Is mother alright?" I gasped, feeling my whole body turning icy cold.

"I'm sorry," the officer replied, moving to sit somewhat closer, "Two people in a pickup truck registered to your father were killed instantly this evening. They were in the wrong lane, when they hit a transport truck head on. We are afraid to say that we think that your mother is one of the deceased. We suspect drunk driving as the cause of the crash. We are so sorry. Your neighbours told us about the recent loss of your father. I think you know Mrs. Allen? She said she was the midwife when you were born. She has kindly offered you a place to spend the night. But because you are fifteen, we had thought about finding you a foster home where you can stay, or unless of course you decide to take Mrs. Allen up on her offer."

I was devastated by the news. My mind swirled, with thoughts that flew in every direction. I even wondered if my mother had had it coming. It even crossed my mind that my dear father had had his final revenge, though in the end, I felt sorry for everyone involved, father, mother, myself, the driver of the transport truck and even foolish Luke, the cause of my mother's demise.

Chapter 11

At Mrs. Allen's

There was no way in the world, that I alone was going to stay in my once beloved home, for it now seemed full of shadowy phantoms and bad memories. How would I be able to stop seeing things that were not there. I would imagine Mother in the kitchen, ever watchful over a steaming cooking pot, and father busy as ever working at his trade, at the kitchen table, just to be near her. I was even full of thoughts about poor Gavin, the brother I never knew, and I felt deeply for him. I wondered what would have happened if mother had never met my father, would I still have been born, and would I have ended up like Gavin? There were no answers to my questions, only opportunities to pose more questions.

"Time will heal all wounds" was the sympathetic words said to me by many locals, who meant well. However, they did not know that the ghosts of both of my dear departed parents haunted me in dreams, offering guidance just as they did in life. Sometimes their phantom selves would speak of regrets, as they appeared to worry about me. Though after a while, their vivid nocturnal visitations became less and less often. There were nights, when I couldn't find rest, and those nights were when I would hear the plaintive resounding call of a wolf, just outside my window. I feared that it must be the same wolf that father used to talk about in hushed tones, describing it as a beast that haunted him relentlessly. But I didn't mention any of this to anyone, not even Mrs. Allen, who I was staying with, and who never seemed to notice that I, in many ways, had become more secretive, like my mother and almost as shy as my father.

Days of living with Mr. Allen turned into weeks, then months. Despite her years, she was sharp, capable and organized. She took care of me and my broken heart, without complaint, as though I was her own child. I often told her that she was 'awesome' and she would laugh out loud. "I'm just neighbourly" she'd, say, "You, my Pet, are a wonderful companion." But all that time, I knew that I was the child she had longed for, even in old age, and had wished that she and her late husband had someone such as myself to spoil and provide for. Being a midwife, helped to ease her sorrow, since she told me how she had guided many children into the world, and at times felt privy to quietly assisting those mothers, since doing so, brought her satisfaction.

I soon became familiar with Mrs. Allen's habits, her trips to the main street, and where she chose to place her tea cups and spoons. She liked to sit for hours in an old twisted wooden chair, near the window and read from the New Testament. She once told me that the chair was her favourite piece of furniture, and that all her furnishings had at one time belonged to someone else. Most were inherited from families she served as a midwife. Even that chair, her favourite one, was given to her by my paternal grandmother, Lucinda Dunkley, who years ago, had welcomed her to Siddon. Mrs. Allen said that for fifty-odd years she had always felt connected to our family, she remembered father as a child being curious and withdrawn.

"I have lived in this house even after my husband Matthew

Allen disappeared some thirty years ago down one of Siddon's mine shafts. He was never found, you know. I even prayed for his return. God rest his soul but even then, he wasn't found. Time helped to heal my grief, though there's nothing I've regretted more than us never having our own children."

Throughout my stay, Mrs. Allen never spoke about my mother or Luke Whitefawn, and she somehow managed to keep me well out of the way of local gossip. She organized a private service for mother, and it was her presence, walking with me to a school closer to her home and back, that silenced wagging tongues.

On most weekends, it was a ritual of ours to sit in silence side by side beside the picture window overlooking the wilderness. The room was often swathed in sunlight and Mrs. Allen would knit fiercely, as though to make the most of that light and I, in my silence enjoyed the steady click of her needles. I often wondered if she had ever, while sitting on her porch, seen my mother's comings and goings into the foreboding forest.

On Sundays, Mrs. Allen cooked my favourite meals, spaghetti swathed in meat sauce and sausages and beans, to try to coax me to eat. I had no appetite; it was noticeable how thin I had become. My body reminded me of an empty sack, with me not wanting anything substantial.

I felt so godforsaken, that I lost interest in music, books and movies; choosing instead to gaze out at the rugged landscape, missing the home I once loved.

Several weeks went by, and it took me by surprise when one morning I awoke with an unusual restlessness I had dreamed about mother, she was travelling from her home in Ireland, all the way to Canada. How happy and beautiful she seemed in my dream, and how young she was, perhaps not much older than myself. I took the dream as a sign from her and I remembered how much she loved me. Somehow it was clear that it was time for me to move on, time to get past things that kept me looking back, even if it meant leaving Siddon.

Chapter 12

Leaving
the Past Behind

"I have to leave Siddon." I said hesitantly, at breakfast one morning, over bacon and eggs I had hardly touched.

"I feel useless, and you know what, Mrs. Allen I turned sixteen a few months ago. I didn't say anything 'cause I didn't want to put you to any extra trouble. I need to try new things and see new places, know what I mean? I even feel that mother would have agreed."

Mrs. Allen smiled knowingly, as though she had long anticipated such talk coming from me. "Where'd you go my Pet?" she said, clearing her throat, as she passed the ketchup. I shook my head and handed the ketchup back.

"I'm serious, you've been more than kind but it's like I can't stay, you know that don't you?"

Mrs. Allen nodded and looked directly at me, her eyes brimming. "By the way I did remember your birthday Pet but I kept it to myself, until the time would be right. That's why I have a little gift set aside for you."

"Seriously?"

"Yes, there's some money set aside for you. But, tell me, where you're planning to go Pet?

When I dared look at Mrs. Allen again, it was my eyes that were brimming, and I rose from my seat and hugged her.

"Mrs. Allen, you're amazing," I said, choking back tears.

"You're very welcome." She smiled and pushed her chair back in place, "Soon enough you will be getting word regarding a trust set up in your name by your parents. But until then, you can make do with this."

"Thanks. I didn't expect a single thing I'm totally floored"

"So where is it that you will be headed Pet?"

"Well for sure I won't be going to Ireland," I laughed, trying to appease Mrs. Allen and make her smile. "I won't go to Quebec either because I don't speak the French" I said, trying to sound French, and we both laughed. "I'm thinking about a city here in Ontario"

"That might be so Pet." Mrs. Allen sighed. "But it can be dangerous in cities. You'll have to be so careful, but come to think of it, Siddon's no better is it? Where on earth would you stay when you get to the city?"

"I'll find a B&B." I said, sounding sure of myself. But honestly I wasn't confident at all.

"Well honey, there's Ottawa and Toronto. Why not try this old trick? I've used it myself. Hold your knife and fork up high, then let them both fall when I tell you to. We'll call the fork Toronto and the knife Ottawa. Whichever one hits the floor first is where God wants you to be. I have friends in both cities, so not to worry"

I couldn't help but laugh at her simplistic resolution but I tried it anyway. It was the fork that hit the floor first and that is how I made up my mind to travel to Toronto. Mrs. Allen told me that wherever I went, her friends would be quite welcoming. Though she neglected to mention that she hadn't heard from either friend in years.

Over the next few days, the sadness that had wrapped so tightly around me began to ease. My thoughts were filled with the anticipation of leaving. Mrs. Allen helped me to pack my suitcase, reminding me to take one thing or another, and one afternoon she stopped at the post office and sent off a note to her friend in Toronto, realizing that she had lost her phone number.

I had hardly cared about my appearance, and it was only when I stood in front of a tall wood framed mirror in Mrs. Allen's hall that I noticed my unkempt nails and that my long straggly curls needed attention. The thin face that stared back at me was unnaturally pale and so like mother's, though my eyes were father's and it awoke fresh longing.

"Poor Mummy and poor Daddy," I sighed, "What's to become of me? Please guide me."

"Come child," Mrs. Allen said in that businesslike tone of hers, seeing me in despair. It was only then I realized that she had been close by, sitting in her favourite chair, keeping one loving eye on me.

"You're over sixteen Kathleen. That's how old I was when I travelled alone from way out west to come here to marry Mr. Allen. He was just nineteen when he proposed and said he loved me. You're a bright girl Kathleen, much brighter than I was back then. Why don't we go over to your house and bring back things you'll need. I'm going to contact a lawyer tonight. I know him well. I delivered him as a baby, he will look after the legal matters concerning your home in case you ever decide to sell or come back again one day."

I still remember how Mrs. Allen cradled her crumpled tear-stained face in her hands and I knew that despite her matter-of-fact exterior, she was soft as butter inside.

"Go make something of yourself" she said, breathing softly, "Siddon's too small, too remote and scandals here could live forever. Every highway leads away from here. Right Pet?"

Was she right I wondered, even though that night I found myself still listening out for the wolf's plaintive call.

Chapter 13

Journey

A few days later, I finally left Siddon. My heart was heavy and I wondered if I had made the right decision to strike out on my own. Trees were bare from the cold and winds were blustery, hardy evergreens were drooped, as though in despair over my departing. I glanced at the skies furtively, and saw that it was stark white and ominous with grey undertones. Not a speck of sunlight peered through and I began to wonder if there might be snow.

Mrs. Allen and I stood braced against the biting wind at the newly renovated bus station outside Siddon. We were startled by the excited honking of Canada Geese that formed a huge V overhead, as they too departed from Siddon. We watched in awe as hundreds of geese crossed the broad northern sky to head south. Even though I had seen many such flights since childhood, the migration had never been more poignant, since this time might be my last. I too, was leaving. The wind moaned as the last of the geese flew over, and Mrs. Allen told me that it surely was a good omen. She held my hand tightly, fussing over the thin fall coat I had chosen to wear.

"Make sure you have your money pouch." She reminded me gently, "And your coat is it really warm enough, you still can change. I packed you an extra one that's more suitable."

I remained silent and felt that there was no need to explain to her that the coat I was wearing had belonged to mother, or that it was more stylish than any I owned. I felt like a child on the first day of school and Mrs. Allen's blue-veined hands holding tightly to mine were comforting.

When I boarded the Toronto-bound bus there were tears in our eyes. I strapped on my backpack and gripped my one roll-along suitcase and tucked it into the storage compartment on the side of the bus, then headed to the back of the vehicle. Mrs. Allen told me that the washroom was located there, and seats back there were the most convenient.

An hour into the journey I found the air at the rear intolerable, so I found an empty seat nearer to the front beside a woman named Mary Cotton. She was quite talkative. As a result I could no longer admire the snow blanketed landscape with its hidden forests and fields that slipped by in rapid succession as the bus sped by.

Mary Cotton introduced herself and asked my name, then immediately informed me that she was going to visit relatives in Scarborough. She told me that Scarborough was larger than anything I could ever imagine. When I asked her about Toronto, she screwed up her mouth in contemplation and after some thought, said that she had never had any reason to visit Toronto. "Why bother," She said, with a smirk "We can get everything in Scarborough."

I slept and woke and slept again then awoke to find that Mary Cotton had placed religious pamphlets on my arm rest. I kept my eyes closed against them, then feeling a slight nudge from her, I read a single page. It was an ornately decorated pamphlet with lilies and silver doves. By sheer coincidence the text printed on the pamphlet were the exact words father had taped on the wall beside my bed years ago. "Let me no wrong or idle word unthinking say. Set thou a seal upon my lips, just for today."

With a trembling hand I returned the pamphlet to the arm rest. Mary smiled and patted my hand, "You'll surely be saved." She said, sounding convinced "I can see that those words mean a lot to you."

"Thanks, they do." I replied, and I buried my face in my hands. What if she knew about my wayward mother, and what would she have thought of my father?

For the next several hours I endured her incessant chatter that lasted through lunch and supper while I ate sandwiches that Mrs. Allen had made. I longed for silence as I slowly ate a slice of apple crumble. Mary Cotton picked at her own food with a plastic fork and I saw that her container had nothing in it but soggy cucumber slices, and a watery chickpea salad.

I offered her a slice of my crumble hoping she would stop talking. She broke the crumble into tiny pieces and played with it on a napkin, while still talking. Sleep finally came between us, and I was able to appreciate the world outside the bus windows. Dark had descended. I could barely make out farms or even fields and I had no idea where orchards blended with the wilderness. Sturdy trees and bush stood black against the sky like silhouettes. Small towns dotted the rural landscape with lonely lights twinkling ,and I must have been the only person, other than the driver, who was still awake when we eventually arrived at Toronto's Bay Street bus station.

I was in such a hurry to leave Siddon, that I did not give much thought to where I would eventually stay in Toronto. Mrs. Allen had not received a reply from her friend, but she wrote down the friend's address and said that I should go directly there, since she might already be expecting me.

Being alone in the city awoke many fears, and I wondered where on earth I should go after leaving the station. I disembarked from the bus and lugged my suitcase from the storage and strapped on my backpack to follow the surge of fellow passengers. Only then did I remember to search my pockets for the address of Mrs. Allen's friend. I glanced at the address several times and thought that it might as well had been on Mars, for I had no idea how to get there. The friend's name was Josephine Ellis and the street she lived on sounded strange on my tongue, as I repeated the name over and over to myself, Sorauren Avenue, Josephine Ellis.

A passing stranger, saw me pondering and in her concern, she pointed out a sign saying Information. I thanked her and approached the information booth. Behind the counter was a middle-aged East Indian man who looked quite bored; it was clear that he must have been asked the same questions over and over.

"Could you please tell me how I can get to Sorauren Avenue from here?" I asked hesitantly. The gentleman looked up from his computer and acknowledged me with the ghost of a smile. "How do you spell that." He said, then he rapidly punched the name into his computer. Looking satisfied, he smiled, "Take the Bay bus up to College Street, then transfer over to the 506 College West bound streetcar. That will get you to Sorauren Avenue. Just ask the driver to call your stop".

"Thanks" I said, memorizing his reply, "But where do I get bus tickets?" I asked, "Can I get them here?"

Before the man could answer, two teenagers, a boy and girl, with identical jet black spiked hair, appeared as if from out of nowhere.

"Hey," The boy said grinning, as they swaggered towards me,

"I'm Jim and this is my girl Heidi. I heard you say you need tickets I've got an extra and we're heading close to Sorauren. Want to buy it? New to Toronto eh?"

"Yes I just arrived on the bus."

"Alone eh?"

"Yes."

"Sweet."

From the way they scrutinized me it felt as though they were playing a game of cat and mouse. I could not have been any plainer looking as compared to them, for they were wearing nose rings and spikes and studs on their chins and wrists.

I remembered father once told me that if a deer stands perfectly still against the forest's foliage, when confronted by an enemy it might have a better chance at surviving by being camouflaged there. I breathed deeply and told myself to be perfectly calm, and imagine that I was fitting in.

"Well take it or leave it, the ticket will cost you five bucks." Heidi grinned menacingly.

"I'll take it," I replied and reached inside my coat pocket for the money.

"Thanks," Jim said, practically grabbing the bill out of my hand. "Let's go then."

"Is that all you brought?" Heidi said, eyeing me and rolling her eyes as though I was totally stupid. "Don't suppose you plan to stay long then."

I was glad that I had a bit of change and small bills in my ample pocket or else those two would surely have figured out that I was wearing a waist money pouch under my coat and it probably was filled with bills. With a smile I silently thanked Mrs. Allen for her suggesting that I wear a pouch.

"Well I haven't made any plans yet. I just want to see how things pan out. You know."

"Right, just look at you, any idiot could tell you're fresh off the bus. Where'd you get that hideous coat anyway?"

I didn't like Heidi's superior attitude or the way she seemed bent on putting me down but since they were supposedly doing me a favour I held my tongue, before replying congenially.

"My mother got this coat in Ireland. It's all the buzz over there. Didn't you know?"

"Really! You could'a fooled me. Are you Irish then?

" I'm half Irish."

"What's your handle?"

"My what?"

"Your name stupid!"

"Kathleen."

"Well Kathleen listen up and listen good!" Heidi said sharply, as she pointed a multi-ringed finger into my face. "Jim here is my man! So don't you be thinking about getting cozy with him! The only reason he talked to you fruitcake is because you looked stupid. Jim's off limits, hear? Don't even entertain any thoughts or you're dead meat!"

"Wouldn't dream of it," I replied and meant it.

"Sure, that's what you say now but aren't chicks like you, always about taking up with unavailable dudes!"

"Hey Heidi, cut the chick some slack," Jim said in exasperation, "This chick definitely doesn't have a thing for me. Look at her, she's like too straight. Let's go catch the bus eh?"

I was more than glad that Jim had the good sense to nip all that process in the bud. I tried to sound interested in their conversation, thought I didn't dare glance in Jim's direction.

I couldn't imagine what Heidi saw in him. He put me in mind of a scrawny porcupine covered in black oil slick.

"So did both of you" arrive on a bus too?" I said, already guessing that they had not.

"Yep, sort of," Jim replied, "Me and Heidi came downtown on a TTC bus. A buddy was leaving town It's like we just saw him off and we plan to crash at his place tonight. You could come too. Jim grinned, "I 'll pull that suitcase for you. Looks heavy, loaded it with bricks eh."

I saw very little of the city that night but I remember how welcoming the lights seemed. It was as if I had travelled into a pool of radiance and though the wind was cold and fierce I somehow didn't even mind. Saddled between Jim and Heidi I made my way to the closest bus shelter. It was a short bus ride from there before we transferred to a streetcar. I felt overwhelmed by the luxury, the spotless red seats, the wide windows and the feeling of being driven in style.

I pressed my face against the cold window and tried to absorb as much of the city as was possible. The whole route was well lit and I saw small shops, cafes, bars and restaurants packed with people. I certainly was not accustomed to seeing crowds out and about at night and soon I was lost in imagining their lives. Heidi and Jim on the other hand were loud and obnoxiously boasting about their plans for the evening. I was sufficiently embarrassed and wished that I was wearing a sign that said, 'I'm not with them.'

Chapter 14

Another New Start

When the driver called out "Sorauren Avenue," I quickly grabbed my suitcase, so as to avoid Jim and Heidi, as I breezed past the driver, thanking him, as I disembarked and stepped out into the night. I needn't have rushed, for neither Heidi nor Jim noticed my departure. I wondered if there was any chance that they had ripped me off, so I hastily checked my pockets and my waist pouch. Thank goodness all was well, nothing was missing. Then it occurred to me that the ticket I bought from them must have been worth a lot less, since there must have been something in it for them and I vowed never to let anything like that happen to me again.

Though I had already memorized the information, I pulled out the folded paper with Mrs. Allen's friend's address and held it tightly like a lifeline. Sorauren Avenue was much longer than I had expected and seemed much darker than downtown Toronto. Buildings that looked like old factories loomed on my left side and on the right were residential houses all built closely together. The street was deserted and I began to wonder if I was the only person still awake. I had no bearings; I couldn't tell if I was going North, South, East or West. Though thank goodness I found myself at the address in less than ten minutes.

The narrow-looking house stood somewhat apart from the

other homes. It had a fenced front garden and ornate metal work that lined its snow-covered walkway, and the porch light was on.

I gripped my suitcase handle tightly, and opened the small garden gate, then went up the steps to the porch. I stood there for a moment, took a deep breath, and I ran my fingers through my hair. I rang the doorbell sharply, there was no immediate response. Perhaps Mrs. Ellis wasn't home I thought. I felt the first wave of panic wash over me. What would I do if she wasn't there, and where would I go at that hour? Then I remembered noticing a small convenience store at the top of the street, and I wondered if the people there might be able to help somehow. I was about to turn around and go back down the steps, when someone pulled back the curtain at the door. Then the door opened with a soft click, and a tall older coloured gentleman stood there in front of me.

"Good evening," he said, solemnly, "I don't want to buy anything or contribute to any causes."

"I'm not selling anything," I replied. "I'm here to see Mrs. Josephine Ellis."

"Well, young lady" he replied hesitantly, "if you've come to see Miss Josephine, you'd better step inside."

The old man ushered me into his small living room and offered me a soft armchair, as he sat down heavily in an overstuffed couch across from me.

"My name's Walker T Robinson." He said, with undisguised pride, as his eyes glinted merrily in the lamplight. "Are you a relative of Miss Josephine?"

"Oh no I'm not related at all. A friend of mine, Mrs. Allen from Siddon, asked me to come see her if I could."

Walker T Robinson hung his head as though a huge weight was on his shoulders and he tightly clasped his long slim fingers together, as I sat and stared at him. He remained perfectly still as though deep in thought. How distinguished he appeared. His short kinky hair caught the shiny light from the one floor lamp, and I saw that his temples were completely white, though the rest of his hair was dark. His unlined features were the exact shade of molasses. He must be about sixty I thought, as he raised his head from his contemplations to reveal extraordinary hazel eyes. I hardly dared to catch my breath and I hoped that he wouldn't take offence at my staring. How was he to know that he, Mr. Walker T Robinson, was the first black person I had ever spoken to?

An awkward long pause fell between us. I was starting to feel nervous when Mr. Robinson finally spoke. "Your friend mustn't have known that Miss Josephine passed on," he said, almost at a whisper, "it's been four years now, as a matter of fact."

I listened intently to the lyrical cadence in his voice, wondering where he was from, and hardly grasping the full potential of the prognosis he had just given. Then all of a sudden it hit me with full force.

"Oh my god," I said involuntarily gripping my armrest and raising myself to a standing position, and preparing to leave. "I'm so sorry to hear. I'm so very sorry. I shouldn't have intruded on you like this."

Walker T Robinson's eyes met mine; and although they swam with tears, they were full of caring, as he waved me back into my seat.

"Don't be sorry. Sit down young lady," he said with authority, "didn't you just come all the way from, where did you say, was it Siddon, and now, have you got a place to stay tonight?"

"No sir, I only just arrived in Toronto."

"What's your name anyway young lady? Don't tell me that at this hour of night, ten o'clock, you don't have a place to stay!" His lips trembled, as he eased himself more firmly into his seat and he let out a deep long sigh. "Don't mind me," he said, sounding apologetic, "I seem to be forgetting my manners. Miss Josephine, good woman that she was, would have welcomed you; and offered you the guest room. I'll honour her memory and do the same. You could stay here if you so choose. It's not really a big room but it has a bed and a bureau, clean sheets and a quilt. It has not been used in quite some time but I'm sure it is respectable. How's about it? Don't mind me I'm getting old and forgetful I'm almost seventy you know. Miss Josephine and I were real close friends for years and years. She lived upstairs and I down here. There was never a finer lady than her, and it didn't make a lick of difference to her that I'm Jamaican. It's a long time now since we pooled all our money and bought this place to share. She is the reason why I have a shelter over my head today."

"Thank you so much Mr. Robinson. I'd be glad for a room, cause I'm really exhausted, and it's quite late. Perhaps tomorrow I could look for a place."

"Call me 'Walker T' everyone else does. So, aren't you going to tell me what your name is young lady?"

"Oh I'm so sorry I'm Kathleen, my last name's Dunkley. It's really a pity that I never met Mrs. Ellis, she sounds wonderful and you know what, she reminds me of her friend Mrs. Allen."

The next morning when I woke up, I was, somewhat confused as to where I was but then I heard the drone of traffic and smelled something cooking, and it all came back to me. One thing was for sure I was no longer in Siddon. I threw on a dressing gown and ventured out of the bedroom. Walker T was already awake and was sitting at the kitchen table. The table was covered with a white tablecloth, and set for two. There were plates of thick brown toast, a jar of jam, a slab of butter and two boiled eggs.

"Good morning Miss Kathleen," Walker T smiled, "slept well?"

"Good morning Walker T, I slept like a log. The bed was very comfortable."

"Then wash up quickly and join me for a bite. The washroom is to your left. The towels are fresh."

When I came back to the table, Walker T rose and pulled out my chair. "Enjoy," he said, taking a pat of butter and dipping it on his egg and toast. "Not much in the house but it's all good."

"Thank you, it looks delicious."

"There's boiled water on the stove and there's condensed milk on the counter. Would you care for some Milo? I always have a cup in the morning."

I didn't have a clue what Milo was, or condensed milk for that matter, but when Walker T made me a cup. It reminded me of hot chocolate, and it was delicious. We ate and drank in silence. When he was finished, Walker T wiped his hands in his broad napkin and finally spoke.

"It snowed again last night while you were sleeping. I watched it coming down for about an half an hour. I like the silence of snow; it reminds me of the sand in an hour-glass. Anyway I'm going to take you over to Roncesvalles Avenue today. It is the main street round here. You might like to find out where to get things in case you need anything. And may I ask how old you are Kathleen? It slipped me to ask you last night,"

"I'm over sixteen. "

"Just as I thought, so you must be a schoolgirl then. Any plans to continue your studies?"

"I haven't thought much about it. I sort of hoped to find work here."

"Education is important young lady. What grade did you get to?"

"I started Grade 12 but I've had a rough time of it lately. So I don't know if I'd settle into studying again anytime soon."

"Well I don't mean to be nosey Miss Kathleen, but what kind of rough time have you been having?"

"No offence taken Walker T, I recently lost both my parents."

"Really! How so?"

I looked into Walker T's remarkable eyes and saw the same concern and compassion I had seen the night before, and there was no stopping myself. I told him without reservation, everything that had happened to me and my family, through a floodgate of fresh tears.

Walker T gripped my hand from across the table, and I felt such strength in those hands of his, and he didn't have to say a word, for I knew exactly what he was thinking.

"You mustn't let it get you down young lady," he said. "You still have a lot to live for. I'm sure everyone concerned would have wanted you to make something of yourself. You are young and strong and good-looking too, and there is so much opportunity for youth here. I thought a lot about it last night. If you like, you can stay in this house for as long as you want. You have my blessings. How's about it?"

Chapter 15

Toronto Living

Walker T and I must have made the strangest pair that morning, for there I was trudging through the deep snow with an older coloured gentleman who was clutching a fedora to his head, looking more accustomed to snow than I, who was born in the north. The problem was my boots; I didn't think to bring my winter boots, considering them cumbersome and the boots I did wear had no grip, being too smooth at the bottoms. We only managed to get all the way down Grenadier Road with all its fabulous three-storied homes, without me once slipping in the snow, because Walker T crooked his elbow gentlemanly, and I hung on to him, all the way to the intersection at Roncesvalles.

"The sidewalk has been cleared here." He said with a smile, "Round here, we just say 'Ronci' not Roncesvalles. It's kind of an affectionate name for the street. But I suspect it's also because the word Roncesvalles can be a bit cumbersome, wouldn't you say? Another thing Miss Kathleen, the neighbourhood used to be mostly made up of Polish and other Eastern European immigrants, but lately it has become more multicultural than it ever was."

"Really?" I said, sounding surprised, even as Walker T pointed out churches, coffee shops, fruit stores, delis, banks and pharmacies and I couldn't believe how lively the street was. The sidewalks teemed with people and it seemed as though every second person knew Walker T.

How unlike my father I was, I thought, since father always talked about the dramatic yet wonderful isolation he found in Ireland, and here I was in Toronto, excited by the hustle and bustle of this booming city.

"One day you might like to stop at the local library," Walker T said. "They might be able to direct you to places that can give you information about jobs. When I was younger I found a brochure here at that library that drove me to enquire elsewhere about a job at the railway. I was a ticket collector, for a long time and after retirement I had a bunch of small odd jobs behind the scenes. I even worked at a part-time job as a nighttime security guard. That's all done with now, though some days I still go down to Union Station to poke around and see the trains. It's a bit of a habit I'd say"

"So is that where you met Miss Josephine?"

"Oh no, Miss Josephine was more respectable than me," Walker T laughed, "she worked at the post office in the Pharmacy that we went past a few minutes back. In those days she used to be a big help when I was still sending packages home to Jamaica. But everyone's gone now, even Miss Josephine. There's no need to send anything anywhere. Miss Josephine used to buy me a coffee and take her break just as I would come in. It was just so that we could have a long chat. We became close friends, nothing romantic mind you, just good friends."

"Was she ever married?"

"Oh yes she certainly was, but sadly she was widowed you know, her husband died three years after they married. Some sort of pneumonia I think. She didn't say much about it, poor soul but she said his name was Andrew Ellis; he worked at the hardware store. I never met him. But from what I heard, he was sort of a big shot but hard-working. He left her a bit of money to live on when he passed."

Chapter 16

Student Help Wanted

The next morning, Walker T and I visited the bank and we conducted 'business' as Walker T called it, for I opened an account and we were just on our way back to Sorauren Avenue, when a sign at one of the local health food stores attracted my attention. It read 'Student Help Wanted'

"Think I should apply?" I said, turning to Walker T "Sure why not," he said jauntily, "it's a reputable shop. They've been here for years."

His recommendation meant a lot to me, though it took me by surprise when he took me by the arm and steered me right up the steps to the store.

How curious it was inside the store. It reminded me of one of those old fashioned apothecaries one saw in books with its rows and rows of medicinal products but there was also health and beauty items, dried fruits, nuts and spices, not to mention, a well-stocked refrigerator. There wasn't a lot of room to move around in but everything seemed to be just in the right place. I was so mesmerized I was taken aback when a friendly salesgirl approached us and smiled.

"Hello Walker T" she said in greeting "Need more vitamins?"

"Not this time I'm actually here to see Carl about the job sign outside."

"Don't tell me you're looking for work Walker T" She said teasingly.

"Oh no it's not for me Susan; it's for this young lady here."

"Well to be honest Walker T, Carl has seen lots of high school applicants. Most of them can't fill the hours he needs. The work is a bit tedious and doesn't pay well enough to make it attractive but what can you expect for just stacking shelves and stuff like that. The person Carl hires would need to be here on the odd morning when the deliveries arrive and some afternoons as well. But if your friend here is still interested, why not go through to the back and speak to Carl."

Carl turned out to be a quiet sort of man with watery blue eyes and a thinning blond patch of hair. His pale round face was dominated by a big dark mustache reminding me of a walrus. His eyes hardly met mine when Walker T introduced us and I couldn't help but notice his slight lisping European accent.

"So this is your first time applying for work? Well, we can train you if you're interested and there is always someone here you can ask about things if you are not sure. All we ask is that you be here when required. Punctuality is very important. We are busy here and we need things shelved and sorted long before we are overrun with customers. Can you do that?"

"Yes I can." I replied fearfully and I clasped my fingers tightly, wondering if I should have elaborated more on my answer. Only then did Carl's eyes meet mine and I found him to be most inscrutable, for not even the slightest change in his expression betrayed his inner thoughts.

"Well," He said In a stern businesslike manner, "You will have to fill out these application forms. One of my girls is going on maternity leave, so you won't start until after she is gone. Is that alright? You'd be on probation though. A lot of young people don't want to wait that long. These days people want things right away. How's that with you?"

"I can wait." I replied nervously eyeing Walker T

"We will see how it goes then eh? We won't need you for another two months. I'll be in touch."

My heart pounded so rapidly I hardly dared breathe and it surprised me when words came out of my mouth. "Thank you sir.," I said "I'll wait."

    ****

That first week in Toronto I took the liberty of phoning Mrs. Allen from the telephone in Walker T's kitchen. She was more than surprised when I told her how things had turned out for me and I could hear her gasp on being informed about her friend Josephine Ellis' passing. I could tell by her voice that she was deeply saddened and perhaps also frightened for me.

"Are you alright my Pet? Are you safe where you are? You can come back here If you need to, you do know that don't you? One never knows when we'll be called by the good Lord," she said. "Poor Josephine. But where are you staying child, are you sure you are alright?"

"I'm staying at the house Mrs. Ellis and her friend Walker T Robinson owned." I said, "He has given me a room on the main floor."

"Who's this Mr. Robinson? Is he a young man? Kathleen you have to be so careful you know."

"Oh no its nothing like that, Mr. Robinson is seventy. He and Mrs. Ellis were close platonic friends, they bought this house together."

"Really! She never breathed a word."

"Mr. Robinson says they knew each other for years."

"This is a surprise but come to think of it I wonder if he would be the coloured gentleman she mentioned in her last letters. She said he's a fine gentleman. But I didn't realize they bought a house. She might have thought I would raise objections with him being coloured. Maybe that's why we lost touch. Is this Mr. Robinson by any chance coloured?"

"Yes he is, he's from Jamaica and very well-mannered."

"Then surely it must be him. Please thank him for his kindness, and offer my condolences though it is a bit late in coming. Poor Josephine I can't believe she's gone."

"How have you been Mrs. Allen? Anything new in Siddon?"

"By the grace of God I'm alright thanks. But the latest news here is that Luke Whitefawn's father has closed down his business. Leaving for B.C. I hear. I think he just wants to get away from all the mess his son caused."

"Well Mrs. Allen, keep well. I'll call again, and I hope by then I'll have more news from this end."

How alien it felt to hear about Luke Whitefawn's father and Siddon while I was living in Toronto. It was as though he and others I left behind belonged to another time and place . I set the phone down into its cradle and wandered into the living room where I found Walker T poring over a thick-bound atlas.

"Look what I found yesterday Miss Kathleen," he said, barely looking up. "Imagine a book like this ending up dumped in a laneway. The things people here throw out! Anyway I got it so you could see exactly where Jamaica is. Like this map says, the island is divided into three counties, Cornwall, Middlesex and Surrey. My folks came from Cornwall. It has lots of white sand beaches and palm trees. But one never knows if the natural surroundings have been destroyed. I heard that they've built dozens of hotels for the tourist industry. So Miss Kathleen, you'll have to remember that the Jamaica I knew might not exist today. But it is my homeland; I still speak of it fondly and enjoy the foods I grew up eating. As a matter of fact I intended to cook us a fine Jamaican meal today."

"Thank you, Walker T" I said, leaning over the book with him, sharing his enthusiasm, "I almost forgot to let you know that I called Mrs. Allen and she sends her condolences and I'd like to pay for the call."

"Nonsense Miss Kathleen I wouldn't dream of charging you. The young women from upstairs use my phone often enough, and at no charge."

"What young women? You never mentioned that anyone was upstairs?"

"Well that's because they are away in Hamilton, they said its some sort of legal business but as a matter of fact, I think they both should be home by tomorrow night. Anyway, do you know that just about every week I come across something useful in the laneway trash? Take that old brass lamp for instance. It was in the trash, can you believe it?"

"Really? It looks a treasure. It's a lucky find Walker T"

"It's not luck Miss Kathleen. It's a miracle"

It was after five the next afternoon that the two women who lived upstairs arrived home. Walker T and I had just sat down to a light supper of spicy tuna and a tossed salad, when I heard a key turn in the front door, followed by the sound of voices.

"Walker T, we're home," someone called out cheerily. "We were lucky to find parking right outside the house."

"Hi Gracie come into the kitchen, we have company," said Walker T, with a broad grin on his face. "Is Claudia with you?"

"She sure is but she just went back to grab her overnight bag from the car trunk."

My eyes were on the doorway but it took me by surprise to find that Gracie, who sounded every inch as Jamaican as Walker T, was a tall Oriental young woman with hair as long and as dark as Luke Whitefawn's. She stepped into the kitchen with confidence born of familiarity and threw her black leather jacket over the back of one of the kitchen chairs before coming over to give me her hand.

"Hi there I'm Gracie," she said with a friendly smile. A whiff of expensive perfume wafted into the room, as I took her hand shyly and found that her grip was firm and welcoming.

"I'm Kathleen," was all I managed to say as I shifted in my seat., suddenly shy.

"Miss Kathleen, Gracie's a top class receptionist," Walker T said with considerable pride. "She works in one of those fancy medical buildings and meets hundreds of people daily. Don't you Gracie?"

"Right," Gracie grinned, as she wagged a finger, "You'd think I was some sort of celebrity from the way Walker T sees things but what he really means is that I work for a private clinic. It's no big deal."

I was impressed with her blatant honesty and more so, when I saw her eyes fill with genuine affection as she quickly embraced Walker T and pulled up a chair beside him."

"Is everything alright?" he said softly addressing her, sounding oddly conspiratorial. Gracie leaned closer to him and smiled. Her long hair hanging like a dark veil across her face wasn't enough to obscure Walker T's bright smile. What an interesting picture they made.

"Claudia's going to tell you everything," I heard her say under her breath, sounding mysterious. "I know you'll like it."

'So it was good news then, Miss Gracie?"

"Walker T, there you go trying to get info out of me, you'll just have to wait, my lips are sealed."

Walker T chuckled softly as he quietly clasped his fingers and didn't say another word, even as he eased himself deeper into his chair. There in the midst of the silence I was acutely aware of the kitchen clock, for it ticked urgently as though in protest against the unbearable waiting. It was with some relief that I heard the front door finally open. There were hesitant footsteps in the hall and instinctively I sat bolt upright, as curiosity got the better of me.

"Where's everybody?" Claudia shouted and from the muffled sounds that followed I knew that she was kicking her boots off.

"We're in the kitchen," Gracie replied loudly, mischief dancing in her eyes, "Walker T has company. Can you believe it Claudia, you and I go away for only a week and already he's found a new friend? She's even a lot younger than us."

I heard Claudia's laugh before I saw her. Her laugh sounded rich and gutsy and somehow reminded me of mother's. But when she came into the kitchen I saw that she was quite unlike mother. She was not as fair. She somehow resembled an Indigenous Canadian, and she was taller, and more muscular than mother.

"So who's here?" she inquired, briskly entering the room and taking us all in with her cat-like green eyes.

"Kathleen's here. I call her Miss Kathleen on account of her being such a nice polite young lady, she's a friend of an old friend of mine," Walker T said, "Come meet her, she's from Northern Ontario and she's staying in the guest room."

"When did all this happen? Pray tell," said Claudia, her lips puckered in a smile.

"It's a longish story Claudia, save it for another time. What I'm interested to know right now, is how things went for you in Hamilton? Don't forget I was right here when you got that urgent phone call to go see your mother."

"Well first Walker T, let me just welcome Kathleen, "she said, lightly brushing her cheek against mine. "Welcome Kathleen," she whispered, before turning to Walker T "Okay, no more suspense Walker T, especially since you already know about Mamma's phone call and her strange message that said I was to drop everything and come. I thought someone in the family was sick or something but Mamma was so cagy I didn't really know what to expect. But as it turned out things were totally insane and amazing, because when I went to Hamilton, Mamma told me that some documents had arrived a few days before addressed to her, from a lawyer's office in Jamaica. There was a letter too but to make a long story short, the lawyer a Mr. Vernon was letting Mamma know that some money was left to her in a will, and that I her daughter had inherited a piece of Jamaican property. Can you believe it! Me inheriting property! Well Mamma who is no fool wondered if it was some sort of scam or a hoax, since the lawyer surely could have contacted me directly. She says she called my dad, who's on a business trip in Miami, and as you know, since he himself is a lawyer. Then he and a few of his colleagues looked over the things Mamma faxed, and apparently, they came to the conclusion that it is all legitimate. But what seems quite curious to me, is that with Daddy being a Jew, and Mamma East Indian, one wonders how come the person who left me the property is a William Chen Loy, who refers to himself as 'Uncle'. I'd safely say he sounds Chinese, so I can't imagine he's related, much less an uncle"

"Perhaps he's a relative of mine." Gracie grinned I'm Hakka Chinese as you know, and Jamaican too."

"Okay Gracie, all joking aside, don't you find the whole thing a bit odd? And to top it all, from what I gathered, the document stipulates that I'm supposed to go to Jamaica to see the property, then file ownership within a month or else I'll forfeit the inheritance."

"So Miss Claudia If you and your parents are absolutely sure the whole thing is not bogus, you should get one of your many male friends to go with you. You shouldn't go alone, under the circumstance, you could be a target for criminals."

"Well Walker T, that is exactly why I am inviting you and Gracie to come down to Jamaica with me. Daddy found out that there's a house on the property, but he has no idea of what sort of condition it is in. He says he believes the property is in a good location, it's not far from Montego Bay. And Walker T, since you know a thing or two about Jamaica, both Gracie and I think you'd be the perfect travel companion, and another thing I know as a fact that unlike some of my male friends, you wouldn't have any hidden agenda. By the way I should remind you that even though Gracie and I were born in Jamaica, we were kids when we came to Canada, we met as kids in public school in Mississauga. We were both immigrant kids, when such a thing was considered a rarity. It wasn't like it is today. Neither of us remembers too much about Jamaica though. I won't mention our present ages but like the island, she and I have been independent for quite a while. But under these unusual circumstances having someone like you there to help negotiate matters would be a big help. Did I mention the fact that no one else I know could go with us at such short notice? I have a hunch that everyone would feel better about things if you were accompanying us, and what better opportunity for you to see your homeland again eh?"

For the longest while Walker T didn't say a single word. It

was almost as though he had stopped breathing but it was clear to all present that he was thinking deeply even as he sat trance-like staring ahead.

"Walker T" I said in a hush, becoming fearful, as time ticked by. "Are you alright?"

"I'm just fine." He replied I just needed to sort things out in my mind and by the way Miss Kathleen I hope you have a passport, because I have no intention of leaving you here alone. What kind of host would I be?"

"So, you won't come without your new friend?" said Gracie, "I should have expected that, for you are really quite the gentleman. Well if that's the only way we can have you, then I don't see any reason why she shouldn't come. It might even be interesting to see Jamaica through a Canadian's eyes. Are you up for it kid?"

Everyone laughed and I wondered if my sigh of relief was audible. "Yes I actually do have a passport, Mother made sure it was always up to date in case we ever needed to go to Ireland. But the only thing is, I don't have enough money to even think about travelling overseas, so don't count me in."

My heart pounded, fiercely I had to face reality. How could I even travel, abroad considering my lack of funds and being without a job in a strange city. I didn't break and dissolve into tears or let my whole story pour out. I had learned to be practical.

"Well Walker T," Claudia smiled, "Regardless of what Kathleen just said. It looks like all of us will be going. This is extremely short notice but I'll be getting tickets for the day after tomorrow. I'm paying. No arguments please, just enjoy. You guys might not know, but I have a friend who works in the travel industry, and she can get us tickets dirt cheap, Kathleen's included."

Part Two

Chapter 17

Off to Montego Bay

A blast of hot air hit us when we stepped out from the Air Canada jet at the Donald Sangster International Airport in Montego Bay. At first I thought the heat was coming from the overheated jet engine, but no, it was the heat from Jamaica's hot salty air. It cleared my winter-clogged lungs, and every breath was soothing. The sun was high in the sky, and everything around us was unexpectedly brilliant and shimmering. When quite unexpectedly, a cool breeze came off the sea to tantalize us, I couldn't help but feel that father would have liked it here. I gazed at distant hills and mountains longingly, his memory very much alive in my heart, though I was no longer in Canada..

It was as if I were seeing vivid colours for the first time. The flowers, people's clothes and the landscape all were aglow, and I immediately fell in love with my new surroundings.

"Thank you, Claudia," I blurted out. "It's like only because of you, that I could be here at all, and it is so amazing."

Claudia pointed skywards, and overhead I saw beautiful birds that I didn't recognize, wheel across the broad aquamarine sky. We all stood together and watched, even as Claudia's fingers gently brushed against mine and she smiled. "You are welcome" she whispered.

On entering the terminal I was surprised that we were

welcomed by groups of musicians playing and singing rhythms that pulsated loudly and shook us to the core. Walker T, who was not as impressed with them as I was, carefully steered us away from that area, making sure we avoided the touristy craft shops, and souvenir stalls. He explaining under his breath that everything there involved spending money, and they were highly overpriced.

The terminal teemed with people of all races. I had never seen anything quite like it, some were visitors like us, and others, perhaps locals judging from their speech.

"Where you people going?" A brown-skinned man cried out, as he rushed towards us, ahead of a group of others who were also attempting to get our attention.

"We're only going as far as Gloucester Avenue," Claudia replied, sounding businesslike.

"Oh you just going on the 'Strip' then." The man replied sounding disappointed. "It just round the corner. Me could'a give you a drive but it wouldn't make no sense"

"Yeah, you're right. The Silver Mermaid Hotel's quite close." Gracie said, "My family stayed there before." and with a show of strength she lugged her huge roll-along suitcase though the crowds, keeping up with Claudia, who was walking briskly ahead of us.

"Well it look like you won't even need a cab." The man said forlornly, as he blended into the crowd and left us.

Only then, did Claudia stop momentarily, "Did I mention to you guys that we will be staying in Montego Bay for a couple of days? It might have slipped me, because it was my friend Anthony in Toronto who made all the arrangements. He also hired a driver who'll take us out to the property from here. He's a whiz at things like that. Hope you all won't mind the little detour."

"Well, Claudia," Gracie smiled, "I guess I was probably the only one of us, that suspected that you'd want to stay at the Silver Mermaid. It is so convenient both our families stayed there and couldn't stop praising its service

"I don't mind staying there," Walker T grinned, "but if I did know we were going to stay in a fancy hotel I would have dressed more appropriately but I suppose being a visitor, my social gaffes will be overlooked."

"Hey did you guys notice how all those taxi guys were staring at us," Claudia whispered, "Its about our money isn't it?"

"Probably," Gracie replied, as she quickly touched up her lip gloss. "Hope I look okay."

"You look fine," I mumbled and I went to stand beside Walker T.

"Miss Kathleen," Walker T said with a flourish, "Don't let all this attention bother you, for if it is one thing Jamaicans appreciate. It is beauty. I'm glad to see that that hasn't changed."

The hotel was more impressive than I had imagined, nothing in Siddon compared with it. I was totally floored, there were strategically planted ornate palm trees at the grand entrance and raised rockeries overflowing with blooms to rival those at the airport. As I looked upwards I saw that there were at least fifteen storeys, all with individual balconies graced with floral arrangements and beautiful shady awnings.

The grounds were well cared for, and a paved interlocking brick pathway sloped down to a long white sand beach, where sunlight dappled the waves that rolled in. Gulls streaked across the sky, as though watching us all below. I was in turn mesmerized by the crowded, beckoning sandy beach. There were tourists congregated under beach umbrellas, and at cabanas near where drinks and snacks were provided.

I watched almost transfixed, though my eyes were drawn to the profuse sprays of tropical flowers that decorated the compound, and I could not help but remember the timid wild bouquets mother often gathered in our Canadian forests.

"Come along Miss Kathleen," Walker T called out to me, "We have to register and get our rooms"

I was suddenly brought back to reality, remembering only then that I was both a spectator and a guest.

"You like it already," Claudia laughed, "just wait until you see inside. You'll be able to explore later"

I walked away from the profusion of butter-coloured flowers that grew in wild abandon at the steps of the hotel and tears welled in my eyes. My thought flew back to the isolated wilderness I came from, that now seemed so far away from the distant mountain ranges that loomed, lush with vegetation I did not recognize. How spectacular it all seemed. "There are no wolves here." I murmured as I tagged along with my companions, glancing back only to glimpse again how the bay seemed to curve like a great arm to embrace the sea and its white-capped waves laden with spray that rushed towards the sparkling shoreline. Fishing boats, I had at first failed to notice, bobbed on the water, as pleasure boats lazily sailed by. How peaceful it is here I thought, as I stepped inside.

"Jamaica is exactly the way I remember it." Walker T said reverently, "But despite all that, I need take a short nap before I head down to the water. I'm sure you folks will find something to amuse yourselves for an hour or so."

Gracie and Claudia decided to go two floors down to the snack patio to enjoy drinks and food. They grabbed me a bag of plantain chips, a burger and a can of pop, and suggested that I should go explore the beach.

"We'll be here for a couple of hours " said Gracie, "this is an all-inclusive hotel, so everything is on the house" You might like to go see what's going on outside. Just try not to get burnt, the sun can be pretty wicked sometimes. The sand is lovely though, you can take your sandals off, you'll see what I mean."

I followed a group of visitors to the elevator and stuck with them as they made their way down to the elegant main lobby.

"Going swimming?"

A little blond girl about ten asked, as she stared at me. "We're going to learn to play beach volley ball." She smiled.

"Have fun" I replied, "I'm just going to hang out on the beach."

"You'll like it" she said, as she walked away briskly to catch up with her family.

The beach was crowded. I slipped off my sandals and dug my toes into the sand. It felt amazing. I kept walking and felt the salt from the sea on my lips, as my hair rose and fell in the sea breeze as though it had a life of its own. Happy people were engaged in a variety of fun activities. From the sound of their high voices I wouldn't have known that I was in Jamaica, since they all sounded as if they were from America, Canada and the UK.

Little cabanas and bright beach umbrellas dotted the beach, though several sunbathers chose to sleep directly under the scorching sun. What could they be thinking? There wasn't much of a chance of my escaping the sun, and since I had left my sun block upstairs, I wandered over to the far end of the beachfront, where it was more inclined to be shady. I soon discovered that an ornate iron fence ran alongside the entire length of the property. There was a sign posted there, it was a warning to remind guest not to go any further than the fencing. I followed the fence line, and went down to the sparkling water. I walked into the shallows and enjoyed the motion of the waves that lapped against my feet, and I proceeded to splash about like a child. I was so caught up in this activity that I did not notice that someone had been watching me, until I heard the sound of laughter. I looked around sharply and heard a Jamaican sounding voice addressing me.

"How come you so pale, you don't have sun where you come from?"

A curly-haired dark-skinned teenage boy approached and I assumed that he was one of the hotel's staff. He was neatly dressed in their signature green and yellow uniform and carried a tray of snacks. He had a friendly grin on his face and I couldn't help but return his smile, as he extended his free hand.

"I'm from Canada," I said with a laugh, "there's not much sun there at this time of the year."

I watched a small worry line crease the boy's forehead, yet his eyes smiled. "So is that why you come here"

"Well I came with friends, and it was a sudden decision, so it's like I hardly had time to think about weather and that stuff."

"So how long you staying then? I might run into you again, cause I work here."

"Yes, you might run into me, we'll be here for maybe three days or so" I said, "what's your name?"

"I'm Peter," he laughed, "I hope you not asking for my name so that you can report me to the office. I'm not supposed to chat with the guests unless they're ordering something."

"Why would I do that?" I laughed "would you feel better if I ordered an ice tea?"

"Yes I could bring you an ice tea on the double. Then they wouldn't say that I was getting too friendly."

"Trust me Peter," I said, "no worries I'm glad just to talk to someone who's around my age. The people I came with are all older that me."

"Is what you saying. Anyway you've not even told me your name and since you not swimming, what is it you like to do?"

"I'm Kathleen, and I guess, I like nature." I grinned, "I like swimming and even walking. But it's like I'm always observing things around me. Maybe one day I'll be a journalist. Know what, we just arrived a few hours ago, so there's lots to see. We will be leaving all this behind in a few days."

"So where you'll be going?"

"One of the women I came with, mentioned that we're going to a property called Santiago."

"Santiago! Are you sure Kathleen? That place is really lonely! It full of bush for miles. My granny live near there. You people must be really and truly brave, cause that property is right next to Rose Hall."

"What's Rose Hall?"

"You mean to say you never hear bout Annie Palmer the White Witch of Rose Hall? She killed her slaves, and her lovers. People say she still haunts the estate, and the Great House where she used to live is called Rose Hall."

"No I never heard of her, but it sounds horrific. How long ago did all this happen?"

"Oh, it was way back in slavery days, be careful out there. How long you going stay there? Maybe next time I visit Granny I could stop by and see you."

"I'm not sure how long we'll stay. It all depends if the house is livable, anyway I guess you could come to visit. I don't see why not."

"Well if you sure it alright, I'll see you one of these days out at Santiago. I better get back to work before I get fired."

After hearing the story Peter told me I wondered if I had been wise to come to Jamaica. It occurred to me that he might have invented the whole thing, though from the little I knew about him, I felt he could be trusted. So I decided to run the story by Walker T, and see what he thought of it all.

Something significant happened when I was making my way back across the beach. I thought I glimpsed Claudia, under one of the beach umbrellas, locked in an embrace with a man who appeared to be Jamaican.

Since it wasn't that long since she and Gracie had gone to the hotel lounge I thought perhaps it wasn't her after all. I took a second look, the woman's, hair was draped across her face and effectively blocked my view. I didn't think much more about it, as I found my way back to the hotel's entrance, and I went through the lobby to the elevators that took me upstairs to our rooms.

I decided to check on Walker T, since it wasn't likely that Gracie and Claudia had returned. I knocked softly on Walker T's door and was surprised when he answered. "Come out here." he said, as he led me out to his spacious balcony. "I had a good rest, and now I'm having tea out here. The view is spectacular."

I was totally taken by surprise by the magnificence of what I saw. The mountains, green foliage, the sea, the beach and the other modern hotels that dotted the strip. "It's awesome." I said, catching my breath.

"Have a seat Miss Kathleen. Did you enjoy your walk? I got us a pot of tea, scones, butter and an assortment of jams. Gracie rang me to say you'll be hungry, so I took the liberty of ordering you that lovely glass of fruit punch and there's assorted sandwiches under that mesh dish cover."

Gracie was right I was famished, though I had eaten on the

beach. The fruit punch was excellent, as were the neatly prepared sandwiches. "Thank you Walker T" I managed to blurt out, as I wolfed down sandwich after sandwich.

" I didn't know I was so hungry."

"The sea air has that effect on people. Enjoy. How was the beach? Think you might go in for a swim? The hotel has a pool too If you'd prefer that."

"Maybe later we could go down to the beach together Walker T But guess what? I met a Jamaican boy on the beach, he works here at the hotel, and he told me a strange story about a place called Rose Hall. The story was about murders and slaves and even a witch, and he says that Santiago, where we are going is very close to the Rose Hall Property. Have you ever heard of the White Witch, Walker T?"

Walker T leaned back in his chair, shielded his eyes from the sun, then pulled a clean white handkerchief from his pocket, to dab at beads of sweat on his forehead.

"Well, Miss Kathleen" he said lowering his voice, "every Jamaican has heard the legend of the White Witch. But mind you, half of it might not be true; though it makes a good story. The legend is propagated in popular books, etc but if you ask me it has got to the stage where it has taken on a life of its own. I remember my own father used to tell us children that he was descended from one of the Rose Hall slaves. He said that his ancestor was a white Englishman who visited the estate to help with the bookkeeping, but it would seem that bookkeeping wasn't all that he was doing there. Rose Hall was a place of debauchery that's for sure."

"So how do you feel about going to stay near such a place Walker T?"

"I don't let it bother me Miss Kathleen and neither should

you," he chuckled. "Those people have been dead for donkey's years and duppy don't have time for me or you. Annie Palmer was half Irish you know, so I hope that with you being from Irish descent, she'll take a liking to us and leave us alone."

"What's a duppy?"

"It's a ghost."

"Really! What a strange word!"

'It might have been derived from the German word Doppelganger. You can look it up on the internet when you get a chance."

As Walker T spoke, I gazed out at the sea and couldn't help but notice that there was a distinct chill in the air. I wondered if he felt it too, but he didn't say a word about it when he excused himself and got up from his chair and went inside.

Later that evening Walker T and I walked down to the beach front, where there was a barbeque and musical entertainment for the guests. Neither Gracie nor Claudia were anywhere to be seen, though somehow, I knew they must be in the company of guests they had just met. Walker T didn't say a word about their absence, so I kept my thoughts to myself.

It was two in the morning, when I finally heard the suite door open. It was Claudia and Gracie; their voices were hushed and conspiratorial.

"She's asleep," Gracie said, as they made their way to the living-room, area, kicking off their stiletto heels along the way. I heard the distinct rustle of their cocktail dresses as they tiptoed across the floor on bare feet. "Kathleen's in the small room and I guess Walker T's in his suite next door neither of them can hear us." Claudia whispered. "Want a nightcap?"

"Actually, no thanks I had too many already," Gracie slurred, "I had to be very firm with Derrick all day, he can be so typical."

I heard muffled laughter and kept perfectly still, as they charged the night air with their whispering. In the darkness it all sounded strangely sinister and I wondered what they would think if they knew about the White Witch, and the close proximity to Santiago.

"Well," Claudia said boldly, "my date's name was Charles, and as far as we were concerned it was a fun day, all day."

As I lay on my bed engulfed in the darkness of the cool Jamaican evening, I couldn't help but think about my home in Siddon, where friendly pin points of starlight would peep in at my bedroom window. I was terribly homesick. I pined for the isolation I was used to, and began to question my spontaneous decision to travel. I even wondered if I should return home, then my thoughts turned to Peter. Would I see him again, and if I did, I needed to know more about the legend of the White Witch. The fact that she had Irish blood intrigued me. Perhaps, a deeper conversation about her, would take my mind off of the things I was missing.

I awoke at daybreak, dogs were barking in the distance, and there was a riot of birdsong. I climbed out of bed and went to the window. I drew back the curtains to a blast of sunlight. Waves were rolling in, and waving palm trees seemed to meet the breeze head on. The sky was an impossible shade of raw orange as a few families already headed for the beach. I watched in silence as gulls flitted above the restless waves rising and dipping in rhythmic motion. I stood perfectly still watching, until finally my rumbling stomach reminded me that I was hungry.

I showered and dressed, while Claudia and Gracie slept, and I dried my hair with a handheld hair dryer provided by the hotel. Despite its droning I managed to hear when someone knocked hesitantly on our door. "Who's it?" I asked, and was relieved to learn that it was Walker T, since Mrs. Allen's words of caution, were still lodged in my mind. "It's me Walker T" came the reply, "I just wondered if anybody's coming downstairs to the breakfast room."

"I'll come." I replied, "the others are still sleeping."

We went downstairs together, where many other guests had already gathered. Some of the people there were dressed for the beach, while others were more conservative. Waiters stood around attentively handling various questions and requests. Walker T and I approached the tables without questions, even as two noisy children ahead of us, made faces at each other. Breakfast was displayed on buffet tables, and the food was kept warm atop electric food warmers.

Walker T's and I were pleasantly surprised by what we found there. The tables were laden with Jamaican dumplings, corn bread, eggs, bacon, sausages, codfish and ackee, bread rolls and butter. There was a separate table for coffee urns, tea kettles, milk, cream and various juices. "What a spread." Walker T laughed, "Think it will be enough for you Miss Kathleen?"

I grinned broadly as we filled our plates and found a tiny nook suitable for two and sat down to our meal. "There's a cornucopia of tropical fruits at one of the tables" I said, "If I have any room left I'll try a few."

"I feel like royalty." Walker T smiled, "but Miss Kathleen, after my meal, I won't need anything else but a coffee."

"Just look at the life I have come to enjoy," Walker T murmured, "as a boy I was dirt poor, we lived over there, near those hills in the distance and I never dreamed that one day I would be allowed into a place like this, much less, be sitting here drinking coffee with fellow tourists."

We both laughed when he said that, though for the next while we were silent, as we watched the beach gradually become more and more crowded with game players, bathers, boaters and launches.

"It's so beautiful here," I said, "it's a pity that Gracie and Claudia, are still sleeping."

"Miss Kathleen, did you mean to say that it's a pity, because we're leaving tomorrow morning? Well I'm sure you're going to love your stay in the country. We can always hire a car if you need to come back into town. You might even make the acquaintance of some young people. You won't want to be spending every moment of your time with an old gentleman like me."

"You're good people Walker T"

Chapter 18

Santiago

A glorious breeze followed us as we headed away from Montego Bay in a hired car. Our driver was called Lalu and though he was clearly East Indian, he spoke in the broadest Jamaican patois. Walker T sat up front with him, while Gracie, Claudia and I, sat in the back seat. The large car trunk was crammed with our luggage. I craned my neck out the window intoxicated by the landscape that flashed by. Lalu pointed out citrus and banana plantations, as well as coconut groves and endless fields of sugarcane that swayed in the wind, reminding me of corn. Palm trees flailed in the gentle breeze as we zipped by.

Once in a while we came upon small country houses with traditional palm thatched or tin roofs. We gazed from the car window in wonderment finding the architecture both quaint and alluring. Then there were sights of large modern flat-topped family homes that sat lonely on top of rolling hills, and I wondered if that was what Santiago would be like.

There was no escaping the brooding purple hills in the distance, that seemed always to keep pace as we sped on. Leafy fruit-bearing trees rustled in the wind alongside us, and through their network of branches we often could catch glimpses of the splendour of the restless, beautiful Caribbean Sea.

The combination of the driver's incessant chatter, the unsurpassed scenery, and the salty air, almost had me nodding off to sleep. I was forced to sit bolt upright, when the car pulled over quickly, and Lalu point out that there in the distance was the Great House of Rose Hall across the expanse before us.

Nothing prepared me for its magnificence. The Great House dominated the landscape and its imposing splendour left me in breathless awe.

"That's where the Witch did live." Lalu announced, his voice charged with emotion. "I don't drive here at night," he continued ominously, "her duppy still roam the bush-land over there. Is a good thing it still morning time now. The house did get destroyed, but them build it up again. People still go see it all the time, cause them don't know that she still there watching. Mark my word duppy live in that there place."

"What nonsense," Gracie said under her breath. "This is the sort of superstitious nonsense that kept my parents away from the island. My mother says she was always terrified when she was growing up here. She heard scary stories about duppies, three-legged horses and rolling calves every night."

"You're so right; it's like Halloween all year." Claudia replied, "My parents remember the same stories you mentioned, but they say that some sophisticated Jamaicans call it being 'dark and stupid'. But since we are neither of those things, we really have nothing to fear. Anyway I'm sure we are both glad that our friends Charles and Derrick are joining us to see the property later this afternoon."

Lalu did not say another word, even as he veered the car off the main paved road, and on to a rocky dirt road with sugarcane fields on both sides. How spooky it felt driving through the tall cane. It was as though the rest of the world was blocked out except for the stark blue sky. Once in a while we saw people, there was a woman carrying a basket of mangoes on her head and another time, there was a man with a machete hacking away at the cane. Neither of them took any notice of us.

"A track through the cane field lead down to the beach." Lalu said. "The water shallow, you can swim and you going notice a small river running past da house. You can use the water for washing. Look. It is ahead of us. That's Santiago."

The car climbed up a steep incline but our eyes were fixed on the house that stood grandly before us. It had a rose garden in front with flowering Allamanda bushes, and fruit trees near the house, and what a house it was! It was two storeys high and rather wide with tall bay windows and wooden columns on the verandah. It was clear to see that the house's old stone steps had withstood the test of time.

As Lalu parked the car, two figures emerged from the house and came down the steps towards us. One was a well-dressed light-skinned woman and the other was a much darker woman who wore an apron over her simple country clothes.

"Good morning everyone," called the light-skinned woman with open arms. "Welcome to Santiago House." Her voice revealed traces of an English accent. "Which one of you is Miss Claudia Haddad? I'm Barbara Foreman, the secretary for your lawyer Mr. Vernon. This is Elfrida, the helper, we thought you might need some help with the daily housework. I'm actually here to get some paperwork signed before you settle in."

"I'm Claudia Haddad," Claudia said, as she quickly opened the car door to let herself out. "It certainly is a pleasure to meet you. I brought some friends along; in case it got lonely out here. This is Walker T Robinson, Gracie Lyn and Kathleen Dunkley; we are all from Toronto, except for Lalu our driver."

"How nice to meet you all" Barbara Foreman said, "Miss Haddad If you don't mind, we could sit here on the verandah where it's cooler and sign the papers in the shade. Then if you have any questions I will be happy to answer them. I'm sure your driver Lalu will help the others with the luggage. Elfrida has made you a wonderful midmorning meal. I'm sure you've noticed the aroma. It is stewed peas and rice with a cucumber and avocado salad and fried plantains. She has also roasted a breadfruit from the garden."

Elfrida smiled shyly and lead the way back up the steps with Lalu following closely behind with the luggage. "The bedrooms are prepared and ready," she said, as though reading from a script, "there is running water in the pipes but don't use too much. We have an electric generator out back, so we have lights but we use the water from the river for washing clothes."

"Will you be staying here Elfrida?" Gracie asked staring at the steep stairs to the second floor."

"Oh no Ma'm, I have to go home every evening to my family. I wouldn't stay out here even if...." But then she stopped short, and in my mind, I filled in the blanks, she wouldn't stay out here at night even if we paid her.

The house exceeded my expectations. The furnishings were antique, as well as the enamel jugs and basins that were in each of the bedrooms. We were amused to find chamber pots under the beds; then realized that using them would conserve water instead of flushing the toilet.

The living-room overlooked the rose garden. Half open windows brought wonderful fragrances into the house. The room was furnished with sturdy mahogany curio cabinets, matching stiff-backed chairs with brocade cushions, though best of all, was a wooden window seat that looked out to the gorgeous garden. My eyes were drawn to the carved book shelves and magazine rack. How comfortable it seemed in the bright sunlight.

I knew right away that I was going to enjoy this room, though it was attached to a rather severe-looking dining room with heavy dark curtains at two large windows which I presumed were to ensure privacy at mealtimes. A large oak table in the centre of that room was set for dining. The ornate mahogany chairs around the formal table seemed out of place, as was the oversized china cabinet that seemed far too auspicious for the likes of us.

Instinctively I wandered into the kitchen, that although much larger, reminded me of the one I left behind in rural Ontario. On the stove was the delicious meal Elfrida had prepared.

"Ready to eat Ma'm?" Elfrida said, catching me off guard, as I stared at her steaming pots.

"I'll ask the others if they are ready. I will be right back." I hurried from the room but took a wrong turn and found myself outside in the yard at the back of the house.

Across the yard from where I was, I saw an old stone well with a wooden lid that fit over the opening. I was walking towards it, when Elfrida called out, waving her cooking spoon in the air. "Everybody's ready to eat,"

When I returned to the house, Elfrida whispered urgently into my ear, "Don't go near that well, the water dry out, and it dangerous."

Elfrida's meal was first rate. All of us over-indulged. Walker T announced that he was stuffed, and would be going into the living room to put his feet up and read the day's paper. "We have to catch up on what's going on here," he said, "People here take politics very seriously and they express it in more dramatic ways than we do back in Canada. There's a lot of poverty here, and then there are also people with more money than you can dream of. I should also check the weather. It looks like it might take a drastic turn. Just look at the clouds outside. Miss Kathleen, did you notice that there is no computer in this house and no television either?"

"Claudia and Gracie brought their laptops." I replied.

"It's a blessing Miss Kathleen, that there's a radio over there on the curio cabinet. I also noticed that there is a telephone way out here in this godforsaken place."

I had not even noticed those details that Walker T pointed out. It was hard enough to imagine that there was no television. It occurred to me that perhaps the evenings would be long and lonely without anything to entertain us.

"So, what you going to do with yourself now Miss Kathleen, are you going to sit and watch the river? If so, you'll have to go there by yourself, because Miss Foreman is giving Claudia a proper tour of the house. As for Gracie, she went upstairs to unpack. I just need to relax for about an hour or so."

"I think I might go see the river," I replied, feeling an urge to be on my own. "It's not too far, I can hear it from here."

There was no mistaking the roar of the river through the open windows and the sound of it took me back to Northern Ontario. Instinctively, I listened for the call of a wolf, or the cry of a loon, then remembering where I was, I headed for the door. I stood there for a moment listening, and heard the distinct sound of a car approaching.

"I wonder who that could be?" Walker T said. I peered out the front door and saw when a car pulled up and two well-dressed black men got out and gleefully dashed up the steps towards me.

"Hello," I said, "how can I help you?"

The men laughed, as though I had said the stupidest thing.

"You're way too formal," one of them said, "you sound like a receptionist. Obviously, you don't know who we are; we're close friends of Claudia and Gracie. I'm Charles and this is Derrick."

On seeing Charles close up I immediately wondered if he might be the man I had seen on the beach with the woman I had thought was Claudia. "Oh," I said, nice to meet you. Sorry I was just on my way out. Claudia and Gracie are here, please come in."

"I'll tell the young ladies that these gentlemen are here to see them." Walker T said, suddenly coming up behind me. "Guess I'll read my paper upstairs after all."

I left the house, and followed a dirt track that lead me through a stand of trees I was not familiar with. Birds flew to hiding places in the branches above, on my approach. At first, I was startled by the sound of their flapping wings, then felt calmer as I approached the meandering river. It flowed much further than I had thought, and was wider than expected. Fields and pastures backed on to the river bank, as did all manner of broad leafy trees. I was startled to see green and brown lizards in the foliage, as well as an occasional brown toad in the slick.

I hoped there wouldn't be any poisonous snakes. Eventually I stopped where lush leafy vines hung from tall trees like a living canopy over the rushing water. There had been birdsong in those vines, until I approached. I went to sit on a huge white sun-bleached boulder that protruded from the shallows. I dangled my feet momentarily in the cool water, only to find that tiny brown fish darted around my toes. They tickled my feet, and I quickly pulled my feet out of the water. The lush wild vegetation in that part of the property reminded me of photographs I had seen in books of rain forests. There were banana trees, palms, citrus and a variety of tangled bushes and vines all clustered together haphazardly in that beautiful isolated place.

I noticed that large rocks of all shapes and sizes jutted out all along the waterway. I felt almost as though I had gathered some unknown mysterious strength in this wonderfully secretive grotto. Then, quite unexpectedly I heard a dog barking, and the sound of children's voices approaching. I waited with much anticipation, as a skinny brown dog darted along the rocks, and splashed through the water to find me. It was wagging its tail excitedly as two local children, a boy and a girl, around nine and ten years old came scrambling after their pet.

"Look dey," the boy cried out, on seeing me sitting serenely on the rock, "A mermaid!" he was rooted to the spot, eyes bulging.

"Dat is no mermaid, dat is a duppy!" The girl shrieked, covering her eyes with fear.

"What's going on?" I asked, slowly rising up from the rock.

"Oh mi God she is the White Witch!" the boy screamed, "I know that she would'a come get us."

Only then did I realize that they were talking about me.

"Hey guys," I called out, "I'm not any of those weird things that you think I am. My name's Kathleen I'm from Canada, and I'm staying at Santiago House."

The children drew a little closer their faces marked with fear; though their eyes were wide with curiosity. "Oh so you is the woman who own Santiago House now?" the boy said. "Our modda did tell we that the new owner coming."

"I'm a friend of the new owner," I said, "she's at the house. I just came out here to see the river."

"Well you lucky you don't drop into a sink hole," the girl said, "see that darkness in the water under them trees? All kind'a cow, pig and goat drown there and it have a duppy boy too."

"Is that right!" I said, "how sad, poor boy"

"Me not going say no more bout him, cause you is from Santiago House, dat's where him did live."

"When did the boy drown?"

"Slavery time...at least that is what we modda did say."

"So where do you guys live?"

"We live over dey, where a goat and a pig a run 'bout."

Do any of you know the name of the boy that drowned?"

"Is what you saying Miss? How come you is staying in dat house, and dunno dat him name was Santiago."

The sun was setting when I made my way back to Santiago House. The two children accompanied me most of the way, claiming to be afraid for my safety. However. It was I, who was afraid for them being out so late.

"We used to dis," the boy had said over and over, as he thrust his bony chest out with pride. "We out to all hours most times." I didn't know if I should believe him; though they walked with such confidence, recognizing every squeal and rustle in the growing dark. I couldn't help but feel some measure of relief when the back of Santiago House loomed in the distance, and there were lights on.

"Thanks for walking with me. I'll be alright from here on," I said, "now that you know that I am not a ghost, perhaps I'll see you again soon."

There was such a smile on those children's faces as they turned and walked away.

On approaching the house, I noticed a couple of lit kerosene lamps on picnic tables in the back yard, and there was a peculiar odor in the air. I drew closer under the cover of bushes, and realized that Claudia and Gracie were outside smoking, and their two were visitors were still with them. The picnic tables were littered with beer bottles and dinner plates. No one seemed in any shape to attend to them, and there was no doubt that Elfrida had already left for home.

"If you like ganja," one of the men was saying, "we can bring you some more in a day or so."

"I love it." Gracie giggled, "it's better than anything."

"Bring it on," Claudia squealed, "I can't remember when I had such a good time."

How strange it is, I thought to myself that neither Gracie nor Claudia seemed the same as when I first met them in Toronto. I was sure that Walker T had never seen this side of them, and the last thing I wanted was for them to see me. I imagined that none of them would have welcomed my presence, so I waited in the flowering bushes, hoping to find an opportunity to sneak back into the house.

However, while waiting for an escape opportunity I inadvertently overheard more of their conversation.

"Is there water in that old well?" one of the men said, coming close to where I was, and I saw that it was Charles.

"Why would that old relic interest you?" Claudia retorted. "My guess is that it hasn't been used in years."

"But have you even looked inside?"

"Well, just to satisfy you I'll take a look."

I watched as Claudia crossed the yard and slowly raised the well's wooden cover. The others got up from their chairs and joined her, when suddenly, Claudia let out a blood-curling scream and fell to the ground.

Charles immediately lifted her into his arms. "What's wrong baby? I didn't think the bottle of rum I put in the well to surprise you, would upset you like this."

"It wasn't the rum you idiot!" Claudia shouted. Her tone of voice harsher than I had ever heard it, "there's a dead woman floating in the water. Look!"

My heart pounded and I could barely breathe, as the others immediately encircled the well. I held my breath while they all looked inside. "There's nothing there but a bottle of rum and the well is dry," Derrick said. "He's right," said Gracie, "you must have smoked too much pot. You're hallucinating."

"Yeah right, you're all crazy! I saw her as clearly as I can see you. Know what, you are all full of it!"

With my heart in my throat I made a dash for the house. The door was open. I literally ran right into Walker T.

"Why you look so frightened Miss Kathleen? You've been gone for hours. I thought something happened to you and just now I heard a scream. I'm glad you are alright. When you were gone I tried turning on the radio, only to find that it is useless. It doesn't even work at all. So Miss Kathleen, we are really and truly cut off out here."

Though Walker T's eyes were filled with concern I felt that I dared not tell him about Claudia and Gracie's present condition.

"I met some kids down by the river," I said, "we walked and talked for hours. I lost track of time. Sorry. That was me screaming I tripped over something in the dark."

"Well, Miss Kathleen, there's some corned beef with rice waiting for you. I made us a quick supper since the others are enjoying themselves out back. They can be quite rowdy but we mustn't forget they are grown women. I'm going to sit down here for a bit, so if you need anything at all, let me know. Your room is the one on the left with plaid curtains."

After I ate my supper I went upstairs and unpacked my luggage in the room that Walker T had pointed out. It was a comfortable looking room, though I didn't feel like sleeping just yet. Not with thoughts in my head about the drowned boy, as well as the possibility that there was a dead woman in the well. Claudia had seemed so sure of it, that it was no wonder both ghosts haunted my peace of mind. I decided to go back downstairs to tinker with the old broken radio that Walker T had mentioned.

Walker T was still awake, He was quietly reading in the living room. I entered stealthily, and retrieved the radio, then went to sit at a table, to scrutinize the mechanism in much the same way father used to do. I cautiously took it all apart entirely by instinct, tweaking wires here and reattaching small things that had come loose.

I surprised myself when I plugged it in. It spluttered momentarily and hummed, before a clear voice came through, speaking about the weather. "It's working again!" I declared.

Walker T hurried over; gave me a quick hug, shook my hand and grinned."What a talent you have," he said in genuine admiration. "We're lucky to have you here. By the way, did I mention that we have an early start tomorrow. Try to get a good sleep tonight."

"Early start for what Walker T?"

"Oh I must have forgotten to mention that a Mrs. Campbell telephoned. She says she is coming here in the morning. She's from an organization that preserves and protects local history. She said that the moment she heard that Santiago House was under new ownership, she felt it was her duty to inform the new owner about the history of the house and property. It would appear Miss Kathleen, that there is a connection with this house and Rose Hall's history. A trusted colleague of hers has written an article about both places, she thought it would be of interest to us."

I headed up the stairs reluctantly. I had a distinct feeling that Claudia would not be in any shape to be up early in the morning, but thank goodness exhaustion over took me, there was no room in my brain to think about spooky things, all I wanted to do was sleep.

Chapter 19

Local History

I awoke in the early hours of the morning from a deep sleep, to find the house perfectly still. I glanced out my bedroom window to find the sky stained with purple hues and only a hint of gold to signal the rising sun. What a spectacle it was. I stood there for the longest time bathed in the beauty.

I felt a presence beside me but I was not afraid, for it was as though father had somehow managed to share the moment with me. I remained steadfast at the window and saw dawn break over the distant cane fields. Suddenly, I heard a shuffling sound behind me, coming from the hallway I turned around quickly, thinking that by some miracle it would be father. Then there in his place, was Claudia!

Claudia's face seemed frozen in an intensely evil expression, and her long hair that usually was well groomed was disheveled and wild. She was wearing jodhpurs as though readying to go for a ride. Despite the tropical heat, a chill came over me, something was not right! I held my breath as she went past my door. There was purpose in her stride, as she headed down the steep staircase to the ground floor. The front door opened, and I heard her go out. Only then was I able to take a deep breath, and I immediately heard the door gently click open again.

In the stillness of that early dawn, the sound of Claudia's

riding boots on the stairs were like restless thundering. She went past my room gripping an old riding whip in one hand, and in the other, a very sharp looking machete. My thoughts were in turmoil, my heart beat like a drum. I don't know what prompted me, when silently I sneaked down the broad hallway, past what I thought must be Walker T's room, Gracie's room and in the shadows, with the door slightly ajar, was a room I somehow knew must be Claudia's. I kept myself well hidden, and saw her slide the dreadful instruments under her mattress. She turned quickly as though alarmed by something. I wasn't sure if she saw me, but I held my ground and stood perfectly still in the purple haze of morning. There was absolutely no expression in her hollow eyes. Her skin was as pale as death. I still don't know how I kept myself from screaming.

Gripped with fear I raced back to my room and bolted the door. I waited but no one approached. I pulled my covers around me like a cocoon and didn't leave the room until later in the morning when I heard Elfrida downstairs announce her arrival. Only then did I quietly unbolt my door and took the stairs two steps at a time to join Elfrida.

"Good morning Ma'm," Elfrida said, the moment she saw me. "You sleep good?"

"Yes thanks," I replied, I had decided not to say a word about the night's activities or even about Claudia's early morning manic behaviour.

"Ma'm, me did see Miss Mattie down the road when me was coming this morning, she say that she pickney dem was with you last night, and you is a real nice lady."

"Oh it's like they were so nice to me Elfrida. They walked me home and I thought I should invite them here for a meal one day."

"No Ma'm you can't do that, dem wouldn't come on account of… well, let me just say dat them is not used to foreign people and all that."

"Elfrida, tell me the truth, are they afraid of Santiago?"

"Everybody round here afraid Ma'm. Is just cause you people is here, why I is here."

"Elfrida, don't you agree that sometimes we have more to fear from the living. " I said, trying to sound confident, as I pushed open the front door.

"Don't stay out too long Ma'm, breakfast going ready soon."

There was a birdsong in the trees. The grass, as well as the low rose bushes and the allamanda, were damp with dew. The air was fresh and the undulating land that lead out to the mountainous countryside was inviting. I was tempted to go to the back of the house to see for myself what was inside the forbidden well, knowing that Elfrida would be occupied in the kitchen and wouldn't have time to check on my whereabouts. I crossed the yard cautiously, and noticed spider webs glistening in the early morning sunlight, and I heard the low moaning of pastured cows. Dogs barked in the distance, and once in a while a lone donkey brayed. There was no doubt that some of the people on adjoining properties were already up and about. I heard a tractor go down the dirt road, and the sound of laughter and people talking, carried on the wind.

I quickly made my way to the well, and with great effort, lifted the wooden cover, being careful not to make a sound. When I peered into the interior I was surprised as to how deep it was. I couldn't even see the bottom, though along the walls was a winding stone stair, not unlike the stone steps at the front of the house; though these went down into the bowels of the well. There was no water to be seen, and thankfully, no drowned woman either. Without warning, a hollow unearthly sound floated up from the depths, and I shrank back in horror. I tried to think rationally, and concluded that a wind tunnel must have opened. I quickly replaced the wooden cover and backed away, retracing my steps to the house. Elfrida was at the front door watching for me, not realizing that I had gone to the back of the house.

"Mr. Robinson is awake," she said, seeing me approach. "I was just looking if you still out there. Come inside and have breakfast with him."

"Thanks Elfrida I'll have a quick wash and be right there."

Walker T and I were already in the middle of breakfast when Gracie came downstairs. "I'm famished," she said, "did you guys sleep well?"

I was about to reply, when Claudia came to join us. I noticed that she was wearing a pretty sundress and her hair was well-groomed. "Sorry to be late," she said. "It's the country air, I slept in. What smells so good?"

"Johnny cakes and codfish fritters." Walker T said, reaching for another fritter. "I only made the coffee, Elfrida made this delicious meal."

"Everything's good," Gracie said, "this is the life, eh?"

"Yes," I nodded, barely even looking up, "so, what are you guys doing today?" I asked.

"Well after that lady comes, what's her name again?" Gracie said, "we could do something. Claudia and I made plans. We want to go snorkeling at the beach near here. Do you snorkel, Kathleen?"

'Is there such a thing in Northern Ontario?" Claudia remarked patronizingly.

"No, I don't snorkel," I replied, as I held myself in check, "I wouldn't mind exploring some more of the property though. Maybe Walker T would come with me."

"Well ladies I'm sorry but I can't take you up on your offers. Today I plan to walk only as far as Bickerstep Cemetery near here. I was remembering last night, that many of the people I knew are buried there."

"Want me to come with you Walker T?"

"Oh no young lady I'll be fine by myself. Besides, visiting cemeteries is no way for a young girl to enjoy herself.

There was a sudden downpour of rain before Mrs. Campbell's visit, although by the time she arrived at the front door, the stone steps were dried, thanks to the hot sun.

Mrs. Campbell was middle-aged and short with a ruddy complexion, and stiff reddish dreadlocks. I was surprised to see that despite the warm weather she was wearing a short-sleeved business suit.

"Thanks for agreeing to see me," she said, as Claudia came to greet her. "I hope you all don't mind that I brought my colleague David Chang along. He's parking the car."

"No worries," Claudia said, "It will be a relief to hear something factual about the place. Because so far, we have been inundated with silly rumours."

When David Chang joined us in the living room, all eyes were on him. His height being most noticeable since he probably was over six-feet tall. I concluded that he must be in his early twenties. He's quite good-looking I thought, trying not to stare, despite his light brown almond shaped eyes, high cheekbones and wavy brown hair. He's clearly mixed race, perhaps Oriental and something else. I pondered, noticing that whatever else he was mixed with, was not betrayed by his slightly-tanned complexion. He somehow reminded me of Luke Whitefawn though as far as I was concerned, David Chang was the better looking of the two.

"Have a seat Mr. Chang." Gracie said, indicating one of the overstuffed chairs.

"Thank you, call me David, there's no need to be formal."

He sat comfortably in one of the living room chairs, not far from Mrs. Campbell's, and leaned forward to speak to us, in a hushed conspiratorial manner.

"I've done lots of research," he said, "and as a result, I was able to find out about, and write articles concerning both Rose Hall and this house. The reason I am here, is that seeing that Santiago House now has a new owner I thought it only fair to share my findings, strictly with the hope that you will agree to preserve its legacy." He pulled his chair even closer, as he fished around in his briefcase.

"No doubt," Mrs. Campbell said, pulling her chair closer as well, "you have heard every rumour and innuendo about Rose Hall, so for the moment we will concentrate on Santiago House, because this house has retained its mystique, and has not given up as many of its secrets as Rose Hall has. That is why David is going to tell you what he has learned about this property. We trust that after hearing what he has to say, you will take great care to preserve the history of this remarkable property for posterity."

David Chang smiled, for he must have found whatever it was he was rummaging for, and it wasn't difficult to read into the approving glances on Claudia's and Gracie's faces, as they fixed their eyes on him, and took in his every word.

"Let's begin with the boy Santiago," He said dramatically, as he gripped a wad of notes in one hand. "The boy was actually smuggled here on a slaver, and brought to Jamaica from Haiti and although Haiti is French-speaking, he only knew Spanish, which lead me to believe that he was home-educated in Spanish. We believe, though not conclusively, that his mother was one Isabella Duarte of Havana, Cuba who was the mistress of one of Annie Palmer's lovers. Miss Palmer herself had spent some years in Haiti where it is said that she first learned the practice of Voodoo from a native priestess. That alone is why some people speculate that she herself might have been one of Santiago's blood relatives. Anyway, history books might refute that claim, since nothing has ever been mentioned about his parentage.

Santiago was said to be a blond with a pale complexion and hazel eyes. But there was talk amongst slaves which was passed on to their descendants that the boy's arrival in Jamaica was to be kept as a well-guarded secret. There was even talk that Annie herself shielded him from the authorities and for a while, kept him well hidden at Rose Hall. She was the one who had Santiago House built. It was to be a sort of refuge for the child. Why she did that, remains a mystery to this day, for Miss Palmer was not in the least sentimental or nurturing. In fact she enjoyed other people's suffering. Stories abound about the fact that she relished watching people agonize as she tortured them to death. Much the same as a cat tortures prey without compassion. Yet the strangest thing is, both her and the boy were often said to be seen walking together on one property, and then, in an instant, on the other in a matter of mere moments. There are those who attributed it to Voodoo magic. Another thing that has been said, is that the slaves who built this house, and there were quite a few of them, all disappeared after its completion. It was whispered that they were all put to death to hide the house's many secrets. No one seems to know if that is true or not, but from what we found out, it was revealed that Santiago was a solitary child, the sort of child who kept things to himself. He entertained himself with books and loved nature. He was often found, face luminous, watching spiders, watching bugs, birds, crickets and lizards. It was as if the solemnity of those activities awoke gentleness in him, for he was careful never to cause harm. It is said that he was six years old when he discovered that the meat he ate was actually carved from the carcasses of animals. A chill must have run through him, for the slaughter of docile animals repulsed him, even as he grew older. He was the exact opposite of Miss Palmer, who often doled out death to anyone, or anything that went against her will. By the time Santiago was about ten or twelve, he could only tolerate beans, lentils, rice and vegetables in his diet. It is said that he became quite sickly at the sight of meat, having at one time accidentally come upon the blooded head of one of Miss Palmer's dead slaves. Reliable sources reported that when he approached puberty he began to keep journals. Those priceless journals were never found. The boy's memories were perhaps sharp, because it is rumoured that those journals would have recalled in exact detail all that had happened to him here in Jamaica, as well as in Haiti."

"How awful for that the poor boy to have to live here alone," I said, "he sounds quite sad; I'm sure he missed his family. I wonder why he was brought here in the first place."

Walker T, who was sitting beside me on the couch, patted my hand reassuringly and David Chang's eyes briefly flew to mine, then back to his notes, before he took a deep breath and continued.

"Santiago didn't live alone in the house," he said, "there was an old docile slave man named Martin Swift who was assigned to take care of him. Don't forget that Miss Palmer never trusted women as confidants and she considered most men weaklings, since they were so easily lured into illicit relationships. She lived a life of contradiction and debauchery, since we know now that she herself was often the main prize of many such unions. She considered old Martin Swift an ideal companion for the boy, because he was no threat to her authority, and could not compromise her sexuality. Even to this day it is still said that Martin Swift, an ancient coal black Negro slave and the young vital Latino boy Santiago, made quite an improbable family.

"I wonder how it is that Santiago never heard gossip about the White Witch and all the disgusting business that went on." Walker T said, with a puzzled look in his eye, "because, even when I was a boy, all we children heard all kinds of stories about her."

"That's a good question," David said, "perhaps Santiago didn't understand much of what he heard, because he spoke mostly Spanish, and as a result, he didn't know a lot about the woman he called Auntie Annie. But he must have figured out that she was his provider, and that even one insinuating word, true or false coming from him could have old Martin or any other slave beheaded or poisoned. It is said that Santiago loved the old man, who reciprocated his caring and gentleness. He did not know that Martin Swift had at one time in his youth lead an uprising against slave owners. Martin was caught and beaten and was badly wounded as a result of a crude castration. Though he survived, he was never the same again."

"It sounds pretty gruesome," I said "poor him. I wonder where he stayed when he was here, and even if the inside of this house was exactly as it is now."

David smiled, and nodded in affirmation. "He probably stayed in the quarters at the back of the house, but as for Santiago, he was in the room at the far end of the hall. I've been here before on tours, and so far the condition of things here is still quite impressive. I'd say, it is exactly the way it was then."

"So, it's like he was in Claudia's room!" I exclaimed, hoping that I didn't sound too startled. David was already speaking and didn't seem to take any notice of my reaction.

"Every stick of furniture here at Santiago House was brought over from Rose Hall. Back then, most of the pieces were previously owned by former tenants of the great house, and some used to belong to Miss Palmer's castoff European lovers who showered her with expensive gifts. As you can imagine, Santiago House was imposing then, and it still is now, just look around you. As long as the boy lived here, he was under the protection of Miss Palmer and her slaves. Not surprisingly though, there was a lot of secret resentment amongst those very slaves concerning the fact that a mere boy owned and lived in a house of this size while they served a cruel mistress and lived in cramped confined quarters. From what some old folks have said, it is believed that there were several plots designed to do away with, or overthrow Martin Swift. But the old man was always vigilant, being a practitioner of African mysticism and Obeah. Even so, he knew that he was no real match for Annie herself. I am holding here in my hand, a copy of something an illiterate slave said he had overheard in a conversation between Martin Swift and the boy. The slave's observation has been passed down from generation to generation.

Here it is:

'Listen to me child, I don't wants you to go get mix up with bad tings, you hear me?'

"I imagine Martin Swift would have said those words gruffly, as he boiled and prepared herbs for healing and protection, for himself and the boy."

"You could be right David." I chimed in.

"There's more," David added, "it is also said that the old man warned Santiago that if there was ever any danger, and he, Martin Swift was killed, the boy should remember to hide in secret places, he previously had pointed out to him."

We were so intrigued by David's story, that we all leaned closer to hear more. David's eyes met mine momentarily, before he continued.

"Every person I've interviewed has told me this same story, about Martin Swift's conversations with the boy. So there is no doubt in my mind that there are secret places not yet discovered in this house."

"So what ever happened to Santiago?" Gracie asked, eyes wide with curiosity.

"Dead like everyone else?" Claudia grimaced.

"It was assumed that he drowned," David said, as a muscle moved in his jaw, and his eyes once again met mine.

"One day, a dozen or more slaves came here with the intention of killing Martin Swift. People say that he and the boy were at the river at the time. It is also said that it was miraculous that the old man heard the murderers coming, though they were about a mile away and he warned the boy to run and hide. Ironically, Martin Swift could not run himself, his legs were arthritic, he was caught, beaten and pelted with stones; his lifeless body was thrown into the river not far from here."

'So where did Santiago hide?" I asked, "did the slaves find him?"

"He was never found. In fact people still have it to say that when he eventually saw the old man floating in the river water, he dived in to save him, and not being a strong swimmer, he drowned in a spot they now call the Sinkhole."

"What a sad story," Gracie said. "If only we could fill this house with love and laughter It might drive out all that sorrow. And by the way, shouldn't there have been a monument or dedication to their memory? "

"There's still time." David said solemnly.

"The sad story of Santiago House has been quite a lot for you all to take in at one go," Mrs. Campbell said, as both she and David started to get up from their seats.

"If you don't mind, we could come back again another day and discuss things further." David added.

"Thank you," Claudia said shaking their hands. "We are off to the beach now, so yes, another day would really be best."

"I was going to mention," David said, as though in afterthought, "I'm going to drop Miss Campbell off to visit friends near Rose Hall, but I'll be going on to the Great House, just to poke around and continue my research. Would anyone like to see the place? I could drive you out there, and be back, for around four o'clock."

"I'd like to see it," I said sounding a tad too eager.

Claudia was the first to turn down his invitation. "Thanks," she said but we already made plans for the day. Gracie and I really need to get into some seawater, we're going snorkeling at Cove Bay."

"Well I'm not going snorkeling." Walker T chuckled, "I'm sorry but I won't be able to accompany any of you, since I plan to do a bit of walking today I'm taking a trip down memory lane."

Then quite unexpectedly a wild-eyed Elfrida came bursting in from the pantry.

"If nobody going be here today, then me not staying in this here house alone! I going go over to the yard on the next property till somebody come back. Me did start dinner already, just some spinners left to do."

Everyone laughed to themselves, knowing that she had been listening to our conversation.

Chapter 20

Rose Hall

Mrs. Campbell sat in the back seat and I sat in the front with David. Although they were speaking together I hardly hear a word. My thoughts were in turmoil. First there was the nagging memory of Claudia dressed in riding gear and hiding the whip and the machete. I wished I had spoken to Walker T about it but there just was never an appropriate opportunity. My eyes were glued to the rearview mirror, watching Santiago House disappear behind us into the distance. "What a mysterious and magnificent place," I thought, yet I couldn't help but be impressed by how imposing the house looked out there in the middle of nowhere. My thoughts turned to the boy, Santiago. How unspeakably strange and lonely it must have been for him, cut off from everything he knew. I couldn't help but empathize with his loneliness, for I too was lonely. I longed to hear the sharp quick bark of a fox or even the haunting howl of a northern wolf.

As we sped along, I imagined black bears, moose and deer following us in the hot tropical bush land, and was somewhat comforted.

We stopped briefly at a small flat roof plantation house that appeared to be caressed on all sides by vines, in a yard where banana, mango and citrus trees grew in profusion.

We entered the property through a rusty iron gate with metal fencing. Barbed wire fences at the back of the house separated the yard from the encroaching wilderness behind.

Mrs. Campbell's friend came out to greet us the moment we pulled up. "David," Mrs. Campbell said, "you won't have to pick me up later." she said, "Mary will give me a drive back to Montego Bay after lunch."

David and I drove down the rough dirt road and headed back to the highway. I was finally alone with my thoughts, as the vegetation grew denser, and Rose Hall would not be far off. I could barely see the sky above, we were driving so close to the tall cane fields and wild bushes.

"So, what do you think of Jamaica so far?" David said, making conversation, though his eyes were fixed on the bumpy road ahead. I gazed out the car window appearing distracted, though I was well aware of the tall windswept fields and coconut groves. I was delighted when the broad blue sky once more came into focus. I turned away from the mesmerizing landscape and smiled. "I like it a lot." I said, "It's awesome."

"Is this your first trip here?" David said, swerving the car to avoid a family of goats. It appeared animals were rarely tethered, since I saw calves, dogs and donkeys running loose, all along the way.

"Yes, it's my first time here." I replied. "I've never travelled before."

"Well I'm glad you came to Jamaica, though I suppose you do know that it can be tough living here as compared to where you came from, but I personally like it here, my family lives here, and with a little hard work we have been able to afford a thing or two. But anyway, if you don't mind my asking, how did you meet Gracie and Claudia and Walker T, for that matter?"

"Walker T owns the house we share in Toronto but I only met Claudia and Gracie about a week ago."

"Is that so?"

"They were already living there, when I first went to the house. Claudia wanted Walker T to come to Jamaica with her, and he didn't want to leave me behind. So I guess that's why I'm here. Just luck"

"Oh, so you don't know too much about Claudia then."

"Not really."

There was a puzzled look on David's face, and I could see the muscle working in his jaw, and it was a while before he spoke again.

"Kathleen I hope you don't think I'm being presumptuous," he said finally, "correct me if I'm wrong but having just met all three of you, I found Claudia a little odd. I'm not sure what it is. I just can't put a finger on it."

"You noticed!" I exclaimed, "I actually feel the same way about her sometimes."

'Yes, Kathleen I noticed."

"Mr. Chang I think she's changed a lot in the few days I've known her."

"Please don't be formal, call me David, and by the way, we'll be approaching Rose Hall in another ten minutes or so."

I don't know what made me want to open up to David, except that I felt that I could trust him with my life. "Mr. Chang." I said. "Oops, I mean David, there's something I'd like to say."

"It is my turn to be apologetic," he said. "there's something I kept to myself back at Santiago House. I was being cautious so I kept it to myself. I am glad I did. The helper was listening, but Kathleen, I can speak openly now. You'll be surprised to hear that it was my grandfather William who left the house to Claudia."

"What!!!"

"Yes."

"Did he know her at all?"

"No, he didn't, the house had been in our family for generations."

"But David, why did Claudia inherit it?"

"Well Kathleen, what I didn't mention at the house, is that back in the days when the boy Santiago lived there, there was a young Coolie woman who used to bring food to the property for Santiago and Martin Swift. Her name was Leila Narasingh. People say that she either was sympathetic to the old man, having lost her own father, or else she must have had maternal instincts for the boy, because, at that time she had no child of her own. When she eventually married a local shopkeeper Samuel Chang, a Hakka Chinese merchant everyone was taken by surprise.

You must also understand that Leila took great risks bringing cooked meals to Santiago House. If Annie Palmer had found out, she would have had her killed for her interference. That dear woman Leila was a godsend, it is thanks to her generosity that the boy and the slave remained fairly healthy in their isolation. You might already have guessed that Miss Palmer, in her cruelty never provided sustenance for neither the boy nor the old man. It was as if she expected them both to fend for themselves.

When Santiago died it was a surprise to everyone to find that he had somehow made a will leaving the property to Leila and her descendants. He must have been well aware that he lived under the threat of death on a daily basis, and it might have been

Leila herself who smuggled a lawyer on to the property to have legal papers drawn up. We will never know the true story. But after Leila and her husband passed away, none of their grown children and their Chinese relatives wanted anything to do with Santiago House and property. They considered the place an inheritance of evil and haunting, yet the will stipulated that the house was never to be sold. It wasn't until years later, that my grandfather William took an interest in the affairs of the place, and he ended up taking great pains to locate the East Indian relatives of Leila Narasingh.

He always said that it would be bad luck for us with Chinese blood in our veins to ever live on such a notorious property. Grandfather William hired lawyers who tracked down Claudia's mother who is a direct descendant of Leila. They later found out that she had a daughter, and at the last minute my grandfather decided to leave the Santiago property to the daughter, not the mother. He felt that she would eventually raise a family there. Your friend Claudia is half East Indian and Jewish you know. It was Grandfather William's involvement in the matter that inspired me to research the history of both properties.

"So David, you are sort of related to Claudia then? Are you ever going to tell her?"

"Oh that won't be necessary. I'm just glad the property has a proper owner now, though. I only hope Claudia is the right person, and up to the task ahead of her. You know what I mean, don't you?"

Chapter 21

Rose Hall Revenge

Rose Hall in its magnificence stood brooding on top of a huge rise in the land, it looked to be deliberately placed half way between the mountains and the sea. How entranced I was by its presence and I felt as though I was totally swallowed up by its grandeur. I imagined that the view from Rose Hall's windows would be nothing short of breathtaking and I was right.

David drew the car to a halt, and as though caught in the moment, he spoke in a voice so hushed that I had to strain to hear him.

"Kathleen let's not forget that this house has become a tourist attraction. It supports a huge staff. There are cooks, waiters, maids, tour guides and even musicians working here. It wasn't always that way. The building was left in ruins after Miss Palmer was murdered in 1831 and was left like that for years. It was not restored until the 1960s when an American businessman and philanthropist named John Rollins took on the task of restoring it."

"Is that right David I didn't realize that this is a restoration. It looks so authentic. They must have really worked hard at duplicating the original architecture."

"Yes, they did a great job. In fact, many parts of the old house are incorporated into the architecture and some of it was looted and lost items were tracked down and restored to their rightful place. I would say that the exterior is pretty much the same as it was in Annie's time. Just imagine, that this is what young Santiago saw when he first came here."

"Wow! That's cool, did Miss Palmer ever try to find out what happened to Santiago and Martin Swift?"

"Not as far as we know, but she herself was murdered not long after they died. The woman was a monster. That is why her slaves eventually turned on her and killed her. See that little balcony; that is where she used to stand in the mornings giving orders to slaves, orders that included floggings, murders and all kinds of torture."

"Creepy. Did she run the plantation alone?"

"Yes but she did have the support of some white overseers. From what I found out they all were in bed together. But Annie also took to sleeping with her slaves. She was feared by those men that she toyed with, because once she tired of them, she had them killed and immediately took on a new lover. As you can imagine Kathleen, slaves were terrified of her. Her attention was never welcomed. Some research claims that her practicing Voodoo was what kept her in control."

"So how was she murdered?"

"The story goes that there was a young slave couple, a young man and woman who were very much in love and wanted to spend their lives together. But you know what; first I should have mentioned that the girl's father was an Obeah man which means he practiced a form of Voodoo. He had become quite powerful in his craft but kept his skills hidden from Miss Palmer. Anyway, as fate would have it Annie noticed the good-looking young man and she set her cap to attract him. It was common knowledge as to exactly what would happen to him if she bedded him. Well, what did happened though is that when Annie took him to her bed she didn't follow her usual pattern of killing her lover the next day or a day or two later. She instead killed him that very night! Some say that the killing must have been done in revenge because the young man must have refused her attentions out of his love for his sweetheart. Needless to say the murder angered his sweetheart and her father and set them into a fit of rage. Perhaps it was under the influence of his Obeah, that vengeful slaves entered Anne's bedroom and killed her in the very bed where she enjoyed debauchery with so many others before having them flogged, then conveniently disposed of in the morning. People say that was her wicked way of hiding her shame from the rest of the world."

"David, that story gives me chills I'm not even sure I'd be comfortable going into the house."

"I know what you mean Kathleen. But there's a restaurant in the basement of the building, perhaps we could grab something to eat. Then you can decide if you want to go upstairs to see the rest of the place or not. No need to feel pushed if you don't want to,"

"Sounds good David, let's do that."

Chapter 22

A Rose Hall Tour

Rose Hall's basement was not what I thought it would be. I thought it would be eerie. Instead, there was a pleasant atmosphere there and a fully stocked gift shop that displayed photos taken by former visitors to the site and there was the restaurant David had suggested. David and I split a meal of fish and chips, since I wasn't that hungry. The whole atmosphere was congenial. Musicians played in the old English pub-styled room and dozens of visitors and their guides were drawn there because of the delicious aroma. All the locals seemed to know David, some even asked if I were the new owner of Santiago House. It would appear that David Chang had made himself well known while conducting his research on Rose Hall. How relaxed it all felt and strangely enough, as I settled into a comfortable chair across from David's, I couldn't help but feel that perhaps I should see the rest of the house after all.

"Could we see the other parts of the house," I said gingerly, "will you come with me, please?"

"It can be arranged." David replied.

The house was cleverly built having various levels, but the first thing I noticed as we went up to the first level was the magnificent chandeliers hanging over the huge double mahogany staircase leading up to the main floor. I whistled softly to myself for though I had found the exterior of the house formidable I hardly expected the grandeur of the interior. There were dark antique mahogany furnishings and panelling, book cases and broad heavy drapery. There were windows and paintings to be admired. Each huge room was more exquisite than the last. There was so much to see, terraces, a very large ball room, a library with leather bound books, a beautifully furnished dining room, guest rooms and even a Gentlemen's room that was once occupied by Annie's husbands whom she was reputed to have murdered. Then there was Annie's red themed bedroom. Red it seems, was the colour she chose to reflect her inextinguishable passion. The room was dominated by her four-poster bed covered with red rose motif bedclothes, the site of her bloody murder. Adjacent to her bedroom was her sitting room boudoir. I stood looking at her things and felt somewhat uneasy. There was a pervading sense throughout, that an unnatural brooding presence inhabited all of Rose Hall. If David had not been with me, I would not have stayed as long as I did.

David told me that not all of the rooms I saw were open to the public, so I should consider myself privileged. He pointed out the secret passages that lead to Annie's rooms and told me that Annie used them to smuggle her lovers in and out of her quarters. It occurred to me, that she might well have used those very passages to secretly smuggle the boy Santiago back and forth between his property and hers. But why, I wondered.

What a view there was from Rose Hall's windows, wild mountain ranges ran along one side while the sea glistened on the other. Down below, there were well-kept lawns, walkways and gardens ablaze with blooms. I was so captivated by the view that I felt compelled to stand at various windows taking it all in.

Then out of the corner of my eye, I noticed someone dressed in riding gear striding across the wide lawn and heading towards the East garden. The person turned round briefly in mid stride, I was shocked to see that it was Claudia!

"Come David look!" I hissed, trying to keep the fearful tremor from my voice, "Claudia's down there."

David came immediately to stand beside me, but when we looked out, Claudia wasn't there at all. I was quite shaken, though I managed to keep my composure, "I must have been wrong" I said, "no one's there now."

"You must have seen Annie Palmer." David grinned.

David and I barely exchanged a word on the way back to Santiago House. Perhaps because I was still reeling from what I thought I saw at Rose Hall. But no matter what David had said, I knew that the person I saw was Claudia.

"So what's your background?" David Chang said finally as we drew closer to Santiago House. His question seemed to come from out of the blue, and it startled me, for my thoughts had been elsewhere.

It took me a moment to answer, "mother was from Ireland," I said softly, as though apologizing since I remembered that Annie Palmer was also half Irish, "My dad was Irish-Canadian." I added hoping that would make things sound better.

"What do you mean 'was'?"

"They both passed away."

"Oh I'm so sorry. I was just thinking that your eyes look so sad for a girl of your age. You're fifteen or sixteen, right? You've seen a lot of sadness haven't you?"

"Yes I suppose I have. I'm over sixteen. I was an only child."

"What a shame. My apologies for bringing it up; it makes sense now why you seem to be so close to Walker T"

"Walker T is wonderful David. He has been extremely kind. But enough about me, tell me about you."

"Things haven't been too bad for me Kathleen. I've been lucky I suppose, and as for my background I'm a mixture of Chinese, Black and English. My dad's Chinese, my mum's a mulatto."

"Cool. What an interesting combination."

"Yes I suppose it is. But we in Jamaica are used to mixed races. Our National Motto just happens to be 'Out Of Many, One People'. But anyway, I guess this is it for now. Santiago House is just around that bend."

Chapter 23

An Attempted Murder?

I arrived at Santiago House to find Gracie sitting on the verandah. She looked quite distraught, drying her hair with a thick towel.

"Oh, there you are." she said, as soon as I came out of the car; and waved goodbye to David.

"Thanks again for taking me," I shouted after David, as he pulled away.

"How was Rose Hall?" Gracie asked, hardly looking up from her task.

"It was quite interesting. David was a good guide," I replied "how was the snorkeling?"

"I almost drowned," Gracie replied flatly.

"What!!"

"Yes, if I didn't know better I would say Claudia tried to drown me."

"You're kidding, right?"

"No kidding I swear she tried to drag me down under the water. I almost blacked out, but to be honest I'm not really sure if she did it on purpose or not. The water was crowded with other divers and swimmers. But when I struggled to the surface, Claudia wasn't anywhere to be seen. But something keeps nagging at me Kathleen, and as a result I'm sort of convinced that it was her. When I was under the water I remember seeing a woman's face that looked a whole lot like her, though she had a rather evil expression. But you know what, Claudia's insane! Can you believe she left me alone at that strange beach! I didn't even know a single soul, and it's not that close to here, if you ask me. If it wasn't for two Jamaican women working in a cane field, who asked if I needed help, then gave me directions, I would have had to walk back here alone. It was clear that they both knew that it wouldn't be safe for a woman to be walking alone on a back road, because they actually left their work, and walked with me through a short cut to get here. They wouldn't even accept payment for their kindness. I can't believe how nice they were. You should have seen how many Rastafarians and farm workers we ran into on the way back. Some of them looked quite scary, though they surprised me by being really polite. Can you believe it?"

"So how did you get to the beach in the first place?"

"Charlie drove us there, he said he couldn't stay because he had an appointment in Mo Bay. I'm wondering if he came back for Claudia while I was still snorkeling. I'm so sick of him anyway."

"Do you think that maybe she went to Rose Hall?"

"Not likely; she's upstairs. I heard her in her bedroom when I came home. I went and had a shower then came down here to get away from her. She's been a bit too spooky lately."

"Yeah, you're right, she has, but how come you're sick of Charlie?"

"It's not just him Kathleen I'm actually sick of Derrick too. He's been trying to get me into bed since day one, all I can say is enough already. I didn't come to Jamaica to make a fool of myself. As a rule I never get too involved with a guy I just met.

Unfortunately I can't say the same for Claudia; she's really got involved with Charlie. At first her fooling around seemed like a bit of fun but if the truth be told I wonder if she's even considered the possibility of repercussions. To be honest, we don't really know a thing about those guys."

I was glad that Gracie chose to confide in me, and not censoring her words. Her candour made me feel accepted as a friend, rather than the tag along kid I must have been perceived as.

"I agree with you Gracie." I said, "Claudia should be more careful. Come to think of it, I can't say I like Charlie that much either, there's just something about him, but I can't put my finger on whatever it is. You didn't hear me say that. Right?"

"No worries Gracie, everything you said, stops right here."

Chapter 24

A Tiny
Painted Red Rose

After that conversation I decided to go upstairs to see if Claudia was wearing riding gear. I don't know what stopped me from telling Gracie about what I had seen at Rose Hall, though I suppose I wanted to be one hundred percent positive before saying anything. I stole up the stairs, all the while listening for movements from Claudia's room. I didn't hear a sound, and when I saw that her door was ajar I approached and peered in. She was not inside. Growing bolder I stepped across the threshold to find the room empty. Perhaps Claudia was never there I thought. Perhaps Gracie had been mistaken. Feeling bolder I jerked open the closet door, all the while looking over my shoulder, only to find that she wasn't in there either. Then I decided to take a look under her bed and when I pushed the bed it rolled aside easily. I went down on my knees and examined the floor boards, all the while keeping an eye on the doorway. I didn't know what I expected to find, but then, there it was. A tiny red rose was painted on one of the floor boards. I would easily have missed it, had I not been on a mission. I pushed against the rose, and some floor boards slid aside, then closed again on its own accord. I was about to examine it further, when

I heard the front door open. I only had enough time to roll the bed back into place before scampering back down the hall to my own room and shutting the door behind me.

"Kathleen is that you up there?" I heard a voice say, and I knew that Walker T had returned from his walk.

"I'm just on my way down," I shouted, as I made a show of slamming my door and I left my room. I practically charged down the stairs, and ran into the living room where Walker T was sitting.

"Good to see you young lady." he said, mopping his brow. "I'm a bit breathless from all that walking, but did Mr. Chang take good care of you? I was thinking about you."

"Oh he was quite sociable; he treated me to lunch before we toured the house. Rose Hall was awesome and terrifying too. I don't think I want to go back there anytime soon."

Walker T chuckled softly, and gestured for me to have a seat. "Young lady I haven't wanted to go back there either. Last time I was there was some years ago. But it seems just like yesterday"

"How was your walk? Did you enjoy it?"

"It was a longer walk than I anticipated young lady, but it was worth it. Some old friends of mine are buried in that old cemetery. I managed to spend an hour or so there, and even left a few wild flowers on the graves. I was lucky to meet one of the dairy farmers from up the road when I was coming back. He stopped his pickup truck when he saw me and he said he heard that some Canadians were staying here at Santiago House. He wanted to know if I was one of them. Nice chap, his name is Jonathan Cousins, he says you all can come see the dairy farm anytime you like, and he gave me his telephone number. Where's Claudia and Gracie anyway?"

"Gracie's here, but it's like I'm not sure about Claudia. Know what, Walker T, you must really be physically fit to be able to walk there and back. It was very hot today, at least I thought so. Anyway, your Mr. Cousins sounds like a nice person. People here have been amazingly kind. My dad probably would have liked it here. He spent time in rural Ireland, and said that those were the happiest days of his life. And you know what Walker T, I'm beginning to feel the same way about here. Anyway, about Claudia, I'm not sure where she is, perhaps she's with Charlie. Know what, I think we both could use a cool drink. Elfrida usually has something cool in the fridge."

Chapter 25

Walker T Tells His Story

Gracie, Walker T, and I were huddled over cold glasses of tamarind juice when Elfrida finally returned to the house. She brought a basket of mangoes for us, before going directly to the kitchen.

"Me only have to make spinners for the soup," She said, "The pumpkin and other vegetables and broth cook up already, and me going serve it with crackers and cheese."

"Thanks Elfrida." Walker T shouted, "I can't tell when last I've had real Jamaican pumpkin soup."

Having said that, Walker T got up from his chair, and softly closed the hall door that led to the kitchen. "Hope you ladies don't mind," he said, "but I like to keep my conversations private. I thought you might like to know why I had to go to the cemetery despite the long walk and the blazing sun."

"I just knew there was something to it," said Gracie, her cheeks glowing with mischief, as she pulled her chair even closer and cocked her head to listen. I noticed that Walker T looked furtively at the closed door, and I was sure that whatever he was about to tell us would be quite personal.

"I was seventeen when I finished High School in Montego

Bay," he said, and his voice was soft and steady, "you should have seen me; you would have thought I had won a million dollars. Nobody in my family had ever gone that far, so you can imagine what a big dinner we had to celebrate the occasion. I can still remember the roast pork done over coals dowsed with gravy and there was rice and peas, macaroni and cheese, and all kinds of salad. My mouth waters, even just to think about it.

To be honest, I was hot as hell walking around in my dress suit all that afternoon but I didn't mind one bit for I was the main attraction. People came from all the surrounding villages to wish me well. My Mamma was never so proud. My daddy had left her, but thankfully saw to it that I finished school. Mamma took in washing to supplement the few pounds he sent from Kingston to help finance my education.

Then there he was at the dinner which was held in the field behind the school, asking Mamma to take him back. Mamma was a big woman, all muscle and fat I don't know who was happier she or me, for she took daddy back. It was a long carefree summer but in September daddy arranged for me to go to find work in Kingston. I had never been away from home and the thought of leaving scared me."

"I never thought you'd ever be scared of anything Walker T" I said, then remembering Rose Hall, added, "except for The White Witch of course."

We all laughed; then Walker T cleared his throat and leaned in, seemingly filled with new vigor.

"I was sent to live in Kingston with some bachelor friends of father who lived on Ballater Avenue In in a residential part of the city. All three men were hard-working, and managed to make ends meet by pooling their earnings for groceries, and to pay the mortgage. I still remember their names, Verley, Lampton and

Cecil. It was such a novelty for me to address middle class working men on a first name basis. The job I ended up doing was a junior position. I helped to file accounts at Times Store on King Street. Verley worked there, and was able to pull a few strings to get me the job. Both Mamma and Pappa felt that I had struck gold. But to tell the truth the work was repetitious and boring. Every weekend I took a country bus home, and those were the best days. One weekend when I went home Mamma told me that a friend of hers named Tessa had invited her to lunch in Montego Bay; she asked me to come with her since Pappa had to work. I was reluctant to go, for being seventeen I could think of better ways to spend my day, but I ended up going for Mamma's sake.

As it turned out Tessa Bramson was one of those fair-skinned Jamaican women with light coloured eyes and blondish kinky hair who, were it not for their Negroid facial features could have passed for white. In Jamaica coloured people of her complexion were referred to as 'red neygaz'. Anyway it was such a step up for me to be in one of those old Montego Bay Homes with spiffy furniture, drapes, crockery and a piano. Mamma and I were out on the back verandah, not far from the kitchen, when Tessa Bramson announced that her daughter had just come home from visiting friends, and would be joining us for lunch. In my mind's eye I imagined that the daughter would be an old spinster looking type, somewhat like her mother. We were drinking aerated water when we heard the daughter's voice, I was surprised that she sounded young. The daughter came bursting through the house, calling; "Mamma dinner smells so good. How soon we going to eat?"

I will never forget the look of surprise on her face when she saw us out there on the back verandah sitting in lawn chairs enjoying the breeze. "Oh," she said, her lips forming a perfect O. "I didn't realize we had visitors. Excuse my manners."

Her mother laughed merrily and beckoned for her to join us, "Come Marceline," she said, these are the Robinsons, Edna does some of our washing, her son's name is Walker; he works in Kingston. Edna is the one who got all our laundry ready for your graduation. This is my way of thanking her."

I squirmed in my seat, feeling somewhat ashamed that Mamma good woman that she was, was perceived only as a washer woman; yet at the same time I was exhilarated because that was the very reason why we happened to be there.

I don't know how I took my eyes off of Marceline; she didn't look one bit like her mother, except for the fact that she was quite fair and blond. But her hair was straight and it hung in a heavy braid down her back. I swore that hers was the face of an angel. She was that beautiful; and she couldn't have been more than sixteen.

All through dinner, my eyes examined the slant of her brow, the curve of her pale hands and the tiny dimple at the corner of her lips. It was as though I was intoxicated by her. I honestly didn't want the lunch to end but it did. When we were wiping our faces and hands in our napkins, Marceline's mother complained of feeling bloated.

"I can get you something at the drug store." Marceline said brightly, "Walker would you like to come with me. We shouldn't be long."

I could hardly believe my luck, and I practically sprang out of my chair, though I hoped I didn't appear too eager. "That's alright," her mother said sharply, "I can make some ginger tea."

"Oh Mamma," Marceline laughed, "let me do this one teeny weenie favour for you, just look at the scrumptious meal you had the maid cook for us. It was the best."

Again I rose from my seat only to flounder in the blueness of Marceline's eyes. She sounded so well-spoken and worldly that I wondered what exactly I would say to her when we were alone, but then she smiled and nothing else mattered.

"Let's go," I said, "I know a short cut."

"Okay," her mother replied patting her bulging stomach that looked as though she had never missed a good meal. "Take your time though; go the long way, because as we all know, we Jamaicans have a saying that, 'short cut draw blood'."

When Marceline and I got out to the street, she laughed good-naturedly and steered me towards the short cut. "Never mind Mamma," she said, "Let's go this way. Know what, Mamma's pregnant; two months I think, but she thinks I don't know. What did she expect with all the sailors she entertains. My daddy was a sailor, he stopped over for two days when I was conceived and she's never seen him again."

"Is that so," I said, "how does she manage, all alone and all that?"

"Ha! If you can call it work, she works every week. She gets money from sailors. She's always there to meet ships when they come in. It's always the same routine; she has the maid prepare a good meal for a sailor, then she gets down to business. Know what I mean?"

I was too startled to comment but Marceline just laughed and threw her braid over her shoulder. "Want to kiss me?" she said and I gulped so hard I almost choked, as I looked at her wide-eyed.

"Don't be such a baby!" she said as she thrust her cheek against my lips. "Maybe one day you will really kiss me," she said, and I stood there all frightened to death.

"Okay let's go get the stomach salts," she said, "and maybe

on the way you can tell me about yourself. I could come to see you in Kingston if you like. My uncle Norman lives there. Mamma would let me go see him if I ask."

"So Walker T did you ever see her again?" Gracie asked, eyes brimming with curiosity.

"As a matter of fact, for the next six months she came to Kingston every Friday evening, and rode back to Mo Bay with me late Saturday evenings on the train."

"So she stayed over with you?" I asked, finding it hard to imagine Walker T making those kinds of arrangements.

"She actually spent Friday nights at her uncle's house but we did manage to spend most of Saturday together. Her uncle owned a large home on Tucker Avenue but he was almost never home. So sometimes we were there, and at other times we were at the house where I was staying."

"So you became lovers then?" Gracie grinned.

"No. It wasn't that way at all. All we exchanged were kisses. Marceline was more straight-laced than her mother."

"Were you in love?" I asked.

"Yes I loved her more than anything and she loved me too. So one weekend when she begged me to come to visit her mother I agreed out of sheer politeness and blind love."

We arrived at her mother's house around six thirty that evening, and I could almost see the thunder in her mother's eyes, as she laid her gaze on us coming up the steps together.

"Isn't this the Robinson boy?" she hissed, as she glimpsed Marceline's hand reaching for mine. "Why the hell is he here? I hope to God he's not pushing up himself on you. Get inside before the neighbours see you!"

But before Marceline could reply, her mother practically dragged her into the drawing room leaving me alone in the foyer, as though it wasn't possible for me to overhear their conversation from there.

"He's my guest Mamma," I heard Marceline insist, "why can't he stay for supper?"

"Just listen here girl I should never had allowed you to go to the drugstore with him that day. Look what it come to! And another thing, he can't be here tonight. The baby's father is coming to see us. His ship, the SS Starsong is anchored here in Mo Bay. He wants to marry me. Can you believe our luck!! He's coming here tonight to tell you all about it himself. We're all going to settle in London, England. What a blessing come down on us! So you see why we can't have this Negro boy here tonight, don't you?"

"But Mamma I'd like him to be here, I love him."

"Love him! Nonsense Marceline, can you imagine what would happen to the family if you and him was to get together. We are almost white, as it is, young Robinson would bring tar blood and disgrace into the family. Your babies would be black as coal!"

'Mamma I'll never love anyone but him, and don't you pretend we don't already have Negro blood in our veins. I want to be with him Mamma, he means everything to me. I'll kill myself if I can't be with him! You'll see."

"Foolish girl, my baby's coming soon, don't you hurry it along any sooner. It's going to be white like its father and he is offering us a better life in England, that's where he is from you know. There will be no more renting for us. We going up in style girl. You'll even be able to afford the piano lessons you always wanted. I'm sure you'll get over that Robinson boy soon enough. Lots of white English boys over there are bound to fall in love with you once they see how pretty you are."

It was at that point in their conversation that I couldn't listen anymore, and I quietly let myself out through the front door.

"So Walker T, what happened? Did love eventually conquer all?" I said, sounding a tad too bright,.

"It was the darkest night of my life young lady. I walked all the way from downtown Mo Bay to our village out of town. I thought I would never see Marceline again but a week later she came to Mamma's door asking for me. Mamma knew the whole story and I can't forget how kind she was to leave me and Marceline alone in the house while she attended to some really unnecessary outdoor chores."

"I came to say goodbye," Marceline sobbed, "we are going to England as soon as the baby comes."

"So what happened with you and Marceline?" Gracie blurted out. "She's so feisty I like her."

"Well here is what happened I remember it like yesterday. Marceline thrust both her hands in mine holding me tightly as we stood there together, our bodies gravitating towards each other as her eyes brimmed with tears. She lifter her head to meet my kiss, and I felt her tears warm on my cheek, as she sobbed.

"Walker darling," she said, "Mamma was just awful. I'm so sorry you had to hear all that rubbish, but it looks as if there's no choice. I'm going to have to go to England with her. But you know of course that there will never be anyone else for me, you know that don't you? Please tell me you know."

"Yes, I know my love; respect is the only thing that kept me from taking you to bed. Marceline I can't describe it but my body aches for you, and I don't even know how we will we ever see each other again. None of us have enough money."

"Let's not think about that Walker, just love me. Kiss me so hard that you'll never forget me. I'll never forget you, and I know I can't live without you."

The afternoon was filled with sweet kisses and regrets, it was the last time I was to see my dearest Marceline. A month or two after she arrived in England, she sent me a letter that I will always carry with me, for after she wrote it, Marceline jumped in front of an Underground train at Piccadilly Station. She is buried here in Jamaica at Bickerstep Cemetery. She wanted to be not too far away from where I lived."

Tears stole down Walker T's cheeks as Elfrida rang the bell for supper. Though he wiped his eyes with his kerchief and managed a smile I could well imagine the conflict inside him. "How nice it is to have you both here with me," he said, as he put his arms around Gracie and me and steered us into the dining room.

"So now we know why you never married," Gracie whispered, and her voice trembled with respect.

The moment we sat down, we all heard footsteps on the stairs. "That must be Claudia now." Gracie said and I was surprised to see that it actually was.

"The supper bell woke me." Claudia said cheerily, as she came into the room and pulled up a chair. "That soup smells so good."

"Where were you today when I almost drowned?" Gracie blurted out, "I had to walk back here with some field workers. Don't you pull that innocent face, where the dickens were you Claudia?"

We all waited for an explanation but Claudia leaned across the table menacingly, "Did you stop to think that I might have had too much sun, and had to leave?" she said, "I almost had sun stroke while you were enjoying yourself. Luckily I got a drive back here. There was no time to consult with you. I had to come back here to rest."

"Right," I thought to myself, "you weren't even in your room. Bet you somehow managed to get to Rose Hall without the rest of us knowing.

Chapter 26

Duppy?

About a week after that incident I decided to go to explore the river again. Even though the vegetation was definitely tropical, the dense growth reminded me of home. I was sitting on the verandah steps slipping on my running shoes when I heard voices coming from the dirt road. I was taken aback to see that one of the figures approaching was Peter. He was walking with one of the cow hands from the farm up the road. "Hi Peter," I called out loudly, and he came running. What a pleasure it was to see him.

"How's it going?" he said as he came level with me, "Seen any duppies? You look healthier than when I did see you last time, country life must be good for you."

I couldn't help but laugh with him, I was delighted to have him for company. "Come inside Peter, let me introduce you to the others. I was just thinking of going to the river. Want to come?"

"Sounds good," Peter grinned, "It's a good thing my granny sent a little something. We could have a picnic there if you like."

"How sweet, what did she send? Be sure to thank her for me"

"You could even thank her yourself Kathleen, because if we're going to the river, we could pass by her house. She lives just a little further along by the riverside. She packed us some escovitch fish and festival."

"Wow that sounds fantastic. But what kind of fish is that and what's festival?"

"Escovitch fish is usually snapper fish marinated in vinegar, onions and allspice and scotch bonnet peppers, then it gets fried. And festival, is a pastry side dish that we eat with food. You going like it."

"I love everything here so far Peter. Come on inside, come meet the others."

We found Walker T inside reading the local paper called The Gleaner. He looked up when he heard us come in. "Well, who do we have here? Hello young man," he said, "I'm Walker T Robinson. Please call me Walker T"

"I'm Peter, nice to meet you sir."

Gracie was trying on a bright straw hat in front of the hall mirror. She was getting ready to go shopping in Montego Bay. Claudia wasn't home though, and I presumed that she might have spent the night with Charlie.

"Nice to meet you Peter," Gracie said, "I'm Gracie; I'm going out with Mrs. Campbell, a lady that Kathleen and I met the other day. She taking me to some shops in town that are not tourist traps."

Peter laughed and shook her hand, "Nice to meet you Gracie but let me warn you. It is hard to find shops in Mo Bay that are not geared towards tourists. Unless of course your friend plans to take you off of the main drag. Prices are outrageous for tourists,"

"Hope I don't look too touristy then." Gracie grinned.

"Well guys," I said, "Peter and I were about to go to explore the river bank. We might visit his granny too. She's not that far along the river from here."

"Excellent" Walker T said, "take good care of her young man."

Peter smiled shyly and shook Walker T's hand. "You can bet on it Sir," he said.

"Well I guess we'd better get going," Peter said, "I'm already looking forward to the picnic lunch."

"You'll have to wait one more minute Peter. I'm going to cut some roses for your grandmother."

"Take some lemonade with you too," Gracie urged, "it's so hot outside, you'll be glad you did."

We walked for about a mile following the river, as the sun streamed down on us through the puzzle of overhanging tree branches. There were places where the river ran swiftly at our side and yet there were other places where the flow was slowed by rock formations. It was at those sedentary places that we saw thirsty animals come down to drink. Further along the riverbank women were hard at work, washing and beating out laundry on the jutting rocks. What a lot of laughter and chatter we aroused as we approached.

"The White Witch going ketch you!" one woman cried out, and I saw that she had no teeth, yet she grinned broadly at us as we waved. I was never sure if the White Witch she was referring to was Annie Palmer or me.

All along that walk, the never ending bush-land was alive with bird cries, buzzing and unexplained rustlings and every once in a while, we'd witness a swarm of small grey birds perform what I called 'a flying ballet' over the water. We finally came to a point where only huge moss covered boulders marked our way. And that was where Peter chose to have our picnic, on a large flattish rock that jutted out over a black slick of water.

"The water's deep here," he said, "if we had brought our swimming trunks we could have dived off from here and had a swim."

An involuntary chill ran through me, for though we had gone much farther along the river in the opposite direction of my previously sojourn, this spot reminded me of the eerie place I heard about, where Santiago and Martin Swift drowned.

"This is a good spot for a picnic," Peter said, and he looked so pleased with himself that I found myself nodding agreement.

"Have you been to Rose Hall yet?" he asked as he spread a small blanket for us to sit on.

"Yes I have. A man named David Chang took me. It's a spooky place alright and you know what Peter, I thought I saw Annie Palmer. But then again I'm not sure because she sort of looked like my friend Claudia, the one who inherited Santiago House."

"Oh that's the one I didn't get to meet. Was she at Rose Hall too?"

"No she was supposed to be snorkeling with Gracie miles away."

"Sounds weird Kathleen; what did Gracie have to say?"

"Better sit tight Peter" I said, and I then proceeded to tell him all about Claudia and her involvement with Charlie, and how I saw her dressed for riding on the stairs and about the machete. I also told him how Gracie thought that Claudia had tried to drown her, and reiterated the fact that I had seen her at Rose Hall. I even mentioned how her personality had changed, and how she somehow disappeared from her room.

Peter's eyes were wide, as I told him about how I discovered the rose floorboard that moved aside under Claudia's bed. I almost could see horror in his eyes.

He shook his head knowingly, and his eyes darted towards the bush, as though making sure we were alone. "Know what Kathleen," he whispered, "it sounds to me like your friend Claudia is possessed. A duppy has taken her over."

Though I had half suspected the same thing myself. It was more frightening hearing Peter voice his opinion.

"You going have to watch her carefully," Peter said, his hand patting mine reassuringly, "it sound like is Annie Palmer herself that take her over."

We sat there in silence on top of the rock dangling our feet over the water, with the lunch, the roses and the lemonade between us, none of us daring to mention Claudia again.

"You like the food Kathleen?" he said taking a bite of the escovitch fish.

"Yes very much, I like spice." I replied, "maybe it's because mother used to eat Indian food when she was pregnant with me."

We both laughed, and our laughter bounced off the rocks, and echoed through the surrounding trees. It was such a relief to think of pleasant things. I told myself to avoid all further talk of Claudia and Annie Palmer.

"So Peter," I said, my mouth stuffed with festival and onions, "last time I saw you, you mentioned that you are a student. What are you studying?" I had to wonder how I managed to get so many words out.

Peter glanced over at me, laughing loudly. "Just look at you. You've got a greasy face from the food. You've been pigging out."

We both thought that was hilarious and laughed so hard I almost fell into the water. "But to answer your question Kathleen," Peter said conclusively, "I'm studying art and design."

"So you want to be a painter?"

"Not really I'd eventually like to get into computer animation but the classes here are full. So I'm sort of doing the next best thing. How about you, are you still in school Kathleen?"

"I almost finished high school. But as I told you on the beach I haven't given much thought to studying further but you know what, lately I've been thinking that perhaps I'd like to be a journalist. I should take some courses I suppose."

"Well you should look into it before the classes get filled up."

"Yes, you're right I should."

After lunch we waded in the shallows and meandered with the river to Peter's grandmother's house. It was a small zinc zinc-roofed brick house just a few steps from the river bank itself. Peter's grandmother was sitting on the tiny porch on a wooden chair. What delight was in her eyes when she saw us coming. "Peter," she called out, "so this is the pretty Canadian girl you tell me bout."

Peter laughed good naturedly and hugged her. "Granny this is Kathleen, yes she is the one I told you about."

"Nice to meet you," I said, "thank you so much for lunch. It was amazing. These roses are for you."

"What a sweet girl to bring an old woman like me flowers. Everybody round here call me Granny, okay? Mek me go inside and put them in a vase. Them look so pretty eh? So Peter, you eat food already? Why you don't offer Miss Kathleen some sweet potato pudding and a glass of aerated water."

The moment she stepped inside, we felt droplets of rain, then there was a huge crash of thunder and rain began to pour in earnest. Peter grabbed my arm and ran up the steps with me.

"It's a rain storm," he said. "You'll be drenched if you stay out here."

As the rain pounded like bullets on the zinc roof, Peter offered me a seat on a small quilt covered couch in the tiny living room. There was only enough room for three pieces of furniture, the couch and a side chair though they had managed to have a small glass cabinet hooked up against the wall with a display of their best dishes. There was no dining room, just the kitchen with a wood-burning stove, a small fridge and a cupboard of some sort and a table with three mismatched chairs. Granny was in one of the two bedrooms closing the window. "Me don't want lightning coming inside," she said, "and we have to cover the mirror too."

The house became almost as dark as night. The storm raged outside, while all three of us huddled beside a kerosene lamp in the kitchen where we picked at our pudding. "I usually turn the generator off when there's a storm," Granny said, "I for one don't trust electricity and lightning together."

The sweet potato pudding was delicious, and I told her so and she promptly cut me another large slice, though I felt as if I was going to burst.

Thunder rolled menacingly above us, I heard cracking noises like tree branches snapping and there was a huge whoosh of wind that shook the entire cottage. "It's a bad one," Peter whispered, "we're lucky we weren't caught outdoors.

"Back in my day," said Granny, pulling her chair closer as her face glowed in the lantern light, "It was dark times like this that people used to talk bout duppy and bout Annie Palmer. Me glad me don't live too close to Rose Hall, cause we still fraid of the White Witch you know. Me own granny used to tell us that the White Witch used to ride on a big black horse in all kind of weather looking for slaves that wandered off the compound. The horse foot would make a sound 'tu tup, tu tup', as if it only have three leg not four. That's why even to this day we still fraid of three-foot horse duppy. Them say she did carry a long whip that she flog slave with if she find any. Other people dem say that she used to use a sharp cutlass to chop slave up with. But you know what, when she find any good looking young man like Peter, she would force him to sleep with har but once them done, she'd kill him. She was wicked can't done. And you know something, my other granny used to say that Santiago must be the bastard son of a Spanish man that Annie Palmer wanted to get into her bed. But since she couldn't get him, she must'a did get smaddy else to kidnap the boy, then she hold him ransom. She build the house to tempt the Spanish man wid it as a gift. But him never come to har, you know. People say that the Spanish man was murdered by Santiago's Mamma before she poison herself. Nobody ever did come looking for Santiago. It's very, very sad I tell you."

What a grizzly past there was to Santiago House I thought. It was a wonder I was even able to sleep under its roof at night. But I kept my thoughts to myself. Peter looked over at me with sympathy in his eyes and I knew that he must have read my thoughts, but before he could say a single word, there was a sharp knocking at the door. "Wonder who that is," Granny said under her breath, "nobody ever go out in rain like dis."

Peter was the one who got up to open the door, and I was so terrified, my heart was in my throat.

When the door opened, two Rastafarians stepped right into the cottage. They were soaking wet, rain streamed from their long locks and beards. "You alright then Granny?" one of them said, "a whole heap a tree blow down near here and a cow drown upstream."

Granny immediately got up from her chair; she was smiling, "Oh is you Isaiah. Me glad you come look me up. Me alright so far; me grandson Peter is here with him Canadian friend Kathleen. Have a seat na."

"So dat's who dat is." Isaiah said eyeing me with suspicion. "Me bring me friend Erasmus in case you need any help. We check out everybody along the way already, so if is alright we could stop here till the rain ease up."

Erasmus the elder of the two men had the scariest eyes I had ever seen. His brows were hooded and bushy and his piercing eyes coal black. He winked at me and reached into a jute bag he carried, I was sure he was going to pull out a pouch full of weed. But instead he pulled out a piece of wood wrapped several times in plastic. He sat down on the couch, wet clothes and all and beckoned to Isaiah "you didn't hear Granny say we is to have a seat."

Isaiah joined him on the couch, as Erasmus pulled out a short knife and began carving the wood. "All kind a bad weather start happening in Jamaica," he said. "and the sun hotter than ever. I don't know what happening but we losing all kinda crops."

"It's the same in Canada," I said, "the climate is changing due to pollution, I personally think too much damage has been done already."

"But this girl have brains," Isaiah said, "you must listen to her Peter. I bet she can tell you a thing or two. I did think she fool fool like some a dem tourist girl."

""Speaking bout story," Granny chimed in changing the subject, "I was just telling these young ones bout the White Witch."

"Granny, me and Erasmus was just'a talk bout the same thing. Even last night some people was a say them see Annie Palmer in the bush these last few days. Duppy walking again Granny, some people say she dress up in riding things, carrying a cutlass and a whip. But nobody dare go close to the duppy except Daniel, who was'a smoke a spliff. Him did want to give her a drag, and him follow her. People hear a whole lot a groaning and them run go hide. But when them see Daniel this morning him full'a deep scratch all bout him body."

"You serious?" Peter said, "but what did Daniel have to say? Do you think it was the White Witch?"

Erasmus grinned a toothy grin that revealed his strong, yellowed teeth. "She is the witch alright," he said, "Cause who else have old time clothes like dat? Tell me which other white woman fool enough to go round bush-land alone at night? No doubt in my mind bout it Peter, dat woman is a duppy."

Though I listened with my heart in my throat, there was no doubt in my mind that the woman they were talking about was actually Claudia, but I didn't dare say a word and when I met Peter's eyes I felt assured that he wouldn't say anything either.

Story after story followed about ghosts and slaves and the White Witch herself. Each story was scarier than the last. The rain kept pouring and the lantern light grew dimmer as nature hammered against the zinc roof and shook the cottage with her fists urging the deluge on.

The weather did not hold up until late in the evening when darkness had fallen.

"We going have to sleep here Granny." Erasmus said. "It too dangerous in this darkness. The river swell up and a heap'a damage all bout. We going leave first thing in the morning. In case you all sleeping when we go, this little something is for Miss Kathleen."

I was taken by surprise when Erasmus handed me a perfectly carved wooden pendant. He hung it on a leather thong, cut from a small roll in his bag. How amazing it was to see that the carving of a girl's head looked every bit like me.

"This is beautifully done," I said, "I will treasure it."

That night I slept in Granny's bed up against the thin wall and she slept beside me. Through the night I heard her ask the Lord for deliverance from the storm, as well as to keep us all safe from the White Witch. Peter and the two men were less than five feet away from us, camped on the kitchen and living room floors. There was no hiding from their snoring through the thunder. It wasn't until dawning before I heard their waking rustlings. The sun peeped in at the window an hour after they left and I arose to have a look outside the window. I eased the latch open to find that the air that seeped in was deliciously fresh and cooler than before the storm.

"You wake?" Peter said, coming into the room, "I just buttered some hardo bread we can have it with Milo, then head back after."

"Thanks Peter. What a dreadful storm that was. Granny's exhausted, she's finally asleep. I'm glad we are all safe I'm sure everyone at Santiago House must be worried about us."

"I know," Peter said, "but there was no storm warning."

We ate quickly then headed out the door. I looked back momentarily at Granny's house and saw that it stood firm, though the river had washed up almost to the doorstep. "Thank goodness it's not in ruins," I said under my breath.

"I left Granny a note," Peter whispered back, as he looked around in awe at the devastation around us. Coconut, citrus and banana trees that stood in the wake of the storm were precariously bent and broken, others were uprooted by the force of the wind, as though they were mere toys. Even the huge thick trunk trees along the riverbank suffered damage. It was as though a giant had come and tossed them aside carelessly. The air was stagnant and there were no birds, nor animals in sight, except for a lone Billy goat bleating in an overgrown field. We steered clear of the river bank, avoiding slippery jutting rocks as we meandered through the thick bush land and pastures, where a swath of destroyed and uprooted vegetation marked the path of the storm.

"Granny needs her sleep," Peter said finally, as though to take my mind off of the destruction around us. "As soon as I have you safely home I'll go back to give her a hand. She going have to be careful to boil her drinking water, cause when the river flood, the water gets bad. Did you see the uprooted trees near her house? They are going to block the river's flow. I will have to get some men to help with that. And by the way if that well at Santiago House was in use, you wouldn't have to worry about conserving water."

"We might have to boil water too and you're right; the well could have served as a catchment. I wonder why they don't use it anymore."

"Nobody tell you?"

"Tell me what?"

"Well Granny told me that everybody stay away from that well because back in slavery days, Annie Palmer filled it up with poisonous snakes so that the slaves wouldn't hide down there."

"Really! I looked down there a few days ago and saw stone steps leading down into complete blackness. Why would anybody build steps in a well in the first place?"

"Did you stop to think that maybe those steps are how the slaves got the snakes down there? I'm sure they didn't just throw them down. Granny used to tell me that slaves carried basket after basket of poisonous snakes down there, then released them. And from that time till now, the well hasn't been used for anything. It is always kept covered, and for all I know the snakes must be still down there."

"But Peter I thought I heard that Jamaica doesn't have many poisonous snakes."

"Annie Palmer brought the snakes into the country from overseas. Some were gifts from her lovers, because they knew that snakes would be just the sort of thing she would like."

"Well it sounds as if her evil knew no bounds."

"You got that right."

"I should tell the others about the snakes. Do you know that the other night a friend of Claudia's named Charles put a bottle of rum under the rim of the well?"

"Is that so, he's lucky he didn't go down there. Yes, you'd better tell the others."

As we continued walking, we came upon local people from the adjoining properties, attempting to gather up things the storm had scattered. Some were herding wandering animals that became lost during the bad weather. Peter and I stopped often to lend a hand.

It was almost noon before we approached Santiago House. Walker T was standing on the broad front steps shading his eyes against the sun and looking anxiously towards the road. Gracie was by his side looking equally concerned. They saw us coming and immediately hurried down the steps to meet us.

"Thank goodness you both alright?" Walker T said, with an audible tremor in his voice. "There was a news flash on the radio, just after you left, warning of severe weather. I hope you managed to find shelter. You must be tired and hungry too."

"Luckily we were at Peter's grandmother when the storm started. We stayed there till it blew over. Peter's grandmother fed us and we were lucky her house withstood the storm, because you should see all the damage on the way here."

"I know, young lady, the radio is full of reports about the devastation. Some people on the East coast of the island lost everything. We just got the tail end of a bigger storm. I suppose we're lucky indeed."

"But is everything alright here? What about Claudia, did she come home?" I said, remembering the stories I had just heard about sightings of the White Witch.

"We haven't seen her," Gracie replied, "more than likely, she's with Charles. I thought I smelled her perfume in her room last night, but when I looked inside, no one was there. Anyway, we should be glad that we didn't suffer any major damages. Except for a small leak in the hallway, there was nothing else to really cause concern."

Chapter 27

After the Storm

When Peter left to return to his grandmother's, exhaustion finally kicked in, I climbed the stairs to my room, where I slept for several hours. A whole day passed before I woke up. The first thing I heard was the breakfast bell, and I sat up in bed trying to remember which day it was. I noticed there was soap, towels and a basin next to an enamel jug of water on my bureau. I proceeded to wash my face and brush my teeth as best I could, then I combed my unruly hair. After that I changed into clean clothes and went downstairs.

"We thought you'd never wake up young lady," Walker T said, as he met me at the bottom of the stairs. "I made breakfast. Elfrida can't make it out here. Buses aren't running. Gracie says she will wash the dishes after, so you can dry. Okay?"

"Did I sleep that long? I can't believe I slept right through yesterday. I must have been really beat."

"You should have seen yourself Kathleen, when you came down that road with Peter," Gracie grinned, "you were totally bedraggled, your eyes were red and your hair looked like a bird's nest. Come to think of it, he didn't look any better."

"Did I look that bad?" I laughed, as Gracie covered her mouth and whispered, "If I didn't know better, I'd have taken you for homeless."

All three of us sat down at the breakfast table laughing at the memory. Over a cup of coffee, Walker T proudly handed round scrambled eggs and sausages. "That's the last of the eggs and we only have about two sausages left. We have a loaf of bread, but no butter. That's alright, its all good. There's lemonade for you young lady, instead of orange juice but that's good too."

"Everything's delicious," I said, as I stuffed my face. "Thank you."

"Yes it's good," Gracie agreed, "thanks Walker T, too bad Claudia isn't here to enjoy this."

Three phone calls came before we finished breakfast. The first was from Mr. Cousins from the dairy farm up the road, apparently making sure we were alright. He offered to bring us milk, butter and eggs if needed. "His timing couldn't be better," Walker T commented. "Dairy products and eggs are absolute necessities and Mr. Cousins says he'll be here before lunch. I knew right away that he was a decent man when I met him the other day. I was lucky we exchanged phone numbers. Maybe we could give him some of our mangoes and oranges. Quite a few fell off the trees during the storm."

The other call came when we had almost finished eating, it turned out to be Mrs. Campbell. She wanted to know if we were alright, and was pleased that we sustained no damages. Then the third call was from Charles, who said he had been trying to find Claudia. I thought he sounded quite unpleasant, there was an unaccustomed harshness to his tone of voice.

"We thought she was with you." I said nervously as I toyed with the telephone wire, as though that act alone would somehow affect him.

"Well let me make this clear, she's certainly not with me," he replied, "so just you tell her, when you see her that she owes me big time. Then get her to call. I'm waiting on payment."

He sounded so aggressive, that I had to wonder what it was that Claudia had got involved in. Where was she I wondered, was she safe? Before I could ask any questions, Charles rudely hung up on me.

"Who was that?" Walker T inquired, though I suspected that he already half guessed.

"It was Charles looking for Claudia."

"She's not with him!" Gracie hissed. "Where on earth is she then? Couldn't she have called? She has my stomach in a knot already."

"Maybe we could try to find her," I said, "she has to be somewhere nearby because as far as we know, no car came here to pick her up."

"Young lady I don't suppose you realize how difficult it would be to try to search the countryside after such a storm. If you still feel inclined to do something, you and Gracie should stick together. We can't afford to have one of you wandering off and getting lost. I'd better stay near the phone in case she calls."

Mr. Cousins arrived in his pickup truck, just as Gracie and I were about to leave the house. To my surprise he looked athletic, tanned and younger than expected. He jumped out of his vehicle carrying a large carton box in his muscled hands. He couldn't have been any more than thirty or so, and from his appearance, curly black hair and creamy coffee complexion I figured he was bi-racial.

"He's nice looking." Gracie said under her breath. She didn't take her eyes off him, even when he set the carton down on the verandah.

"Thought you could use these," he said, momentarily glancing at us, and returning Gracie's smile. "Hope you don't mind my leaving this here on the floor, I have to get another box from the truck."

Gracie waited as he brought the second box. "Want these in the kitchen?" he asked, "I'm Jonathan Cousins. There's fresh milk, butter and some eggs from the dairy farm my dad and I operate together down the road. From what I heard. It will be difficult to get anything in town, for a few days. We thought this should tide you over."

"Thank you so much.\," Walker T said coming out to join us. "Our helper couldn't come today. We've been doing the cooking ourselves. We're already running out of things. Much obliged."

"My pleasure, don't mention it. These ladies must be the Canadians you mentioned were staying here?"

"Yes, please excuse me, where's my manners. Mr. Cousins, meet Gracie and Kathleen. They were just going out to search for Claudia, the new owner of the house. We haven't seen her since before the storm."

"Is that so? Do you think she might have got lost or something? I sure hope not. Anyway, please call me Jonathan."

"I'll take the boxes inside," Walker T said, "none of us know for sure if Claudia is lost or not. We thought she was with a friend, but as it turned out, that is not the case. Anyway I told these ladies that I would stand by the phone while they try to find her."

"That basket of mangoes and oranges by the door are for you. We have so many, now that the storm blew them down."

"Thanks I appreciate it, though it sounds as if I could be of some help since I have my pickup truck. As a matter of fact, why don't you ladies jump into the back, we could drive around and have a good look. Are you alright with that?"

Gracie could hardly conceal her pleasure, watching Jonathan swing the heavy basket of fruit into the pickup truck. She then hoisted herself up and was the first aboard the truck. Once I was aboard, she and I sat on a sturdy built-in bench that must have been intended for carrying cylinders of milk. There wasn't a divider that separated the driver from the hold at the back where we were, so it easy to speak with Jonathan as we drove.

"I suppose you've heard there's been a lot of looting," Jonathan said, "times are desperate. One can't be too careful."

"Is it Rastafarians doing the looting?" Gracie asked. Her eyes wide with fear.

"Not necessarily," Jonathan replied. "All kinds of people loot at times like this. You'll hear about it on the radio. Looting happens when people who have nothing get desperate for something. That is part of the reason why yesterday my dad and I distributed free milk to the poor. People came from all around. The way dad and I look at it, is that we might have lost some income but in the end, we gained a lot more. You should have seen the children with milk on their faces. Priceless."

I couldn't help but be impressed with Jonathan's way of looking at things, and I thought what better time to tell Gracie about the Rastafarians I had met at Peter's grandmother's house

"Well Gracie," I said testily. "I actually met two Rastafarian a day or so ago, one of them carved this beautiful pendant for me. At first I thought he looked as scary as anything. So it really surprised me when I found out that he and his friend were going around giving a hand to people, as a result of the storm."

"Is that right? That's totally unbelievable Kathleen! I would never have imagined that they would help out, and I must say that pendant is gorgeous. How much did he charge, an arm and a leg?"

"No Gracie he didn't charge anything. It was a gift."

"Really? Who would have thunk?"

"No doubt that must have been Erasmus," Jonathan laughed, "everybody round here knows him. He's talented, you should see his paintings. He gives away most of his work. Sometimes I wonder if it's because he doesn't want to get too dependent on financial gain."

We didn't say much more, being completely occupied with keeping our eyes on the road and the surrounding bush for signs of Claudia. Years seemed to go by as we drove, though we occasionally had to stop the truck to clear storm debris from the road and ask passersby about Claudia, but despite all that, we were no further ahead with our search.

It wasn't until we were returning to Santiago House, that I happened to see the two children I had met at the river. They were walking nonchalantly along the embankment of the dirt road, minding their own business. Not even the approach of the pickup truck attracted their attention. I somehow had an urge to speak with them.

"Stop the truck Jonathan!" I said urgently, "I know those kids."

"Oh that's Maximilian and Olive," Jonathan replied, "I didn't realize you'd met them. They live on my property."

The truck slowed and startled the children, but when they finally looked up, they recognized me at once. "Miss Kathleen," they squealed, "is nice to see you Ma'm."

"Nice to see you too," I replied. "I was wondering if any of you have seen a light-skin lady with long brown hair wandering around?"

"You mean the White Witch?" Olive said; her voice trembling, and her face gray with fear. "Everybody say dem see her and I hear dat the witch bruk into a stable down the road. But the horse dem make one big noise dat wake the Busha man, and him frighten her, cause him had a gun. So is must be the witch dat bring the storm to kill all of we."

"Who's the witch they're talking about?" Gracie whispered.

"It's probably Claudia," I replied, "we all know there isn't any real witch around here."

"But why would they even think that Claudia is a witch?"

"Well it's like everyone round here is obsessed with Annie Palmer? Maybe they think that Claudia resembles her."

"You know, you might be right Kathleen." Jonathan said softly, "I'm sometimes inclined to think that both the adults and children around here associate every foreign white woman with the Witch."

"They might be on to something Jonathan." Gracie smiled, "but Claudia isn't white though. She's Jewish and East Indian, but I'd say she looks more Jewish."

The children drew closer, perhaps to better overhear our conversation. I leaned over the side of the truck and handed them some sticks of gum I brought from Canada.

"So, did you guys see the witch?" I said, as they stuffed the gum into their mouths. "Did anybody see where the woman was going, or what she was wearing?

Maximilian, the braver of the two stepped forward, as he worked his thin jaw around the gum. "Me hear dat she was going down the Rose Hall road," he said.

"An she was'a wear riding tings." Olive added.

"Are you sure?" Jonathan said, hoping to coax out a fuller story from them. "Know what I think, maybe both of you should come with us, just in case you remember something else."

Though the children's eyes lit up at the prospect of joining us in the truck, they hesitated, and chattered amongst themselves in rapid-fire patois, which I didn't understand, but to my relief they finally climbed aboard.

"They didn't want to come with us," Jonathan translated, "they thought we might steal them away, but it was only because of you Kathleen, that they decided to trust us."

What a pleasure it was for me to hear that, and I smiled at the children and they reciprocated.

"Any sign of anything?" Jonathan asked as we turned a bend in the road. "No, not really," Gracie replied, and we sped on towards the dreaded Rose Hall.

I had no desire to visit Rose Hall again. I hated the gloomy atmosphere there, and after the disturbing stories I recently heard, it was the last place I wanted to be. As if in answer to my prayer, we rounded a sharp hairpin curve and almost ran into a huge roadblock. There were a couple of policemen and a few civilians standing in front of it.

"Stop!" one of the policemen shouted, "you can't go further than here."

"What's the problem?" Jonathan asked, craning his neck out the window.

"There's been a landslide Boss," a man said, coming over to the truck, to scrutinize us. "Nothing going through," he said, "too much mud, rocks and fallen trees and a tourist bus get trapped in the middle of it. So that is why them can't allow any more vehicles to try pass through."

"Are the people alright?" Jonathan asked, trying his best to see further than the huge pile of rubble and debris that blocked our path. "Looks like the whole side of that hill came down."

"So far them only had to treat minor injuries. That's what the medical people at the site say, but where you was going Boss?"

"Rose Hall."

"Sorry, but nobody's going to Rose Hall today."

What a relief I thought to myself. "See what we mean," Olive hissed, "is the witch do that too." I didn't laugh, for my mind was on Claudia, and I wondered if she might have been hurt in the landslide. "Were there people other than the passengers caught in the slide?" I asked, fearful of the answer.

"Yes, of course" one of the policemen replied, "but they have all been accounted for, except for one woman, perhaps a tourist out sightseeing. She took off into the bush, and wouldn't wait for help. People say she was suffering from shock. We plan to send some men on foot after her."

"I wonder if that was Claudia." Gracie whispered, "It scares me to think what could happen to her."

"Was she a young woman?" I called out to the policeman.

"Well, she might think she young but from what people say she was 'getting up there.' Them say she dress like a 'Mother Young Gal'"

"What does that mean?" I asked turning to Jonathan.

"It means she's an older woman who dresses like a much younger woman," he grinned, "So at least we know that's not Claudia. Maybe we'd better head back. Would anyone like to come to the dairy farm for a quick bite to eat?"

It was only Gracie who accepted his invitation, since the two children suddenly remembered that they were sent on an errand, and I declined in favour of returning to Santiago House. "Call us if you hear anything," I said to Gracie, as they dropped me off, before heading to the farm, and leaving a cloud of dust behind them.

When I entered Santiago House it was unaccustomedly still. The silence was so thick it was almost palpable. "Walker T" I called out, but there was no answer. I proceeded to the living room, then the dining room calling his name but I was only greeted with more silence. Where could he be? I wondered, as I checked the kitchen and the pantry but declined checking the outhouses and servants quarters. I slowly climbed the stairs, with Walker T's name at the tip of my tongue. By then, there was no doubt in my mind that the house was entirely empty, and that realization was disturbing. I am alone with spirits from the past I thought: the dead slaves, Santiago, Martin Swift and even the coolie woman who brought food to the house. I grew more fearful by the minute. I forced myself to remain calm, and the image of my own dead parents slowly took over my consciousness and their unwavering love for me gave me strength. It was as if they were actually there protecting me, and my heart stopped racing.

"Is anyone here?" I called out sounding more confident and hopeful, but there was still no answer. I looked down the long hall at the top of the stairs and it seemed as though all the bedroom doors had slowly yawned open. I was mesmerized as I slowly walked towards Claudia's door, and was barely at the threshold when I heard the front door open with a tremendous bang. I knew at once it wasn't Walker T, not with such a determined crash of the door. The air turned cool, as quick footsteps pounded across the downstairs hall causing me to turn away from Claudia's door. Retracing my steps I went to stand at the top of the stairs and looking down; I was startled to see a pale looking boy charging upstairs towards me. His greenish eyes were wild and full of terror.

Chapter 28

Disappearing into the Floor

"Socorro! Socorro!" he shouted, and his words chilled me to the bone, even though I didn't understand them. "Who are you?" I shouted as he brushed past me like a cool summer breeze. He looked neither left nor right, his bare feet drumming against the wooden floors, as he ran directly into Claudia's room.

I still don't know what made me follow him, but when I did I was in time to see when he pushed the bed aside and slid open the floorboards. "Ven." He urged, staring directly at me and beckoning.

There was no way that I could have stopped myself, for my body was like an obedient puppet, ready to obey him. I crossed the floor and pushed the floor boards aside, and saw that beneath was a descending wall with rungs that allowed one to find footing. I stepped down into the dimness and the floor boards closed over me. At first I panicked, and would have tried to claw my way back out of the hole but then I heard the boy's voice below me reassuring me. "Don't be afraid," he said in accented English. "When it is necessary to return, touch the middle board."

"Thank you," I said, as I continued to descend another rung or two. "Cuidado." The boy shouted from below, and he somehow guided me as I went further down holding tightly to rocky indentations in the wall and finding footing on the rungs. It wasn't long before I realized that I was directly under the front rooms of the house. I heard peculiar noises above me that grew in intensity, to sound like rumbling thunder. I froze against the underground wall hardly daring to breathe as I heard voices bellowing above me. It must have lasted less than ten minutes but I held my breath listening. "Claudia not here," a man's voice shouted, and another responded. "Okay boys, put the guns away. We going have to come back. Nothing of value here anyway."

I couldn't help thinking that one of those voices sounded a lot like Charles.

My heart almost burst out of my chest, realizing that gunmen were in the house, and I was fearful of what could happen if Walker T or anyone else returned home. I covered my mouth and stifled the scream that threatened. In frustration tears stung my eyes, and I shuddered in the dimness. Surely I would have been raped or killed if I had been found in the house alone.

It felt like an eternity before there was silence, followed by the sound of a vehicle departing. Only then did I entertain the thought that the men had left the house. Looking around I found my bearings and noticed for the first time that the wall I was leaning against came to an end a few feet below me. It veered off into two tunnels; one went left and the other to the right. All at once I remembered the story about the snakes in the well, and I wondered if snakes were in the tunnels. Returning to Claudia's room wasn't an option, for what if one of the gunmen had remained behind in the house. There was no doubt in my mind that I had to take my chances and I pressed on.

I chose the tunnel that veered right, because it seemed shorter and wasn't as dark as the other. When I entered that tunnel I was sure that I heard the boy's excited voice shout 'Excellente'.

Almost as soon as I set out I came upon a huge magnificent stone set into the wall-face. It was taller and wider than I, and covered with carvings. I was compelled to stop to admire it, for the carvings were well-executed renditions of Jamaica's flowers and fauna. What a treasure this is, I thought. It shouldn't be hidden from the rest of the world! I caught my breath, as I leaned against it and it occurred to me that the stone might well be a doorway. I pushed it with all my might but it seemed like wasted effort, for it didn't even budge. However I was taken completely by surprise when after a third try, the stone laboriously swung aside. It dislodged years of caked-up dust, dirt Insect debris and matted cobweb in its wake, as it opened into a cave-like room with dirt walls. An old ladder was propped up purposely against one of those walls.

I entered the room with much trepidation, and on examining the ladder, found it to be sturdy. I climbed up, and saw that there were boards above me that looked like flooring. Even in that dim light it was possible to see that there was a small rose painted on one of the boards. It looked exactly like the one on the floor in Santiago's room.

I knew at once this would be my escape route and I felt hugely indebted to the boy who had guided me out of harm's way. Where was he I wondered, an uncontrollable fear washed over me, as the penny dropped. I had been alone, all along, the boy whose help had been so invaluable, was none other than the ghost of Santiago!

Fear got the better of me; I shot out of the cave room and ran towards the rungs. Realizing only then that climbing back up could prove to be foolish. I came to my senses, and retraced my steps to quickly climb up the ladder. I was soon level with the flooring boards that ran across the ceiling. Remembering Santiago's words I pushed against the rose on the middle board I was flooded with relief when the trap door slid aside.

Emerging through the opening I found myself in a small room. Sunshine streamed in at the one window, accentuating cobwebs and dust particles. The room proved tiny and claustro-phobic, there was only space enough for a small cot and a couple of old crates. Having become accustomed to the underground half-light my eyes smarted against the light, as I braced against the room's heavy wooden door. It opened easily despite old rusty hinges. A blast of fresh air immediately hit me in the face. I stepped out to find myself at the back of Santiago House. The well stood lonely not far from where I was, and I immediately surmised that I had just been standing in Martin Swift's room.

Chapter 29

White Witch

Keeping close to bushes I stealthily made my way towards the front of the house. I was reminded of the fateful day in Siddon when I had heard my parent's arguing. Here I was again in a conundrum, but this time more fearful of going into danger, and at the same time wanting to warn the others. I wondered what would happen if the men returned.

A fragrant aroma from the rose bushes wafted in the air to belie the dread that consumed me. I went to hide in a clump of guava trees. I had a good view of the verandah, as well as the dirt road. I heard the river gurgling and I told myself that its song was sent to calm me, and keep my mind off things. Green lizards basked in the sunlight on tree branches, and noisy wild birds hungrily ate ripe fruit. I kept as still as possible, attempting to blend with the surroundings. I watched beautiful butterflies flit in the air looking like tiny guardian angels and I listened intently, and heard rustling noises in the bush-land behind me. I was unperturbed because I knew it most likely was pigs, goats and cattle furrowing.

Like mother, I felt akin to the creatures of the land, believing in some small way that they played a role in preventing my coming to harm. I found myself wondering what Luke Whitefawn would have thought of Jamaica, though his face had gone blurry in my memory. The face I saw in my mind's eye was that of David Chang.

I was concerned with watching the road when a loud bang from the house attracted my attention. It was the front door pushed open with extraordinary force. I saw a tall gangly man dressed in black, step out onto the verandah, shading his eyes against the sun, while speaking on a cell phone. I wished I could have heard what he was saying, but he was too far off. He stood there for the longest time, not moving an inch, except to occasionally shade his eyes and survey the surrounding property.

I became fearful that he had caught sight of me, for he stared intently in my direction, and then began descending the steps. I didn't dare move an inch. I prayed the foliage would somehow camouflage me. I watched him reach the bottom step still staring, and I wondered if he heard the drumming in my heart. But then another sudden sound broke through the tension. A vehicle came humming up the dirt road, followed by clouds of dust. Please don't let it be Gracie I said to myself. But when the car drew up to the house, I could see that it wasn't Jonathan and Gracie. The driver was known to the man on the front step, for he quickly put away his cell phone, and hopped into the car. They were gone in a heartbeat.

It was fortunate that I hadn't gone back into the house, for it was clear that the lone man was left behind to give the house a thorough search. Even after the car shot down the dirt road and out of sight. I couldn't get myself to budge. I just kept waiting, and wondering where were Walker T and Claudia? When dusk came, bringing mosquitoes and night bugs on the wing I was still crouched amongst the trees.

Darkness fell quickly, but because we were so isolated, it wasn't until stars came out, that I finally heard a vehicle approaching. When it came into view, I saw that it was a pickup truck, and knew it must be Jonathan. The truck drew up to the house and despite the dimness I was able to see Gracie climb down from the back. I also was aware that besides the driver, there were two other darkened figures in the truck. I wondered if the river children had come along for the ride. I found my legs and charged towards them shouting: "Wait, wait!"

Jonathan immediately cut the engine and came out of the truck. "What's up?" he said, not half realizing the enormity of what had happened.

"Are you alright?" he said, and he came, to stand beside Gracie, his hand seeking hers. Only then did I see that it was Walker T, who was in the back of the truck and the person in the front seat was a woman I didn't recognize.

"Is everything okay, young lady?" Walker T said, leaning out of the truck, his face lined with concern.

"I'm alright now," I panted, "but I have to warn everybody about what's been going on here."

"Well if it is a medical emergency, you'll be glad to know that we are on our way to the hospital in Montego Bay." Jonathan said, "So climb in Kathleen, you too Gracie. As you can see, there is a lady in the truck. She is suffering from shock. We think she is the tourist who disappeared near the landslide. It was Walker T who found her. He brought her to the dairy farm. But we wanted to make sure you're alright, since we realized you'd be here alone in the house."

I didn't respond immediately, it was as if I had gone mute, though I practically jumped into the back of the truck to sit across from Walker T, I was visibly trembling all over. Gracie put her arm around me. "You're terrified, what's happened Kathleen ?"

"I have to warn you guys." I said, my voice quivering, "Something dangerous happened today. A bunch of gunmen came to the house looking for Claudia. I hid from them in the house, and after I thought they'd left I hid outside just in case. By then I was too scared to go back inside."

Everyone was shocked by what I had to say, though I couldn't bring myself to mention anything about Santiago, or the painted rose on the floorboards or even about the carved rock underground. My caution concerning the matter stemmed from the fact that I didn't really know anything about the strange woman who was in the truck with us.

"You've been very lucky young lady," Walker T whispered nervously. "You know of course we will have to leave Santiago House, or else hire a guard to stay there with us. This is serious business, and this dangerous situation affects all of us."

"I know," I whispered, "right now I'm so shaken, I don't even know if I can trust the lady sitting up front. How did you meet her? Do you know her Walker T? Has she said anything at all?"

"It's a long story young lady, but no, I have no idea who she is. She has not spoken even one word."

"Did gunmen come to the house when you were alone Walker T?"

"No, no young lady, nothing like that. What happened is that I was quite alone in the house I was having a quiet lunch in the dining room, when all of a sudden I heard a sharp banging at the window. I wondered what on earth it could be, I pulled back the drapes and saw the blurry outline of a woman wearing a white riding outfit. She was standing a little distance away from the house, and my first thought was, how did she move away from the window that quickly? I wondered if it was Claudia, playing some kind of joke. I was about to call out to her, but the thick foliage around her blurred her even more. To be honest I was becoming less sure that it was Claudia, but the woman somehow mesmerized me. She beckoned urgently, and poor me I wasn't even sure that I was the person she was calling to. She persisted, so I went to the front door and saw that she was still a short distance away, though her back was turned towards me. Every now and again she turned round slightly, keeping her face concealed and still beckoning. What sort of game is Claudia playing I wondered. I stepped right out onto the verandah, and heard her say my name in a soft whispery voice that sounded vaguely familiar.

"I walked slowly towards her, hoping to catch a better glimpse of her. But each time I got within a few feet of her, she would suddenly appear to be much farther away. I must have been in a trance, because I followed her dog-like all across the property, through the bush and over to the riverbank. I couldn't get a clear fix on her. I kept wondering who on earth she was. Ages went by without my thinking of the distance that separated me from Santiago House. I even saw the tombstones at Bickerstep Cemetery loom on the horizon, but then the river veered off and so did the woman."

"Isn't that just creepy Kathleen?" Gracie hissed, "Jonathan thinks it's weird too."

"Well young lady," Walker T said, leaning forward; and it was obvious that the road had been cleared, for the sound of Jonathan gunning the engine filled our ears. "I've never experienced anything quite like it before. I arrived at a fork in the river, and heard someone crying. I couldn't imagine who it could be. But curiosity made me go look amongst the rushes that grow at the very centre of the fork. So you can imagine how shocked I was, to find a frightened woman there up to her ankles in water. She was rocking back and forth, and her exposed skin was covered in dried blood and scratches. She was wearing a blond wig; it had gone askew and was covered with burs and twigs. But as for her clothes they were badly torn and muddied. She was so traumatized ,she didn't say a single word. She's lucky to be alive though, because after the storm, the river is swollen and hungry. I used a short bamboo pole I found as leverage, because the riverbank is nothing but slick and mud."

"O my god Walker T, all that took a lot of courage. That poor woman must have been scared out of her mind and the devastation from the storm must have frightened her."

"You are perfectly right young lady, she was actually trembling, much the same as you are. However I'm not sure if I'd say I was courageous, perhaps I was just foolish, I had to do what had to be done, and I used my handkerchief to clean the woman's face and hands as best I could. I spoke encouragingly to her and told her I was there to help. She looked so frightened, I wasn't sure she understood. It dawned on me that we were closer to the dairy farm than to Santiago House, so that's why I decided to take her there. I helped her to her feet and had her lean on me for support, as together we navigated the muck and debris and headed towards the farm."

"But what happened to the woman in the riding gear? Did you see her again?"

"No young lady I didn't see her. But the oddest thing is I didn't even have time to think along those lines since I was deeply concerned with the task at hand. My one thought was to take this woman to safety and to make sure she was alright. I feel much better now that we are taking her to the hospital."

Chapter 30

Hiring Armed Guards

As the truck drove through the silky darkness, we felt a stiff refreshing breeze from the sea on our faces. Coconut and banana trees flailed in the wake of the wind and the moon chased us overhead. The lush foliage along our route appeared ragged and blackened, and over my right shoulder, the angry sea shone silver.

I felt as one with nature out there in the open riding in the back of the pickup under a canopy of bright comforting stars. It reminded me of nights in Northern Ontario when father and I used to watch the skies and listen out for the cry of wolves. It was times like that I sometimes forgot where I was, for my mind was there, and my heart was here, as we sped on unhindered. Diligent labourers must have spent most of the day clearing the road, for there were no major obstacles. Jonathan's hand was unwaveringly steady at the wheel. Once in a while, Gracie would softly touch her fingers against his broad shoulders. It was clear for us all to see that they shared new found camaraderie.

As we cut a swath through the night, the woman in the front seat remained mute. I longed to voice my speculations out loud. I wondered if the woman in white that Walker T had seen might have been the White Witch, and not Claudia. I held my tongue, remembering that I had seen Santiago, and had not said a word about him. The urgent cranking of the pickup truck's engine reminded me of the last ride mother took with Luke Whitefawn speeding away from our cottage, and as a result of those thoughts, I became silent, as though retrieving something from within myself; something that couldn't be shared. It is no wonder that I was the last to know when we arrived at the hospital.

"I'll take her inside," I heard Walker T say when Jonathan pulled the truck over and parked in front of the entrance, "they'll want to examine her. It shouldn't take too long and I'll stay if I'm needed. Perhaps you could check back in an hour or so, I'd be much obliged."

From the truck we watched as Walker T accompanied the frightened woman into the well-lit building. He stopped momentarily and waved at us, and we waved back, then he took her through to the Emergency entrance.

"We have some time to kill," Jonathan said sounding quite serious, and he put the truck into reverse, "hope you don't mind but I have to stop and speak with some buddies of mine in town."

I wondered why Jonathan would want to go visiting, but then he told us that his friends worked in Security. "I didn't want to scare that poor woman any more than she already is," he said, "but what happened at Santiago House today is very serious business. I intend to ask my buddies if any of them are available to come out to Santiago House with us tonight. I'm pretty sure that based on our friendship, a couple of them will be more than willing to help since we all went to Cornwall College together."

We left the hospital grounds and drove through the busy modern tourist sections of the city. What a spectacle it was at night with neon lights and sidewalks teeming. I imagined it was somewhat like being in Miami. But then Jonathan turned off from the strip, and took us to the older part of town. "There's an old creek here," he said, "old folks here used to say that a mermaid lives in that creek. Don't laugh Gracie, because who can say one way or another, considering that lately we have been hearing about the reappearance of Annie Palmer. I for one can't be too skeptical; I'm quite open-minded."

We drove to a house located at the foot of a small hill on Humber Avenue. One could see that many of the older homes there had at one time seen glory days. I longed to stretch my legs, but thought it best to remain in the truck. It was Jonathan who stepped out, and came to the side of the pickup where Gracie was, and patted her hand. "See you in a bit," he said, then he went into the house alone.

"I like him a lot," Gracie whispered, "it might sound strange, because I've only just met him but I'll be darned, I like him a whole lot."

"It's obvious he likes you too," I said, "no doubt about it."

Gracie's smile broadened, "van't wait to tell Claudia about him. He's kind, down to earth and smart. And by the way, it doesn't matter a bit that he isn't Chinese like me."

"I didn't think that would matter."

"Well it's just that sometimes people just assume. Have you ever felt like this about someone Kathleen?" Gracie laughed, then slapped her wrist, "what am I saying, aren't you just sixteen? Time enough I guess."

"Well don't assume anything," I grinned. "and, for your information Gracie, my sixteenth birthday was months ago, and to answer your other question, yes, there's someone…"

I didn't get the opportunity to finish my sentence since we saw Jonathan coming back to the truck, and I knew that Gracie's attention was completely diverted.

"So what's up Jonathan?" Gracie said, "everything alright?"

"Yes, things went well, and it took me less than fifteen minutes. Two armed guards are going to follow us in their car back to Santiago House, and I found out where Claudia is."

"Is that right? Where is she?"

"I'll tell you in the truck. You never know who's listening."

"True enough."

I couldn't wait for Jonathan to get back behind the wheel, and when he did, he pulled out from the curb, just as two burly black men emerged from the house. And although it wasn't obvious to anyone watching, we knew they would be following us, and I felt more at ease with the situation.

"Apparently Claudia's been hanging out with one of my buddies named Raymond Alexander. Raymond works in security, and has an excellent reputation" Jonathan said, keeping his voice low, though there was no possibility of being overheard. "A few days ago, Raymond took Claudia to St. Thomas, a Parish at the other end of the island to get her out of harm's way. From what I understand Claudia made connections with him through her father, a brilliant lawyer. These guys here told me that Raymond was recommended in case Claudia should run into trouble down here. My buddies also pointed out that when she first came to them she was agitated and mumbling something about the White Witch. She told these guys that she was threatened by drug dealer idiots and was warned not to contact anyone at Santiago House in any manner or else you all could be murdered. It might be nothing but a bluff on their part, but regardless, there is cause for concern since they actually came to the house. It seems they didn't count on her leaving the Santiago property."

"Well let's hope she's safe. Why would those guys want to kill us, we didn't even have anything to do with them," I said, hoping

Jonathan didn't think of me as some kind of idiot who just didn't see the big picture.

"You've got a point Kathleen but it is possible it is all nothing more than a threat, but we can't be sure can we? Those dealers are well aware that Claudia came into money inheriting the property. I think they intended to milk her out of every penny. But then again, sometimes these criminals just want to make an example of someone."

We all became silent; we drove near the beachfront, none of us that comfortable with prospects for the future. The brightly lit hotels, shops and restaurants filled with tourists, made Montego Bay appear carnival-like and oblivious to our dilemma. When Jonathan stopped the truck and picked up some jerk chicken dinners, the two burly guards were still on our tail.

"Wouldn't you say it's time we go get Walker T?" Jonathan said, reversing the truck and steering towards the hospital. "My guess is the woman has been seen to by now."

"I'd say," Gracie replied, munching her chicken, "it's been hours, and besides Walker T must be starving. It's a good thing we bought dinner for all of us. It's so good, I'll have to go back there again. What was the restaurant called?"

"Glad you enjoy the food Gracie, I eat at 'Miss Matilda's Kitchen' quite often. Anybody who is anybody round here knows the place... I'd be happy to bring you back anytime you like."

We arrived at the hospital to find Walker T standing at the entrance under the bright lights.

"She's been admitted for observation," he said solemnly as he came over to the truck. "She probably lost her passport so we still don't know who she is. But none of the hotels have reported a missing guest. Anyway I took care of her bill, and told the staff I'd check on her tomorrow. One of the emergency nurses said that a friend of a friend told her that the woman might be English, because someone on a tour bus said that the woman protested when people tried to prevent her from going off on her own, and she had an English accent."

"Well it sounds like we won't know anything about her for a while." Gracie said, "Anyway we brought you dinner Walker T It might be a long night ahead."

Exhaustion got the better of me, I fell asleep on the drive back to Santiago House. I only awoke when we were parking in front of the house, and the two guards were pulling up in their car

"Well folks," Jonathan said, "these buddies of mine are Sonny and Glenville. Don't anyone go inside until they have checked it out. Don't worry about accommodations these men are used to being posted outdoors. They will keep an eye on the property, and occasionally check on us indoors."

After about twenty minutes, we all filed into the house and the guards immediately took up posts outdoors. I was surprised to find that the house was in good order. I quickly climbed the stairs and went to my room; it was exactly as I left it. "All's well here," I shouted.

"My room's good too," Walker T said coming out into the hall, "I guess there's nothing left now young lady but to settle in. Have a goodnight."

The last thing I heard before closing my door was Gracie saying Goodnight to Jonathan downstairs. "Thank you for everything," she said, "you've been wonderful." There was a long silence and I imagined they were kissing and I smiled.

Chapter 31

Buying a Dress

I slept well that night and only awoke when Elfrida began clanging pots in the kitchen. I knew she was hard at work preparing breakfast. A delicious aroma wafted up the stairs and coaxed me out of bed. Things seemed so normal it was hard to imagine that not only were there were guards on the property but I had seen Santiago, and Walker T might have had an encounter with the White Witch. Did I imagine it all, I wondered, but no, for when I looked out my window I saw that the guard called Sonny was standing nearby smoking.

I quickly washed and changed and went downstairs to find Gracie and Walker T already up sitting in the living room.

"Good morning, I must have slept in," I said.

"Not really young lady, Gracie and I woke very early. I had a very light sleep, but Jonathan called Gracie early this morning to see how we are. He's coming later. The guards are going back into town, and another two will take over. Anyway Elfrida's is making breakfast for all of us, the guards too."

"It smells delicious doesn't it Kathleen?" Gracie said, "Elfrida says she's making festival, ackee and cod, plus bacon and eggs. Man, I love Jamaican breakfasts."

"Me too. Is Jonathan going to join us?"

"Oh no, he has milking and herding to do, as well as see to his chickens and pigs."

"Don't they have hired help?"

"Yes, they have a few farmhands, and a maid, but Jonathan is a real 'hands on' type of farmer if something needs doing, he's there."

"Is it a large farm?"

"I'd say. And his dad has a couple of horses, so they have paddocks and pastures. Yeah the farm is a good size."

"You didn't mention his mother, what's she like?"

"Well Jonathan and his dad didn't say much about her. But from what I gathered, she had an affair and ran off years ago. She recently died from cancer, and neither Jonathan nor his dad ever saw her again after she left. That sort of thing is so sad and is bound to affect those left behind, wouldn't you say?"

"Yes I'm sure it affects everyone in the household. Trust me."

"Well young ladies I must ask to be excused. I have to let the guards know breakfast is almost ready."

The moment Walker T left the room, Gracie smiled mischievously. "I can't wait to see Jonathan today," she said, "I can already see us getting really close and I don't even want to think about what will happen when I have to leave Jamaica."

"Who knows what will happen," I said sounding philosophical, yet at the same time, wondering about my own life.

Four days later, the house was still under guard, yet life at Santiago House continued as normally as possible. I didn't wander too far from the house choosing instead to accompany Gracie and Jonathan to the beach on occasion, or else to go to the river on my own. Elfrida brought word that most of the roads were cleared, and tourists were once again visiting Rose Hall.

I didn't see anything of the river children, and wondered what had become of them. My thoughts even turned to Granny. I was taken by surprise when Jonathan brought word that the children's mother had been injured in the storm, and it was the children who were looking after things at home. Jonathan said that he had taken them much needed food supplies, and a couple of live chickens, and he thought the mother would soon be on the mend.

Walker T developed the morning routine of driving with the guards into Montego Bay, and returning later in a hired car with a driver. He felt obliged to be at the hospital each day to check on the mystery patient. From what he told us the woman seemed to be making good progress, though she hadn't spoken. One morning I accompanied him into town. I arranged to meet him at the hospital, after I had an opportunity to have a look around the shops.

The guards were kind enough to drop me off on the strip instructing me to be cautious, and not take up with strangers. They needn't have worried for everywhere I went, people were courteous and helpful. I bought a few trinkets to take back to Canada, and I was contemplating buying a colourful summer dress, when I glimpsed Peter going past the store with a friend. I hurried out and called out to him: "Hi Peter, how's it going?"

He was surprised to see me in town but was clearly pleased, as he came and hugged me.

"Hi Kathleen, what you doing in MoBay?"

"Just a bit of shopping, I was just about to buy a dress when I saw you."

"This is my friend Debbie. We... work together at the hotel."

"Nice to meet you Debbie."

"Likewise. What dress were you buying?"

"That one in the window."

"That one! Did you look at the price Kathleen? I can take you to a place that's more reasonable."

"Really! But aren't you on your way to work?"

"Peter and I were just killing time. We start at 12:30"

She's nice, I thought to myself and attractive too, with her coal black complexion, long braids and full figure. I was however somewhat taken aback when Peter took her arm in his as we set out.

"I told Debbie how you came and met my Granny," he said, "and guess what; I think that is why Debbie and I got closer." When he laughed, I joined in.

"Kathleen, what Peter's trying to say is that I was jealous, but I wasn't, honestly. I just thought that now is a good time for Peter and me to start acting the way we should. I always knew that he cared about me, but I played it cool. Kathleen, I have you to thank for what's going on with us now. I like him a lot."

Peter shyly blew her an air kiss, and I was happy for him. I had never thought of him as anything more than a friend and it was clear that I hadn't lost his friendship.

"I'm very glad for the two of you," I said meaning it and I squeezed Debbie's hand.

"Now about that dress I'm looking for. Think you could help me find something bright with thin straps and not too tight fitting? I have a pair of plain black sandals I could wear with it."

Debbie seized my hand and smiled., "I know just the place," she said excitedly. "My cousin Beverly always shops there it's called Doctor Bird's Palace and it's cheaper than these tourist joints."

"Well let's go there then, and it had better be good."

"No problem."

Doctor Bird's Palace was exactly as Debbie described. It was situated off of the beaten path, and jam-packed with clothing. Trying to move around in there was a major undertaking but the locals who shopped there didn't seem to mind. Doctor Bird, as it turned out was a tall skinny albino guy who wore a top hat, and walked around on stilts. He somehow managed to weave in and out of the shoppers, laughing and chatting, while making not too subtle suggestions as to what to purchase. "This would suit you," he'd say or else "Forget bout dat. It don't look good on you."

I found two dresses, one with pale green fern leaf designs and the other in bright aqua with pinkish fishes. Both seemed exactly what I wanted, but that was until Doctor Bird came over to me.

"Why you playing it so safe pretty girl?" he said, "Try this one. It will bring out the colour in your eyes, and look at the neckline. It was made for you."

He was right too, for when I tried on the deep purple dress he chose with its thin straps and a plunging neckline I knew at once that I had found a winner.

"I'll take it," I grinned, thanking him.

"Why not get one of the other one's too." Debbie coaxed, "Because this one's so fabulous, you'll will want to keep it for special, but you can wear the other ones anytime."

"Excellent idea." I said, "And you know what, the two of them together will cost less than twenty-five Canadian dollars. That's totally cool. Thank you so much Debbie."

"Debbie's clever." Peter chimed in, "She's working her way up to head chef at the hotel. That's why, now more than ever I want to make something of myself."

"You still can." I smiled.

Chapter 32

Luckily Nothing Happened

I met Walker T at exactly twelve noon as was arranged. "Everything alright?" I said coming to sit on one of the benches beside him. He looked gray-faced, as though he'd lost a battle. "She's alright is she?" I asked hopefully.

"She must be. She's checked out. They couldn't stop her, she was well enough to leave."

"So where did she go?"

"They wouldn't tell me. All they said is that it had something to do with patient confidentiality."

"But they don't even know who she is. Do they?"

"Young lady, that might have been so at the beginning, but more and more I began to get the feeling that they knew more about her than they were letting on. Anyway, what it boils down to is no more trips out here for me every day. I was kind of getting used to it, and by the way, Gracie mentioned that she thought you had a birthday several months ago, but didn't seem to have had a celebration. We'd like to invite some folks to the house to celebrate. Turning sixteen is a milestone."

"Sweet. But that was long ago, I'm sort of closer to seventeen now." That was all I could say. I was so choked up.

When Walker T and I returned to the house, we found it empty, though the two guards were still posted outside. We found a note from Gracie pinned to the living-room door that read:

'Out at Jonathan's. Will be there till six. Don't save supper. Love Gracie.'

"So we're alone." Walker T sighed as he settled down to read the newspaper. I went into the living room and sat down in the chair nearest to his.

"Walker T," I began hesitantly, "It wasn't just my birthday that I didn't tell you about, and I don't want you to be the last to know anything. So I'm going to tell you something I should have told you before."

"What's it, young lady? If it concerns your birthday, we can start phoning folks around two o'clock or so. There's still time"

Oh no. It's not about that. Something happened the other day when the gunmen came."

"What do you mean? Did they hurt you or do anything to you?"

"They didn't even see me Walker T, don't worry. I saw something, and I found out that there is a trap door in Claudia's room that leads to a tunnel underground and that's where I hid while the gunmen were here."

"But how on earth did you figure out there is a trap door and a tunnel there young lady?"

"Well Walker T, you'll probably find this hard to believe, but then again, after what happened to you I could be wrong. But here's what happened. Santiago appeared to me in the house, he was screaming something I didn't understand. I knew that whatever it was, it was urgent, and he wanted me to follow him. I saw him run into Claudia's room, and then he went through the trap door. At the time I didn't know who he was, but I followed him and found the tunnel. That's when the gunmen came. Santiago must have known they were coming, and it was his way of warning me. When I was underground, I saw a huge carved stone door that lead me into a room with a ladder, and when I climbed up the ladder, I found that I was in a small room in the quarters at the back of the house. I'm almost certain it was Martin Swift's room. I quickly left his room, and hid outside, until you guys came."

"Sounds like you had quite an encounter young lady. Are you sure it was Santiago you saw? Because if it was, we are talking about a ghost, you do realize that don't you!"

"Yes I'm sure it was him. Besides, who else would know Claudia's room as well as he did? It used to be his room, remember."

"Well, thank goodness he's a benevolent spirit. He actually saved your life. Do you realize that?"

"Yes, he did, didn't he? But Walker T don't you go forgetting that it must have been the White Witch Annie Palmer that led you to that woman you found, so you must have seen an apparition too."

"To be honest I hadn't given it much thought, but you might be right in thinking it was her. Do you remember I told you about a relative of mine who was a bookkeeper at Rose Hall back in slavery days? Well you would be right, if you assumed that he was one of her many lovers. He was an Englishman, as I've said before, people say I have his eyes. He was one of the poor saps Annie couldn't bring herself to murder. He ended up marrying a local girl who was black as an ackee seed and that is how the Jamaican side of my family started. Through the years, my family always joked, and say that Annie Palmer would never harm a hair of anyone of us, because of how she felt about my ancestor."

"Cool. But you know what I found out today Walker T? Peter has a girlfriend."

"Are you surprised? He's a good looking young fellow."

"No, not really surprised. I ran into them today and his girlfriend seems nice, she even helped me find a place to buy a nice dress."

"Well that's kind of her but don't you go feeling sorry for yourself. Someone will come along for you soon enough."

"Yeah, sure. To be honest though, it's like I never had those kinds of feelings for Peter in the first place."

That afternoon I spent less than half an hour calling and inviting the few friends I made to my birthday gathering. At first I almost could have counted the guest list on one hand, but then one or two other people would come to mind. Besides Walker T and Gracie, there was Jonathan, Peter and Debbie and Mrs. Campbell. I would have asked the river children if I was able to get hold of them, but by now I knew they wouldn't come. Then I remembered Erasmus' kindness and thought perhaps Peter could get word to him, since I had no other way of contacting him. I hadn't forgotten David, not for a moment' but I had begun to feel self-conscious about inviting him. So in the end, when I spoke to Mrs. Campbell I suggested that she could bring her colleague along if she wanted to, and that said, it took the onus out of my hands. I was so excited, that I couldn't wait for the day to come.

The celebration was set for the coming Friday, and that morning I awoke early, I opened my window to the accustomed sound of bird song, roosters and barking dogs. The sky was a purple haze, and I marvelled at its beauty. Poinciana trees on the property were in full bloom and their vivid orange blossoms reminded me of a bright flame. Not too far from the house sugarcane swayed in the morning air, and the faint lilting voices of field workers reached my ears. How far away I felt from home. I was homesick, remembering past birthdays.

I quietly climbed down the stairs and went out on to the verandah. The air was fresh and warm. and as I looked towards the fields I witnessed a panorama of flowering plants, as well as cane, banana and fruit trees that filled me even more with missing. Perhaps it was because I was only weeks away from returning to Canada, and was in the exact state of mind as father must have been when he was leaving Ireland. He too must have wanted to take it all with him, though fully aware of the impossibility.

My eyes brimmed with tears as I gazed towards the dirt road, and my heart became heavy despite the sweetness of the river's incessant gurgling and murmuring, as a large white bird sailed across the skies. I went down the steps, thinking I would take a better look at the bird, but it was soon lost to my view, due to the density of the surrounding foliage. Disappointed I turned back towards the house and caught my breath in wonder; for the house, bathed in the glow of the dawning sky looked spectacular.

I suddenly heard a sound that reminded me of leaves crackling underfoot in the Canadian Fall weather. It took me a moment before I realized that someone was walking in the bush near to where I was. I was alarmed when a deep male voice intruded into my reverie and said, "You not fraid to be out here alone at this hour?"

I was so startled; it brought me right back into reality. I could hardly breathe, even though I saw that it was one of the guards. His expression was dark and serious, and reminded me that I had forgotten about potential dangers.

"What time is it?" I said, sounding foolish as he approached and I stuck my hands into my pajama pockets lest he might notice that I was wearing a watch. My first thought was to make small talk, as a cover for my bad judgment. "I was a million miles away just now," I said, "couldn't help myself, everything looked so lovely."

"Well you lucky nothing happen to you. Anyway, you all will be glad to hear that Charles and his cronies were arrested last night in Mo Bay. One of the gang members named Derrick turned the rest of them in. He says he owes it to Gracie, but he didn't elaborate. Anyway we were just about to go back to town. You won't need us out here anymore. We just called Jonathan."

"Are you serious? Everything's back to normal, that's awesome."

"Be sure to read the story in the Star this evening. Those fellows prey on unsuspecting tourists all the time. They're like a disease if you ask me."

"Well the fact that they are arrested is the best news ever. I'll wake the others and tell them."

"Give them our best."

"So you won't be coming to my birthday gathering?"

"Sorry, thanks for thinking of us, but we can't make it, we have another assignment. Good luck and many happy returns"

"Any news of Claudia?"

"No, we haven't contacted Raymond as yet."

Chapter 33

Remembering
Past Birthdays

That afternoon the aroma of baking filled the whole house. Elfrida outdid herself. She made me a chocolate cake and baked a sweet potato pudding. Then she set into preparing a pot of curry goat, rice and peas and roast pork. Gracie too, was hard at work fixing a salad with ingredients from the garden. I was given instructions to stay out of the way, so I went out to the verandah and read old magazines. Walker T was out of the house for most of the afternoon, he had gone into town to see if there was any word from the mystery woman, and he said he would be back in time for my celebration.

"Is Erasmus that send the goat meat." Elfrida said proudly, "People give him all kind of thing in exchange for him art work and is Mr. Jonathan that supply the pork leg. Everything going eat nice."

The guests were instructed to arrive at five-thirty, so at three-thirty I went indoors and had a long shower and washed my hair, determined to look my best for the occasion. I slipped on my new purple dress, hardly believing that the image in the mirror was mine. What I saw in the mirror, was a confident young woman looking back at me, with her shiny long lush hair and extraordinarily blue eyes. The dress was seductive without being blatant, Doctor Bird was right. It did do justice to my eyes. I couldn't help but smile, as I strutted in front of the mirror in my black raised heel sandals. Not bad, I sighed and I put on a thin coat of lip-gloss.

When finally, I looked at the time, I saw that it was already four-forty-five. I wondered who would arrive first, and if anyone would even come. What a difference this belated birthday was as compared to my previous birthdays. Birthdays in the past had all been spent in our rustic kitchen in Siddon, with just my parents and me. One or the other of them would usually have rustled up a cake, and that would be followed by what became our traditional walk in the forest. Father used to mark notches on a tree trunk as evidence to my height and age. But mother on the other hand always brought along a chunk of cake in a biscuit tin to feed to small animals. 'Why shouldn't they celebrate too' she'd say. Then afterwards we always went home to enjoy apple cider and talk long into the evening. However, now that I think of it in retrospect, I wonder if the cake mother used to take to the forest was actually meant for Luke Whitefawn.

Chapter 34

Pearlsand Other Presents

I was sitting on the edge of my bed dreaming of what was, and what might have been, when Walker T came up stairs carrying a long package under his arm.

"Happy Birthday" he said, "These are for you. You're a real young lady now. Just look at you. And by the way, I hung a string of storm lanterns on the verandah. It will give us a bit of ambiance don't you think."

I laughed, thanked him and tore open the package to find a stunning arrangement of orchids and anthuriums. There was a small gift box amongst the bright blooms, and inside the box was a single strand of beautiful pearls that brought tears to my eyes. "Thank you so much Walker T these gifts are like so cool. Thank you again."

I immediately slipped the pearl necklace around my throat, and Walker T fastened the catch. "You are most welcome." he said, his voice charged with emotion. "I knew this necklace was made for you, when I saw it in the store window but hurry, come downstairs. Someone else is here."

With Walker T leading the way I followed with bated breath and found that Erasmus was waiting in the hall at the foot of the stairs. His face lit up the moment he laid his eyes on me. "Is you that?" He said with a wide grin and a toss of his locks, "You look like big woman now. Happy Belated Birthday I did bring you something this morning."

"Yes you did, didn't you? Thanks for the goat meat. Elfrida cooked it and it smells delicious."

We were about to go into the living room when Peter and Debbie arrived at the door. They were laughing, singing and banging out the tune 'Happy belated birthday to you' on the doorframe. They thrust a portable CD player into my hands and handed me a stack of CDs.

"We brought you music. All these CDs are for you."

"Thanks so much. I was just thinking, like we should have something to listen to."

"Is mostly Bob Marley." Debbie said, "He's cool. But we throw in a few Rhianna."

"Sweet."

Jonathan arrived and Gracie must have heard him, she came flying down the stairs dressed in an off the shoulder green dress. She looked amazing, Jonathan couldn't take his eyes off her. "Happy Belated Birthday," he said, following Gracie's every move with an appreciative smile. "This is for you Kathleen," he said.

I tore open the flat box he handed me and found that it contained a linen tablecloth with matching serviettes embroidered with Jamaican motifs. It was the sort of gift I would treasure. I gave Jonathan a huge hug as we all retired to the living room where Elfrida had strategically placed trays of snacks and a bowl of rum punch.

"We should eat outside," Peter said and everyone agreed, the house seemed a bit too formal. We moved out to the verandah and with the music, laughter and chatter, there was no doubt everyone was enjoying themselves. I kept watching the dirt road at the corner of my eye and keeping my fingers crossed, and hoping. My hand flew to my mouth when finally I saw dust in the air, and heard a car approaching. I could have jumped out of my skin with excitement, for my heart was beating so rapidly. I continued my conversations haltingly, trying my best to sound interested, when all the while, all I wanted to do, was to see who was in that car.

When the car purred into the parking spot alongside the verandah I couldn't even look at it. I was suddenly consumed with self-consciousness and shyness. I bit my lip so hard I thought it might bleed, and feeling light headed. I steadied myself by holding tightly to the verandah railing, which is how I managed to force myself to look towards the distant mountains, and not at the car. I prayed for strength, and heard voices murmur around me, as the music pulsated. All of a sudden, everything was completely shattered by a scream of delight from Gracie. Only then did I allow myself to glance at the car and it took me by complete surprise when two of our former guards emerged. Something must have gone wrong, was my first thought, and I couldn't suppress a shiver. My heart almost stopped when Claudia stepped out from the back seat. Nothing could have held me or Gracie back, as we flew down the steps and embraced her.

We stood together for a long time crying our eyes out, and the other guests came down the steps to join us. What a welcome it was.

"Let's party," Claudia laughed, sounding her old self, as she lead us back up the steps. "Happy Belated Birthday Kathleen. I'll tell you about your gift later. Don't let me forget."

Just then, Elfrida came out to the verandah and announced that dinner was ready. All the men set into arranging tables buffet style, then Erasmus and Jonathan went to help bring the food out. What a spread it was. I was in the middle of serving myself when another car drew up. My plate almost fell out of my trembling hands, because it was David Chang and Mrs. Campbell.

There was a flurry of introductions and hugging and air kissing, then David came up to me and removed the plate I was holding from my hand. "You look gorgeous," he said, slipping a tiny box into my hand, "here's a little something for your belated."

"Is that a ring?" Debbie shouted, and everyone laughed, and I must have turned beet red.

"I wish." David replied with a grin.

With trepidation I slowly lifted the top of the small box, my fingers were cold with sweat but my eyes popped open with delight at the sight of the contents. "It's a sapphire brooch!" I gasped, and David immediately came and pinned it on my dress. "It is almost as blue as your eyes." he whispered, and what a rush of emotion I felt with his hands so close to mine. I couldn't help but hide behind my hair to somehow compose myself. "Thank you so much David," was all that came out from my throat, and I stood there looking aloof, though I longed for nothing more than to hug him.

Chapter 35
Cake For all

"Have some punch," Gracie said bringing over a cup and laughing up into David's face. "Come, meet my buddy Jonathan."

I watched jealously as Gracie, Claudia, Jonathan and Walker T engaged David in lively conversation, while I practically slinked away to find Erasmus. I chatted with him for a while and it was interesting to note that in the present situation Erasmus' English was much less patois accentuated that it had been at Granny's.

"So what have you been working on lately?" I asked, and Erasmus with a drink in hand, happily indulged me. "I've decided to make a sculpture of Santiago." he said, his eyes practically challenging mine. His gaze was intense, as though he knew my thoughts and insecurities.

"This Santiago?" I replied nonchalantly, yet at the same time wondering what could have prompted him to explore such a subject; because from what I had heard, Erasmus was more accustomed to painting landscapes and carving small objects.

"Yes man," he said, reading my thoughts, "I mean the Santiago that lived here. I got interested in him lately when I heard that new people were living here. I have a feeling he would approve of the work I'm doing. But the only drawback, is that I can't quite seem to get his face to look right. Yes, I know I have never seen any likeness of him, but even so, I want to create an angelic face, because that is how I think of him, and the face I made just can't live up to the one in my imagination."

"I know what he looks like." I blurted out and my hand flew to my mouth, as though that action alone would prevent my having to offer further explanations.

"You have a photo of him then?"

No, no, I saw him."

"You mean to tell me that you've seen a duppy."

"Well it didn't seem like it was a ghost. But let's just say that I saw him."

"So is it a secret then? I have a feeling you know something and not telling the rest of us. But maybe you could help me with my work. I wonder if you could ask the owner of the house if I could work on the sculpture here on the property. This place would really inspire me. I just know it."

"I'll ask Claudia for you, but personally, I don't see why she wouldn't agree."

Just then Peter and Debbie came over and joined us. "That was a nice gift from that guy David." Peter said, "Did you meet him here in Jamaica?"

"Yes, to both questions Peter. It's a lovely brooch, and yes, I actually met David here at Santiago House. He was the one who took me to see Rose Hall."

"I think he likes you," Debbie joked, "Any fool can see that."

"I don't know about that Debbie, he is always nothing short of being a gentleman around me."

"Well you must be just plain blind Kathleen. The man is as handsome as anything; and look at the way him look at you like you is a queen. Sort of like how Peter look at me."

We all laughed though my heart raced hearing what Debbie thought about David, and I hardly dared believe a word of it.

I quickly moved away and went in search of Claudia. She was at the other end of the verandah with Walker T She smiled as I approached. "How are you?" I said, handing her a cup of punch. "I'm fine." she replied but there was a look in her eyes that told me not only that she felt drained, but that there was something else I couldn't quite put my finger on. No doubt she wasn't quite herself, not with the way she would furtively glance towards the mountains, or was she somehow drawn to Rose Hall in the distant landscape.

I wanted to ask her so many questions but I was prevented by everyone loudly singing Happy Belated Birthday. I saw someone, perhaps Gracie, bringing in the cake with its candles blazing. The cake was passed hand over hand until it reached me.

"We added a blue candle, to the sixteen pink ones," Gracie said, "We know you are over sixteen, and wanted to acknowledge that"

Everyone laughed, I sought out David, and his smiling eyes met mine.

Though the soft glow emitting from Walker T's storm lanterns, was enchanting, they were no match for the sparkle on that cake. It was he, who set the cake down on the table nearest to me and I was excited to hear him whisper: "Blow the candles out young lady."

I blew so hard I blew them all out with one breath and a huge cheer went up. "Who will cut the cake with her" Claudia shouted, and suddenly, David was there by my side. Two sharp knives were plunged into the middle of the cake as David and I stood facing each other across the table. I took hold of one knife and he took the other. "One, two, three go." Everyone shouted as we quickly cut our way down the cake. My knife was the first to hit the plate and another cheer went up. Everyone had a slice and I felt so exhilarated I drank a cup of punch.

"Let's go to the river for a moment." David whispered, "I just need to get some air."

"Okay." I said, "we can't be long."

Chapter 36

Longing to be with David

We slipped through the house and went out through the back door, then crossed the yard to the river. The water looked deep, dangerous and dark in the failing light, the moon shimmered through the web of tree branches, and a star stood over us.

"Nice here isn't it," David said, "I worked at Rose Hall today, there's still so much to learn about that dreadful place. Annie Palmer's life continues to be shrouded in so many mysteries and everything on that property has a story. That's why I'm writing another article about it. Don't mind me though Kathleen, sometimes I'm just too exhausted to be much of a companion, but despite that I didn't want to miss your special celebration. Turning sixteen though belated, is a milestone. I'm five years older than you, have you thought about that?"

"No, but I wondered when you'll let me read your work."

"I'll give that some consideration Kathleen."

"Don't forget I'll be going back to Canada soon."

"I'll take that into consideration too."

I couldn't think of anything else to say, after he said that, and David had looked so weary, I allowed him to think his own thoughts. The dusk deepened to darkness around us, the moon reigned silver in the skies, and I heard the drone of flying insects in the air, as a donkey brayed in the bush nearby.

Though we were alone, David and I were never close enough to touch each other. The sound of our laughter mingled and bounced against the night as the dreadful braying continued. It was only when we gathered a pile of smooth pebbles did our fingers briefly brush against each other's, as we threw pebbles into the dark water, not knowing or caring where they would land, as we collapsed in shared laughter.

All was silent, the moon was our only intruder, once in a while I stared at David in the pale light intrigued by his beautiful countenance. Filled with wonder I contemplated his eyes, wondering what he thought about the tangled waves in my hair, or the pallor in the curve of my cheek, or even the silver bow of moonlight on my lips. His mere presence awoke emotions in me I didn't fully understand and I shivered in the hot night.

"Let's go back to the party." David sighed, sounding spent. "They'll be missing us by now."

His sudden decision to return to the house took me completely by surprise. How could he not know that I wanted nothing more than to be out there with him? Reluctantly I got up from the rock I was sitting on, and followed his lead through the ever-lengthening shadows, convinced that those few moments with him, were the happiest of the evening.

By nine o'clock guests began to depart. First it was Jonathan, and he offered Mrs. Campbell a ride. Then like a domino effect Erasmus left with Peter and Debbie in her car. The guards had long gone taking Elfrida with them, and last to leave was David.

He gently squeezed my hand, then turned on his heel and headed down the steps. He hesitated momentarily, as though forgetting something, but then he continued on his way, before stopping again.

"May I call you at about 1:00 tomorrow?" he said, running his long fingers through his hair, and looking somewhat perplexed.

"Yes, I'll be here," I replied, sounding a little too much like an eager child. "I expect I'll be home all day."

"I'll call you then," he said, as he disappeared into the night.

I remained out on the verandah, feeling David's presence, though he had gone, and I occupied myself with extinguishing the flames in the storm lanterns. Gracie snuck up behind me; and her breath was heavy on my cheek as she leaned against my ear and whispered.

"So, did he?" She giggled, as she grabbed my wrist to tug answers out of me. "Did he what?" I asked innocently.

"You know?"

"No I don't,"

Come on, did he give you a Belated Birthday kiss?"

"No Gracie, and I didn't expect one."

"Well I thought he would. He was saying such nice things about you."

My cheeks were probably glowing when Gracie and I, with shared laughter went back into the house. A strong unexpected camaraderie had developed between us and I was thankful for it, since I had never had a young confidante back in Siddon.

Chapter 37

Claudia
Tells it Outright

We found Walker T pouring coffee in the living-room and Claudia was sitting rigidly beside him. She was holding her cup in both hands as though warming herself. Her hair framed her face and she looked lovelier than ever.

"Come join us," she said, "I have things to tell you."

Walker T handed us each a steaming cup, and motioned us to take seats. We sat together like family going over the day's events.

"So what did you think of my Jonathan?" Gracie smiled, lowering her eyes as she addressed Claudia.

"He's different, that's for sure. He seems genuinely caring, and no doubt he feels for you Gracie. Grab on to him girl, he's a keeper."

"Thanks for the encouragement. I like him a lot, my only concern is how am I going to leave here without him."

"Well if it's that serious, don't leave."

"Easier said than done."

"Why?"

"Well we'll just have to see how far we want to go with this. He has a say in the matter too you know."

"I don't think it likely that we'll find a solution tonight," I said, "but I only hope you all enjoyed the evening, and everyone else for that matter."

"It was an excellent evening young lady," Walker T said, as he poured Claudia another cup. "We all enjoyed it, and it was good to see your friends here. Anyway, I've got the distinct feeling that Claudia needs to tell us something now that she's been assured of our love and caring. Did I mention how lucky we are to have her safely back with us?"

"I'll drink to that," Gracie laughed. "Me too," I chimed in.

I sat there with bated breath in the dim living-room waiting for Claudia to speak, and at the same time anticipating David's call. Claudia was in no hurry, she took her time; sipping coffee as though it would be her last. It wasn't until she drained her cup that she finally spoke.

"For some time now," she said softly, "I have been thinking that something is not right with me. I can't quite pinpoint it but something changed in me the moment I landed in Jamaica. You must have noticed it Gracie. I became full of bravado, and I was never like that. I also became seized with an urge to destroy and dominate evreryone, especially men who came within an inch of me. I struggled within myself, because I knew that you all are good people but it wasn't difficult for me to turn vicious with the likes of Charles and other guys I met here. At first I put it all down to my occasionally smoking pot but something inside me knew that it went much deeper than that.

I became quite ruthless not just with Charles I even tried to hurt you Gracie, and I'm so sorry about that. You're not going to like this but there were other men whose names I can't even remember, that I toyed with, and hurt. I'm ashamed to admit that I roamed these properties like a wild beast on a hunt for prey as I ravished guileless men. I actually enjoyed clawing my way out of their arms determined to find someone stronger, and with an appetite for passion to match mine."

"But Claudia," Walker T said calmly, "that hardly sounds like you at all. You have always been kind and generous, and you used to keep to yourself so much I never thought you'd even have a boyfriend. The person you are describing to us is the exact opposite of the person I know you to be. Mark you; it was bad judgment on your part to get involved with Charles. But I put that down to a bit of holiday fun. However none of us was surprised to hear that he was a drug dealer, he took advantage of you, and would have tried to destroy us. Don't be so hard on yourself. It is clear that you're already regretting your improprieties."

"But Walker T, someone like Kathleen who didn't really know me before we came here, might think differently, and I'm bound to come off looking sordid. Thank goodness you and Gracie knew me before all this. Trust me Kathleen, the person that has been with you guys since we arrived here is as much a stranger to me, as she is to you, and I have so many regrets. I know now that there was something weird going on inside me. It goaded me on, and played wicked games with my head. But I now know exactly who it was that was fooling with my mind. But I'll come to that later. Just hear me out."

"Claudia, we've been friends since we were kids, and honestly I can't say you've ever been this candid. I think a lot of terrible things have been happening, and it makes me feel badly about being ecstatic about Jonathan, while you are obviously going through a lot of pain. I feel helpless under the circum-stances."

"Gracie, you are the best buddy a girl could have had.

Thanks, I appreciate your support as always and I want all of you to know what has been happening since I left here. I told myself I wouldn't cry but there I go, please try to ignore the tears stealing down the corners of my eyes."

"Claudia, don't worry about your tears, we are crying too inside and out."

"So I see Kathleen, so I see."

"Here's a clean handkerchief of mine Miss Claudia. Wipe your tears."

"Thanks Walker T I have a lot of contacts back in Toronto but it was my dad that I called when I saw that I needed help. He suggested that I contact the Security people here to get protection. He also wanted me to come home, but I couldn't bring myself to ruin your vacation, though a lot of strange things had started happening to me."

"Like what?"

"Gracie, this is totally weird but I would suddenly find myself at Rose Hall!! I don't know how I got there, or even remember thinking about the place or anything like that. But there I was, dressed in riding gear, going through the Rose Hall Great House and property, as though I knew the place like the back of my hand. I even found myself in Annie's bedroom which is the creepiest, most horrific place of all. There are beautiful roses on the bedding and the antique furniture seems ordinary enough, but the scent of death lingers in the walls and in the very air. I swear there is a presence there that watches our every move. The first time I went there, I caught a glimpse of myself in her mirror, and didn't even recognize myself. A dreadfully evil creature looked back at me, and when its wicked eyes met mine, I was shaken to realize that it was me! From that moment, a change came over me, and incredulously I began to feel quite at home in that room. It was as if Rose Hall its properties and the things in the house were rightfully mine. I instinctively knew where every secret thing was located. I sought out my brush and my comb, and found that my whip was already firmly grasped in one of my hands. A great hunger came over me, leaving me wanting nothing more than to hear the delicious sound of that whip cracking through the air. Feverishly, I longed to gloat over the blinding pain I could inflict on potential victims. How beautifully and swiftly my weapon could crack down, to split skin open in its passage and spill rich warm clotty blood to drench me with the taste of that delicious salty brine on my lips. There is no describing the heaven in that anticipated thrill, or the awfulness of the disappointment I felt when I would suddenly find myself ensconced back here at Santiago House. I remember being totally terrified in my room upstairs, as I changed into my own clothes, never quite sure if I was awake or dreaming. But there was always the riding clothes to contend with. I stuffed the despicable garments out of sight underneath my bed, not wanting to be exposed for the fiend I had become. Later in lucid moments, I'd find that the riding clothes had disappeared, and I thought I was taking leave of my senses."

"What a weird story Miss Claudia. I only wish I had been aware of your suffering, what an ordeal it must have been for you to go through alone. But why on earth didn't you confide in one of us?"

"Because Walker T, I was afraid. I was terrified even when the security company assigned me their best guard. I was babbling like an idiot, and almost tried to run away from myself. Do you know that I was this close to revealing everything to the people at security? Thank goodness that in the end, I held things back, for what would they think of me? I wouldn't want to bring that disgrace to my family or even to myself. That is why I didn't offer any arguments when they decided that it was best for me to leave Santiago, that same day. We drove directly to St. Thomas. That Parish is quite different from here in St. James. It is definitely not a tourist destination; there are much more sugarcane fields, farmlands and rivers than here. I was taken to a place called Serge Island Estate; the guard has family there who live in a rambling old house. I've rarely met nicer hosts than Glenville and Helen Murray who are both accountants on the estate. We were situated near a factory, and all day long I could hear the droning hum of machinery and it seemed to calm me."

"So was rest and relaxation all you needed to recover? You seem to be your old self again."

Oh no Gracie. It wasn't just rest. There's more. The Murray's had a maid named Janet; it was strange to me to see her always dressed in long white skirts and a huge white head wrap. It was obvious that she was different from the other maids, because, for whatever reason, they shunned her. While I was there, I tried acting as normally as possible, though it didn't surprise me that Janet knew that something was wrong.

One day she came to my room with two large preserve jars. Each jar had something floating inside and when I looked closely, I saw that one jar had two snakelike creatures inside. She said they were called snake waiting boys, and if I kept it in my room, they would be sure to keep away any evil that dared to torment me. In the other jar I saw a disgusting combination of scorpions and poisonous snakes and she said that those would take the sting out of any illnesses I had contracted. She said I should keep the jar close by. I knew then that she was a practitioner of the black arts, but despite that, I thanked her and accepted her gifts.

"One night the Murrays invited me to accompany them to a movie in Morant Bay a small town nearby, but I was so exhausted, that I took a pass. I knew full well that I would be in the house alone, because Raymond the guard had gone to play dominoes with friends, but I wasn't afraid in the least, not after Rose Hall anyway. So after a light supper of codfish balls and okra I went to bed, and slept only an hour before I awoke to the sound of a drum. It was a hypnotic drumming that reverberated throughout the house. I couldn't go back to sleep, the pounding seemed to be calling to me. 'Claudia, Claudia' it chimed louder and louder, and there was no possibility of my resisting. I threw off my bed covers, slipped my feet into sandals, found my day clothes and dressed quickly. And still the drum called. I stuck my head out the window, and saw a huge procession of people dressed in white, with head-wraps much the same as Janet's. Some were carrying lanterns while others held flaming torches in their bare hands. I watched for a moment as they wended their way up the hillside, and the droning sound of night insects grew so loud it was as though they too were mesmerized.

"My feet knew no better than to follow the procession. I ran through the house in a shiver and recklessly gave myself over to the drum's command as I stepped outside."

"Claudia, this is getting creepy. If you weren't here in the flesh I would have thought you were a ghost. I just hope nothing bad happened to you."

"Kathleen I'm compelled to tell this story, even though there are dark sides to it. I just cannot abandon the telling outright. But perhaps if you look at is as a learning experience it might be easier for you to swallow."

"Yes, young lady" Walker T interjected, "sometimes in life we have to learn to take a little vinegar with the honey."

"Now where was I? Yes, I had just left the house. I hit the ground running as it were, for I chased that procession and caught up with them on the crest of a hill. They took no notice of my presence as they continued on their march. Occasionally I joined in with their chanting as the rhythm of the drum soaked into my skin, and pounded the walls of my mind. I might not have been chanting the right words but in my mind it sounded pretty darn close.

"We walked in that manner for about a mile, until they stopped under a massive tree, referred to as a 'Cotton Tree'. Its humungous limbs and branches was where in days of old, slaves were hung by their white masters for the flimsiest of crimes. The air there was charged with the scent of remembering, and a dreadful moan rose up amongst the marchers as they assembled under the tree. Horrific groans reached my ears as the marchers began to writhe against each other as though in an orgy. The drummer continued the drumming frenzy, never ceasing though some people fell flat on the ground and rolled in the dirt unmindful of soiling their garments.

"My heart couldn't but follow the beat of that dastardly drum, and like a puppet I danced and writhed amongst the others. Then suddenly the rhythm changed, and became even more hypnotic, people around me guided by the tempo, began to walk a slow mournful walk, and I followed. They proceeded in single file counterclockwise around the tree, while someone lit a fire off to the side of us. The flames shot up hungrily and every now and again someone would leave the circle, as a voice over near the fire would shout out: 'Testify'. Then the poor soul who had left the circle would suddenly begin to gyrate and babble in tongues as though part of them had truly left this world. On and on we marched around the tree, though the circle grew smaller and smaller as a result of the ongoing testifying."

"Have some water Miss Claudia; your throat must be dry from all this talking. It sounds like you were amongst some Pocomanians. Are you sure you want to continue your story tonight?"

"Thanks, Walker T, I'll take a sip of punch. I probably won't be drinking after tonight, I must finish the story I can't hold it in much longer."

"But what's, Pocomania, Walker T,?" I questioned.

"Young lady. It is an old religion brought over here from Africa by slaves. It blends factions of Christianity with Voodoo and other Afrocentric beliefs. It continues to thrive here despite the fact that it is frowned on by the average Jamaican."

Realizing that Claudia was in urgent need to spill out her story, Walker T got up and fetched the punch bowl. There was still some punch left with chunks of pineapple, lemon and pitted cherries in the juice. I watched as he carefully ladled out four cups and handed them to us.

"I'll just take a drop," Claudia said, pouring most of hers back, "I want to be clear-headed" she sighed.

I took a sip of mine, and felt the last of the rum that had accumulated at the bottom of the bowl burn down my gullet. All at once my thoughts turned to David. I wished he could have been there with us, though at the same time I was filled with uncertainties and insecurity. Why did he mention the gap in our ages, was that significant and was I just a child as far as he is concerned?"

I was suddenly jolted back to Claudia's story, for she stood up quickly, and banged her foot against the floor and shouted: 'Testify' as though to regain our attention.

"That is what someone screamed in my ear," she said, "before two people came and led me away from the relative safety of the tree. They brought me over to the fire, where I could feel sweat run down my body like rivulets, as a result of the heat. In the midst of the chanting and writhing I threw off the bolero I had worn against the chill of the evening, and kicked off my sandals, only stopping short of hoisting my skirt as everyone congregated around me.

"My hands were no longer under my bidding, for in a frenzy my fingers explore every part of my body, my head, my eyes, lips, breast and even between my thighs; the drum beat grew wilder as the chanting grew louder. I spun uncaring in and out of the congregated marchers, until in a fantastic frenzy I began to shiver and call out words I had never heard before. Words formed themselves on my tongue, and spat themselves out into the air as I fell down to the ground foaming at the mouth, and weeping uncontrollably.

"When I looked upwards I saw a long silver cord extending out of my body. It pulsated in the night air as it rose higher and higher above me yet remaining rooted to me. I couldn't move couldn't speak, even when I saw the cord transform itself into a human shape in the air. I couldn't even close my eyes against it. I was totally terrified, to see the cord take on the appearance off a woman in riding gear. She had in her hand a long sharp whip and out of nowhere a huge black horse appeared at her side. She sprung up on the horse's back cracking the whip both left and right. Its sound breaking through the horror of the night.

"A dastardly great scream reached my ears as the assembled marchers looked up in horror and saw her: 'She's Annie Palmer! She going kill us!' they screamed, as they shrunk back in terror.

"The thing that was Annie Palmer rode roughshod over them, cracking her whip indiscriminately. People panicked, and stampeded unmindful of things left behind such as bibles, lanterns, clothing, and me.

"Within minutes I was alone on that desolate dark hillside unable to move or speak. After a long silence, I heard the sound of a vehicle approach. I felt hopeful, and prayed to God that help would find me. The vehicle which was a jeep stopped next to me, and I heard the door open. From where I lay on the ground, I could only see the person's sandaled feet. I looked up, and at the same time tried to avoid glimpsing the apparition floating above me. But instead of Annie Palmer I saw the bluest eyes I had ever seen look back at me in the dying glow of the fire. The expression in those eyes was gentle and compassionate and I knew even then, that I could trust the man behind them. Was it Jesus himself, I thought; just then I saw his clerical collar and knew he was a priest.

"'Don't be afraid,' he said softly as he lightly touched my shoulder and brought a sense of peace over my whole being. I watched as he stepped back, perhaps in shock, for his eyes must have at that moment confronted the dreadful creature. Only then did I realize that he had been leaning on a wooden staff, which he raised high and shouted:

"'Be gone from this woman, you remnant of darkness. May the Lord God of light take away all her torment and troubling. Grant her peace O Lord in this world and in the next, in the name of the Father and the Son and the Holy Spirit. May thy will be done, now and forever more. Amen'

"I immediately felt a tremendous ripping and tearing sensation all along the length of my back. It was as though something was extracting itself right out of my skin. The pain was horrendous, but when it subsided, a gush of tears flowed out from my eyes, and I finally felt at peace with myself. 'Who are you?' the priest said bending over me. When I opened my mouth, no words came out. 'Where do you live?' he asked, but I was incapable of responding. He saw my distress and showed compassion by taking me by the hand. 'I'll have to take you to the nuns.' he said, 'They will take care of you, and aid in your recovery.'

"He helped me into his jeep and we drove to Aqua Valley about an hour's drive away. My eyes and my mind were unfocused; I never saw or heard a single thing along the way. It was only when we arrived at the Aqua Valley Convent, that I was aware that six nuns came out to meet us, for the priest must have called ahead.

"'My name is Father McConnell,' the priest said, addressing me. 'This convent is a house of compassion. The nuns here are good people who do the service of the Lord. If you should want for anything, just let them know and the nuns will send word to me.'

"Though the convent truly was a place of holiness and worship I had no memory of my past. As a result I quickly became accustomed to and anticipated their strict routines, and it grounded me. I rose early in the morning at 5:30am and knelt with the nuns at rosary. Afterwards we attended mass in the small chapel there, then had breakfast in an adjoining room. A junior school run by the nuns is located on the same property, and I found that I enjoyed helping out in each classroom until noon. In the afternoons, I was assigned to the kitchen helping with the preparation of meals. Following that, Mother Superior and I, and three other nuns worked in their vegetable garden. Later in the evenings I would find contentment participating in Benedictions or Novenas. But over that seemingly short time my voice and my memory gradually came back. The first thing I asked was to be allowed to participate in the Sacrament of Penance. I had been away from the confessional for years, and desperately needed forgiveness. It was Father McConnell who heard my confession. Afterwards I contacted the guard Raymond, as well as my hosts the Murrays. Yesterday I went to Morant Bay to see a lawyer, and today here I am."

"What an amazing story Claudia. Here I was thinking you were kicking up your heels and having fun all this time."

"No, Gracie. It was nothing like that at all. In fact I have being considering making some rather serious decisions about my life, and one of my decision gives major consideration to the nuns and their Holy order."

"Seriously!"

"Yes, I couldn't be more serious."

Chapter 38

Claudia Gives Away Santiago House

A more serious tone fell over Claudia's story as she continued.

"One of the things that I have mulled over in my mind is, I want you and Kathleen to have this house. I've already signed the release papers. I have to sever all ties to this place. I don't want to be even close to Rose Hall. Something evil that festers there has obviously targeted me. I suppose that is because from what I have been hearing, I resemble her...you know who I mean. No doubt when I relay the news to my parents they will be shocked at first, but I'm sure they will come to realize that it is for the best, since I will make it clear that this is the only way for me to escape the evil that took up residence in me. Thank goodness I met Father McConnell, because if not for him I would have continued to be a pawn in some wicked game."

Gracie immediately responded "But Claudia, though I appreciate your wonderful generosity I cannot accept your offer. I want to be with Jonathan, more than anything else. He has taught me so many things and he loves me. I am so lucky to have found such kindness and compassion all in one person. I'm looking forward to living on his farm. I already know that he is hoping I will decide to stay. He probably thinks it's too early in our relationship to propose marriage but I'll wait. I am quite comfortable on his farm and his father and I get along well. They have a huge farmhouse; ultimately it will need a woman's touch. But whatsoever it takes, I know that I never want to be away from him.

"Kathleen, do you remember that sometime back I said that Santiago House should be kept as a monument to both Santiago and Martin Swift? Well I think that you, as a person with a good head on your shoulders; should be the one, with assistance from Walker T, who would bring such a dream to fruition. That's why I'll gladly give over my share of ownership."

"Are you for real Gracie?" I gasped, "this is totally an unexpected surprise. Do you really have such faith in me! What an honour! Did you seriously think things over before you decided? I'm blown away; really I am, just to be considered as an heir."

"Kathleen I have already signed the house over. All I'll have to do now is add an amendment so you will be sole owner. I'll also mention that you'll be getting guidance from Walker T until you feel capable of handling things yourself. I'm not sure what the legal terms are, but whatsoever it is, my lawyer will take care of it. I'd better give father a call. Tomorrow, I'll have to return to St. Thomas."

Four days later, Claudia returned from her brief trip. We knew she had been visiting her lawyer, and that she had made arrangements to also visit with the holy sisters at the Aqua Valley Convent.

Her face was radiant. 'You'll have to come to St. Thomas the day after tomorrow Kathleen to see my lawyer," she said, over dinner, "he'll want you to sign a few papers so everything will be official. You're not busy then are you?"

"No I haven't been busy; I've just been hanging around the house."

"Really! If it were me, I'd be… okay, let's not go there. Just throw some things into an overnight bag. We could stay over for a day or so. But by the way, what's this I hear about you and David Chang?"

"Oh, there's nothing happening with me and David I haven't even heard from him. Last I spoke to him was at the party."

"Silly man if you ask me."

"That's alright; he probably thinks I'm just a kid."

"Not from the looks of you Kathleen. You've blossomed here. Have you seen yourself in a mirror lately? You're gorgeous, you remind me of a young beautiful actress I saw in a movie, and by the way, girls over sixteen, are not kids. Not on your life!"

"You're kind, thanks for the compliment. Anyway how are we getting to St. Thomas? I still can't believe this is really happening."

"Raymond's taking us, but we'll be staying at the Aqua Valley Convent."

Chapter 39

Gunmen Are Coming

"Well young lady it seems we can believe in miracles." Walker T smiled, as he folded his napkin and put it aside. He was about to excuse himself from the table, when there was a sharp knocking at the door. The urgency of the knock startled me, though I hardly could imagine who or what it could be. After all, Gracie had left earlier to see Jonathan, but even so, she had a key and one thing was for sure. She wouldn't be knocking down the door like that.

"I'll get it," I said, hardly containing my curiosity, as on wobbly legs I approached the door. I opened it and was surprised to find the river children standing there glassy-eyed and out of breath. "Miss Kathleen" the girl panted, "We was just down by the river, and we hear something real bad."

"Calm down," I said, "What's happened?"

"Some man dem was down at the river, we hide in the bush, cause them have guns, so we keep real quiet." The boy added. "Dem didn't see us, not even when we run."

"But we hear them say that them coming to Santiago House to kill the White Witch that live here. You better hide now! We going run home quick."

"Thanks. I'll tell the others right away. When you get home tell your mother to get Mr. Jonathan to call the police immediately." The children nodded, then dashed off and scrambled through the rose garden, and in no time were lost from view as I closed the door. I bolted it, and ran into the dining room.

"Quick," I shouted, "we have to hide. Gunmen are on their way here!"

"What! Who said so young lady?"

"The children I met at the river. They overheard the gunmen saying they are on their way here to kill someone."

Walker T and Claudia both looked at me with horror in their eyes, and though I didn't say so, we all knew that the men were after Claudia.

"But where would we hide?" Claudia said nervously, "Surely they'll find us here. We haven't got a vehicle, and there is no time."

"I'll call the police" Walker T said, heading for the phone.

"No! No time for that," I shouted, "I've sent word to Jonathan to call them. We only have moments before the gunmen get here. Follow me; I know where we can hide. Trust me on this one."

All three of us immediately went upstairs, and when I led the others into Claudia's room I could see surprise register in her eyes.

"What's the point of hiding in here?" Claudia said, "they'd only have to break down the door to find us."

Walker T smiled reassuringly and patted her hand. "Don't worry Claudia," he said, Things will be alright. Kathleen recently told me that there is a way out that you might not have noticed."

"What are you both talking about? There's no way out of here except perhaps through the window."

"Wait Claudia; this is an emergency. Listen to the young lady.

You'll have to trust her. I already do, I think you should too."

I squatted down on the floor and easily rolled the bed aside and found the painted rose. What shock I saw in Claudia's when the trap door slid aside. "You go first Claudia," I hissed, "I have to be last I'll set the bed back in place so no one will know we went this way. Claudia looked down into the darkness below us, and hesitated for a moment; then she closed her eyes as if at prayer and let her feet guide her. "Open your eyes Claudia," I said, sounding very much like a person in charge, "you'll need to try to see where you're going."

Walker T followed soon after, and his agility surprised me. "Be careful," I whispered, go slowly." Next was me. I pulled the bed back into place, and closed the trap door, we all heard a tremendous bang at the front door. "That sounds like a gunshot!" Walker T said, attempting to lower himself even faster.

"Maybe they shot the lock off the door." Claudia replied from below

"Who knows," I said, trying to remain level-headed "perhaps they shot into the air to scare us. Its like, they still don't know we're not in the house."

It was pitch-black inside the opening, perhaps more so because night was falling outside. Not a sliver of light penetrated the silky blackness. "Keep going, " I urged a hesitant Claudia who no doubt had just heard the sound of feet running through the house above us. "They're inside now," she hissed, "may the good Lord protect us."

"Hear, hear," Walker T responded, as we slowly inched our way along the walls and finally came upon the carved stone door and the two tunnels. "Where do we go now?" Claudia whispered nervously, "two tunnels are ahead of us and there's this huge stone."

"Too bad there's no light Claudia, because you'd see that the stone is intricately carved. It's like really an awesome find, but obviously this is not the time to see it.

"But which tunnel should we take? Do you think those guys can hear us?", Claudia said nervously.

Before I could answer, we were shocked to hear shots ring out above us. Were the gunmen shooting in desperation I wondered, or were they perhaps riled up because they couldn't find us?

"They can't hear us," I said softly, "at least I don't think they can, but that tunnel over there only leads to Martin Swift's room. That's no good for us; they'll search the entire house. We'll have to take the other tunnel."

"But where does that other one go young lady?"

"I don't really know, but we don't have any choice. Are you game Walker T?"

"Yes, I suppose so, seeing that there's no real alternative."

"I agree," Claudia nodded, "but I just hope there are no dangerous insects or snakes down here."

"Yuk; I'm not going to think about that Claudia, I'm just going to concentrate on getting as far away as possible."

"I suppose that's best, but Kathleen but how did you find out about this labyrinth anyway?"

"It a long story I'll tell you as soon as we are safely away."

Entering the unknown tunnel was like entering into the blackness of space. Not even a chink of light reached us. Our only reassurance was hearing each other breathe and listening to the soft thud of our footfalls; our eyes strained to become accustomed to the dark.

"I'm almost afraid to speak," Claudia sighed, "something weird could fall into my mouth."

"Don't gross us out," I said softly.

We continued to probe our way through the darkness when Claudia felt something under her hand. "I think I feel a handle of some sort." she said excitedly, "I think there is a door here on the left side. Should I try opening it?"

"Yes Miss Claudia, go ahead, open it. What have we got to lose? Need help?"

"Thanks, I think I have it."

The door opened easily, we peered inside; and we saw a familiar looking set of steps that led our eyes upwards. A long way off above us was the moon, a mere sliver in the sky. Without a doubt we were in an opening at the very bottom of the well.

"I don't think we should go that way." I said firmly, "We'd be in the backyard and the gunmen will search the grounds. We'd be better off to keep going."

It was with some reluctance that we continued along the tunnel not knowing where we were going. Minutes slipped by; though none of us said a single word, until finally I heard Claudia squeal in delight: "There's a door here."

Together we eased the door open. The room it led into was too dark for us to judge its size. We stumbled over various pieces of furniture, and scattered books, as we felt our way in the darkness. There were rows of shelves along one wall, stacked with what felt like canvases, paper and tins of various sizes. There was no sign of a way out. I thought we would be better off retracing our steps, despite the fact that Walker T decided to venture further into the darkness. However, after a few steps, he stumbled and almost fell. He had come upon a hurricane lantern left carelessly on the floor. He grabbed hold of the frame of a low bed; then turned his attention to the lantern.

"Wish we had matches." he said, "We could have used this

for light. There's still a little kerosene oil in it." He began to examine the bed, running his bare hands over a dark mound in the bedding. I hoped that whatever it was, was not a snake. But I was immediately shocked out of my wits when Walker T suddenly recoiled.

"Let's get out of here!" he hissed under his breath, heading back towards us. "Ladies, there are bones in that bed. Someone died there!"

"God rest that poor soul." Claudia murmured, as with hearts thumping we retreated from the room. The thought of having been in a room with dead bones, was more than I could stomach, though I kept my thoughts to myself.

It was a long lonely walk in the darkness, each of us thinking about the dreadful bones and none of us wanting to speculate about it. It was quite a relief when we came upon another door. We carefully eased it open, hoping for respite as we went inside. But the air there was thick and stuffy as though a sea of dust got in the way of our breathing. All we could make out was a huge stack of some sort, that went from floor to ceiling.

"Wonder what that is," Claudia said, keeping well back as Walker T went to have a better look, "it seems that whatever it is has been covered over with sailcloth," he said cautiously.

"What's under the sailcloth?"

Do we really want to know, I thought to myself as I lingered near the door.

Keeping well back, Claudia and I watched as Walker T gingerly raised an edge of the cloth. Nothing could have prepared us for what happened. Walker T's knees buckled; he almost collapsed right there in front of us.

"Are you alright?" I called out in fear. Moments went by, before he staggered over to us and I could have sworn that his legs were nothing more than rubber bands.

"Bones are under there," he said, voice shaking. "Nothing but bones from floor to ceiling!" And he covered his mouth and nose with his hands. "Close the door," he said softly.

"Are you alright though? Do you need to rest?"

"I'll be alright young lady; I couldn't rest here if you paid me. I'm just a little shaken that's all. No doubt those are slave bones, and we all know how they got there. Let's keep going."

"But you can barely walk..."

"Don't worry about me Miss Claudia I'll manage."

It was another hour or so it seemed, before we reached the end of the tunnel, which left us no choice but to try to go through a huge door in a wall that barred the tunnel's opening.

"Hope this doesn't lead to more bones," Walker T said under his breath, as he approached the doorway cautiously.

"Please Lord," Claudia murmured, "deliver us into safety."

I myself had no expectations, not even when Walker T called out: "Come, give me a hand. This door is stiff as anything."

This time, we all put our shoulders to it, and pushed the door with all our might. "Keep pushing," Walker T urged, "if I am correct, it feels like it is easing a bit. I feel a draft like air at my feet."

Walker T was right, the door opened on our next push and we found ourselves outside and above ground in a wild clump of bushes. Tangled twigs and branches barred our way, as well as camouflaging the opening. It must have gone unnoticed for years. We wondered where we were, though the air was rife with the night noises we had become accustomed to since coming to Jamaica. Those noises had never sounded as sweet, as they did then. I looked skyward, and saw that like a sentinel, the moon was watching over us, just as it did, the night I last saw David.

By starlight, we saw our way clearly as we moved through the thickly wooded area until it gradually gave way to a clearing. The land dipped dramatically, we went downhill practically running, as we glimpsed an edifice some distance ahead of us. As we drew closer to the building, it loomed ominously in the moonlight, and we realized that it was Rose Hall.

Chapter 40

Safe at Rose Hall

We had no choice but to keep on going, the property was isolated and help would be a long way off.

"Some people might still be there at Rose Hall," Walker T said, as though remembering that we were on the very grounds where Annie Palmer was reputed to have run roughshod over her slaves. "There are always tourists and curiosity seekers at the house at all hours night and day," he added, as though to reassure both himself, and us.

"We won't have to go inside, would we?"

"No young lady, we probably won't have to, but what about you Claudia, this is no way to cut ties with a place is it?"

"It certainly is not, the nuns gave me a scapula medal to always wear for protection, and Father McConnell gave me this chain I'm wearing with a silver crucifix."

"Good, we don't want anything bad to start happening again."

"I trust that I'm well protected Walker T"

"Should we say anything about finding the bones?" I said nervously, noticing that there were cars parked near the house, and people were taking pictures, much the same as they did in the daytime.

"Personally young lady, I think we'd best save that

information for the likes of Mrs. Campbell. She will know how best to proceed. I sure could use a glass of water though, how about you ladies?"

"Yeah, water would be great just about now."

"If you feel like anything else, I just happen to have my wallet in my back pocket."

"Oh my gosh Walker T, that reminds me I left my bank card in a suitcase under my bed."

"Well let's hope they don't find it. As a matter of fact young lady, that's probably not what they are after anyway, but how about you Claudia, you okay for cash?"

"Yes thanks; I'm okay I'm wearing my money pouch."

What a shock it must have been for the people gathered outside Rose Hall, to see us come out from the dark, looking filthy dirty and bedraggled.

"Does anyone here have a phone we could use?" I said, my voice sounded husky and as hollow as the tunnel we had emerged from "We just had a terrifying experience, our house was invaded by gunmen, we're just coming out from hiding."

All eyes turned on us, all of a sudden we were more interesting than Rose Hall itself. "So what happened?" An older woman asked, holding tightly to a child.

"We own a property further along the road. Gunmen broke into our house. We managed to escape, but we have been hiding until now."

A middle-aged man in a dress suit came over and joined us. "Would you by any chance be Canadians? You sound just like my brother-in-law from Guelph." he said, "I'm a journalist. Mark Stewart's my name. I just took some extraordinary shots of the house."

We hardly had time to respond, when a girl around my age

quickly handed me her cell phone, and while Walker T spoke with the journalist, I called Jonathan on his cell. I could hear relief in his voice when he learned that we were alright. He quickly told me that the children and their mother had filled him in, and given him the message to immediately call the police to go to Santiago House. He was already at Santiago House, and Gracie was there with him. "There's been a shooting here," he added, "Two gunmen were in the house, they had an argument, they couldn't find the person they were looking for. One of them wanted to rob the house; the other was more intent on thoroughly searching the grounds. They ended up shooting at each other, one was hit in the leg but the other ran off. Fortunately for us, he didn't know the property, he got lost in the dark. Police dogs caught up with him down by the river and he was arrested there. As for the other guy he was captured, and taken to hospital. It looks like they were the last of Charles' gang. They have all been accounted for now, but where are you calling from anyway?"

"Rose Hall."

"What! How did you get there?"

"We walked."

"Right! Gracie and I will come get you. But seriously, how did you get there?"

"It's true, we walked but I'll tell you more when we see you."

A group of curiosity seekers surrounded Walker T, trying their best to squeeze as much of our story out of him. Knowing Walker T, I knew he would be careful not to reveal anything significant, except to say that we were visiting from Canada, and had just escaped a home invasion. I thought it significant that no one approached me or Claudia. Was it some sort of divine intervention, I wondered or had people grown accustomed to news about crime? Perhaps that might explain why Claudia and I, despite our presence, seemed to have completely dodged out of the path of potential questions.

When I looked for Claudia I glimpsed her heading towards the front door of Rose Hall. How ominous the night felt then. There was no escaping the mood emanating from the very stones of the edifice, as the house loomed dark and brooding, as though engulfed in something monstrously evil. I held by breath, Claudia stood at the entrance, she appeared inexplicably drawn by some unknown power. I watched in horror as she desperately tried the doors, as though attempting to rattle them off their hinges. She looked wistfully at the windows; deep longing tainted her expression, and there was dejection in her stance.

I was relieved when she retraced her steps, though my respite was short-lived, for Claudia was pulled back again to those stalwart doors by a force stronger than her will. What a battle must have raged inside her. I knew then without doubt, that Annie Palmer the White Witch of Rose Hall was behind whatsoever it was that was trying to regain possession of Claudia.

I immediately wove my way through the crowd and reached her side. I reached out and held her hand tightly. I almost could feel her breath on my cheek but when I looked into her fierce eyes I was startled. She reminded me of my feisty and defiant beautiful mother and I knew that whatever I was going to say would have to cut to the very core of her being. My words came out like a ball of fire.

"Remember Claudia," I said, "the words the priest spoke to you in St. Thomas. He called upon powers stronger than the evil that inhabits these walls. Also remember that he was as strong as a warrior, he fought for, and restored your humanity. Whatever you do, you must not allow the darkness of that witch to steal it from you again. Fight Claudia!" I hissed, "fight with all your might!" After I spoke I felt Claudia's cold hand squeeze mine reassuringly, warmth was returning, though I felt her shudder against me.

"She was calling me," Claudia said softly. "She wants to get under my skin. I was merely a puppet under her hand. But this time I'm prepared I will not give over to her, I mean it Kathleen! May the Lord God and his holy angels walk with us, and keep us safe from her harm."

"Thanks Claudia," I murmured under my breath. "We sure can use all the help we can get, and by the way, Jonathan's coming. He'll get us away from here."

The people gathered must have seen the hollow look in our eyes, for they were kind enough to offer us coffee, sandwiches and a great deal of sympathy. "Try to get your friend to a hospital" a woman whispered, nodding towards Walker T "He's in shock you know. It wouldn't hurt to have him looked at."

"I'll suggest it," I said, as Claudia slipped her hand into mine.

"Yes, let's insist that he be checked." she said, "remember how shaken he was after what he saw in that room. To be honest I was more worried than I made out."

"So was I," I said and I looked over to see that Walker T was by himself. He was looking quite frail, leaning against one of the parked cars. Evidence I thought, that our story was already taking a back seat in the minds of those present. How forlorn he looked, there in the moonlight, though his face was painted luminous.

"Think he'll be alright Claudia?" I whispered.

"I hope so Kathleen. Perhaps the hospital will give him a sedative or something."

It was a little more than half an hour before Jonathan and Gracie arrived. "So, are you sure you're all alright?" Gracie asked, practically jumping out of the truck. "We want to take all of you to Jonathan's farm for the night. There's lots of room, we are sure none of you will want to stay at Santiago House. The place is crawling with cops and journalists."

"Thanks Gracie, we'd appreciate that," Claudia said, stepping forward, "but Kathleen and I think Walker T should see a doctor first. He's had a nasty shock."

"Was he injured?"

"No, not in the sense you are thinking but he's not quite himself. Just look at him. We all saw some awful things on the way here, things that we can't talk about just now. Too many listeners if you get my drift. We've already downplayed the whole thing, so as not to get into the horrific details."

"Really? Was it something you saw along the road?"

"Sorry Jonathan; as I said, it is best not to discuss it here. I'll explain everything once we are in the truck. Just look at Walker T, he really needs to be seen to."

"You're right. Let's get him to a doctor."

"He doesn't look himself does he?"

"I was about to say that myself Claudia," Jonathon admitted.

"Here, let's help him into the pickup."

"Okay Kathleen, let's all give a hand. We'll all go with him right?"

"Yes, Gracie. Thank you"

Chapter 41

A Visit
to the Hospital
for Walker T

That night after undergoing a barrage of tests at the hospital, Walker T was advised to stay overnight. Doctor Morgan Pagan who examined him said that Walker T had a significant rise in blood pressure. But he assured us that prescribed medication would lower it considerably in conjunction with rest.

"Did he go through some sort of trauma?" Doctor Pagan asked pensively as he approached Claudia.

"Yes, he has." Claudia replied, "We had a home invasion. We only managed to escape in time."

"Well in that case you are lucky to be alive then. I don't know what's happening to our country. The crime rate seems to be rising daily, some people are comparing the loss of life to a war-zone. Is everyone else okay?"

"Thanks Dr. Pagan. We are alright. None of us was hurt, but I think it's a good thing I'm going to St. Thomas for a few days rest."

"Rest is always an excellent idea after trauma Miss Haddad. Is Mr. Robinson going with you as well? It would be advisable.

A change of scenery would be quite in order. Anyway, whatever you decide, you can collect him at about noon tomorrow, and I can assure you; you'll be surprised at the difference in him."

I was impressed with Jonathan's father who welcomed us like family. I had imagined him to be overweight and portly; but no, he was far from that, being more like a dapper country squire or a gentleman farmer. I found him soft spoken and cordial, reminding me at times of my own father. However he was not as easy to read, as I first thought, for he seemed guarded as though carrying a great deal of private pain. I wondered how he would react when informed that he would be hosting overnight guests.

"Good evening ladies," he said the moment he laid eyes on us, "I'm Roland, Jonathan's father." He eased himself out of his chair and shook our hands in greeting. "It's such a pleasure to entertain you Canadians. I'm hoping you'll join me for a cup of cocoa, and a slice of bun and cheese?"

"Oh that would be nice," Claudia said, as Jonathan pulled up some chairs around the coffee table, where cups, plates, a teapot and bun and cheese slices were arranged.

"Hope you like Jamaican fruit bun, couldn't think of a better snack at this hour. Jonathan called, and brought me up to speed," his father said, nodding towards the spread.

"I had in fact just put the TV news on," he said, "but the incident at Santiago House was only mentioned briefly. Perhaps because a double murder in Black River took precedence. Which reminds me, I just let our guard dogs out, so don't go back outside for any reason. The dogs don't take kindly to strangers. But anyway, how's the older gentleman, Jonathan has been speaking so highly about?"

"Not to worry dad, though Mr. Robinson was admitted to hospital. It will only be an overnighter. His doctor assured us that Mr. Robinson's extremely high blood pressure would improve with prescribed medication."

"Poor chap. Hope he'll be alright."

"I hope so too Dad."

Chapter 42

Beyond
the Cache of Bones

"By the way Dad," Jonathan said, "let me ask you something, since you've lived here all your life, and have seen several renovations. Gracie and I and Kathleen and Claudia were talking in the truck and wondering if any remains were ever found of the slaves that Annie Palmer murdered?"

"Well to be honest Jonathan, most of what I heard was merely rumours based on folk tales, but no, I can't say that there were any excavations or anything like that. From what I've seen through the years, people here have been content to give over the land to farming, and as you can see, a little community has already started to be established here."

"Well Dad, you'll probably be as surprised as I am to learn that earlier this evening these ladies and Mr. Robinson had come upon a cache of bones in a tunnel not far from Santiago House."

"A cache of bones! Jesus, Jonathan! That's gruesome! Have you told the police?"

"No, not yet Dad. These ladies want to contact a historical society first, because according to Kathleen here, other things might be in the tunnel that would be better kept for posterity at Santiago House, before vultures descend and take everything."

"She might be right. Do you know anyone at the society you can trust?"

"Yes, there's a Mrs. Campbell and a colleague of hers, David Chang."

"So Kathleen, you actually saw those bones?"

"Yes sir, Claudia and I, and Mr. Robinson all saw them. There was a whole room full of them."

Jonathan's father cringed and lowered his head, as though unable to bear the pain of it all. "God have mercy on those poor souls," he said softly, "and to think that those bones could be the bones of our ancestors. We'll have to contact your Mrs. Campbell first thing in the morning."

I had difficulty sleeping that night. I kept seeing piles and piles of bones before my eyes. Claudia and I shared one of the three guest rooms, since none of us wanted to be on our own. We must have tossed and turned until dawn, before we fell asleep. When I finally awoke, sunlight was streaming in the window. Outside was a lovely mound of zinnias, clumps of ferns and coronations just under the window.

A herd of skinny brown cattle sauntered by, followed by a young cattle-hand on the way to pasture. I heard well-fed chickens contentedly clucking and scratching in the yard and it occurred to me that Jonathan and his father had long since attended to their morning chores. I wondered where they might be, and if the guard dogs were still on duty.

I was so caught up with the activity outside, that only then, did it dawn on me that Claudia was no longer in the room. I crossed the floor on bare feet and cautiously went to stand at the bedroom's half opened door. I heard Claudia and Gracie's voices coming from down a wide sun-filled hall and I ventured out.

Along one side of the hall were sliding glass doors that afforded splendid views of the undulating farmland. I couldn't help but agree with Gracie, the farm was indeed special. At the far end of the hall I came upon the breakfast room, where everyone else was gathered around a huge rustic round table.

"Good morning," I said, sheepishly entering the room, still dressed in yesterday's clothes. No one took notice of that, as they looked up from broad ceramic plates of eggs, bacon and fried dumplings. "Good morning." They replied.

"Pull up a chair Kathleen." Gracie said, obviously quite comfortable in her surroundings.

"Don't worry, we saved some food for you." Jonathan laughed. "The breakfast is Gracie's treat. She was up early cooking," he said proudly, "I'm glad you got up before noon. I have something important to say, and it shouldn't wait too much longer."

"Did you contact Mrs. Campbell then?"

"Oh It's not about that Kathleen." Jonathan said, biting his lip and there was no hiding the slight tremor in his voice.

"Okay, shoot." Gracie grinned, "If it is about the dumplings, yes I did use quite a bit of milk in the batter."

But Jonathan didn't respond as quickly as I expected, and his deliberate pause brought about a heavy silence at the table as we all collectively held our breath. It felt like an eternity before he smiled and winked at his father, and the tension eased. "Dad," he said, "thank you for welcoming Gracie into our home, and her friends too of course."

"You are most welcome son. These are good people, and Gracie is a very special lady."

"Well Dad; having heard you say that, here goes."

All our eyes were on Jonathan, and none of us was prepared for it when he went down on one knee on the tiled floor. He was bathed in the morning sunlight, yet something he held in his hand shone brighter, like a shining star.

"Gracie darling," he said, " I know it is only a few short weeks since I first met you. However there are times when it only takes a moment for a person to realize what is and what is not meant for them. With that in mind, dear Gracie, would you do me the honour of spending the rest of your life here with me as my wife and partner? I hope your answer will be yes since I love you so much, and I wanted your friends and my dad to witness this very special moment in our lives."

None of us expected Jonathan's proposal, least of all Gracie. I saw her eyes brim over with tears that quickly spilled down her cheeks and Claudia and I soon joined in. Smiling through tears, we held each other's hand tightly, happy as clams, though we almost broke each other's fingers.

Gracie could not have been more bowled over. She pushed her plate aside, and stood up, and with lips quivering, made her way over to Jonathan.

"Oh Jonathan yes," she said, "I feel the same way about you. The world would be meaningless without you. Yes, Jonathan I'd be honoured to be your wife. Anywhere you are, that is my home."

There was a great deal of weeping and heartfelt congratulations at the table as Jonathan gently slipped an engagement ring onto her finger, then kissed her right there in front of us all. I felt something stir inside me as I watched them, tears stole softly down my cheeks, and I felt an inexplicable longing to see David.

It took us a while that morning, to get around to calling Mrs. Campbell. Breakfast had evolved into a celebration. Amidst laughter and chatter we hoisted shot glasses of Tia Maria and wished the couple well for more than an hour of revelry. Despite all that, I was to be disappointed later when we called Mrs. Campbell's number. Jonathan said that there was no one there, only a voice message.

"The message says the office is closed for a week, due to an unfortunate sudden passing." My heart almost stopped. What if it was David who had passed away, after all, there hadn't been any word from him? I didn't say anything about my fears to anyone, and I kept to myself for most of the afternoon. No one was aware of my misery, Gracie and Jonathan happily went to make rounds on the property and an exhausted Claudia had retired to the bedroom.

I would have liked to have gone to see the pastures but remembering the guard dogs I went to the sitting room instead. I found a bookcase there stacked with ancient looking volumes and I nonchalantly pulled out one titled 'The History of Our Pasture Lands' by Tomas Pinto. The book was mostly about farming, and the cultivation of Jamaica's crops through the ages. Needless to say it wasn't all that interesting, until suddenly as I flipped through it, two sentences practically jumped out at me.

'Soil on the Santiago property in St. James; might not be suitable for cultivation. The earth there is not deep enough to support proper growth, and one could speculate that there are underground rocky caves there.'

I quickly looked up the publication date. It was 1920, quite a while back I thought, as I slipped the book back on the shelf and closed my eyes in contemplation. I wondered if the author was on to something back then, but perhaps couldn't pursue the topic further due to limited technology. No doubt he knew nothing about the tunnel under Santiago House. But come to think of it though the land at the front of the house supported the rose garden and the lawns, but no crops, except for wild bush, one or two fruit trees and short rooted plants, everything else was set back from the house or along the side. I was deep in thought when Jonathan's father came into the room.

"You alright?" he said, "want a cup of green tea?"

"I'm alright thanks, I was just thinking."

"Are you a bit out of sorts after your experience last night?"

"No, not really but it was hard getting to sleep. I'm glad Claudia was with me."

"Do you need to contact your parents?"

"No sir, I'm an orphan."

"My apologies but is there anyone you'll need to call."

"Thanks sir but there isn't anyone."

"Not even a boyfriend?"

"No one."

"Want to see the rest of the farm? Jonathan and Gracie are down near the pond where the animals drink. Let's go see the calves there."

"Okay thanks, but though I'd have loved to… I'm not really up to it just now. I was thinking about Santiago and all that has happened there, and I've come to the conclusion that must certainly, it must have a lot of secrets. Did Jonathan tell you that I'm going to be the new owner, and that one of the things I was considering, is to have Santiago kept as a museum or historical site. What do you think?"

"I think you have a very smart head on your young shoulders. Perhaps the historical society could help to bring your dreams to reality. "

"Yes I hope they can. The house has a lot of potential. I can also see some of the space reserved for artist's studios. I have a friend, an artist who could work there."

Chapter 43

Walker T
Released with a Letter

When Jonathan, Gracie and I went to pick up Walker T at the hospital it was about twelve-thirty in the afternoon. Claudia stayed behind; she and Jonathan's father were driving over to Santiago House so she could get an early start getting her papers and clothes together for her impending return journey to St. Thomas.

Though I would be going with her, I wouldn't have much to pack, just a pair of jeans, T shirts and small things. All that would take less than ten minutes.

When we arrived at the hospital, we found Walker T at the discharge desk settling his account. What a smile was on his face when he saw us.

"How are you feeling?" I said, practically tripping over myself to get to him. "I'm just fine," he replied, reaching out his hand to steady me. "Dr. Pagan's prescription is a miracle worker. How is everyone?"

"You'll be pleased to hear this Walker T, Gracie and Jonathan got engaged. It was so sweet."

Walker T's eyes lit up, and he immediately shook Jonathan's hand and hugged Gracie. "I could have seen this coming." He laughed, sounding like a sage. "Congratulations and as for you Jonathan you are as fine a man as I'll ever know. Take good care of our Gracie. When's the wedding Gracie?"

"We haven't set a date yet, but it can't be too soon for me. I love Jonathan so much."

"And you know what Walker T, man to man, that's the way I feel about our Gracie. I want you there dancing at our wedding," Jonathan said, "all ready to go?"

"Yes, thanks, let's go, didn't bring much, but from now on I'm now going to have to take pills once daily to keep the pressure down."

"Well it's good they can control it." Gracie said, winding her slim fingers into Walker T's gnarled hand as we strolled down the hall together like family.

"Yes I guess that's true Gracie, at least it can be controlled. Where's the truck parked anyway Jonathan? The legs are still a bit wobbly."

Just as Jonathan was about to answer, a rather serious looking nurse came lumbering down the hall towards us. "Wait," she said, "you are Mr. Walker Robinson, are you?"

"Yes I am, is something the matter? My bill's been paid."

"Oh no it's not the bill. My name is Nurse Lisa Pendergrass, my colleague Nurse Abrahams in Discharge just mentioned your name, and I suddenly remembered that a letter was left here for you. I was away yesterday when you were admitted, so I hope it is not too late to give it to you now."

"Well what does the letter concern?"

"Actually Mr. Robinson I don't know. It was left here some weeks ago by one of our former patients. She didn't know how to get in touch with you, but thought you'd probably gone back to Canada. She took a chance and left the letter just in case we ever heard from you."

"But why would that person think that the hospital might hear from me?"

"Well she said that you were the one who brought her here, and came to see her many times. Here's the letter sir and it's quite a bulky one."

Walker T grasped the letter and thanked the nurse but made no attempt to open it. It wasn't until we were well on our way back to Santiago House before he began fumbling with the envelope. "Wonder what this is all about," he said while staring at the blue line of the sea as we shot by. "I wouldn't worry about that right now," Gracie said, "I have some good news, I was talking with Claudia and she says it would be nice if you could come along with her and Kathleen tomorrow. They're still going to St. Thomas, you know. The change of scenery would be good, don't you think?"

"She's actually invited me along? Well if that's not the best news that young woman could have given me. Do you know I was just thinking that it would be nice to get away for a few days? But even if I went with Claudia, where would I stay? "

"Claudia said there is a smallish three bedroom house, referred to as the priest's house, not far from the convent. Priests usually reside there one weekend a month; otherwise it is used for guests. So I imagine that's where you'd be staying."

"Has she cleared all this with the nuns?"

"You bet. She is the most organized person I know."

"Well I have to agree with you on that one. With that in mind, I'm sure she'll practically be expecting me to be ready to leave immediately, which means I'll have a little packing to do as soon as we get to Santiago. Guess I'd better read this letter now that I have an opportunity."

I kept my eyes on the distant mountains as they chased along with us on our journey home. How I wished I was as solid through every circumstance. I often chastised myself for being too soft, though I hoped that my sombre mood wouldn't raise questions concerning David Chang.

"Well young lady," Walker T said, reaching over the seat for my hand, "you seem a long way off, but I know that you, Gracie and Jonathan must all be as curious as I am to find out what this letter's all about. So if there's no objection I'll read it out loud."

None of us said a word, as we nodded approval, and with my hair trailing in the wind we sped towards Santiago. I tasted salt in the air and saw trees bowing to meet the breeze that accompanied us. I looked skywards, fearful of an impending storm. There were the usual gulls and black crows crisscrossing the sky, and it surprised me as to how accustomed to Jamaica I had become.

The hum of the motor seemed to fill our very beings like an anthem, even as Walker T cleared his throat and vigorously began to read.

'Dear Mr. Robinson,

Let me start this off by thanking you for all the kindnesses that you have shown me. I have been telling everyone about you, because not only did you rescue me after that terrible storm but you spent so much of your precious time with me when I was hospitalized.'

"Well Walker T, no doubt that's the woman you helped. It's good that she is giving you some recognition and gratitude."

"Yes, Jonathan I appreciate it. Maybe as I read further we might find out who she is."

As though fired up in search of clues, Walker T held the letter closer to his eyes and continued reading. Though I knew he must have been feeling somewhat self-conscious about the words that followed.

'How commendable that a gentleman such as yourself, who never knew me; would be so generous. I was told that as a result of trauma I experienced temporary memory loss at the time. I am so grateful that I am well now and I only wish I had thanked you sooner. I know that there is every possibility that you have returned to Canada, because the nurses have since told me that you were a visitor from Toronto. I hope that somehow this letter of thanks will find its way to you, because my late husband always used to say that if it is God's will, then it will be so.

I recently came to Jamaica to visit the past and renew old friendships. But what I found is that many of my old acquaintances have either passed on or left the country.'

"Well folks I can sure identify with that, because since coming here I myself have not had occasion to run into a single soul that I knew as a young man."

"Walker T, that must be so strange for you, sort of like being the last person alive and losing all your landmarks. It's hard to explain but I'm sure you get my meaning, I said."

"You've hit it on the head young lady. But what it really boils down to is, I have become a tourist in my own country. I don't know anyone here, and no one knows me."

I was about to mention the fact that even in Siddon I might have been considered an outsider, much like Luke Whitefawn and his father. But I held back, considering it would involve giving way too much information. So I was somewhat relieved when Walker T began to read again.

'Things have changed a lot since my first visit to Jamaica fifty years ago on my honeymoon. I was married to a fine Jamaican gentleman I met at home in England. In those days it was frowned on in some circles if an English woman like me married a mulatto man from the colonies, despite his fair skin.

Montego Bay was where we made wonderful new friends that included the Chambers, the Lightbodys the MacKenzies and many others. Since then I had always wanted to visit the island again. But I am a widow now; my husband was laid to rest these past twenty years in St. Martin's cemetery in London alongside his beloved sister.

My husband and I had no children of our own and perhaps that is why we became so involved with his sister and her dear young son Terence.

My husband originally came to England as a result of very sad circumstance which I won't go into just yet. But it was because of that visit that we first met. I was a neighbour of his sister, though we never spoke but as a result of the tragedy I went over to the house to offer condolences. While there I met this rather portly Jamaican blondish gentleman, who turned out to be my neighbour's brother. I fell in love with him immediately and he must have seen something in me, because within six months we were married in South Kensington, on the happiest day of my life.

When my sister in law's son Terence was little. It was a pleasure for me to be doing one thing or another for her baby. My maternal instincts kicked in, though doctors sadly told me that I would never have a child of my own. But in the end it was a blessing that I loved that child unflinchingly, because when Terence was just six years old, his father was arrested and charged with murdering my sister-in-law. Apparently her husband had long suspected that the red-haired child Terence was not his and though he himself was no saint, he was unforgiving of missteps in others. My sister-in-law unfortunately must have turned a blind eye to his faults, when she expected nothing but forgiveness and sympathy after she foolishly confessed her many past indiscretions to him. As a result of her naivety, her husband flew into a rage and shot her dead in the bathroom of their London home. He was sentenced to life imprisonment but passed away a few years into his sentence. My husband Norman and I ended up bringing up their child Terence and he couldn't have been more loved.

I am proud to say that today Terence is an established London architect. Last year he visited Jamaica with his family, so they all could see where his mother grew up. They ended up visiting many 'off the beaten track' sites in St. James. Not to mention old cemeteries where some of their relatives are interred.'

"Gosh I wonder if that is why you found her near the Bickerstep Cemetery. Maybe she was trying to visit the same sites that Terence and his family had gone to."

"Jonathan I'm sure you are right I was just thinking that very same thing myself and you know what I'm getting a little jittery about this letter."

"Why?"

"Young lady, there are things I'm reading between the lines here that are giving me Goosebumps."

"Is that so? Then read some more Walker T because I for one will be listening more carefully. I'm good at getting to the bottom of things."

"Okay Gracie, listen up. But bear with me, and please excuse the water that is filling my eyes."

"Want me to read then?"

"Thanks Gracie, but I think I can manage."

Walker T's hands shook as he grasped the letter as though it were a lifeline. My heart pounded with the waiting, and there was no disguising the tremor in his voice when he eventually began reading again:

'Terence and his family had planned a return visit to the island this year. I was supposed to accompany them. But unfortunately, at the last minute he was called away to Belfast to help with building restorations there. He said it was a brilliant career opportunity and he decided to take his young family along to Ireland with him. But I decided to travel here alone, because to me it felt as though I was coming home to my Norman. Some of our best days were spent in Jamaica and I knew that he would have wanted me to visit places in Montego Bay, such as St. James Parish Church and even Cornwall College, Rose Hall and of course Bickerstep Cemetery.'

"Just as I thought." Jonathan said with satisfaction and in the rearview mirror I saw a faint smile on his cheek, "There it is, she had to have been influenced by what Terence had seen."

"No doubt." I said and I leaned in as Walker T again cleared his throat and set in to reading.

'My darling Norman's niece is buried in Jamaica. It was because of her untimely passing that he first came to England. From what I was told, the poor girl was in love with a Jamaican chap whom my sister-in-law didn't approve of. Apparently she thought he was too dark-skinned. That is why my husband's niece was hastily taken from Jamaica to England and as a result the distraught girl committed suicide at one of our Underground stations within weeks of her arrival. My Norman told me that his niece was quite fair with long blond hair and no outsider could ever have guessed that she was a mulatto. She sounded strong and commendably faithful to the boy she loved and I regret never having met her. I often wonder what happened to the boy she fell in love with, though no one ever mentioned his name.'

Thanking you again for you kindness,

Irene Reynolds Bramson

Walker T could hardly get through reading that last paragraph. His hands flew to his eyes as if that alone could arrest the spillage that erupted from his eyes.

"She's Marceline's aunt-in-law" he said at a whisper, "I didn't even know."

I reached out tentatively, and could almost feel Walker T crumbling. "You should contact her." I said, "her address might be on the envelope."

"No, it isn't," he replied.

When we arrived at Santiago House, Claudia was waiting on the verandah. "Welcome home Walker T" she said coming down the steps. "Looks like the hospital stay was just the ticket. Except of course; you seem to be getting all teary-eyed on us."

Gracie quickly emerged from the car and pulled her aside, perhaps hoping to bring her up to speed regarding the letter, but Walker T himself interrupted them.

"What's happening?" he said, "Do I look that bad?"

"Oh not at all," Gracie said, "I was about to tell Claudia about the letter."

"I'll show her the letter myself Gracie, but thanks."

Chapter 44

The Last Lunch

Just then, Elfrida came out to the verandah, relief written all over her face. "Is nice to see that Mr. Robinson is alright." she said, "I have some patties warming up for lunch. Miss Claudia did just tell me that this could be her last lunch here as owner."

"That's right Elfrida, thanks. My goodness me, I almost forgot that our young lady here will be signing the official transfer of ownership papers in St. Thomas. I imagine that all this impending serious business is too much for my brain, So I guess we should take a break and go in to enjoy Elfrida's lunch."

"I'll second that." Jonathan said, and with his arm around Gracie, we headed inside.

"I've been having a slight headache all morning." Claudia said in passing, "Perhaps lunch will perk me up."

"Did you take anything for it?"

"No Gracie If it gets worse I'll be sure to take pain medication I brought along from Canada.

"So did Elfrida spend hours making the patties herself?"

"No, not really. She bought them, but she did make a little chicken soup to go with it."

That evening Jonathan and Gracie stayed up late at Santiago House. Walker T and I went upstairs early to pack for the next day's journey.

When I came downstairs I grabbed a bottle of pop from the refrigerator and found Gracie and Jonathan still in the living room, heads together.

"Are you planning the wedding Gracie?" I said casually, and I went to sit in one of the comfortable chairs, still clutching my drink. Gracie looked up, and nodded at me, smiling. "You know of course we'll want you and Claudia to be in the wedding party. You could be bridesmaids I guess, but my Canadian cousins and my parents will want to be in the thick of things too. I'm planning to walk down the aisle on daddy's arm, but I hope Mamma will be content with being just a terrific Mother of the Bride, sort of thing, because we mustn't forget that Jonathan's relatives should be included."

"Hey where's Claudia?" I said noticing for the first time that she wasn't there in the midst of the planning.

"Oh she'll be the chief bridesmaid of course."

"No, what I meant is, where's Claudia right now?"

It was Jonathan who looked up from the stacks and stacks of papers they had been scribbling on. His eyes were red and weary. "She's probably had enough of our planning." he said stifling a yawn, "She stepped outside for some air."

"At this late hour!"

"She's only on the verandah. We can see her from here. If we go over to the window."

"Wonder if she could use some company?"

I didn't wait for Gracie or Jonathan to respond, I slipped out to the verandah and saw Claudia illuminated in the moonlight leaning against the rail looking quite forlorn. "Hi," I said softly, "Beautiful isn't it."

The moon was high in the sky and its silver glow visible over the entire rose garden, creating a reverential ambiance. There was a hush around us, "Yes, it is lovely here," Claudia said, not once diverting her gaze from whatsoever was holding her attention. She sighed deeply, when she turned to face me, there was a hint of sadness in her eyes.

"These extraordinary nights are among the things I will always remember about Jamaica." I said softly.

"I can see why." Claudia smiled, "Do you know, just now I was having a bit of a headache, so I came out here to clear my head, and this magical night has worked wonders."

"Are you sure you're alright?"

"Yes, I'm as alright as I'll ever be, and we mustn't forget that at this time tomorrow, this will all be behind me. I was just looking at the mountains; they look so majestic etched against the dark. But I must confess that I couldn't stop myself from looking towards Rose Hall. Sometimes I compare myself to an addict, but on the bright side I know without a doubt that I am strong enough to move on. I was just whispering a silent goodbye to everything here. I know I will be well-cared for at the Aqua Valley Convent, and I was told that it has stood there for many years and the Mother Superior, a darling woman, seems always to have been there weathering disasters. Even the floods of 1951."

Claudia's eyes swam with tears as she backed away from the railing, and the views it afforded. "I'm so happy," she said, "someone as caring as you, will be looking after this place. You have my blessings Kathleen, always remember that."

"Thank you."

Claudia's hand felt warm, almost feverish, as she took my hand in hers, and led me back inside where Gracie and Jonathan were waiting.

Chapter 45

A Visit from Santiago and David

That night, alone in my room I could barely sleep but it wasn't because of the horrific cache of bones nearby, or because I lay there in the dark contemplating the coming journey; thoughts about being the next owner of the property was weighing heavily on my mind. I wondered how I, a rather inexperienced Canadian teenager would manage things. I tossed and turned eluding sleep, until quite unexpectedly, I became aware of a sound like someone sobbing,

I leaned on my elbows, and surveyed the moon-filled room, wondering if the sound might be coming from one of the other rooms. I had every intention to slip slowly out from under my bedcovers but I was jolted on to my feet when I saw Santiago!

Santiago was crouched beside my half-opened bedroom door. Seeing him there pale in the moonlight, was almost enough to convince me that he was no ghost; his features were as distinct and as solid looking as my own. How sad he seemed, there was no mistaking the childlike longing and loneliness in his eyes. He covered his mouth, as though attempting to hold back the sobbing but he didn't once move from his post. When his eyes met mine, he slowly pointed towards the hallway.

Somehow I wasn't in the least afraid, even though his old-fashioned clothing tended to cast him as an entity from another time.

He beckoned more urgently, and I sensed that whatsoever he wanted, was quite important. I hoped he wouldn't want me to follow him down the rabbit hole again. I nervously felt for my slippers, and was surprised when Santiago addressed me. "Come wit me." he said in a thickly accented voice.

A shiver ran through me, he clearly enchanted me. I pulled on my slippers and a light robe. Santiago's finger was over his lips silencing me. I followed reluctantly on tiptoe down the dark hallway and just as I thought, he led me to Claudia's room. Her bedroom door was slightly ajar, Santiago stopped momentarily and beckoned furiously. I came to stand beside him, and wondered if he was aware of my heavy breathing. He pointed into the room, and to my surprise I saw that someone with their back towards us was in the room. Though the room was dimmer than mine, I could see that Claudia was asleep in her bed, while the intruder was draped over her menacingly. My heart pounded, I had to grab hold of the doorframe for support. I don't know how many moments went by before my legs somehow carried me over the threshold.

"What the heck are you doing?" I hissed, as I entered the room, bearing nothing more than my two clenched fists for defense; and without any thought for my safety.

The figure turned to face me. I knew without doubt it was the White Witch! Her bloodshot eyes mocked me even as a small trickle of blood careered from her cheek. Did Claudia somehow manage to scratch her I wondered, but no, Claudia was sound asleep, her head resting on her white pillow where droplets of fresh blood clung to the silver cross on a rosary that lay beside her. I shuddered at the sight, and turned my eyes away only to see the witch spontaneously disintegrating into tiny fragments that soon dissolved into a misty looking substance that hung briefly in the air, then completely disappeared.

I was terrified; I leaned over Claudia protectively and accidentally brushed my sleeve against droplets of blood. I froze in fear. I heard every drumbeat of my heart, though I told myself to relax and be consoled by the fact that Claudia was asleep and unharmed. Her protective rosary was beside her. Where was Santiago I wondered, noticing for the first time that he was not there with me.

I returned to my room wondering if I had imagined it all, even though the blood-stained evidence was right there on my sleeve.

As the moon waned I sat upright at the side of my bed and searched out Santiago in the dimness. But to my disappointment, he was not there. It was then that I heard the distinct call of a wolf echoing in the darkness outside, leaving me shivering and wondering if the wolf that had haunted my father had at last found me.

I awoke at about 6:30am the next morning, to the sound of the phone ringing downstairs. I sprang out of bed and raced down the stairs, but the ringing stopped before I got there. If it is important they'll call back I told myself, and I waited for about twenty minutes but it didn't ring again.

Elfrida arrived a short while after that; she immediately began to prepare breakfast. "Morning Ma'm, everything alright?" she said, as she bustled about in the kitchen.

"Morning, Elfrida," I replied, "I'm okay thanks. How are you?"

Elfrida smiled in response, and I went to the old curio

cabinet's drawers and grabbed cutlery and a fresh tablecloth to set the breakfast table.

"Ma'm," Elfrida said pensively, "I put some fresh flowers in the dining room. It will help brighten up the place. But I just want you to know that I won't be staying here alone when you people gone to St Thomas. So if is alright I going come back in bout four days if that okay."

"That's alright Elfrida. Mr. Robinson is coming with me and Claudia, Gracie is going to stay at the farm up the road. We'll be locking up the house entirely. Mr. Jonathan says he'll post a guard here on the grounds while we're gone."

"Miss Kathleen I did forget to tell you that somebody phone the house yesterday but since nobody was here, me didn't answer."

"No worries Elfrida, they'll call back if it is important."

By midmorning Claudia and I and Walker T had piled our small travel bags onto the verandah, ready to go. Gracie and Jonathan were the last to wake up, and they were lingering over coffee at the breakfast table.

Walker T, Claudia and I took on the task of making sure all the doors were securely locked and bolted. We were in the process of double-checking the windows, when we heard a car approaching. Raymond's here I thought, and since no one else made a move. It was I, who went out to the verandah.

The moment the car came into view, and drew near the house, I knew it wasn't Raymond. The driver caught sight of me, and speeded up. When it parked I noticed that the windows were shaded. I couldn't make out whosoever it was at the wheel, at least, not until the driver practically bounded out of the car into the sunlight. It was David!

I barely moved from the top of the steps. I was both stunned and happy to see him.

"Good morning, Kathleen," David said, hurrying towards me. "I owe you a big apology. I was away in Florida. Mamma's father had a stroke. I tried calling here several times, even early this morning, as soon as we arrived home. But there was never any answer. I didn't know if you'd gone back to Canada, so I came to see for myself."

David stopped in mid-stride, and stared with disbelief at the luggage beside me. "Your'e leaving?" he said, in surprise.

"Apology accepted David. We're not going back to Canada, not yet anyway, we're going to St. Thomas for a few days, staying near the Aqua Valley Convent. But how's your grandfather?"

"Grandpa's doing better now, thanks. His doctors in Florida said that he didn't suffer any brain damage. He's surrounded by loving family such as Mrs. Campbell, who closed down the organization while we were away, but I had to come back because..."

"Mrs. Campbell went too!!"

"Oh yes, she's married to a cousin on mother's side. We are a close-knit family."

"David, you never said a word about being related to Mrs. Campbell. But never mind, I guess it wasn't relevant. Anyway, that's good news about your grandfather. I have to go going to St. Thomas because Claudia wants me to sign some legal papers there. She says the convent would be a nice peaceful place to stay."

"I don't really know the place Kathleen, but I heard that it is scenic and peaceful. How are you getting there anyway?"

"We're going with the guard Raymond, remember him from my party, he's coming to pick us up any minute now."

"So how many of you are going?"

"There's me, Walker T and Claudia."

"Would you like to drive there in my car Kathleen? Surely one less passenger for Raymond, would give the others more room to rattle around in. I could call Mamma on my cell-phone, so she'll know my plans, then pick up a few things at the house. If we leave right away, the others could meet up with us at my place. Agreed?"

"Sure David, though we'll have to first tell Claudia about the change of plan."

I was flabbergasted by his offer, though I could hardly take my eyes off him. Not for a moment did I consider how like an excited schoolgirl I must have seemed. Claudia smiled knowingly on hearing the arrangement, and Gracie full of humour let out a low whistle, not unlike the whistles Jamaicans used to show appreciation for a woman. Walker T chuckled at her audacity, though none of that mattered; what mattered to me was that I would be together with David for a few precious hours.

After waving goodbye to everyone including Elfrida, David and I headed out. I barely looked at the landscape zipping past us, my eyes were content with sneaking glances at David's strong hands on the wheel. I sat well away from him on the passenger side, and occasionally would force myself to glance out the window, though I was more content with watching him.

"Nice day for driving," he said, "we had some bad days in Florida. Heavy downpours it's the hurricane season you know."

"We didn't have rain here, but we did have a break in at the house. We had to escape through an underground tunnel."

"What underground tunnel?"

For the next few minutes I recounted to David the details of our escape, mentioning the ornate stone door, the cache of bones and the other small underground rooms. I told him about how Walker T had gone into shock and how after a brief hospital stay, had found out about his high blood pressure and need for rest. David was most concerned for my safety, and I could see relief all over his face when I told him that the last of Charles' gang was now remanded in custody.

I went silent as I contemplated whether or not to tell him about the role Santiago played in my discovery of the tunnel. But realizing that it was impossible for me to keep anything from him, I took the plunge, and told him everything.

He was rather still as he listened to my story, never once interrupting. As we approached Montego Bay, he pulled the car over, and came to a stop on the grassy banking that edged the road. We sat there not saying a word as other cars whizzed by. Then finally he spoke.

"Thank goodness you're safe Kathleen. I don't know what I'd do if..."

But I didn't let him finish his sentence. I leaned over intending to tell him how I felt, when he gently took my hand. His fingers were warm against my skin, and I might as well have sizzled.

"Kathleen," was all I heard him murmur, as he held my hand in a warm grip, unmindful of the passing traffic, the salty breeze or even the relentless sea that rushed to the shore not far from us.

"We'd best get on our way," he said, "they're meeting us at my place, remember?"

Chapter 46

Visiting David's Parents

Breezes followed us as the car turned towards the hills overlooking Montego Bay. The houses there were large, and spoke of money. Some had outdoor pools and boasted large rooftop patios and manicured lawns, behind tall green hedges.

"Is this where you live?" I asked incredulously, as the car navigated the precarious hillside road. David slowed the car and smiled as he patted my hand reassuringly.

"Yes, my parent's home is here. I have my own little apartment attached to their house. It is a suitable arrangement."

"This is like so posh," I said under my breath, my eyes wide, staring at the opulence around me. "Who'd have thought a place like this was up here."

"Yes Kathleen. It is rather nice, but don't forget it took a lot of very hard work on the part of my parents to be able to afford to buy property here. I myself could have gone and lived elsewhere in the city, with their help. But I chose not to. My family is close-knit. I wanted to be close, for peace of mind and safety's sake. It doesn't hurt that there is a security contingent that oversees these properties. Anyway, see that house there on the left, the one with the tall metal gates. That's our property, Mamma's home, I see her car's in the garage."

I was hit with a sledgehammer of nerves when he said his

mother was home. How would I manage to be myself, with David beside me. She'd see it written all over me, that I was just a teen. As though reading my thoughts, David squeezed my hand, Mamma's cool." he whispered.

The details of the house's appearance escaped me. I was more concerned with the upcoming introduction. I stepped out of the car on wobbly feet. David opened my door for me and waved at his mother. "Hi Mamma" he said.

I could barely steady myself, when his mother carefully came down the winding verandah steps to the car. She was younger-looking than I imagined. There was a warm smile on her face. Her curly, honey-coloured hair was unexpected. She was mulatto I thought, even though she was more Caucasian in appearance. Somehow or other I had wrongfully presumed that she would have been Chinese.

"Pleased to meet you at last." she beamed, extending her hand, and affectionately brushing her cheek against mine. "I'm Georgia, I have heard so much about you."

"Likewise," I said, "so sorry to hear your father's been ill."

"Thank you," she smiled, "daddy will be fine. He's quite the fighter. He came from a family of strong military men from the UK. Do you have time for a cool drink?"

Before I could reply, David held her hand in his and hugged her affectionately, "Next time Mamma," he said softly, "Thanks, but we only have a moment. I just came to quickly grab some stuff from the apartment. Kathleen and I have to hurry to meet her friends."

"Well next time you come Kathleen, you'll have to stay longer. Okay?"

"I will," I said and I felt David tug my arm to lead me round to the small apartment attached to his parent's house. It was modern looking and might well have been called a condo back in Canada. "That's my apartment," David said with a smile, and he went up the narrow steps and looked back. "Wait here," he said and my heart raced, for I had been wondering what would happen if we were alone.

"I will be a second," he reassured me as he stepped inside alone.

He emerged in about five minutes carrying a small overnight bag. "Just a few things," he said, "in case when I get to St. Thomas I decide to stay over in a hotel near where you'll be."

It hadn't occurred to me that he might decide to stay over in St. Thomas but the thought of it was almost dizzying. For the first time in a long time I thought of mother and her unquenchable passion for Luke Whitefawn. I wondered if this was how it was for her, but then stopped myself, feeling as though even my thoughts were a disservice to father. I had to remind myself that I was not even David's girlfriend by any stretch of the imagination.

Chapter 47

Pondering Life
and the
Blind Girl

We met the others at a designated crossroad half way between Santiago House and Montego Bay. Raymond the driver was first to see us waiting there, he waved from his car window and pulled up beside us. "You been waiting long?" he said sounding apologetic. "Not that long," David replied, "we got here less than five minutes ago."

Peering into Raymond's car I saw that Claudia had the back seat to herself, Walker T was up front with the driver but Claudia seemed to be leaning in a manner that would suggest that she was tired. I wanted to believe that she welcomed the extra room. She smiled wanly when she met my eyes, though I noticed she was wearing a thin blue sweater around her shoulders against the warm day.

"David, you better drive extra carefully with our young lady," Walker T called out; his resonant deep voice sounded sincere yet playful, and it temporarily distracted my attention from Claudia. "Don't forget that now that our young lady's about to become a property owner, she's precious cargo. Isn't that right Miss Claudia?"

"Yes sir, as soon as she signs the papers in St. Thomas she'll be a new woman. You ain't seen nothing yet."

Everyone laughed, including Claudia, and David squeezed my hand reassuringly.

"So that's what this mysterious paper signing is about," he whispered, "Claudia's handing the property over to you. That's a big responsibility Kathleen. How are you going to manage?"

My words came out in a rush as I held tightly to his firm hand. "I was hoping you and the historical society would help."

David smiled; without embarrassment, leaned over. "That's a given," he said.

When I glanced over at the other car, I saw that everyone was smiling at us, even Raymond who revved up the engine. "Okay love birds," he shouted, "time to go, my car will take the lead I happen to know a little hole in the wall place along the way; where we can stop and get a good lunch."

"Good enough," David replied, tooting his horn in approval. We set off behind them into the bright day to head east across the island.

Coconut, banana, sugar and citrus plantations dotted the ever-changing landscape. At times we were confined to narrow roads that were little better than dirt tracks, where trucks laden with produce took up all the room. Cows, goats, pigs and even stray dogs roamed freely on those mountainous roadways. More often than not, locals would come along carrying huge heavy baskets laden with fruits and vegetables on their heads.

Once in a while we crossed over sturdy concrete and wooden bridges that spanned across swiftly moving rivers and dried gullies. It seemed inevitable that there would always be streams, meadows and endless bush-land just around the next bend. It became clear that we had somehow lost sight of our companion, the sea that had so faithfully dogged us in St. James. Onwards we plunged through the island's interior as our cars bore us away, through small villages and towns unmindful of the coastal shoreline left behind.

When Raymond's car finally slowed, so did we. Children magically appeared along the roadside to come running to our cars carrying oranges, bananas, tangerines, cashews and even dried spicy shrimp for sale. "Buy mine Sir, buy mine Ma'm" they shouted and what delight was in their eyes when we purchased from each of them and tucked our treasures into the car trunks before heading off again.

We came to a halt about three miles down the winding road, a good distance from where the children were, and parked the cars in a one street village that David said was called Kingdom Come. There were two or three shacks set back from the road, a tiny cemetery, with perhaps six headstones and a miniscule schoolhouse and a small church. Up a little dirt road, visible from the cars was a small lean-to-shack with a sign over the top saying Heaven Hollow.

Raymond came over to our car and pointed at the shack. "That's the place," he said, "nobody going pester you here, and the food is unbelievable. Try the tripe."

None of us tried the tripe. We sat at a small makeshift table behind the shack and enjoyed Dip and Fall Back, a mackerel dish with boiled bananas, which was followed by fried chicken with plantain and rice and peas. What a feast it was. "I haven't had food like this since I was a boy," Walker T said, chewing on his chicken bones. "Let's thank the Lord for this wonderful meal," Claudia said, bowing her head in prayer, and I noticed that though she shivered slightly, her forehead was beaded with sweat.

"We are almost there." Raymond said, "Once we pass Sugarloaf Mountain we are home free. Anyway David if you need a place to stay I have relatives in St. Thomas who would gladly put you up for a couple of days. What you say?"

"Thanks man," David replied, "I'll gladly take you up on the offer, because I was going to look for a hotel or something but you've saved me the trouble. Thank you."

"Nothing to it man, you like the food here?"

"The food's first class," David replied and when he said that, I could well imagine him sitting down daily to upper-crust meals prepared by servants. But then again, there was something quite independent about him, and I wondered if he ever cooked.

"This fried chicken is almost as good as mine," he said out of the side of his mouth, as though reading my thoughts "you'll have to try my cooking sometime Kathleen."

I smiled and squeezed his arm affectionately. "Perhaps I shall," I said, passing him the plate of fried plantains. "Seriously," he said, "Mamma likes you. She'd be glad if you'd come for dinner. I'd do all the cooking. When are you going back to Canada?"

"We're leaving at the end of next week. But I could try to come before we leave."

Those words tasted bitter on my tongue, because the thought of leaving the island weighed heavily on my mind. I felt tears well in my eyes and I turned my face away from David.

"Jackie, come back inside!" a woman's voice shouted, just as my fork dangled half way between my plate and my lips. "Nothing outside there baby. Come inside!"

Like a knee jerk reaction we all looked towards the shacks that stood on a small ridge nearby. We saw a skinny little girl about eight years old, feeling her way down the incline with a white stick. The stones and rubble appeared to be familiar to her, as she made her way fearlessly towards us. There was no doubt that she was blind, and the white stick was her only guide. The woman whose voice we had heard began to scramble down the rocky slope after her. and eventually came abreast of the girl, just as she reached us. "There's people here having lunch Jackie," she said apologetically, "we mustn't disturb them."

It could well have been an awkward moment, since none of us was prepared for the intrusion. But I smiled brightly at the woman, and nodded at the child, though knowing she couldn't see either gesture. "It's alright," I said but the little girl stood stock still, as though finding her bearings, then she lifted her sightless eyes and thrust a knobby hand out and pointed at Claudia. "Something bad is here Mamma," she said in a monotone voice, "Something real bad that want to kill people."

"No, no Jackie," the mother pleaded, already embarrassed by her child's perception. "These is good people Jackie, them just having lunch, don't bother them baby."

But the child would not budge an inch; she wrung her little hands furtively and dug her heels in. I wanted to assure her that all was well, but something about her stubborn stance prevented me from making overtures.

"Mamma something real bad is here." The child wailed but the mother quickly apologized and led her away. My heart pounded with fear, the incident was totally disconcerting, and I watched as the child turned round as though to look back at us with her strange white eyes. "A wicked thing's here, a very wicked thing." She sobbed as they departed.

None of us had much of an appetite after that episode. We toyed with the remainder of our food, before leaving a hefty tip and a little something for the blind girl. "We're going up to Aqua

Valley Convent," Raymond told the cook, "the meal was exceptional"

Neither David nor I had much to say for the rest of the journey, each of us must have been mulling over the events at Heaven Hollow. We had long gone past Sugar Loaf Mountain and were nearing the convent, when David finally spoke; but there was a worry line across his forehead.

"That was bizarre wasn't it?" he said, "imagine that little blind girl coming right over, and pointing out Claudia. I've heard it said that blind people's perceptions are more heightened than ours. Wonder what the girl meant about something evil? Guess we'll never know."

He put an arm around me protectively and there it remained for the rest of the journey. "Hope nothing bad happens," he said, and instinctively I rested my head on his shoulder.

"David," I said softly, "I have a feeling that whatever it was, it had something to do with the White Witch. What else could it be? Don't forget she was in Claudia's room last night"

We arrived at the convent within moments of that conversation, to find that word must have spread in advance about our arrival. As we pulled up, both cars were surrounded by a swarm of nuns. Their happy murmurings putting me in mind of buzzing bees pouring out from the depths of a hive. What a welcome it was for Claudia. Every nun's radiant face greeted her with welcoming smiles. With the utmost of care, they helped her out from the car, as though already knowing that she had not been well.

"Doctor Farthing is waiting for you," they said, and I wondered if he was some sort of church official.

Chapter 48

Meeting the Nuns

The nuns had prepared afternoon tea, we were taken to the dining room where plates of sandwiches and raw vegetables with various dips awaited us.

"We have tea and coffee," a young nun smiled, gesturing towards the tables. "if you prefer aerated water, there's cola-champagne and cream soda with ice."

After the lunch at Heaven Hollow, it was a wonder any of us could have taken another bite. But Raymond ate heartily, much to the admiration of the nuns. Walker T took tea, and a small plate of sandwiches to a window seat at the far side of the room. From there he could admire the views of the lush aqua tinged valley, the vegetable garden and the distant mountains. Mother Superior went over and joined him. "Hope you'll enjoy your stay," she said, sipping her tea, "it is rather a quiet existence here, mostly prayers, fasting, meditation and teaching young ones. It is a rare occasion that we entertain visitors. Besides priests, Claudia was amongst the first we've had in years. I could be wrong but I suspect the Lord has a calling for her."

Walker T returned her smile and put his cup down. "Mother Superior, this sort of place is exactly what I need right now," he said, "the peace here is hard to come by. We all could use prayers, so as far as I am concerned, I've come to the right source, I cannot thank you enough for your kind hospitality. But tell me something, who is this doctor that's waiting to see Claudia?"

"She didn't tell you?" Mother Superior responded, raising an eyebrow. "Why, he's her physician. It is common knowledge here that Claudia has a rare blood disease. Dr. Farthing has already diagnosed it as being possibly fatal. You see, when she was here last, we had to send to Morant Bay to get a doctor. Claudia had been having dizzy spells, heavy night sweats, and devastating headaches. Dr. Farthing has already informed her, and us too, that her test results were not good. Her only hope is some sort of experimental drug though to be honest, I don't think he's convinced it will work."

Walker T went ashen, he set his plate aside and cradled his face in his hands. "Poor, poor girl, where is she now, anyway?" he said noticing for the first time that Claudia had not joined us in the dining room.

"Dr. Farthing's examining her upstairs," Mother Superior replied, "We plan to hold a vigil for her this evening, and wondered if you would like to join us. Would you by any chance be Catholic?"

"No Mother Superior, I'm not a Catholic, but under these circumstances, prayers are prayers. I'd be happy to join you. You know of course I'll have to tell the others about Claudia. They will be as shocked, and as caring as I am," he sighed, "our poor dear Claudia, she obviously didn't want us to worry."

Chapter 49

An Angel Called Elo

Early next morning Claudia invited me to see the beautiful flower garden in front of the convent. She had hinted that it would be a good place to await our ride into Morant Bay. I sensed that she wanted an opportunity to speak to me privately. At first, it seemed that she was concerned about the darkening sky and cool air that had descended into the valley. She moved reverently from flower bed to flower bed, examining each bush and flower.

"Things grow so well here," she said, running her hands over leaves and gently caressing flowers. "I helped feed and water these," she said, "look at the Cannas, the gerberas, the lilies and the roses how healthy they are. It is wonderful to have contributed to their survival. I hope bad weather doesn't come and waste out efforts."

She took my hand, and her hand was cool and clammy. Her eyes were partially closed as though in prayer, a smile played at the corners of her lips.

"Kathleen," she said softly and I knew she had at last found an opening for her intended conversation.

"I know I should have said something sooner Kathleen, about my health. I meant to, but I didn't want to upset anyone, and then there was Gracie's wedding plans. Forgive me, but it is just as well that now we both know there isn't much hope. You also must have realized that earthly possessions don't mean a hell of a lot anymore. It is not like I don't have a good doctor. Dr. Farthing is the best. He has been like a father and protector, so if I am to die, there isn't any other doctor I'd rather have beside me. I also want to let you know how happy I am that the Santiago Property will be yours, you have my blessings. As for you and David, I just want to say that you couldn't have found a finer young man. I just know that he will care for you and love you for the rest of your life. Now don't you start crying Kathleen; dry your tears. I haven't gone yet, have I? I'm still very much alive."

It was with much solemnity that the legal papers were signed in the law office of one Joseph Lambton QC. His office was near the Morant Bay court house, a site immortalized in Jamaican history because of a slave rebellion. But instead of the violence of that long ago event, here I was being welcomed, and congratulated and shaking firm legal hands. Try as I might I couldn't hold back tears. "Wouldn't it be nice to have a shot of Appleton" Claudia said, perhaps attempting to divert attention from my swollen eyes.

"This is an occasion for champagne," Lawyer Knowlton, the junior assistant in the office said and as if on cue Barrister Lambton immediately rang for the secretary. "Bring the champagne in," he said with a laugh, "champagne glasses too please; then join us in congratulating this young Canadian woman, who now owns a prime piece of Jamaican property."

There were ten of us in the office that morning. Champagne was served accompanied by various cheeses and crackers, as well as Solomon Gundy dips. Was a signing always like this I wondered, though it occurred to me that Claudia must have been the brainchild behind the celebration? My only regret was that David wasn't there. I knew of course that he would be at the convent later in the afternoon. I would have so much to tell him. I was caught off guard when the young lawyer Justin Knowlton, who judging from his accent was perhaps from the UK, suggested that we could meet for lunch in the late afternoon. "Thank you," I said, "but I have already made other plans."

"Well perhaps some other time," he murmured, and his congratulatory hand grasping mine felt as soft as a woman's.

That afternoon, while Claudia rested, one of the younger nuns Sister Serena a Chinese Jamaican, took me and Walker T on a tour of the convent property. The grey skies had cleared, and fluffy white clouds scuttled across the hemisphere. From our location we had a good view of the distant blue mountains, that surrounded the valley. It felt as though we were in the bottom of a deep aquarium. The green valley stretched as far as I could see, though every now and again bright flowers peeped from underfoot as well as in the wild bush-land. Far in the distance was the promise of the sea where the sky met the aqua green horizon. Remembering northern Ontario I wondered what kinds of animals inhabited this wilderness, and I longed to see a flash of deer or hear the call of wolves and owls, as I had been so accustomed. Only then, did I remember that I had indeed heard the call of a wolf back at Santiago House.

"We are like a world unto ourselves here," Sister Serena said, "we grow our own food, and we even have chickens, and a couple of dairy cows, they are cooped and pastured in another part of the valley. It is a hike getting there in these shoes; I should have thought to wear rugged boots. So today I will show you the beautiful mountain spring where we get Mother

Superior's drinking water, and the cassava cultivations, as well as our avocado and ackee orchards. Some people have said that this place is heaven on earth."

"They might be right," Walker T said tapping his chin in contemplation, "so far I have found the peace here to be unsurpassed."

"Where were you staying before coming here Mr. Robinson?"

"We were at Santiago House, close to Rose Hall."

"I've heard of that place, pardon me if I'm wrong, but I heard it is supposed to be haunted. Isn't it?"

"You could be right Sister Serena. I suppose that would be the only explanation for things that occurred there."

"Well Mr. Robinson, may I suggest that you let the owner know that the house should be blessed."

"Sister, this young lady, Kathleen is the new owner. You perhaps haven't heard that Claudia officially handed over ownership to her this morning."

"Really, well congratulations Kathleen, you must have heard me just saying to Mr. Robinson, that Santiago House should be blessed. With your permission, we could contact a priest in that parish, to do the honours."

"I think that would be appropriate, but does such a thing really work Sister?"

"Yes, Mr. Robinson most definitely it does. In fact I myself have had experiences that warranted those same drastic measures."

"Care to talk about it Sister?" Walker T said, keeping pace with the young nun whose nimble steps led us over rocky inclines and through grassy fields. Walker T's lively step soon matched hers, laying testament to the fact that his interest peaked.

"Seeing as I'm not Catholic," he continued softly, "I haven't had much experience with that sort of thing but I wonder if this young lady, Kathleen has?"

"Put it this way Walker T," I replied, a broad smile on my face, "My mother was from rural Ireland, not only was she Catholic, but she brought a lot of the local mythology over to Canada with her. I was reared with beliefs in nature spirits, angels and ghosts and of course fairy folk."

Sister Serena turned her head eastwards, her cheeks bright and eager for a telling.

"See that stream over there," she said, "the locals call it God's Waterway. It is supposed to be the purest water on the island. Some even say it was brought here by an angel."

"Do they have proof of that Sister?"

"It is mostly based on faith Mr. Robinson. There is something I must show you that might convince you. See that stone, the great black one that juts up above the water? Look carefully at the shape it makes. It is an angel with a trumpet. We Sisters heard it said that the angel was called Elo. Local legends say that long ago in the dim past long before slaves were here In the days of the Arawak Indians, there was a great drought and famine here on the island. The Arawaks were a meek and docile tribe who had great respect for the land. They were somewhat skilled in the art of irrigation and some managed to survive on fruit and vegetables that thrived here. But soon rivers and streams began to run dry, until nothing was left except dry gullies and tribes began to dwindle. The Arawaks turned to prayer, and one day an angel came from the skies and descended into this valley. With a wave of the hand the Angel restored the water's flow. Then from out of nowhere, a huge demon appeared, with a head like a hydra and a thousand great eyes. It was bent on destroying the land, the people, and the angel. A great fight began, rocks and boulders were strewn for miles around and the valley itself was gouged even deeper into the land between these mountains. Thunder split the skies, and the Arawaks had nowhere to hide from dangerous bolts of lightning. They fell on their knees and entreated God's mercy. The skies opened, and out of the heavens came an angel equal to Elo, bearing a shining sword of gold and a huge shield. It is said that the Arawaks called that angel Olem. As a result of the battle that ensued, the soil, the trees and all the waterways were overturned like the mixing of a great stew. In the end, Elo and Olem triumphed, and the ferocious demon was destroyed. With the golden sword Olem carved that rock into the shape of his companion angel to guard the waterway in his stead, while Elo set right the landscape and thus it remains to this day."

"So Sister Serena that means we are actually standing on holy ground"

"Yes, Kathleen we are, and that is why a convent was built here to forever worship and praise God's goodness, whether it is the God of the Arawaks or the God of Israel."

"But Sister," Walker T interrupted, sounding somewhat skeptical, "as a nun, do you believe that the events in that legend actually happened?"

Sister Serena listened to his words and stopped dead in her tracks, her eyes wide with sincerity, as though gathering wisdom from God himself.

"Mr. Robinson," she said gravely, "there are stranger things between here and heaven. Who am I to dispute it and you must admit the rock appears not to have been formed by human hands."

Chapter 50

David Arrives
at the Place of Miracles

I instinctively knew that David was somewhere near the convent. I looked out towards the meandering roadway where it rose dramatically over a small hillock, and what should I see, but a car approaching. "David's here." I said, quickening my pace to return to the main building.

"I hope you'll excuse me," Walker T said wearily, "I think now's a good time for me to retire to the priest's house and rest."

When Sister Serena and I returned to the convent, I saw that David had parked, and had already entered the building. I went directly to the drawing room and found David bent over a cup of coffee with Claudia beside him. The nuns were occupied with their assigned duties, and affording their guests much needed time alone. Sizing up the situation, Sister Serena immediately excused herself, and went to join some other nuns in preparing the evening meal.

What a wealth of information there was to share with David I thought.

"Been exploring?" he asked, looking up from his drink. "Sort of," I replied, "It was more like a learning experience. I'll tell you about it later. First, Claudia has to tell you about the signing this morning. Right Claudia?"

"Yes, it was very significant, and memorable," said Claudia, sipping on a glass of water.

"So how was it?" David said, looking me in the eye. "Was it one of those boring things that you just can't wait to be over?"

"There was a bit of that David, there was endless paperwork but in the end it was alright."

"How so?"

"Well they threw a celebration for us."

"Really?"

Seeing how keen David was to hear what happened, Claudia and I laid it on thick about the celebration. She named in detail all the snacks provided, and the brand name of the expensive champagne. Then she mischievously mentioned about how I was asked out to lunch by one of the young lawyers.

David set his coffee aside, and I saw that the muscle working in his jaw.

"Did you accept?" he asked, sounding calm. I answered with a laugh, and said, "and miss Sister Serena's tour? Not on your life!"

David smiled, and held me in his gaze. "That lawyer might be after an heiress, wouldn't you say? Claudia and I laughed. The ambiance in the drawing room was so uplifting, that I felt it was the perfect time to tell both of them about the legend of the angels.

I started with recounting the story about the Arawaks, the famine and the drought, then I went on in a more dramatic manner to tell them about the coming of Elo from the skies, and I ended with Olem the warrior and his mighty sword that carved the immortal angel in the rock. To my satisfaction, they were intrigued.

"Imagine, I was here before any of you guys, and no one told me that wonderful story" Claudia whispered, "perhaps they thought I was too ill to listen, but having heard that story, I am inclined to believe that this place is built on consecrated soil, much like Lourdes."

"I was thinking the very same thing," David said, as he reached across the coffee table and took Claudia's trembling hand, "Claudia, you might be right, this place could be a place of miracles."

"If David is right Claudia, this is the perfect place for you to be."

My voice was charged with hope, and with my hand on top of David's and Claudia's, it felt as though we had formed a trio of co-conspirators.

"I wonder what would happen if you took a bath in these waters Claudia." I whispered.

"Well." Claudia replied hesitantly, as she cleared her foggy throat, to find her voice that had gone quite husky.

"The nuns only use the spring water for Mother Superior's exclusive drinking." she said, "The water in the pipes come from a reservoir close by in Danvers Pen."

"But just for the sake of argument," David continued, "Is there's any way you could get enough water for a good soak. You never know, this water might be better than the mineral waters at Bath near here."

"I've heard about Bath," Claudia replied, "the water there is full of antioxidants and very active minerals. However, even so if there were miracle waters here in Aqua Valley, wouldn't local people already know about it?"

"Well, not if the nuns kept it as highly confidential information. They might have gone to lengths through the years, to preserve the peace here. Don't forget, they have occupied this valley for donkey's years."

"You might be right David; I can't see them wanting hoards of people, coming here expecting miracles, but what's to stop us testing the water on Claudia. Think it's worth a shot, what have we got to lose?"

"Only my life." Claudia smiled, still as mischievous as ever.

"How's your headache anyway?"

"It's manageable Kathleen; thanks."

David left us at dusk. He said that he wasn't comfortable travelling on country roads too late at night, and besides, he wanted to be on time for dinner with his hosts. It was clear that he was enjoying his stay with them.

"They've treating me like family." he laughed, as he waved goodbye, and I saw the sun, a humungous ball of gold, tingeing the mountains in its glow, and hanging impossibly low.

"You should see how they fuss over me," David shouted out the car window. "They mean well though, so not to worry."

Before he was even at the end of the driveway I missed him.

Chapter 51

A Vigil for Claudia

Doctor Farthing arrived moments after David left, they might well have tooted horns at one another on the desolate country road. Claudia immediately got up to go upstairs with him for her daily medical examination. "So sorry I'm late," Doctor Farthing muttered, "it couldn't be helped, rounds are taking longer, though nothing would stop me coming to see this special patient."

A pale smile crept across Claudia's luminous face, though her hand that gripped her armchair trembled.

"Thank you Doctor Farthing," she said, softly, "I knew you would come, no matter what."

I watched as slowly they climbed the stairs together, and noticed how gently Doctor Farthing took Claudia's frail elbow as they climbed. It hurt my heart to see how thin she had become. She leaned her aching head on his broad shoulder as though to catch his every word. How professional Doctor Farthing looked in his dark suit and tie and how gentle was his mustached face. No wonder Claudia trusted him with her life. It was more than obvious that this sandy-haired middle-aged man of Scottish descent was extraordinarily concerned with her welfare

Claudia had promised David and me that she would propose

the idea of the bath to the doctor. If he was agreeable, she knew that he could easily arrange for a donkey to traverse the sloping land with a local man who could draw the water and bring it back to the convent. But could a local man be trusted to keep things to himself?

It occurred to me, that perhaps it might be better to take Claudia to the water instead.

Later that evening, the sanctuary bells rung, and a tall dark-skinned sister came to the rooms to let us know that the vigil for Claudia was about to begin. I grabbed a thin scarf to cover my head and went downstairs. Dozens of nuns were scurrying to the prayers. Walker T was steadfastly waiting at the bottom of the stairs.

"Young lady, you won't believe who came." he whispered as I drew abreast of him.

"David?" I asked. "No, not David," Walker T replied, "Remember the little blind girl from Heaven Hollow? It seems she and her mother have somehow managed to make their way here. I suspect they walked most of the way, though they probably occasionally had rides in the back of donkey carts."

"But why are they here?"

"I don't know young lady, I have been wondering about that myself, though I overheard a nun say that they were following a calling, and that's that."

"Wonder if we'll find out why? But anyway, is Claudia already in the chapel?"

"Yes, she's sitting with Doctor Farthing. I'm afraid she's starting to look like a wisp of dandelion fluff. So I'm glad the doctor's helping to keep her comfortable. You should see how lovingly he's cradled her in his arms, and brought her down the stairs. It's all good."

He's a kind man Walker T; I admire him, thank God for him. It's like I've been afraid to admit to myself, Claudia's slipping away from us, and it scares me."

"Hush young lady," Walker T said gently, he slipped an arm around me and managed to stay the tears that stood in my eyes.

"Young lady, we have to believe that the Lord brought Claudia here for a good reason and as for Doctor Farthing, surely he is an instrument of God's goodness."

Side by side, Walker T and I slowly made our way down the hallway to the chapel. As we entered the house of prayer, incense wafted in the air, and nuns bent their heads reverently.

Chimes continued to call, when I saw Claudia sitting in the front row, cradled against Doctor Farthing's strong shoulder. There was a faint smile on her face as she acknowledged us.

The altar was elaborately decorated with a lace altar cloth, and vases of red roses and white lilies, strategically placed against flaming tapered candles. Solemnity crackled in the air, strains of organ music began to swell and the nuns raised their voices in song.

Two priests ascended the raised altar platform; then turned simultaneously to face us, and made the sign of the cross, to signal the beginning of the vigil. We fell on our knees in the auspicious candle-lit atmosphere, and I noticed that the little blind girl was sitting nearby. There were tears streaming from her sightless eyes.

One of the priests dramatically raised his hands heavenward in salutation; his voice dominated the silence.

"Praise be to thee our Lord God. We ask of thee, to come into our midst and cleanse our hearts, forgive our sins and free us from infirmity, especially the suffering of your servant Claudia Haddad whose life hangs in the balance."

The service lasted for a little more than half an hour, and Claudia was blessed throughout. Despite the good intentions, I could see that her cheeks were flushed with fever, and her eyes half closed. Doctor Farthing's hazel eyes were especially weary, and his face was as crumpled as sheets after a night of insomnia. His brown hair that was usually slicked back, had lost its hold and was hanging untidily across his forehead. He was not thought of as a handsome man, though his thick mustache, distinguished him. There was no mistaking the caring that radiated from him. I wondered if he had begun to have feelings for his patient.

We had intended to return to Claudia's side, when we became aware of the little blind girl's stick tapping on the tiled floor approaching us. Doctor Farthing stopped momentarily, "Poor little thing," he said shaking his head, "both her eyes are covered with cataracts."

In a moment the girl's mother was at Doctor Farthing's side, "we can't afford no surgery," she said sounding apologetic, "that's why we had to leave things alone. The only reason we come here, is because Joyce my daughter, had a dream"

"What kind of dream?" said Doctor Farthing, and I could see a spark of curiosity in his eyes.

The child's mother moved in closer, as though to impart something totally confidential. She lowered her eyes, and when she opened her mouth her words gushed out like a stream.

"My daughter say that she did had a dream that she was alone by a river, and all of a sudden, she hear a woman telling her that she fall off a horse and couldn't get back in the saddle. The woman said that she can't find somebody to help her get her back on her horse, and everybody going suffer, cause of it. My daughter say that she try to help the woman climb on the horse, but the woman was too heavy, like a rock. Then the woman tell her that only one person can get her back on the horse, and that person is the sick woman that was at Heaven Hollow recently. That's why we come here, cause we know she is here. But we don't know how a sick woman, like that, can help with anything. Anyways, bad things start happening already in Kingdom Come. The cook at the restaurant break him leg yesterday, and him can't work no more, then an old woman name Agatha get knock down by a car and she dying, so we had was to come quick to find the lady."

But how can Claudia help I wondered, because as it is, she could barely even lift a spoon to her mouth. "Well," Doctor Farthing said softly, "I'm the sick woman's doctor. She is in dire need of assistance as you can see, and that is why we are taking her somewhere in the morning to see if we can get help there. Perhaps you and Joyce could come along, but mind you, not a word to anyone else. Okay?"

"You have my word, doctor."

It was a bad night for Claudia after Doctor Farthing left. Nuns scurried in and out of her room with cold and warm compresses, and towards morning she rallied.

"Doctor Farthing's taking her to get help," one of the older nuns whispered. "She really needs professional medical attention I hope she'll respond."

I lay in my bed and thought about things, Claudia was uppermost in my mind. I hoped with all my might that she would be well again.

"If she survives," a young nun sighed, "maybe she will join our order."

"If it is God's will, then so it will be," said an older nun, "but then again, God might have other plans for her."

At five thirty in the morning the bell rang for prayers, and at last, the nuns left the room.

I went over to Claudia's bed, and stood there momentarily watching her.

"Claudia," I whispered in the half-light, she didn't respond and I panicked. Then I was relieved to hear her soft breathing. "Are you alright?" Again there was no answer. I realized that she was sleeping peacefully at last.

Breakfast was at nine I washed my face using water from the jug and basin provided. As I brushed my teeth, I wondered if the water was from God's Waterway. I remembered that Sister Serena had said that they only used that water for drinking. I changed my clothes and went downstairs to the dining room to join the sisters in a breakfast of scrambled eggs, fried dumplings, bacon, juice and coffee. Two nuns took a tray up to the room to feed Claudia some eggs. Later, we were told that she was not able to manage anything more than two teaspoons of food and a sip of water.

At a table set with fine silverware, sparkling dishes, starched white serviettes and a pristine tablecloth, the nuns spoke in hushed voices about housework, gardening, the way of the Lord and Claudia's impending outing with Doctor Farthing.

I didn't say much to anyone, and having lost the edge on my appetite. I excused myself from the table and eagerly went to shower and get ready for the day. I wondered if Walker T, over at the 'Priest's House' was doing the same.

By the time I returned to the bedroom, Claudia was propped up on pillows, looking gaunt.

"Look at the sunlight," she said, "it is almost like something holy, the way it streaks into the room touching everything. How are you Kathleen?"

"I'm good Claudia, how about you? Are you up to the trip ahead?"

"More than ever Kathleen I only wish I wasn't so tired."

"You slept a lot, Claudia, though maybe it wasn't enough."

"Perhaps not, Doctor Farthing will be calling David, to arrange things with him about this morning."

"Did he really?"

"Yes, they are planning things together."

"Is that right? Try to get a good rest before they arrive."

Chapter 52

Claudia's Journey to God's Waterway

The nuns were busy gardening, cooking and teaching, when Claudia and I were finally left to our own devices. I sat at the edge of my bed watching her breathe, as she slept. Her breath was laboured, and I was full of a thousand and one concerns. Please let her be alright, I whispered. It was with great relief, when I saw that her breathing was occasionally more normal.

By ten o'clock nuns returned to the room to sponge her down and prepare her for the journey. It was clear that they were under the impression that Doctor Farthing was taking her to a hospital or some other medical facility. I didn't say a word to the contrary. To avoid unwanted questioning, I left the room in search of Walker T Making my way downstairs I was surprised to find Joyce sitting on the bottom step waiting.

"Good morning Joyce," I said, "did you sleep here at the convent last night?"

Joyce turned her head towards me as though trying to have a fix on my location. I saw that she was smiling. "Mamma and me sleep in a room down here and early this morning the Sisters give us breakfast. Them is nice people. I want to be a Sister when I big."

I smiled to myself and wondered if her small dream would one day be realized. I was so moved by her sincerity that I sat down beside her on the step. "Perhaps you will be a nun," I said, and just then I saw one of the sisters hurrying towards us. "Doctor Farthing has arrived," the nun said.

Looking down the hall I saw both Doctor Farthing and Walker T coming through the main entrance. Doctor Farthing hurriedly greeted the nuns near the doorway, and Walker T beckoned to me. I got up immediately, he was gesturing to me to step outside.

Once outside I saw that the sky was white, though ominous dark clouds threatened at the edges of the horizon.

"Young lady," Walker T urgently whispered, "you know of course I won't be coming along with Claudia. Doctor Farthing got hold of David, he should be here soon. He'll be a big help to the doctor and is trustworthy. Doctor Farthing doesn't want to arouse any suspicions, that's why he's going to use Joyce as a ploy and bring her along. The folk here will assume she is going somewhere to get medical attention. He is probably telling her mother that he plans to take her with us to get some special medicine for her."

Looking skywards I saw black clouds increasing in size. "Hope we make it before there's rain," was all I said.

Off in the distance where the road snaked up to the convent I saw David's car approaching. Walker T saw it too and began to retreat towards the building. "Young lady," he said with a wink, "I'll go in to give Doctor Farthing a hand. Most likely they'll need towels and a pillow for the seat in the van."

When David arrived, he parked his car and called out to me.

"Morning Kathleen, I'm leaving my car here, all of us will fit in Doctor Farthing's large van."

He emerged from his car, took my hand, and leaned down. His cheek brushed against my hair. "You alright Kathleen?" he said softly, as he looked towards the main entrance.

"I'm fine David, thanks, how are you?"

He squeezed my hand in reply, and my heart raced. I wasn't sure what the rules were in close friendships, though I found myself tipping to peck his cheek. David smiled, and the warmth of him stayed on my lips, as arm in arm we approached the convent.

"Walker T went upstairs to give Doctor Farthing a hand. They'll want to bring blankets, towels and a pillow for Claudia. Think this water thing might help?"

"It won't hurt." David replied, sounding quite confident. "However, Kathleen I have a feeling the Mother Superior is on to something. Doctor Farthing believes she's been here much longer than the other nuns. Just look at her! She doesn't look a day over thirty-two. She should be in her late fifties or thereabout."

"Seriously! Well come to think of it, Mother Superior is the only one allowed to drink that water, and now that you mention it, I remember Claudia once saying that Mother Superior has weathered many of Jamaica's natural disasters, some of them way back. If that is the case, that should make her closer to seventy or more! But how can that be? She doesn't look all that much older than Gracie and Claudia."

"The whole thing baffles me Kathleen, but right now my thoughts are centred on Claudia's well-being."

"Mine too."

It wasn't long before Walker T emerged from inside the convent carrying some folded towels a blanket and a pillow. I was about to say something, when he put his finger to his lips to silence me. In a moment I realized why. Immediately behind him were three nuns with more blankets and behind them, was one of the priests from the previous night's service. The nuns padded the last seat in the van with the blankets and the pillow to make it more comfortable for Claudia. Then the priest introduced himself.

"Good morning," he said, "I'm Father Carlos Muniz, visiting from Brazil. I hope you won't mind but I have to travel with you, since it is necessary that I get to Morant Bay today. A priest there has secured me a drive to the airport in Kingston. I leave for home tonight. Doctor Farthing has kindly offered help. Are you relatives of Claudia? No?"

"No, Father," I said nervously, "we're not related. I'm Kathleen, I'm visiting from Canada. Claudia's a friend and this is David from Montego Bay." I couldn't help but wonder how on earth we would be able to visit God's Waterway, with the added unexpected hurdle of Father Muniz accompanying us in the van but I didn't say a word to anyone about it.

Father Muniz smiled broadly oblivious to my concerns as he shook our hands, "May God bless you both," he said, as he assisted the nuns with his luggage.

Joyce and her mother and a smattering of nuns soon joined us, and it was then that David left my side, to return moments later with Doctor Farthing cradling Claudia in their arms.

"What a lot of trouble I've been," Claudia sighed, and I saw how heavily her head lolled, giving her a lopsided appearance, and I felt sick inside.

I could barely watch as she was carefully lain across the seat, before the rest of us took our places inside the van. Father Muniz was up front with the doctor, David and I were in the seat behind them hardly daring to breathe. Joyce and her mother seemed shrouded in silence behind us and in the last seat in a fetal position was Claudia.

Doctor Farthing didn't say a word to any of us as he pulled away from the front of the convent. We waved enthusiastically at the gathered nuns and Walker T, who had all come to wish Claudia well and buoyed by their positive feelings; we headed down the road into the wild countryside. It wasn't until we were well out of visible range of the convent; that Doctor Farthing finally spoke.

"Father Muniz," he said softly, as he ran his long fingers through his slick-backed hair, "seeing as you're Brazilian I'm sure that on occasion you have come up against things that are completely unorthodox."

"That's true," Father Muniz nodded, "Brazil is a haven for supernatural, as well as other unexplainable phenomena."

"That's exactly what I thought," Doctor Farthing said sounding grave, "that is why I know that you would understand if I told you that there is someone who is in love with a woman who is dying, and the only thing that might save the dying woman is something quite unorthodox. If you knew someone in that situation Father, where everything conventional has failed, I wondered if you'd be willing to suggest taking a chance with the unorthodox. Do you understand what I'm trying to say Father Muniz?"

Father Muniz clasped his fingers together in deep thought; moments went by before he finally spoke.

Chapter 53

Marriage on the Fly

"Doctor Farthing," he began, "my understanding is that you are in love with the woman you are speaking about. In that case, my advice is, it is necessary that you do whatever it takes to save her, for that too is God's will."

Doctor Farthing slowed the vehicle, the skies were slowly darkening, as he pulled over to the side of the road, as though resigned. "Yes, Father you are absolutely correct, I am in love with Claudia, and I can no longer bear to see her slipping away from me without my trying all that can be done to save her life."

"Well Doctor Farthing it is possible that I could marry you and Claudia right here in the van. The paper work can be done later. Just look outside, at that lovely bank of wild flowers beside us, an untamed landscape produces such beauty. Love is another way of expressing the beauty that God wants from us. Go this moment and discuss my suggestion with Claudia as it is urgent. If she accepts your proposal, we have witnesses right here with us."

Neither David nor I dared even whisper; we were awed and elated by the turn of events. We sat in silence as Doctor Farthing left the vehicle, and went to the side of the van to open Claudia's door. By the sound of her breathing, I surmised that she had been resting and was probably unaware of the doctor's conversation. Then I heard low sounds as Claudia's tired voice spoke in little more than a hush. The deeply sincere tones of Doctor Farthing's whispering followed, and combined together with Claudia's in an unexpected romance of words. David and I held hands, each in our own way hoping for the best outcome, as their warm, loving murmurings held assurance.

With prayer book in hand, Father Muniz stepped out of the van into the moist air and went round to the back seat to be with them. He was on one side of Claudia and Doctor Farthing on the other. "So you want to marry this man?" he said, his dark eyes blazing, and Claudia nodded."

"All we need then is a ring" said Father.

"I have my parent's wedding ring," Doctor Farthing said triumphantly removing a gold band from his little finger.

Claudia Haddad and Doctor Cedric Farthing were married there in the van under oppressively rainy skies. Remembering the bank of wild tropical blooms outside, I opened the van door and hastily gathered a bunch for the pajama-clad bride. Then the sky finally opened, and rain lashed down on us in sheets.

"What wonderful rain," Claudia sighed as it roared around us and Doctor Farthing hugged her protectively and smiled. "The past is being washed away darling," he said, "after this; everything for us will be a new beginning." The man's a poet I thought to myself. I watched in admiration, as with gentleness he relished his first moments of marriage.

We were still parked at that very spot long after the rain tapered off, and were still there even when a hint of blue finally tinged the sky.

"Congratulations newlyweds," David and I said, as we went to shake hands with the happy couple.

"Thank you. Thank you so much," Doctor Farthing replied, his voice choked with emotion.

Chapter 54

Pushing on to the Waterways

Claudia in her weakened state acknowledged our sincere wishes, though we knew she wanted nothing more than for us to move on.

"Where's the Waterway Kathleen, we need to get there soon," she said, barely speaking above a whisper. "Do you think you can find the way from here?"

"Yes I'm sure I can," I replied and I eagerly gazed out into the rain-drenched landscape with fresh eyes, and recognized landmarks nearby that Sister Serena had pointed out. David leaned over the seat, eagerness in his eyes. "I'll help carry Claudia" he said, "When I was a kid we used to play a game carrying other kids around in two sets of hands. Perhaps we could try that with her."

"Well we could give it a shot," Doctor Farthing said, "But we'll have to park the car in the bushes. I don't like the idea of leaving an empty van on the main road. Criminals you know."

"What are you planning?" Father Muniz said cautiously, and it reminded me that none of us had explained to him about the true reason for our journey. Father Muniz looked at me expectantly as he carefully wrapped his prayer book in a square of black silk, before slipping it into his jacket pocket.

I nodded towards Doctor Farthing, who cleared his throat, kissed Claudia's cheek, then spoke.

"Darling," he said, patting Claudia's hand "I'll have to tell Father Muniz everything, because now he is as much a part of this as we are."

Claudia smiled at him in approval and Doctor Farthing continued. "Father Muniz, there is an interesting stream, here that was located in the time when Arawak Indians inhabited the island. It is said in legends that an angel came from the heavens, and created the waterway. The Arawaks had great respect for this valley considering it highly significant and holy, especially since there is a rock formation in the shape of an angel that appears to be guarding the stream. But to come to the point Father Muniz, all of us here are inclined to believe that the water might be miraculous. It seems possible that the nuns have suppressed information about the water's properties. To make a long story short, what I'd like to do, is take Claudia to the stream. It might be her only hope for survival."

"So why are we waiting then Doctor Farthing?" Father Muniz said enthusiastically, "I am a descendant of the native Indians of Brazil and we too now live in a culture of suppression. We must find this stream immediately."

"So Mrs. Farthing," beamed the doctor, "are you ready?"

We all saw Claudia's smile of approval, and even Joyce and her mother who had been silent for the whole journey, applauded loudly.

Doctor Farthing drove the van along a dirt track that snaked further down into the valley. Trees and bush grew wild on both sides. At one point in the meandering, Doctor Farthing decided it was not practical to drive any further. It was clear that the track deteriorated into wilderness.

"We'll park here," Doctor Farthing said.

We didn't have much further to go. Already I could hear birdsong, and instinctively I listened out for sounds in the wilderness ahead of us. In my mind, I heard wolves call, and bears trampling, and I had to remind myself that I was thousands of miles away from home. On and on we tramped through bush and grass land, until at last I heard the silver tinkling of the stream.

"It's over there," I shouted as we all surged forward to see the stream with the carved angel shining in the sunlight at the bottom of a small rise.

"Not much further now?" Claudia whispered.

"I hear the water darling! I hear the water!" Doctor Farthing shouted enthusiastically, "David, let's go."

David and Doctor Farthing hurried forward with Claudia in their arms, as I, Father Muniz and Joyce and her mother came up from the rear bearing towels and blankets, unmindful of the tangled overhang. Then, there it was, the stream, lively and slippery, bathed in sunlight.

"We're there at last." Doctor Farthing said, already breathless.

Father Muniz fell to his knees in rapture. "This indeed is the Lord's place," he said, "His presence, and that of His angel, are all around us."

"We need to take Claudia to the water's edge," Doctor Farthing said urgently, and I immediately preceded him and lay some towels down at the very edge of the stream hoping to protect Claudia from the harsh gravel, lumpy stones and gritty sand.

The air was dry, as though completely depleted of moisture, and all around was an unexplained stillness.

"The stones are warm," David whispered, marvelling at the change in the temperature. Father Muniz made the sign of the cross, and Portuguese prayers tumbled off his tongue filling the air like a mantra.

Meanwhile, Doctor Farthing lovingly and carefully extracted Claudia from David's arms, and carried her by himself, as he made the few steps down towards the shallows, and set Claudia down. The water embraced her immediately. She closed her eyes, as though either in pain, or ecstasy. She appeared fragile and nymph-like, as water slowly crept round her, coursing from her toes to her torso. David's presence beside me was my reassurance. His hand was close to mine, and it somehow gave me strength. I wanted to believe more than anything that Claudia would be well again.

My heart was in my throat as I watched her, since after only a moment or two in the crouching stillness, she appeared unnaturally prone. I became extremely nervous, and racked with doubt. I wondered if we had been wrong in throwing caution to the wind, and I was afraid for her.

"Darling," I heard Doctor Farthing say, and though his voice came out strong, his words were coated in caution "Is the water too cool my love? Are you alright in there?" Not receiving a reply, he absently began to occupy himself fussing with the objects in his pockets. Perhaps that was the only way he could have prevented himself from plunging into the stream to join his new bride.

Beads of sweat on his brow, bled into the deep worry lines across his broad forehead and I saw fear peep out from his weary eyes.

Seeming unable to restrain himself any longer, he stepped forward on wobbly legs, with his shoulders stooped and a clenched jaw that held back tears.

"I should take her out," he murmured, consoling himself and us; though sounding defeated.

How many times had he faced down death and won I wondered, even as Father Muniz's prayers roared in our ears syncopating the doctor's every step.

"Holy, Holy, Holy Lord God of Hosts, Heaven and Earth are filled with Your glory!"

Chapter 55

A Thunderous Black Stallion

We were suddenly startled to hear a great rumbling sound that jolted across the sky. Kip plop, kip plop, kip plop it came. It drew nearer, and grew louder as it drowned out our thoughts and fears. We are all facing death I thought and I clung to David with my nails dug deep into the flesh of his forearm. I felt his warmth against me, felt his quick breath and I was consumed by the nearness of him, as he patted my hand. "Don't worry Kathleen, I'll take care of you." He said reassuringly, and I wanted to believe him, even as I saw sheer panic in the faces of Joyce and her mother.

I heard a great thunderous pounding reverberate in the landscape, though no tangible source could be seen. "David," I whispered, "what have we done?" Together we stood at the edge of God's Waterway in the midst of the dissonance. Holding each other as though it might well be our last chance to do so. The noise grew to a clangor; we had no choice but to cover our ears reeling from the unwanted intrusion.

"What's going on?" I cried out but no one heard me, even as I looked skyward expectantly. The sky that recently had turned blue; was now transformed into an iron gray sea of anger, and a broad mist was beginning to gather around us. The mist was soon as thick as porridge and appeared impenetrable. There was no way out. I couldn't see any further than my nose and it alarmed me.

"David!" I shouted but the only sound I heard was the sound of my own heart beating. "Doctor Farthing!" I cried anew afraid to step in any direction, lest I might inadvertently fall into the stream.

Only then did I feel the warm clasp of a hand around my wrist and I knew instinctively that it was David. "It's alright Kathleen" he said, "I'm here." I clutched his hand afraid of letting go, and as I glanced around, I saw that the mist was slowly parting. It reminded me of a great curtain, and I wanted it to hurry, though it took its own time unfolding.

"What's happening David?" I shuddered, as he pulled me against him, wrapping his arms around me.

"I don't know Kathleen. But I would hate for anything bad to happen to you."

I was beginning to feel safe. The sound of David's voice was reassuring. I urged myself to be calm. Then my knees buckled. A humungous black horse galloped towards us!

"That is the horse from my dream!!" Joyce wailed, "I can hear it galloping and snorting!!"

We crouched in fear, as the horse, a muscled black stallion, drew abreast of us to rear up on its hind-legs, that were as large as pillars. It stared down at us, and whinnied and snorted menacingly.

"It going kill all of we!" Joyce's mother screamed. David shushed her; holding me tighter to shield me.

We shivered with relief as the horse backed away to slowly make its way along the banks of the stream trampling grasses and bush in its wake. It drew near to Claudia, and I held my breath at its every step.

Without warning, the horse leapt! I cringed in fear; my hands flew to my face imagining the danger. Nervously I peeped through my fingers and saw the magnificently muscled beast straddle the broad steam like a living bridge. Claudia had not come to harm. I gazed in awe at the tremendous arc the horse made over the water, and it brought to mind, the gigantic bridge structures that spanned open waters back home in Northern Ontario.

This must be the witch's horse I thought, as the horse's saucer-sized eyes loomed above us and regarded and stared us down before once again turning its attention to Claudia. Father Muniz stepped forward bravely, and fell to his knees, elevating his rosary to the heavens.

"Let us pray," he said, "Lord we are your servants and vessels of Your love. Have mercy on us." The horse shook its wild mane and turned its eyes upon the priest "In God's name have mercy!" Father Muniz cried out, his rosary dangling from his fingers like an offering. "Our Father who art in heaven," he began and the rest of us joined in.

The great horse did not waver. It again fixed its eyes on Claudia, like a faithful dog awaiting instructions from its master. None of us dared look away, even as it lowered its great head and audible plaintive whimpers escaped from the animal's dark throat.

"My wife, my wife!" Doctor Farthing spluttered, "please don't hurt my wife." He attempted to get to Claudia, only to be stopped in his tracks by one look from the horse's fiery eyes.

"It seems to want to protect her from me," Doctor Farthing shuddered, "My poor, poor Claudia."

None of us knew what to do or say. "For God's sake we've got to help her!" he yelled in frustration, though his words lacked conviction.

"The horse has mesmerized us all." I sighed, squeezing David's hand, feeling as helpless as Doctor Farthing.

"The devil's amongst us!" Father Muniz proclaimed, furtively glancing at the giant horse. He made the sign of the cross, before falling on his knees praying.

David drew me close, "Kathleen," he said, with a catch in his throat, "We have to be careful; the horse is a duppy. You know what a duppy is don't you?"

I didn't answer; I was too caught up with what was going on. Seconds turned into minutes and it seemed that years on an invisible clock ticked in my ears, until finally I spoke. "Yes David I know about duppies; just hold me." He held me closer still, and I felt a warm wave of contentment flow softly over me. I had not even noticed that Joyce and her mother were mute with fear.

"Look!" Doctor Farthing shouted, jolting me back into the moment. I followed his eagerly pointing hand to see that down in the hungry gushing waterway, Claudia had moved for the first time.

"She's not dead!" I shouted and watched as she slowly arched her back, appearing to be under tremendous strain. Seeing her in that contortion frightened me. I began to wonder if she might split in two but even so, I couldn't take my eyes off her.

I turned to David for reassurance, digging my fingers into his unflinching flesh, only to be caught off guard when a horrific scream escaped from Claudia's throat, followed by a jet of black liquid that shot out of her mouth and spewed into the water around her. The horse watched in silence, and waited.

The spew congealed reminding me of thick petroleum. Claudia started coughing. Her cough was ragged and harsh; it hacked like a relentless pick-axe, never ceasing until something dislodged in her throat. A cold shiver shot through me, and a cloud of what looked like black smoke burst out of Claudia's open mouth like a fist! Claudia struggled and writhed like a worm under a hatpin. Before any of us could attempt to make a move to help her, the horse comforted her. It bent its humongous head level with hers and nuzzled her.

I was in awe. Claudia lifted her stick slim arms and shakily embraced the animal as though greeting an old friend. This can't be Claudia I thought.

My eyes were riveted on her, despite the comforting warmth of David's nearness. I knew without doubt that any intervention would be pointless, because it was clear that this was not Claudia, but none other than the White Witch of Rose Hall a supernatural creature with powers totally unknown to us.

"My dear wife what is happening to you my dearest?" Doctor Farthing pleaded but none of us dared even fathom an answer. It was as though we were all tied and unable to be of any assistance even as the black spew began to weave and braid itself into the form of a woman. It happened so quickly it was impossible to follow the progress. There before my eyes, was a fully formed shimmering giant woman, completely coated in the black slick of the recent spillage! Her appearance was all too familiar; she carried a long thin whip, and she was dressed in riding gear.

The horse's neighing and bellowing was an assault on our ears as the animal triumphantly declared recognition of its master. With great skill, the woman mounted the creature and rode bareback, to sit regally atop her mount, as though finding her rightful place in the universe. She dug her heels into the horse's side and the horse reared at her every nudge, its mane flying in the breeze like a victory flag.

A great flash of light shot across the valley like a lightning bolt. It illuminated both the horse and the rider, as they charged skyward. The witch has finally abandoned Claudia I thought, and relief flooded through me.

"Did you see that?" David asked.

"Yes. It was scary." I replied,.

Out of the corner of my eye I saw Doctor Farthing running towards the river. He clambered over jagged rocks in order to let himself down into the water. I watched as he waded out to where Claudia was. She looked pale, and spent, even as Doctor Farthing cradled her waif-thin frame in his arms; whispering and weeping.

David and I immediately waded out into the water to join them. Claudia's lips were extremely pallid. Doctor Farthing bent and kissed her, "she's alive!" he sobbed. "My wife is alive! I felt her lips, she's alive."

I couldn't take my eyes off Claudia. She appeared as limp as the swaying weeds floating in the water. I couldn't have been more startled when she slowly opened the tiny slit that was her mouth and words tumbled out. "I'm hungry," she said, "when are we going to eat?"

Joyce and her mother broke out into an infectious laughter, having heard Claudia and what Claudia had said, even from where they were. They were probably thinking exactly the same thoughts as Claudia, as they celebrated her survival, hugging each other and laughing.

Filled with sunlight, the valley was transformed. Birds wheeled across the endless sky, chirping and singing, as though sharing in our joy.

Chapter 56
Claudia's Recovery

That afternoon we said goodbye to Father Muniz, who assured us that his lips were sealed, as to the happenings at the stream. He reassured us, and gave the doctor and Claudia his silver rosary as a wedding gift. We were sad to see him leave, though we knew he was full of the wonderful anticipation of going back to his homeland, and he was at threshold of that long journey.

Before departing, Father Muniz kept his word, he witnessed Claudia and Doctor Cedric Farthing's signing of the legal papers that would declare their marriage official. He stood proud and happy as the newlyweds embraced, assuring him that Claudia was well on her way to recovery.

Despite his exhilaration over Claudia, Doctor Farthing did not forget Joyce. In thanksgiving, he promised that he would be making arrangements with a colleague who would be able to perform the sight-saving surgery that would remove her cataracts, and restore her vision. How I longed to tell Walker T all about what had happened.

Later that afternoon, David and I lunched with the newlyweds at The Serge Patio, an upscale outdoor eatery near Morant Bay's seacoast. Tourist attractions along the route reminded me of those in Montego Bay. Though there was no mistaking the untouched rustic landscape of St Thomas that edged so close to habitations.

Unlike Montego Bay, many locals including office workers, market women, and field-hands were present on the streets. Cars and milk trucks jostled with pushcarts, bicycles and combine tractors.

It was quite hot on the patio I could feel sweat creep down the back of my T shirt. I wondered if I looked as ragged and spent as I felt. Sitting across from Claudia and Doctor Farthing I had to admit that despite her recent ordeal, Claudia had never looked better. There was colour in her cheeks, and her eyes were bright, achingly reminding me of my mother. I was almost weak from my remembering.

"I like it here." Claudia said, unaware of my thoughts, and my longing for what was. "I hope we are going to be living here in Morant Bay." She said, sliding her chair closer to the doctor's. "You know of course, I don't want to live anywhere near Rose Hall."

"Darling, you have nothing to worry about." The doctor replied kissing her hair, "the home where I grew up and my practice are not far from here. We'll be staying here for a few days; just so I can be sure you're well enough to fly."

"Fly?"

"We are going to Brazil for our honeymoon."

Chapter 57

Departure, Plans and Promises

That evening, David and I and Walker T left the convent for the last time. Mother Superior and most of the nuns came outside to see us off.

Little Joyce and her mother were still there as the first stars pricked the sky.

"We going to Morant Bay in the morning." Joyce's mother said. "Doctor Farthing's friend is going have a look at Joyce. Them feel they can do surgery that will help her. Praise be."

"All the best," I shouted, as we drove off into the evening, "thanks for everything."

David and Walker T shouted their thanks, perhaps missing all present already.

Not a word was breathed regarding Claudia's return to health, or even the appearance of the huge horse and the bold rider. The nuns were surprised enough already, to learn that Claudia had married her doctor, and wouldn't be returning to the convent. Walker T was as surprised as they were, though he seemed to take it all in stride, admitting that he had seen small signs of their affection, though he kept it to himself. It wasn't until we were entirely alone that David and I recounted to him all that had taken place at God's Waterway and there was no hiding his amazement.

We continued to wave from the car windows even as we headed down the long drive down into the valley, to eventually cross the island. The stars and the moon above us seemed to mark our way as small towns, plantations, fields, rivers and streams slid by. I tried to hold precious memories in my mind, considering there were only a few days left before I would be going home to Canada.

The lights were on in Santiago House when we arrived later that night, having cut a swath through the dark heading home. Walker T slept for most of the journey, though he awoke just as we were arriving, and he and I wondered who might be in the house. "One thing is for sure," he said with a laugh, "It is not Elfrida. We all know how she feels about being there at night."

We were surprised when it was Gracie, who came flying down the steps, followed closely by Jonathan. I had imagined that she would have been staying at the farm, knee deep in her planning.

"Welcome back," she said breathlessly, "we have something to tell you."

"We have something to tell you too," I said, "but you go first."

"We called off the wedding."

"You did!"

"Yes, we gave it a lot of thought; things were moving too fast, we seemed to have got caught up in unimportant things. What we really need to do is to get to know each other better first. That's the most important thing. Don't you agree Jonathan?"

"She's right. We've decided to wait a year, that's ample time, and we won't be making any major plans, we just want to enjoy each other and have a proper courtship. Gracie and I adore each other; we will be burning up the skies between here and Toronto."

"She's going back with me!"

"Yes, Kathleen, she needs to attend to a few things there, but I'll be flying there as often as possible. I know it will be hard being apart but in the end it will be worth it."

Walker T was the first to hug Gracie, and shake Jonathan's hand, "I guess if that's what works for you, then go for it. I wonder how soon you two will start missing each other too much. I wish you the best anyway. Just you wait until you hear about Claudia."

"Yeah, where is she anyway? Is she still sick? Did she join the nuns?"

"No, no, nothing of the sort Gracie."

"Well?"

Walker T turned to me and nodded, and I who had thought that I couldn't wait to surprise Gracie and Jonathan, was suddenly self-conscious and tongue-tied. Every night noise around us sounded louder than ever, telling stories richer than mine, and I almost could feel the night air grow thick and clammy around us.

"Claudia's married," I blurted out, squeezing Gracie's hand and relishing the look of surprise that loomed in her eyes, and then there was Jonathan.

"What! Are you for real! Who did she marry?"

"She married her doctor, Cedric Farthing, he lives in Morant Bay."

"I never even heard mention of him. Has she known him long? Claudia's a real dark horse isn't she?"

"More than you know, Miss Gracie," Walker T chimed in, "from what I overhear she is quite happy. She might even send us a postcard from Brazil."

"Brazil! Why on earth would Claudia be in Brazil?"

"She's on her honeymoon Gracie. It's seems she's beaten you to the altar. Who would have thunk?"

That night, David slept in Claudia's old room, too exhausted to drive back to Montego Bay. I wondered if he had entertained any thoughts about it being Santiago's old room, when Walker T had insisted that he stay over. I saw how tired he was, and knew that such thoughts were the farthest from his mind.

I could hardly sleep knowing that he was at the other end of the hall. I kept reminding myself that we were just friends and had no business thinking such thoughts.

Once in a while I'd hear the sound of Gracie's and Jonathan's voices coming from downstairs, and I longed to be with them. I was more exhausted that I had thought, and could only manage to remain exactly where I was. I remember occasionally nodding off, then waking up resisting sleep; full of imaginings and anticipating the coming morning. That morning, when I finally awoke, David was already gone.

Chapter 58

Back to the Tunnels

Two days went by before I saw David again. He and his trusted colleague Mrs. Campbell arrived at Santiago House at around ten that morning bringing pickaxes, flashlights and shovels in their company jeep.

"We wanted to start investigating the tunnel before you leave for Canada," David said, as he greeted me with a smile. "I've told Mrs. Campbell everything and she is as excited as I am about your find. But how are you, I wondered if you'd want to join us."

Mrs. Campbell hopped out of the vehicle and met me on the steps. She seemed both businesslike and elated. "Good morning, Kathleen," she said, extending her hand, "what an excellent treasure trove of information you have unearthed. David and I are both hoping that you will come with us, considering you already know the layout of the tunnel and all. We'll want to catalogue some things, and set some aside for display purposes. David says you're thinking about eventually opening Santiago House to the public."

"Yes, it seems like the right thing to do and as well, I would like to establish some sort of studio space for local artists but I'm not sure how to go about doing any of this, though I

315

imagine that while I'm away David and you would be helpful in establishing contacts here."

"You're right, Kathleen, we do have some connections, and there are people who would give of their time, as a contribution to our historical society, isn't that so David?"

"Yes I can think of a few people who'd help, but first let's see what size of a cache of objects we'll find down there. We will of course have to report things to the authorities. This find of yours is major. It will surely benefit the island's tourist industry."

"I'd like to come David," I whispered, "though to be honest going down there again would like give me the willies."

"I thought as much" David replied, "that is why I want to reassure you that I will be right by your side the whole time. Remember how brave you were at God's Waterway? It will be like that, I promise."

There was a lump in my throat, words wouldn't come out, all I could do was nod, and David knew I would join him. Little did he know that I was not in the least bit brave at God's Waterway. I actually felt like a coward. He hugged me briefly, as though quite proud of me. "Thanks," he said, "you're a real sport."

What David didn't know is that I had become accustomed to having him nearby, and that perhaps was the silliest reason for me agreeing to go back underground.

"Who's going to be using all that equipment?" I asked, "Surely not you Mrs. Campbell." I laughed, as she stood there looking quite smart in her khaki pants and army green shirt. Surely, she would not be soiling her hands or her crisp clean clothes.

"Oh," she said, "David should have mentioned that your friend Peter's coming to give us a hand. At this stage of our explorations, we'd rather only involve people that can be trusted. I'm sure you understand."

"Peter's coming along?"

"Yes, he was quite excited when we told him about your findings. He should be here any minute now. Raymond's bringing him. We thought Walker T and Gracie might feel safer in the house if Raymond was here while we went down there. Not that there is a problem mind you, but just for peace of mind."

Walker T was sitting on the verandah sipping coffee and poring over the paper when Peter arrived half an hour later. After David and Mrs. Campbell had taken some of their equipment into the house I went to stand on the verandah breathing in the scenery, the glimpses of the distant mountains, the pastures, the cane fields and the rose garden. "It's going to be another hot day," I said, looking towards the horizon. "I'm going to miss this when we're back in Toronto."

"I will too, young lady. We'll soon have to start packing for the journey," Walker T murmured, and just then, we saw Raymond's car arriving. I quickly went down the steps, and there was Peter, my refuge against talking about going home. I heard the front door open behind me and glancing back, saw David and Mrs. Campbell. They must have heard the car arrive, and were coming to join me on the verandah.

They were right about Peter; he was trustworthy and not one to spread gossip to all and sundry. I descended the steps, the heat of the day sizzled in the air and the thought of the cool tunnels below was almost welcoming.

"Good morning," Peter shouted from the car, "everybody ready?"

I felt David at my elbow, and together we went to meet Peter and Raymond. "Good morning to you both. Come inside," I said, "let's have some guava juice before we go down."

After our pleasantries, the bed where David had slept just a few nights ago; was rolled aside; and the small painted rose was exposed. Without explanations I pushed the floorboards open, and in no time, found myself leading the others down the shaft into the bowels of the tunnel.

"This is one major discovery," Peter hissed in the dimness as he reached for his flashlight, "you realize how many mysteries this going solve?"

"Yes, it is going to be big," David replied, "and there is so much we will have to do once everything is confirmed. It will keep us busy for months on end."

"Perhaps we should start with the room that Santiago used as a studio." I said, "There are tons of papers, paints and other things there that could be valuable. We'd need to spend a lot of time in there."

"What about the bones," David whispered, "wouldn't that freak you?"

I opened my mouth to reply, knowing there was no doubt in my mind that everyone else was most interested in exploring that very room.

"Okay let's go," I said, sounding braver than I actually was. David took my hand and that was all the reassurance I needed. "First we'll go to the room I call Santiago's room."

"I brought face masks." David said, "We're going to need them, we might as well put them on now. Ready?"

I don't know why I thought the room might have been different but it wasn't. It was stunning by flashlight and lanterns, far more intriguing than when I first I saw it. Shadows danced along the walls as the room slowly revealed its secrets. There were neatly stacked experimental charcoal and watercolour sketches and canvases alongside some finished landscapes. It was clear that the lonely boy was both prolific and talented.

David and I quickly glanced through a stack of canvases and found realistic drawings of the river meandering under lush green overhangs. Some were of sun-kissed pastures and raw sunsets set against distant mountains. Amongst them all were six completed canvases. One in particular held my attention. It was a startlingly realistic rendition of a house, not unlike Santiago House, or even Rose Hall standing proud against a purple sky where small brushstrokes seemed to dance and dip with blatant yellowed flecks of orange and gold. To me it suggested the coming of sunlight at dawn and I stood there in awe staring. How amazing it was to imagine that these works must have helped Santiago the solitary child, bide his time, when there was no one except an old slave man for company.

"This is lovely." I said, "If I'm allowed to keep anything from this collection, this would be it."

David leaned over my shoulder with his flashlight, there was no doubt he, too was captivated by the beauty of the piece. "Everything here is signed by Santiago," he said softly, "there's no doubt, that these are his work. He must have been a prodigy."

"Why would that poor boy resort to painting down here by lantern light?" Mrs. Campbell said, dusting off debris from the piles of canvases, "I wonder what brought on such secrecy. I guess we will never know the answer."

"This cache of artwork has probably never seen the light of day," I replied, "they could easily have been lost forever if not for us."

"Look!" Mrs. Campbell shouted from the other side of the room. Her excited voice distracted me momentarily from the splendid paintings.

"What's going on?" David yelled.

"Come see this David, you'll have to see it for yourself," she gasped, "this portrait leaning over here, must be none other than The White Witch. Do you realize that all these pieces of Santiago's have historical value?"

"Yes, I know," David replied, "this whole place is a goldmine. Santiago still has his secrets though. Why would he choose to paint down here, when the house has sunlit rooms upstairs? I just can't figure that one out."

"I guess we'll never know David," Mrs. Campbell said, pointing her flashlight directly at the painting. "My guess," she continued, "is that the White Witch wouldn't have approved of the fact that he was enjoying something. Because, judging from what we've heard about her, there is nothing she enjoyed more than torturing others. Surely the boy would have known that. Can you imagine how scared he must have been? I wonder if he knew that the room right next to this one was stacked with human bones, but to be honest I don't think he did"

"Kathleen, I think she's right," Peter hissed, "we'll just take another quick look round, then leave further inspections for professionals. It's too creepy down here. Hey but there's something that look like a cot over in that corner, maybe that was where him sleep."

"I wouldn't go over there, Peter." David said urgently it's dark there, and it looks like there's something in the cot. It could be a snake!!"

"Could it?" I said, "Peter, you'd better listen to David I'm, like scared of snakes. Let's go chill upstairs."

"Never mind Kathleen I don't think it is a snake after all, that dark mound in the bed is too big to be a snake. I think we should have a quick look."

"Are you sure David?"

"Yes, quite sure."

Mrs. Campbell was the first to reach the cot. The rest of us came up behind her with our flashlights at a ready. I, was probably the only one of us dragging my heels, not being sure of what to expect.

My heart took a jolt when Peter cried out. "It's a skeleton!"

"Yes. It looks like a preteen's skeleton!" David said grasping my hand.

"It must be Santiago," Mrs. Campbell surmised, "everyone thought he drowned!"

"That could have been a local rumour," David interjected, "this could open up a whole new can of worms."

With flashlight in hand, Peter illuminated the cot, bringing into focus the final remains of the boy Santiago, his bones white against the dust and dark bedding.

"He's been here for a long time," I said, as a wave of sympathy came over me. I felt that I had somehow come to know him. A shiver ran through me. Proof of his fate was almost too much to bear. This pathetic pile of bones was not how I had wanted to envision him, not after having seen him in the house and hearing his voice full of life, as though he was truly alive.

"Thank goodness he can now finally be laid to rest," Peter murmured, "the proper authorities will preserve all his stuff. Some of his artwork are so fragile they could easily crumble, but they will know what to do to save some."

"That is why they should be handled with care," Mrs. Campbell said, "even the implements he used, such as his paints and brushes, are of historical value. All we can do today is to make a rough list of our findings. People from forensics will have to be involved to do tests, as well as date and catalogue these remains."

We didn't return to the house until late afternoon feeling dusty and dirty. Fortunately, everyone had brought along a change of clothing. After showering and washing, we were pleased to find that Elfrida had prepared a meal for us.

Raymond was helping in the kitchen, we found him stirring a steaming pot of oxtail thick with gravy and white beans. Elfrida transferred a pot of rice to a deep serving dish, where she had placed fried plantains around the mound of rice.

"Everything alright down in the tunnel?" Raymond said the moment we walked into the kitchen. Before any of us could say a word, Elfrida handed him a dish of cucumbers marinated in vinegar. "You can take these into the dining room now," she said with a flourish, as though that action alone would stall the conversation.

We didn't say a word about our findings until we were at the table and Elfrida was well out of earshot. We all knew that if she heard anything, she would be even more nervous around the house than she already was. So it was as though we all had come to a decision to shield her from revelations about Santiago's remains, the artwork and even the portrait of the White Witch. Surely all that talk would have been too much fodder for her rich, rampant imagination.

Walker T, who had been overwhelmed and physically affected by his experience in the tunnel, did not shy away from what we had to say. He leaned in with newfound curiosity, his eyes flashing with personal memories.

"The room is splendid by flashlight," I said, "There are so many paintings and drawings that really should be in galleries and museums and of course, on permanent display here at Santiago House. In fact Walker T it looks as though the authorities will really have their work cut out for them."

"Yes," Mrs. Campbell nodded, "I suppose we all realize that it will take the proper authorities to save and preserve the things there. I'd say, we were the key that literally opened the door, but that is only the beginning. I am grateful for the honour of being among the first to have seen it, but no doubt curators and restorers will be able to give all the things in that room the exposure it deserves. Right Kathleen?'

"Yes I agree; and perhaps Santiago would have wanted that too."

"Know what?" Peter said, "I could start a journal and take pictures of everything as we go along. I have an excellent camera that we use for tourist shots at the hotel. It would be perfect for this. The things we found inspired me, and I have a feeling that a lot of people would want to see and read about this find."

"Know what Peter; I think you're on to something. We'll have to make sure that you are the official photographer for the project. You might even end up with a book, or something like that. People always like to have something tangible that they can enjoy at their leisure."

"You right David and you know what, you just hit the nail on the head, because that is exactly what I wanted to say. Even though taking on this project's going to be a heck of a challenge I get the feeling that it is something I should do."

"But anyway," I said, "Walker T and I are going home to Toronto in a matter of days."

I was unable to prevent my voice quivering I hated to even think about leaving, and now, the day was drawing even closer.

"Couldn't you extend your stay?" Peter asked, "Tourists do it all the time. It shouldn't be a big deal."

"And if it is," Mrs. Campbell said, chewing on an oxtail bone. "I have connections that can speed things up for you and Mr. Robinson.

Chapter 59

The Future Unfolds

In the end, applying for an extension to our stay went without a hitch and it was Gracie who travelled alone, after a sad farewell at Montego Bay airport. "Don't worry you guys," she said "I'll look after everything at home. Jonathan, I love you, don't forget me. See you soon."

As the plane cut through the shining white clouds, thoughts of Toronto played in my mind, and I remembered the job that was lined up for me at the health food store. How distant that all felt, though I decided to send a postcard of apology to decline the job offer.

Jonathan was beside himself, as he turned away from the departing plane. "Why did I let her go." he said, his eyes brimming, "nothing will be the same now I might as well had cut my arm off."

"You should go to see her soon," I said, "she would like that."

"I know, but the days here are going to be long, even though my dad and I cannot help but continue to prepare everything for her return. You know something? She is the best thing that ever happened to me."

A day or two later, while David and Mrs. Campbell were occupied with contacting the proper authorities and organi-

325

zations regarding the findings in the tunnel, Walker T and I found ourselves alone. We were sitting on the verandah, watching what had started off as a light drizzle, grow strong enough to keep us at home. Lightning streaked across the sky ominously, and I felt Walker T's eyes on me.

"Storm clouds are racing toward us," I said, "perhaps we should go in."

Walker T didn't move from his chair, the look on his face seemed more concerned about things other than with the weather.

"So young lady," he said cautiously, "what do you plan to do with your life? I'm sure you know that though you're a property owner, you'll need brains and intellect behind you. I know David and Mrs. Campbell are there to help, as am I, but my mother always used to say that one should try to help themselves first, before reaching out to others. Have you thought about further education? I remember you were of two minds when I first met you."

I was caught off guard by his question. I drew my chair closer to his. It occurred to me that I hadn't given much thought to anything. Walker T's concern was legitimate; and for the first time in a long time I had to give due consideration to the future. Even I was surprised when as though finding my stride, unexpected words came out of my mouth.

"I could take some college courses in Art History and Creative Writing," I said.

I was pleased to see a faint smile of approval on Walker T's lips. "But where would you plan to study young lady?" he asked, looking me right in the eye, expecting a serious answer. I didn't disappoint him.

"I could start off by sending away for Correspondence

Courses from Canada, since right now I want to be here while the business involving the findings in the tunnels is underway. Later on, I'd be more qualified to get into a full time programme."

"Good, but what about David, will he allow you time for your studies young lady?"

"No question about that Walker T, David and I are good friends. We enjoy chilling together, he'd approve of higher education, he's a college graduate himself, and besides he's involved with the work in the tunnels. Another thing Walker T, Claudia and I have not said this to anyone, so keep this to yourself, though she and I signed papers, the house will not be handed over to me legally until I turn eighteen. I can sign things on Claudia's behalf of course, but ownership is another matter."

"I thought as much young lady. I'm glad to see that you have a good head on your shoulders, and I look forward to seeing you studying."

Later that afternoon Walker T ventured out into the garden, the roses were bowed and heavy from the rain, though already bird song emanated from the trees as the land shrugged off its wet mantle.

"The earth smells amazing." I said, as I came down the steps to join him, "all it took was rain."

"Yes, young lady, rain usually clears away anything putrid in the air. But I'm also enjoying the sunshine, for I can stretch my legs and appreciate the things around us."

We were deep in conversation about the Jamaican weather, when we noticed a postman pedalling towards us on a bicycle. He rode right up and handed us a stack of letters. One letter was from Claudia. It was addressed to me, so I didn't think twice about the other mail since I couldn't wait to tear it open. It was

Walker T who thought to tip the rider who pedalled away, holding his head high, as I impatiently tore the envelope open.

"You might want to hear what she has to say Walker T" I said, clutching the letter tightly and began reading.

'Dear Kathleen," it began, "I hope this will find you well. Please give my warmest regards to Walker T, Gracie, Jonathan and of course David.

I am very well I have truly experienced a miracle. I am grateful to God. Cedric has been wonderful; without him I don't know what would have become of me. We are enjoying our life here in Morant Bay and looking forward to our honeymoon in Brazil. We could be leaving as soon as next week, since Cedric has booked off work.

Everyone here calls me Mrs. Farthing; it is difficult to convince them to just call me Claudia. As a doctor's wife I can already see myself becoming a vital part of the community. I have been asked to help in the local library, and I have approached schools regarding volunteering in literacy programs. Cedric says I should go slowly, though I feel I have the strength to take on these projects.

By the way, some of my family will be coming to spend a few days with us when we return from Brazil. Cedric has asked the servants to see to all the preparations, since he is fearful that I could suffer a relapse. I'm being careful Kathleen, and that is why everyday between the hours of 2:00pm and 3:00pm, you will find me napping. Not to mention that every night it is early to bed with Cedric by my side. There is no need to worry I have never felt better. Needless to say, every day I thank God for my blessings. Did I mention that I have resigned from my job in Toronto? They didn't want me to leave and said there would be a position there for me if I should decide to return. But that won't happen I have found true happiness here.

I almost forgot to mention that some of the nuns from Aqua Valley Convent came to visit us. They brought bouquets of flowers and a beautiful family bible as a wedding gift. I felt badly, since I was well aware of the fact that they had hoped I might have joined their order, but when Cedric kissed me at God's Waterway I knew I was his for life. He loves me dearly, so I am sure the nuns realize that God had other plans for me. Cedric is all and everything I could have hoped for.

Would you believe that we are hoping to conceive a child in a year or so? I am looking forward to the possibility, because I know without doubt that Cedric will be the best father any child could have. Can you believe it Kathleen I who was such a 'party girl' am talking like this? Don't laugh though. I am serious.

By the way, the nuns told us that Joyce's vision has improved after her surgery. At first, everything was blurry and clouded. Now she is making out forms and people's faces. They have high hopes for her and I can't help but feel that years from now she will eventually join their order. They are convinced that Cedric had a hand in my recovery too. The things they don't know. Another thing Kathleen I have no regrets about signing over the property to you, though it will be two years before it is legally finalized. I have all that I need now. My intention is to give back to society as much as I can. Did I mention how much I love Cedric. LOL.

I look forward to hearing from you and with God's grace we will see each other in the near future.

Much love to everyone I miss you all.

Claudia'

"Sounds like Claudia's prayers are answered young lady. She is happy and well loved. She sure has come a long way from when I first met her. You might not know it young lady but she used to only live for having fun. Mind you, there's no harm in moderation, but Claudia could party for days. Gracie couldn't keep up with her."

"I figured as much Walker T, since one night when we first came to Jamaica I heard her and Gracie talking and their conversation surprised me. It made me think about mother, and I wondered if Claudia and mother had something in common."

"How so?"

"Well don't forget that I once told you that mother loved men Walker T. She even carried on an affair all the while she was married to father. Sometimes I'm convinced that she loved her lover more than she loved my father."

"Really?"

"Yes, her lover was a handsome indiginous man. She thought the world of him. Honestly Walker T I don't know how often I saw her pacing the floor, wanting to flee to him. It was as if our house was nothing more than a cage that kept her from him. They died together in a crash you know."

"I'm so sorry young lady. You have had to bear so much unspeakable sadness. Why don't we take a walk down by the river? It might do us both some good."

"I'd enjoy that Walker T, though I must say I don't think Claudia would ever have affairs. She obviously adores Doctor Farthing."

"True enough young lady, but what about you? Are you afraid of falling in love because of your parents?"

"I don't know Walker T sometimes I think I'm too young to be thinking about such things."

"Young lady, Marceline and I were mere children, and I still love her. Does David know how you feel?"

"David! Oh no I'd never speak about stuff like that with him. It's like we are buddies, he's a few years older than me. It is just as well that we just chill together, and not get too close. For all I know I might just be a kid in his eyes."

"Well young lady, the way it sounds to me is that the young man is to be admired. He's not taking advantage of you, personally I believe that people who care deeply about each other should be friends. I know what you're thinking and yes, Marceline did kiss me the first day I met her, we certainly became really close friends. I miss her you know, every day of my life. But don't mind me, sometimes I get too teary-eyed; I guess it is because I empathize. I know you miss David every moment he is not here."

"You might be right Walker T I miss him all the time. I even wonder how Gracie can stand being away from Jonathan. I also wonder how Claudia knew that Doctor Farthing was the one for her. I'm confused by all of it. But in the end it all boils down to the fact that I always miss David. I've never had a boyfriend, so is this crazy or what?"

"Young lady there is no doubt you have feelings for him. Love is sometimes like a waltz and you just have to follow your partner, never going too fast or too slow. Just follow gracefully"

As we drew close to the river I grabbed hold of Walker T's arm, and in that manner navigated rocks and weed tufts that would have marred our passage. The air was fresher along the waterway, and the canopy of vines held moisture in check and we were refreshed.

"I'll never forget this place," Walker T said softly, eyes brimming. "Just look at the small rapids over there, young lady. If views like that are not a slice of heaven I don't know what is."

"Know what Walker T, you should think of this place as your second home. Many Canadians come south to escape winter, so why not you? Seriously, this property could be your refuge; whenever you want."

When I looked up to meet his eyes I saw that tears had spilled onto his cheek.

"Not to worry," he said, "these are tears of happiness. You and I have come full circle."

Chapter 60

A Deeper Connection

Four days went by before I heard from David. He telephoned to say that he and Mrs. Campbell had continued to be cautious as to whom they'd share information about the artifacts in the tunnel. As such, they were lucky enough to enlist some good people. David also said that the excavations could start as soon as the next day. I was excited to hear from him especially since my stay on the island was no longer limited to a specific departure date.

"That's awesome news David," I said, "although now we will have tons of people trooping through the house."

"Not really, Kathleen," he replied, "we plan to construct an entrance to the tunnel from the yard and we also will be setting up temporary toilet facilities at the back of the house and there will be running water installed."

"You've thought of everything David, haven't you?"

"Well Mrs. Campbell and I are used to doing this sort of thing but here is something I'm not that used to doing."

"What's that?"

"I'd like you to come to dinner with me and my parents this evening. Mother said you'd think it's too short notice but I assured her that you are not like some other girls."

"Oh I'd love to come," I said without hesitation, sounding a little too eager but not caring. What did he mean about me not being like some other girls? Was it a compliment or what? A dozen reasons crossed my mind as to why I shouldn't have accepted but I felt there were a lot more reasons why I should. After he hung up I contemplated going into town to buy a new outfit but in the end I decided against looking too staged. I chose a pair of black jeans and paired it with a black T-shirt. My only accessory was a strand of pearls, and I had no doubt that I would be presentable, and I was right.

"Walker T," I called out, heading upstairs "David's asked me to dinner this evening. Will you be alright here? I'm still not comfortable with any of us being alone here."

It was a moment or two before Walker T answered, and I was surprised that he sounded almost as excited as I did.

"I'll be just fine young lady, especially since I've just decided to accept Mrs. Campbell's family's dinner invitation to supper. She kept insisting that the invitation was only for me, so I had hesitated accepting on account of you. But I'll call her now. It was not clear to me why she was being so insistent. She even went as far as to say that neither she nor her husband likes driving late at night, so I should stay overnight in their guest room. It would be nice for me to get out, so young lady, from the look of things I don't expect either of us to be back here tonight. Here's the Campbell's number if you should need to contact me."

It occurred to me, that the whole thing had David earmarked all over it. I smiled to myself, and held my tongue, too caught up in the excitement of the events to care.

Mrs. Campbell and her husband arrived at 5:30, just after we had finished our rounds locking the windows and doors. "Sure you'll be alright? Walker T said hesitating on the steps. "Not to worry," I replied, sounding more confident than I felt, and I followed behind him to greet the couple.

I watched as their car disappeared down the dirt road and I sat there on the steps feeling excruciatingly lonely. Thoughts of Santiago, and the many slaves buried underground raced through my mind and I thought of the White Witch and remembered how horrific she was on her horse, and suddenly I felt fear. Every crack or snap in the bush startled me. I looked around suspiciously at the slightest rustle, but as far as my eyes could see there was not a single human in sight, just a couple of stray dogs and a lone cow lumbering towards the dark pasture.

I gripped my purse grateful that I had not forgotten it in the house. I knew I would be equally afraid inside listening to the bones of the house rattle and shift in the emptiness. It was a heart stopping half an hour before I heard David's car approach. With enormous relief I sprang up from my perch and raced down the rest of steps. David pulled up, parked, and stepped out from the car and I ran into his arms.

"What's up?" he said full of concern as he gripped me and I could feel myself trembling. "I was afraid David. I was alone, Walker T left already."

"I'm here now," he said, "I should have come sooner. It sure can be lonely out here. I can see why you'd be nervous. Are you alright now?"

He squeezed my hand reassuringly, before opening the car door for me.

"Ready?" he smiled.

All I could think at that moment was that I was no longer alone. All fear drained out of me, and when he reached over from his seat and tapped his fingers on my hand, tears came to my eyes.

"I'm ready," I said as he took hold of the steering wheel, and we headed off into the darkness.

"My father has been looking forward to meeting you," he said softly, "he is a people person. Any excuse for a conversation. Be prepared for a lot of questions. I'm sure you can handle it."

I wasn't sure I could handle things as David seemed to think. After all I had grown up in an isolated neck of Northern Ontario and my closest companions were my parents.

We arrived at David's, to find both his parents waiting for us in their garden. They came to the car and greeted me with warm hugs and smiles.

"So you're Kathleen," David's father said, his arm around my shoulders, "you're as beautiful as David was saying."

I felt somewhat embarrassed, but managed to catch David's glance, and he was smiling. His father was tall, with pronounced Oriental features I could see something in him that David resembled.

He was like a fountain bubbling over with mirth. It was clear that he liked me.

"So you didn't think a Chinese man like me, would think you're beautiful?" he laughed, "you look shocked Kathleen, didn't David warn you about me? David tends to warn any friends he brings home, but barring all that I show appreciation easily; no bones about it. Just look at my wife; she's absolutely beautiful, and I never forget to tell her so. I have no idea what she sees in an ugly Chinese man like me but just look at our handsome son."

I broke into a grin at his audacity, only to see wonderful pleasure lines crinkle at the corners of his eyes.

"Nice to meet you," I said, "I'm glad you invited me."

"So did David warn you?" he persisted and paused at the front door.

"No need for warnings," I grinned, "because if David is as nice as you, then there's no worries."

"Well I can tell you're special," David's father said and he gripped my hand and pushed open the door. "Between you and me Kathleen, you're the first girl David's brought home to dinner."

"Come on Daddy," David's mother chimed in with a laugh, "Don't embarrass the young people. Dinner's waiting." 'Kathleen," David's father said addressing me, "I hope you like roast beef, rice and peas and chop suey, we also have a cucumber salad."

"Now darling," David's mother replied, "get to the point and tell her how David slaved over the chop suey all afternoon, before making a fruit punch. You might not know it, but usually Daddy is the one that does the cooking. I like making Chinese dishes but he likes to have something Jamaican. He's an amazing cook. Do you cook Kathleen?"

"Well…just basic stuff. I used to watch my Mum. I can bake an apple pie, make spaghetti and meat balls and a few other basic stuff."

"Well David," his father laughed, "you have your work cut out for you."

David nodded agreement, as we entered their spacious dining room. He pulled out a chair from the table for me. "No lessons today," he said, "all Kathleen has to do is enjoy the food. Right?"

I gulped hard and sat down, finding it hard to believe I was actually sitting down to dinner with the Changs, while trying to occupy myself with unfolding my table napkin, hoping my heartbeat wasn't audible.

"So how old are you Kathleen, eighteen?" David's father inquired holding his fork as though he wanted to pin down my answer.

"Dad," David interrupted, "Don't go there. Didn't you once tell me never to ask a lady her age?"

We all laughed and David's mother rang a little bell. and the servant came into the room bearing a tray with the various dishes. The servant smiled knowingly, and took a good look at me, before she left the room and I saw that there was the ghost of a smile on David's mother's face. "Never mind Agatha," she said, "she's been with us since David was born. She's just curious as to what you look like, since David's always talking about you. Anyway, let's say Grace"

"Mother...." David retorted, as we bowed our heads in prayer. I closed my eyes, and was surprised when I heard David voice leading them in prayer.

"Lord we give thee thanks for these thy gifts which we are about to receive. Bless our food and our family and our very special guest, Kathleen."

"Amen," we all responded and I smiled, as I felt the reassuring touch of David's foot against mine, under the table.

We all stayed up late, watching a DVD that David's dad suggested. Exhaustion set in and David's mother begged out of watching it to the end.

"Kathleen," she said, "Daddy and I had better go up to bed, we can barely keep our eyes open. But anyway I've prepared the guest room for you here on the ground floor. The roads aren't that safe at night as you know. Sleep well, we will see you in the morning. We enjoyed the evening."

"Good night," David's father added with a wink, "don't let the bed bugs bite In fact don't let anything bite."

"Good night. Thanks for a lovely evening I enjoyed it." I said with a smile as I watched David's parents walk away arm in arm looking very much in love.

"Sleep tight," David called out, as they climbed the stairs.

"We sure will," his father replied stopping momentarily, to playfully plant a kiss on his wife's cheek.

"Mom, thanks for everything and you too Dad." David said.

At long last David and I were alone. "Where's the guest room?" I asked.

"Kathleen," he said sounding excited, "You're amazing. My parents liked you, you know that; right?"

"I suppose so, though it's like I'm just as tired as they are."

"Really! Well the guest room is at the end of the hall. It has a bathroom attached. It's getting late. I'll see you in the morning."

I smiled wanly, as he waved from the doorway and stepped out into the night. Chock full of emotion I found my way to the guest room and flicked on the lamp to find a huge bunch of yellow roses on the bamboo bedside table. Propped up against a crystal vase was a handwritten note that said, 'Warm wishes from David' it brought tears and a smile.

Though the room was beautifully decorated with silk and lace bed coverings and fine furniture I couldn't take my eyes off the handwritten note. To my surprise I saw that a brand new silk pajama was folded on the pillow. I didn't know if I had David to thank, or his mother. I just knew that I had never worn anything as luxurious. I slipped into them enjoying the cool feel of the silk as it brushed against my skin. I thought about going to find David to thank him, but chose instead to remain exactly where I was.

I don't remember falling asleep. I jumped out of bed at

about seven the next morning. Cutlery and dishes were rattling and I thought I was back at Santiago House. I soon realized that I was still at David's. I proceeded to straighten the bed and showered before pulling on my day clothes.

When I crept out of the room, Agatha was in the kitchen. It looked bright and luminous with sunshine pouring in through two large windows. Agatha had just placed a vase of beautiful yellow and orange zinnias at the centre of the breakfast table, and when she saw me, I knew she was somewhat startled.

"Morning Agatha," I said softly, "need help?"

"Good morning Ma'am," she said with a slight bow of her head, "No thanks I don't need help. You sleep good?"

"Yes."

"Well I just finish di cooking. Mr. David says you like dumpling and codfish fritters, an him ask me to make some ackee too."

"It sounds yummy."

"Well I hope you like it, cause I know Mr. David care what you think. Him say that him never meet anybody like you. So don't you go break him heart."

I felt flush. It had never occurred to me that I could break his heart, and I turned away from Agatha, to stare out of the window, feeling suddenly self-conscious.

"Anyway, Miss Kathleen," Agatha said reassuringly, "I hope you have feelings for him. But you don't have to say nothing. I hear the Missus coming, so I better shut up, and go call Mr. David."

Chapter 61

Fire in the Tunnel

The excavation on the land at the Santiago property began about two weeks after that dinner. Some trusted labourers hired by Jonathan, came to dig the new entrance to the underground tunnels. Walker T was pleased, since the new entrance would prevent people traipsing through the house and constantly disrupting our activities. I had started my correspondence study program. I hardly saw David, though he was on the property every day with Peter, occupied with photographing and cataloguing the artifacts underground.

Raymond was recalled as our main security guard during the night hours to prevent trespassers from coming on to the property. Things were relatively back to normal. I did not even give much thought to the White Witch. Claudia wrote again to say that she and Doctor Farthing were helping to set up a small preparatory school in Morant Bay. All I could think is, that she had returned from the brink of despair after being possessed, and I was grateful.

We received mail from Gracie, who informed us that she was missing Jonathan, and had been seriously thinking about returning to the island. She said she was lonely in Toronto and wondered if Walker T would mind if she advertised for a roomer to take over Claudia's old room.

I could hardly remember how life had been in Toronto, though I knew that if I were there I too would be desperately lonely, although at the same time, I knew that I could not stay in Jamaica indefinitely.

It took a month to complete the excavation but it was not without drawbacks. The labourers complained of experiencing strange sightings, and seeing unexplained darting lights. Some went as far as to say that they heard movements and whispering voices. How much was imagination, and how much was based on reality, was under speculation though none of it surprised us. Still, we did not divulge the fact that the bones of dozens of slaves and Santiago himself were found underground. Then one night, after the entrance way was finally completed, Raymond roasted yams, pork and chickens on an outdoor spit and invited the men to join him in celebration. Walker T and I were included, though after an hour Walker T retired to bed, complaining of exhaustion. I knew that he had begun to spend his evenings writing long letters to friends, and I wondered if he was missing Marceline and Toronto, and needed time to himself.

I chose to stay up with the men, knowing that both David and Peter would soon return from the tunnels perhaps armed with more pictures, scribbled notes and small artifacts. But by nine o'clock I was exhausted, and could barely keep my eyes open. I reluctantly said goodnight and went into the house to sit in the living room. Though I found myself nodding off. I could hear laughter outside as the men gossiped and joked. There was still no sign of David or Peter. I fell asleep in a chair by the window only to be rattled into wakefulness when I heard Peter's cheerful voice outside.

"How's it going?" he said addressing the men, as it was his custom. I imagined that they gave each other high fives.

"We leave dinner for you and Mass David," one of the men said, and I heard the soothing murmur of their voices interlaced with the sounds of night insects. "But where is Mass David?" Raymond inquired and I held my breath as Peter seemed to hesitate.

"He was with me, but he went back to get something he wanted to bring to the house. He shouldn't be long."

Peter's words brought assurance, though I couldn't help but feel a tight knot in my stomach. I knew I wouldn't be comfortable until I saw David face to face. It was no wonder that I got up from my chair and approached the doorway.

"Well I going go smoke," I heard one of the men say, "Me going take one of the kerosene lamp. Me not going far."

I hesitated at the doorway, my hand was on the doorknob, I backed away and returned to my chair. It wasn't an hour before I was jolted by the sound of piercing screams! It frightened me to the core, I ran to the door and burst out into the night. Looking eastwards, I was startled to see a ugly red glow lighting up the entrance to the tunnel, all the men were running towards it. I chased after them, heart pounding, knowing immediately that the tunnel was on fire. In the distance I saw the black outline of a man running towards us. Though I prayed that it was David, I knew that it was not. It took me a moment to realize that it was probably the man who had gone to have a smoke.

"Run!" the man was shouting, "Get help! A weird white woman grab me kerosene lamp, and throw it in'a the tunnel, an now the whole place a burn!"

"Oh my God, David's inside!" I cried out. Raymond grabbed me, and restrained me, fearful that I might have run right into the flames. "David's going to die!" I screamed as I struggled against him, tears streaming down my cheeks.

"Take it easy," Raymond said, as his strong hands held me like a vise. "We going do everything we can. Some of the men going get water from the river. The workmen have pails, buckets and pans out here already."

It seemed like hours before help arrived. Amongst the crowd that came was Jonathan and his father, the river children, Erasmus and several other locals who formed a human chain to battle the shooting flames. Thank goodness Walker T was awakened by the screams, and he had the presence of mind to phone for help. I saw when he came to join the chain of helpers, and I ran to meet him. "David's underground!" I cried hysterically. Walker T put an arm around me. "Hush," he said, "don't give up hope. Everybody's doing their best. We have to pray."

I soon learned that the man who had gone to have a smoke was called Willy Lions, there was talk that he was a compulsive drinker. No doubt that was the real reason he went off by himself. He reeked of alcohol and looked slack-jawed and wild-eyed even as a dozen or so locals surrounded him, eager for information. Willy's yellowed eyes could barely focus. I wondered how much he had had to drink, when a young boy came running brandishing an empty rum bottle in his hand accusingly. Willy trembled in fear when he was confronted with the bottle, he covered his eyes, as though that alone was enough to hide the evidence.

"Willy usually do good work, and him is trustworthy," a man near me said, "but once him have a drink, that is the end of everything. So I don't believe one word him saying."

"I never going smoke again," Willy said, trying to drown out the voices around him. "I was just a stand over there minding me own business, when a white woman sneak up on me. I swear I saw her, cause she was half naked, an when I look at her, she grab me lantern from me and fling it down the hole. The whole thing frighten me so till."

"You should be frightened," a woman said, "you burn down all the hard work that was going on here an now you trying to blame the whole thing on a woman nobody else see. Where is she now? Don't tell us she ride off on a pink elephant, you drunken fool. The fire could'a spread to the house."

"Maybe Willy want us to think that him saw the White Witch!" a loud mouth man interjected, but he was quickly hushed up by the others as I approached.

"David Chang's down there," I shouted, and everyone turned to look at me, as though suddenly realizing that things were worse than they first thought.

"Lord me God," a woman said clutching her chest, "s'maddy going dead tonight." she wailed pitifully, and from the murmur of grief that permeated the gathering, it was clear that most of the locals had come to know David, perhaps as a result of his frequent visits to the area, and his work over at Rose Hall.

"The whole place down there must be full'a smoke," a toothless woman said, coming over to place her broad hands over mine. "If him is down there I sorry, but him is a dead man now," the woman said gravely.

I didn't want to hear what she was saying; so I turned away and hid my eyes, "I have to tell his parents," I whispered.

"I'll come with you?" Walker T said, and with his arm around me, he must have felt me trembling and knew that I barely had strength enough to put one foot in front of the other, as we sadly made our way back towards the house.

"Do you think he could still be okay?" I said hopefully as we went up the front steps.

"It is possible young lady but who am I to say."

Walker T stood beside me as I gripped the telephone, unable to dial, then he sat me down in a chair and fetched me a glass of water. "This will help to settle you," he said, "I took the liberty of adding a drop of brandy, just take a sip."

"Thanks Walker T, my whole insides are shivering. I can't stand not knowing what's happened to him, and I'm afraid to know, if things turn out bad."

"Young lady, you are mature beyond your years, but this is a terrible experience. It is clear that you are quite shaken. So let me speak with his parents for you."

"Would you?" I said weakly, as I thought of the shock that awaited David's mother, and his mischievous father, and even poor Agatha. I couldn't help but wonder, if in the end they would inadvertently blame me for the mishap.

"Of course I'd do it for you young lady. Meanwhile you might want to go out to the verandah and keep watch. Somebody might come with word about David before I even hang up the phone."

After making the call, Walker T came out to the verandah. He looked spent, though he probably tried to keep a brave face. "They are coming," was all he said and we stood together in silence. It wasn't long before someone came running towards us through the dark, and though I kept fingers crossed it turned out to be Peter.

"Kathleen," he panted, "some firemen went down into the tunnel wearing protective masks, and they said there is no one down there!"

I felt my head spin, and the star-studded sky seemed to exchange places with the solid ground. I held myself in check, not knowing whether to be relieved by the information Peter brought, or to be more frightened. One thing was for sure I couldn't find words to respond and I was grateful for Walker T's presence.

"But Peter, how could that be possible?" I heard Walker T say, echoing my very thoughts. I was unable to control myself, as I broke into fresh tears. I knew when Peter took my hand, he was trying to reassure me, and I pressed his palm in gratitude.

"I don't know why they didn't find him, but I know for sure that he turned back, because when I had glanced back, I was in time to see him disappear into the tunnel."

"Peter I'm so frightened for him, his parents are on their way. What am I going to say when they come? I feel as if I should go down into the tunnel myself. I know the place as well as anyone."

"Don't be foolish Kathleen, the air down there is toxic and most likely the whole place is covered in ash and soot. I wouldn't let you do that."

"But Peter, it's David we are talking about. I can't leave him to die."

"And you think I don't know how you feel Kathleen? Trust me, the best thing we can do for David is to let the firemen do their jobs. For your information, they wouldn't allow you to go down there anyway. I'm just as worried about David and I feel absolutely useless."

"No Peter, you don't quite understand what I've been trying to say. The thing is I care a whole lot about David."

When David's parents arrived, they found me with Walker T and Peter at the fringe of the crowd beside the burnt out tunnel entrance. I couldn't even imagine what to say to them. Their faces were ashen, and his mother was wringing her hands with worry. I became suddenly shy, afraid that they would see the feelings that were raw on my face. I don't know how I managed to reach out and embrace them both, though tears lingered on my cheeks; then I felt warmth as they returned my embrace.

"Any word; is he alright?" David's mother whispered full of concern and her husband pulled her close and clutched her slim hand.

"Are they sure he's down there?" his father said, his voice crackling with faint reassurance, though his posture spoke volumes, his shoulders were stooped and his eyes were unusually downcast and saddened.

"The firemen didn't find him," I blurted out, wanting to be optimistic, though at the same time, I gave them the facts as I knew them "Peter is certain he saw David go back into the tunnel. They'd just finished work down there, when David decided to go back down."

"But why'd he go back?" his mother sighed, "David's usually quite thorough, surely that's not like him to want to go back."

"Mrs. Chang," Walker T said sagely, "I'd say it is hard enough accounting for one's self; much less for someone else. People often do things on impulse. David must have thought there was something important that needed attending to. He is a bright young man but who knows what he was thinking?"

"Well I suppose you are right, but I hope to God he is alright." his mother said, a tremor creeping into her voice, as she turned towards me. "Oh, are you alright Kathleen? You'll have to excuse my bad manners. I forgot that this incident is difficult for you too. David is so fond of you, and it is obvious that you have feelings for him a well."

"I'm... bearing up" I said, remembering the words I had said so often after my parents passed away. But no doubt my feelings then, as they were now, were transparent.

As if to confirm of my thoughts, David's father gently took

my hand "Kathleen's obviously as distraught as we are darling," he said, gripping me more firmly and I wondered if he had noticed that I had begun to tremble. "Kathleen's important to our son," he said squeezing my hand. "That's all that matters. Hope you don't mind keeping each other company for a moment I think I'll go talk with that fireman guarding the tunnel entrance, maybe he's heard something new."

I watched as Mr. Chang made his way through the crowd and despite the circumstances, I couldn't help but empathize with the Chang family.

It was well past midnight, when at the insistence of David's parents, the firemen continued to search the tunnel and the underground rooms. In the end, the news wasn't any better than earlier in the evening. We were told that everything below ground was destroyed, and covered in soot. Though there was still no sign of a body, I took small comfort from that fact.

I remained steadfast alongside the Changs. I watched as Walker T went to the house accompanied by Erasmus and two other locals who kept vigil with us. They returned bearing tea kettles with hot mint tea steeped in honey. What a sense of camaraderie there was amongst us. At first neither David's parents nor I wanted to have any tea, we were too concerned for David's safety, too wound up and welled with growing grief. "Have some tea," Walker T insisted, "You'll need your strength. It's what David would have wanted."

His words resonated, I felt that he was right, since no doubt David would have wanted us strong and able to keep our spirits up. That is why we eventually drank the soothing tea that proved effective in bolstering us against the chill in the night air, as we awaited word.

Hope we'll hear something soon," I sighed, as the Changs nodded agreement.

By 1:00am it was clear that the firemen had done as much as they intended. It was with a heavy heart that we had to accept their conclusion that David was not underground. We dragged our heels, contemplating the worst as we headed back to the house, hoping perhaps to hear a shout, a whistle or even a faint call that would save us from our torment. But nothing came.

At first we sat on the verandah, Peter, Walker T, the Changs and me, The night was full of insect noises and moans from animals in the pastures. None of us said a word, not even when occasionally the stars and moon peeped out from behind cloud cover, leaving me to wonder if there might be rain. I longed for the familiar reassuring night noises of Northern Ontario, sounds that would have lulled me to sleep. I listened intently, though still there was nothing in the cool worrisome tropical evening to comfort me.

"Perhaps we should go inside," Walker T said finally, and we headed indoors into the living room, each of us choosing a comfortable chair to settle in. Peter was soon asleep in a chair by the window and Walker T dozed fitfully in his favourite high-back chair and the Changs reclined on the broad sofa bearing up each other in a tangle of arms. I propped myself up in the softest chair, though a comfortable bed upstairs awaited me.

Neither the Changs nor I slept that night, even the slightest night noise outside sounded like an alert, and every creak and sigh in the house's foundation signaled urgency. Even tree branches tapping against window panes created something of a troubling sensation.

The next morning, Elfrida arrived, and without question, prepared coffee, knowing without doubt, than none of us would feel like eating. Word had spread concerning David's disappearance.

"Thanks for everything." Mrs. Chang said as Elfrida poured, coffee after coffee. "We'll have to get home. What if David is there waiting for us."

"Darling if he was there, he would have called. Let's search outside before we leave here I'd feel better if I did that."

After coffee we searched outside, the once lush landscape seemed bleak and lonely since David wasn't there. Even the muddy grounds, including the heel marks and footprints from the crowd of the last evening, seemed melancholy, against the downtrodden shrubbery at the tunnel entrance. A caution barricade was set up there to prevent trespassing.

"There's no sign of our boy," David's father said in despair after an hour's search. "We might as well head home darling. Nothing left now but to pray."

After the Changs left the property, Peter too reluctantly took leave of us. Walker T and I were the only ones left in the house, for even Elfrida had gone, perhaps to gossip with other locals about the happenings at the Santiago Property. I couldn't face eating anything, and I didn't want to go back outside either, because the whole landscape seemed too empty, and besides, the light wind that blew, seemed to be saying, 'David's not here'

Eventually, Walker T went into the kitchen to boil an egg. I curled myself into a ball on the sofa, unaware that the dampness that flowed from my eyes settled into the sofa's fabric under my hot cheek. Life hurts I thought, as I drifted into a deep sleep, even as the fragrance of roses wafted in at the half open window. I didn't awake until the next day.

"Kathleen, wake up," Walker T said and through half-opened eyes I saw that he was brandishing a cup of steaming liquid. "You've been sleeping for more than a day young lady. Jonathan's here, he brought some chicken soup. You'll need to have something or you'll fade away."

"Is David here?" I spluttered pulling myself up, "is he alright?"

"There's no word as yet." Jonathan said coming into my line of vision. "We've sent out search parties all over the Santiago Property."

"I not hungry," I said weakly and I saw a look in Jonathan's eye that reminded me of the look father used to give me when he was determined about something. "Okay I'll have a sip." I said and I sat up feeling both weak and groggy.

"Come, come," Jonathan coaxed, "You'll have to drink the whole cup, you won't let us down will you?"

It took ages to sip the broth, and still Jonathan would wag his finger insisting that I drink more. When at last he was satisfied, he smiled. "Go upstairs and wash up and change. There's somewhere I think we should go. So shake the cobwebs out of your head, and think positive thoughts."

"Did anyone hear from David's parents?" I asked and my voice sounded as thin as a reed. "They've been calling," Walker T replied. "No doubt they are at their wit's end with worry."

"Hurry, Kathleen," Jonathan urged, "we're going to take a little trip in the truck. Walker T's volunteered to stay here in the house just in case, but Erasmus is coming along with us. He's outside in the jeep."

"Where are we going Jonathan?"

"No time for explanations girl, just you get yourself ready, the truck's purring outside.

In less than an hour I was sitting upfront in Jonathan's truck; intent on watching the narrow road zip by, as the fields, pastures, plantations and meadows, swiftly disappeared from view. I found it difficult to admit even to myself that I was still searching for David. A light breeze chased us as we travelled; wafting as fragrant as the sea, and sweet as sugar cane.

"So where are we going anyway?" I said, as we barrelled over bumps in the road. I barely even turned towards Jonathan. His long silences electrified the air, until finally, he cleared his throat.

"We're going to Rose Hall," he said, "we're taking a back road." Although his voice was steady, something in its timbre caused my heart to leap, and a sinking feeling settled in my gut.

"Why are we going to Rose Hall?" I blurted out quaking inside, and feeling completely helpless as the truck sped on, after all Rose Hall was the last place I would have wanted to go back to.

"Jonathan," I said feebly, "Remember what happened to Claudia? Shouldn't we steer clear of that place?"

I searched Jonathan's face, but he continued staring straight ahead. Not even the ghost of a smile, or any slight change of his expression invaded his countenance.

"We're going, because I remembered something Kathleen," he said, sagely and his eyes still never left the road for even a second.

Chapter 62

Back to Rose Hall Looking for David

Though we arrived at Rose Hall in a blaze of sunlight I felt there was something ominous in the atmosphere. We drove through the huge metal gates and the building in the distance stood ahead of us looking more imposing and foreboding than I remembered.

"Doesn't the house give you the chills Jonathan?" I said, hoping that with a change of heart, Jonathan might decide to return to Santiago House.

"To be honest," Jonathan said, "I wasn't thinking about going inside the house. We have other business here."

"So when are you going to tell me what's going on?"

Before Jonathan could respond, we were interrupted by a low buzzing sound.

"What's that?" I said. "Is it your pager?"

"Yes it's the pager, and it looks like Walker T 's calling. I'd better answer, something must have happened back at the property. Let's hope David's turned up."

I gripped the seatbelt tightly and held my breath, hoping against all hope that there would be good news about David.

"What's up Walker T? Jonathan said, pressing his phone close to his ear.

I wished I could hear what Walker T was saying, because there was no mistaking the horror in Jonathan's eyes as the conversation continued. "Stay indoors," Jonathan said firmly, "There's nothing we can do now. But we'll come back as soon as possible. Yes I'm sure more people will begin to congregate there. But someone should make sure they stay clear of the rubble. It's obviously not safe. We'll be finished here soon."

"What's going on?" I said, unable to curtail my curiosity, as Jonathan quickly pocketed his phone and the seriousness in his eyes alarmed me. C'mon Jonathan tell me." I said, and I was relieved when he pulled the truck over against a clump of bushes and turned off the engine.

"Let's step outside" he said, "you too Erasmus, you might as well hear this, because, as you know I was just talking to Walker T. He said that a few moments ago he was having a cup of coffee in the house, when a heck of a noise like rumbling thunder frightened him, and the house was shaking. He thought it was an earthquake. When he looked out the window he saw a humungous cloud of dust in the yard and somehow he knew that the tunnel must have collapsed, and the dust in the air was the residue. He closed all the doors and windows but he could still hear crowds of people running through the property coming to investigate. I warned him that things might not be safe, so as we speak he is calling emergency services. Personally I think that the underground foundations must have weakened and caused some sort of shift. I really hope that David wasn't down there, because he'd be a goner now for sure."

"So, shouldn't we be going back to help. It sounds horrible. Perhaps we should call David's parents or something?"

"We'll do that Kathleen, but just give me a second here; I can't have come all this way, and not do what I'd plan to do."

"But Miss Kathleen's right, somebody might need help back at the property."

"You could be right Erasmus, but as I said, emergency services have been called, and right now we have to do something we should have done already."

"Okay boss, whatever you say."

"What are we doing here? I'm dying to know Jonathan?"

"Okay, Kathleen I didn't want to say anything in case I'm wrong, but try to remember that I'm just acting on a hunch. If it was Gracie missing, I'd be going crazy doing everything in my power to find her. So just bear with me alright. And by the way, she's coming back; we're having a small wedding, no fanfare or anything, but enough about that, the thing to do now is to find David."

"Here?"

"Sure why not, David knew Rose Hall well didn't he?"

"So why'd he be here? Be serious!"

"Well as I said I have a hunch, but bear with me, let's search the bush-land anyway."

"But he couldn't be here, he'd have contacted us."

"True enough, but what if wasn't able to."

"Well boss, to tell the truth, I didn't think of that."

"See the bushes just over there, that's where we're headed."

"It looks more like a jungle Jonathan."

"Yeah it does."

"Well boss is a good thing I bring me machete, cause we can chop through some of the branches to get through."

"Are we allowed to do that?"

"I don't see nobody here to stop me, Miss Kathleen."

Erasmus chuckled, as he brandished his machete, and we all headed towards the tangled bush each with our own thoughts.

"I hope we won't have to split up," I said, as the shrubbery gradually became denser; it swallowed us up waist deep, then shoulders and all.

"It's kind of dark in here. Can you guys see anything at all?" I said sheepishly

"Just keep following us Kathleen," Jonathan murmured, "Erasmus is on a roll. Maybe as we go further in you'll start to recognize your surroundings, though it is probably different in the daylight."

"You don't mean to say that this is the bush where Claudia and I and ....?"

"Precisely."

Erasmus whacked away at overhanging vines and gangly overgrown weeds as we slowly penetrated the bush in the thickly forested land adjacent to the Great House. The land was permeated with yam vines, fruit trees, weeds and a tangle of trees that I didn't recognize, but still we pressed on.

"Don't be surprised if you see mongoose in here," Erasmus said with a grin, "sometimes they come looking for snakes."

"Are there snakes here Jonathan?" I said nervously pushing leafy branches from out of my face.

"Well Kathleen, Erasmus might be right, snakes could be here, not to mention scorpions, lizards and spiders. But if I were you I'd try not to think about that right now, just keep going."

"But are the snakes dangerous, and what about the mongoose?"

"Well Miss, the snakes them not too bad, but is the mongoose that is the fighters. People did bring them from India back in the old days to help kill snakes, but now the mongoose start taking over. But if you just stay clear of them, they won't bother you."

But how can I steer clear of them if I don't even know where they are I thought, and my every step became more cautious than the last, as silently we made our way through the bushes. I was taken by surprise when Jonathan finally spoke.

"Know what Erasmus," he said, "right now I don't want Kathleen thinking about snakes, mongoose or anything I just want us to concentrate on finding David." I couldn't have agreed more.

After a while I noticed that the ground was becoming steeper and it occurred to me that Erasmus was leading us into mountainous country. I began to regret wearing short sleeves since my arms were becoming more and more scratched and cut by brambles and thorns. "Can we stop for a moment?" I said, "My arms are bleeding." The moment I said that, I regretted it. I hoped that the two men wouldn't think that I was some sort of softie. "It's the blood, not the pain that bothers me. It might attract wild animals."

"Here's an old shirt of mine," Erasmus chuckled, barely looking over his shoulder "put it on. It will help sop up the blood." Then he stopped momentarily and threw a shirt to me that he had been carrying slung through his belt. I was so grateful for it, that I immediately pulled it on.

"By the way, Kathleen," Jonathan said, "this isn't Africa; there are no wild animals here, unless you want to count wild hogs and strays. We all broke into laughter, as we pressed on. There was no sign of another human but after a while we came to a clearing, and through the gap in the trees, we could see right down towards the Rose Hall Great House and the parking lot.

"What a view," Jonathan said, coming to stand beside me.

"It sure is," I said and as my eyes searched the landscape. It began to seem strangely familiar as the light and shade reassembled to jog my memory. "I know this place Jonathan," I said under my breath, "I remember it now."

Jonathan turned to me triumphantly, I saw that he was smiling, "So do you think you can find the opening now?"

"What opening boss?" Erasmus asked, as he put down his machete and wiped thick sweat from his brow.

"Kathleen knows what I'm talking about Erasmus, don't you Kathleen?"

"Yes."

"There's another entrance to the tunnel here Erasmus. But the thing is; I wasn't sure we'd find it again. Think you can Kathleen?"

"I think so…"

"Well you'll have to lead us now."

It was another ten minutes along the slope through some of the thickest vegetation we had encountered so far, before we came upon anything worth stopping for. The landscape had proved daunting, yet somehow familiar, and it inspired me to press on with the men following closely behind.

Then there it was, a large rock surface, worn and scratched deep, through years of exposure. It was partially hidden behind vines, moss and undergrowth. However, there was no doubt in my mind that we had finally stumbled upon the Rose Hall entrance to the tunnel that led back to Santiago House.

Jonathan was the first to try to push the large flat rock hoping to manipulate it into opening. "It's not budging," he said, sounding dismayed and disappointed. Erasmus stood by his side looking somewhat confounded by the problem, though I almost could see his brain ticking over.

"If this rock is really covering an opening leading back to Santiago Property, there must be a way to jimmy it open. Let all of we try pushing it together."

We expended a great deal of effort pushing against the stone, but it wouldn't dislodge not even when Jonathan charged at it with renewed vigour. He was obviously frustrated by the problem when he eased out his machete, and slid the sharp edge along the sides of the rock face where it protruded from the hillside. Even that was to no avail. I saw him cock his head as though listening intently.

"I hear something,' he said, his eyes glazed as he cupped his ear with one hand and listened.

"Is the sound coming from behind the rock?" I asked, all at once eager for good news, and scared that it might be bad..

"No Miss," Erasmus replied and my stomach tightened, "it sound like it coming from right over there. You must remember that as an artist I'm used to listening keenly, and observing things," he said pointing towards a tangle of bushes over the rise and with great strides he headed there, signalling us to follow.

"I hear something too! I gasped, as we approached a thick patch of thorn bushes. "But it sounds like the lonely call of a dove back home."

"That don't sound like no bird to me Miss, but you better be careful, makka can jook you!" Erasmus said not turning even once to look back at me, and I didn't have a clue what he meant, until Jonathan translated. "He means you should be careful, the thorns on the bushes are sharp."

Though I was extra careful, I hoped that we wouldn't end up finding nothing more than a wild hog or some other animal caught in the thicket. But despite my misgivings, we began running when a low mournful sound reached our ears. It increased in intensity as we drew closer, and I heard a sudden flutter of wings, though the birdsong and the rustlings in the tree branches above us continued. Jonathan immediately leaped over rocks, low brambles and thorn bushes, "that was a John crow!" he shouted, "something's dead over there, or the crows are waiting for something to die!" I almost fainted hearing Jonathan's words, and I momentarily stumbled. "You alright Miss?" Erasmus shouted but somehow I found my footing and continued on. "I'm alright." I panted.

Erasmus must have had legs like a gazelle, for he raced ahead of us with such power and grace, that he was the first of us to see David.

David was sprawled on the forest floor, practically surrounded by thorn bushes. One of his legs was twisted in an unnatural position, and it was clear that it was broken. His torso was partially resting on a large backpack that he always carried whenever he went down into the tunnels. I had often seen him bring back little artifacts in that very bag and it was the same bag he used to carry his lunch in. I wondered momentarily if crumbs from his lunch had attracted a trail of ants, because there were ants all around him. At first I was afraid to look too closely at him. I didn't want to see his pain, or perhaps see the pallor of death on his handsome face. But my efforts proved useless, there was no resisting him, and when finally I looked closely, I was startled. He looked awful. He was as pale as a corpse and reminded me of a broken rag-doll. But when I saw his chest heave, and I knew he was still alive, I was hysterical with joy.

"David, David!," I cried out, "thank God we've found you!" And I dissolved into a rush of grateful tears.

Chapter 63

Finding David

"We shouldn't move him ourselves," Jonathan said taking command of things, "seems he's broken some bones."

Erasmus stood guard as Jonathan made calls on his cell. "I'm calling an ambulance, they'll know how to lift him," he said, "It's a good thing the hospital's not far. "Want to act as lookout Kathleen?"

I didn't answer right away, preferring to remain steadfast beside David. "I need to be here." I murmured and I hardly heard a word of Jonathan's conversations, though he even called David's parents. I was too preoccupied with being down on my knees, with a cool hand barely touching David's hot forehead, and wanting more than ever to touch his dust-stained cheeks and whisper words of encouragement, but I was consumed with shyness in the presence of Jonathan and Erasmus, and in the end, restraint ruled.

"I've called Walker T," Jonathan said as he gently took my hand. "He's very glad that we found David, and he says that things are alright at the property, the dust is clearing. He also says that the tunnel has been sealed permanentl by the landslide. The emergency services are finished there, and people are dispersing. He said he wished he could be with us, so I've called father to pick him up, and meet us at the hospital."

"That's cool," I said, as I reached out tentatively and squeezed David's hand. "David knows I'm here," I said, "I know he does."

"You might be right," Jonathan smiled, "he looks more at peace now than when we first found him."

"Do you really think so?"

"Yes, I do."

"I hear the ambulance coming!" Erasmus shouted, "I'll go meet them, and bring them here."

"David," I whispered, the moment Erasmus was out of sight, "help is coming."

As I gazed at David, thoughts of my parents flashed through my mind. I wondered what they would have thought of him. I even wondered if they, though absent from this earth, had had anything to do with our finding him. It occurred to me that David was perfectly still, and not moaning. Why then did we hear such distinct moaning sounds earlier on?

I watched over him lying there disheveled and broken with only his beautiful hair to pillow him, and I was taken aback at how much he reminded me of Luke Whitefawn. Mamma, I said to myself, surely you and Papa, know that I might never feel for anyone, the way I feel about David. So please tell me if it was it you that signalled us with those moaning noises that sounded like a dove? Because if it was you I want to thank you from the bottom of my heart.

We followed the ambulance all the way to the hospital with the sound of the siren wailing as it cleared the way for us. On arrival, David was hurried inside the building on a stretcher steered by orderlies, and I caught glimpses of his parents practically running behind them down the hallway. By the time we caught up with them, David had been wheeled into Emergency for examination.

"Thanks so much. Thank heavens he is alive," his mother spluttered through tears, "he's unconscious so he's not in pain. They'll probably have to operate."

"Please accept my thanks too," his father said, standing sedately apart; as he wrung his hands nervously.

"He could have died up there alone… .you know that don't you? I love my boy very much. I hope he knows," his husky words came out with a choke.

It seemed like hours, though it was probably less than a half an hour later that a doctor Chin Loy came to the waiting area to tell us that David's x-rays showed that his leg was broken in two places and that he was having a high fever, and would have to be operated on immediately, and there wasn't one of us who wasn't frightened for him.

We were all still in the waiting area when Walker T and Jonathan's father arrived and to our surprise Mrs. Campbell accompanied them. "You alright, Kathleen?" she whispered, coming over to join me after a murmured conversation with the Changs.

"I have some soft mints Kathleen" she said, her breath warm on my cheek; "they'll help soothe you. I know how you must be feeling. I lost a boyfriend years ago to appendicitis, he was Chinese, not that his race matters but I've never been able to love like that again."

I sucked on the mint, and that solitary occupation felt like meditation. Walker T came and sat on the other side of me. "Young lady, it seems we're always here at the hospital," he chuckled, "perhaps we should ask them to set a room aside just for us. All joking aside, how's David?"

"We're still waiting to hear," I said softly, and I rested my head against Walker T's shoulder feeling at long last overcome with exhaustion. "I really care for him you know," I managed to whisper before nodding off to sleep

David's surgery went well; he was not allowed visitors except for his immediate family. I was disappointed, and felt left out but I didn't let it show. I waited for word from his parents.

"He's resting well," his father said. "He looked like a little boy," his mother sighed, "but he has a lot of stuff hooked up to him. My poor baby."

David would have been embarrassed to hear her refer to him as a baby, but I kept my thoughts to myself. Later that evening, Jonathan took us to his farm to spend the night there.

"Best to let the dust settle over at Santiago House before going back," he said, "it can be bad for the lungs you know."

Chapter 64

Here Comes the Bride

The next morning I awoke to hear Jonathan on the phone, and when I looked at my watch I saw that it was almost mid-day; Jonathan sounded elated and I wondered if there was word about David. I threw my covers off and approached the living room, Jonathan saw me and waved. "Morning," he said, a wide smile on his face as he gripped the phone.

"Kathleen," he said beckoning excitedly, "It's Gracie, she's here in Montego Bay. she wants us all to come get her; you, me, dad and Walker T. It's as if she's up to something but I don't know what it is. Perhaps she's bought something new, maybe a pet of some sort. Anyway I told her I could drop you off at the hospital to see David, and she said, not to worry, she'll meet us all at the hospital, she'll take everything there. I'm not sure what she meant but she said wear something nice, so if you and Walker T can get ready quickly, dad and I can head out."

"Where's Walker T?"

"He and dad are on the verandah discussing politics or something like that."

"Hungry? Grab some fruit and a drink of orange juice. Dad has some bun and cheese cut already, so just help yourself."

Jonathan hurried to his room to change out of his work

clothes. I grabbed a small mango, and two slices of bun with cheese. I quickly washed it all down with orange juice. Too bad I don't have a change of clothes I thought, and about fifteen minutes later Jonathan came into the room carrying a nice new sun-dress. "I had bought this for Gracie," he said, "she left it here, since the weather up in Canada is cold right now. Don't think she'd mind if I give it to you. She's never worn it."

"It's lovely," I said, "are you sure I can have it."

"Why not, I intend to buy many more for Gracie."

"You look spiffy Jonathan, Gracie will be pleased. Thanks for the dress"

In less than twenty minutes we were all ready, me with my mane of red gold curls, setting off the pink and green pastel colours that splashed across the dress, and wearing my black flip flops. I looked in the mirror and saw how tanned I had become. I even looked taller and leaner than before arriving in Jamaica, and come to think of it, I was well past sixteen now. Jonathan came up behind me. "You look stunning," he smiled and Walker T joined him, and grunted approval.

"Take your eyes off her," Jonathan's father joked, "we mustn't keep our Gracie waiting. Let's go."

We all laughed as we got into the car, and left the pickup truck behind. "The car's better for this trip," Jonathan said, with his hands firmly on the wheel. "It's more comfortable for all of us and besides, you know Gracie. She's probably got lots and lots of luggage."

What a cool morning it was; clouds that looked like sheep sailed above us as we headed down the long narrow country road. I craned my neck out the car window, as we went past Santiago House, and thought that the house looked lonely. Cradled amongst foliage with its impressive columns, I had to affirm that it was one of the nicest houses I had seen. There was very little evidence of the dust Walker T had told us about, since no doubt breezes coming in from the nearby sea had dealt with it effectively.

Out of the corner of my eye I noticed a huge scar in the landscape where the earth was raked over and mounded and I knew then that that was the exact spot where the excavation had taken place, and collapsed. The full gut-wrenching impact of the accident was not lost on me. With tears in my eyes I imagined what could have happened to David.

"All the treasures underground are lost forever," I whispered, " I'm not going to disturb anything again, the dead can rest in peace now."

"Hear, hear," said Walker T, and Jonathan's father seconded it. "Well, Santiago House can become a family home now, or a historical site." he said.

"It might best be a historical site." I said, "I can't really see any family wanting to live there with so many dead underground, a stone's throw from the house. It would be like living in a cemetery."

"You are one smart young lady," Walker T said, nodding approval, "I've always believed that about you."

"Well I have to agree with you," Jonathan's father said, "So I guess we all know that it's not just because she is good-looking, that David Chang cares for her."

"I already knew that," Walker T smiled.

"Walker T, trust me I've seen them together," chuckled Jonathan

"Enough already!" I grinned, feeling somewhat embarrassed to be the main topic of the discussion. "Let's just go get Gracie; we all know she's the love of Jonathan's life."

We arrived at the hospital well after two o'clock, since we stopped to get gas and bottled water, the day was that hot. As we walked into the hospital a smiling nurse with a clip board came up to us. "Are you visiting David Chang?" she said.

"Yes," I replied, feeling all at once nervous that something bad might have happened to David. "We are also meeting a friend here," I added, seeing that the nurse was still smiling congenially.

"Would your friend be called Gracie?" the nurse asked, "yes," I replied.

"Well she's in the main waiting area. Follow me."

"Thanks," said Jonathan as we followed behind the nurse and strode towards the room. When we entered the waiting area I saw that it was huge and attractive. There were bouquets of flowers everywhere. "Wow! It's nice here," I said under my breath, "and look; its French doors lead outside to a beautiful garden!"

"True enough but where's Gracie?" Jonathan said, "wonder if she went to see David?"

"Not likely," the nurse replied sounding mysterious, "he's still not allowed visitors, except for family. Gracie could be in the Ladies room, so feel free to enjoy the garden meanwhile."

When we wandered out into the garden, we saw that there were many other people there taking advantage of the sunny weather as they sat on lawn chairs on the manicured lawn.

"What's keeping her?" Jonathan said, and he began to pace alongside rows of coronations and zinnias.

"I'll go check the Ladies room." I said, and I went back into the building feeling almost as impatient as Jonathan.

I was taken by complete surprise, when who should I see hurrying towards me but Doctor Farthing! The moment he saw me he hurried even more, and gathered me in his arms laughing. "Good to see you again," he said.

"What are you doing here, are you here because of David?" I asked incredulously.

"No, not really," he replied, "But I've been to see him though. He's coming along nicely."

"Oh that's so good to hear, how's Claudia?"

"Well, you could ask her yourself, she's here." He laughed.

"She's here! Are you serious?"

"Yes, she's in the Ladies room."

What's going on? I wondered, when just then a woman I didn't know approached us. She was smiling broadly.

"Are you Kathleen?" she said.

"Yes, that's me."

"What a pleasure to meet you," she said, as she shook my hand. I'm Eva, Gracie said you'd be here. I'm sort of a friend. I met Gracie a few hours ago."

Eva was wearing an artificial orchid in her curly hair. I looked around the room hoping to be clued in as to whatever it was was going on. Eva followed my glance and smiled, "We have flowers for you," she said, "Gracie's wearing a white rose and Claudia chose violets, so I guess these daisies are for you. I'm helping them to dress. Look, Doctor Farthing chose a rose for his buttonhole. Isn't it pretty?"

"What's this all about?" I said, but Eva didn't answer. "Let's go see the rest of the garden," she said, as with arms intertwined with mine, we walked slowly admiring the lush garden. What a look of surprise was on the faces of everyone there, as we approached. Eva retrieved a mandolin from behind a leafy Oleander bush, and began to play softly. One or two more persons joined us seemingly attracted by the music, and it took me a moment before I realized that she was playing 'Here Comes the Bride.'

I looked around to see if there was a bride, and was in time to see an attractively dressed brown man, with a salt and pepper beard, step forward. From the look on his face it wasn't hard to guess that he was part of some sort of conspiracy.

"Is everybody ready?" he said and all of us present replied "Yes," though I had no clue what was to follow.

"Today we are gathered together to celebrate the marriage of our friends, Jonathan and Gracie. In case you're wondering I'm Joshua Reed, Justice of the Peace and I'm authorized to conduct this very special ceremony."

It is hard to imagine anyone more surprised than Jonathan. His jaw dropped open, and he started laughing, when Gracie entered the garden, from the far end, and practically ran into his arms.

"So, shall we do it? she said with a laugh, "sure, why not?" Jonathan replied, and when I looked around, I saw Walker T smiling, as was Jonathan's father.

Even the Changs came to join us, and I wished David could have been there too.

Beautiful mandolin music accompanied the vows, and I had never seen Gracie or Jonathan look as happy. Afterwards catered finger food was brought out into the garden, and the guests stood around enjoying jerk chicken wings, cocktail patties, shrimp on a stick, and pleasant conversations.

"They're giving all the flowers to the hospital." Claudia whispered, coming over to join me. "Doesn't Gracie look smashing?"

"She sure does, Claudia but when was all this planned?" I asked.

"It's been a few days now, but we've had to change the original location at the last minute. We heard David was in hospital and we knew you all would want to be at the wedding. So this is the compromise. Brilliant eh, and guess what? This is just between you and me but Cedric is going to see to it that you'll at least get a glimpse of David today."

"Really!"

"Yes, really."

While the festivities continued, I followed behind as Doctor Farthing stealthily led me through hospital corridors, staircases and a maze of adjoining rooms, until at last we stood in front of a door with a huge glass window.

"Have a quick look now," Doctor Farthing said, "David's in there."

I could hardly believe my ears even as I eased up to the window, and sure enough, David was there. He was in bed, sound asleep, one of his legs was elevated. He looked strangely vulnerable; his hair was slicked back exposing his face. My heart skipped a beat, there were tubes, and a drip attached to him, and his parents were with him. They must have slipped away from the celebrations, much the same as I had. After a few moments his mother, who must have sensed our presence, looked towards the door. She waved, and smiled and I waved back.

"We have to go now," Doctor Farthing said, giving my elbow a tug, "rules are rules." He sounded professional and there wasn't even a trace of a smile on his lips.

"Thanks so much, Doctor Farthing." I said, squeezing his hand and spontaneously kissing his cheek, "I am so happy," I beamed. There was no doubt in my mind that despite his demeanour, Doctor Farthing was pleasantly taken aback by my gesture.

"It's a pleasure," he said smiling, "now let's get back to the party."

We returned to the garden, to find Gracie and Jonathan surrounded by well-wishers.

"If we had known about this, we would have brought gifts." Walker T was saying as he hoisted a glass of champagne.

"I'll have you know that Jonathan is the best gift anyone could have brought me." Gracie laughed, and I embraced her as well as Jonathan, "Lucky ducks," I said, meaning it. "Congratulations."

"You're just in time for me to throw the bouquet Gracie grinned, "But every other woman here is married or spoken for. So I might as well just give it to you."

"Really?"

"Of course. Let's hope it brings you good luck. How's David?"

"I saw him just now, he was asleep. I couldn't go into the room, so I sent him good thoughts."

"You really care for him don't you?

"Yes."

"Well, we'll all have to think good thoughts for both of you."

"Thanks."

Jonathan handed me a glass of champagne. "Have a drink," he said, "it's a special occasion, and by the way, Gracie and I have booked rooms at a hotel here in town. We'll be on our honeymoon for a few days. Dad will be happy to take you and Walker T back to Santiago House later. Okay?"

"Cool."

I was about to say something else, when Claudia joined us. "Cedric and I are also staying in Montego Bay for another day.

We'd be delighted if Kathleen and Walker T would join us. We all could use a little pampering.

"That sounds inviting." Walker T smiled, "it's nice of you to think of us, but what do you think young lady?"

"That would be amazing. Thank you, are you sure you'll want us to join you?"

"Why ever not, Cedric and I spend loads of time alone together. We could use some company, and besides, after tomorrow we'll be going home to Morant Bay."

"Well now that that's sorted out," said Jonathan, "let's introduce Kathleen and Walker T to Gracie's parents."

Chapter 65

A Long Needed Respite

Later that afternoon, after we had settled into our rooms at the hotel I decided to go buy pajamas, a tee shirt and a pair of jeans, since there was a plaza near the hotel. It didn't take me long to get everything I wanted, but as soon as I came out of the store, there were beggars and market people outside jostling for my attention. Fortunately I remembered that Walker T had at one time told me that I should just keep walking and take no notice of such solicitations. Though I took his advice it didn't seem to have much effect. It wasn't until a formidable looking black woman who must have heard the uproar, came out from one of the stores, and she shouted at the peddlers in patois, that they dispersed.

"Thanks," I shouted to the woman, and she laughed. A big gutsy laugh.

"They won't bother you now or they'll have to answer to me." She said sticking her ample chest out as she marched back into the store. I looked around furtively and realized that the place was familiar, I was in the vicinity where Peter worked, and I decided to visit him.

When I walked into Peter's hotel from out of the hot sun I must have looked worn out after all the activity at the hospital.

"How can I help you?" a haughty sounding blond British receptionist said and effectively stopped me in my tracks.

"I'm here to see Peter, he works here," I replied, trying to sound equally as haughty.

"Peter the waiter! What has he done now? You couldn't be a friend of his, could you?"

I didn't even respond to her comments. I just stood my ground and waited, until finally she lifted the telephone and raised her eyebrow, as she made a call. After a few minutes, Peter came carefully down the stairs carrying a tray of glasses.

"Hi Peter darling; good to see you." I shouted with exuberance, all for the sake of the nosey receptionist.

"What a nice surprise," Peter said, catching on to my charade as he put down his tray, and came to hug me. "Good to see you Kathleen, darling."

I was sure the receptionist was scratching her head, as together Peter and I walked away out of earshot, and headed outside to the beach where we had first met. Neither of us could stop ourselves from giggling.

"So what was all that about?" Peter grinned.

"That woman was so uppity," I said, "I just wanted to bug her."

All at once, Peter became pensive, "Was she rude to you?"

"No not really, but she seemed really nosey if you ask me."

"Yes I suppose she can be, but enough about her I heard David's in hospital. He's lucky to be alive. I'm hoping to be able to visit him soon."

"You're right Peter, he's very lucky, and you know what, today I caught a glimpse of him. He was asleep; he didn't even know I was outside his room I think it really sucks that he can't have visitors."

"Well at least, you got to see him briefly, how come you're here alone?"

"Oh, I forget to tell you, Gracie and Jonathan got married at the hospital. Don't laugh, I'm serious, they had the ceremony out in the private garden. It was a very small gathering, but Claudia and her husband came, and they invited me and Walker T to spend a day or so with them at a hotel not far from here, so I thought I'd come to see you."

'Which hotel are you staying at?"

"It's The Shell Fish; it's small but comfortable."

"Oh I know the place. It has nice rooms and a lot of palm trees going up the driveway. Are Gracie and Jonathan staying there too?"

"Oh no," I laughed, "They are staying at the very posh Pride of the Caribbean Hotel. From what I hear it is absolutely luxurious with spas, gyms, games rooms, beauty salons and even tennis courts. Anyway I'd better get back to our hotel before everyone starts worrying."

"Well if you'll wait half a second I'll sign out and walk back with you. Sometimes things can get a bit rough even in these tourist areas."

"Really!"

"Well it's not as bad as some other places but there's always vendors pestering you to buy stuff and they could rip you off."

"Well Peter, Walker T once told me that I ever felt pressured like that I should just keep walking and not give in but you know what it doesn't always work, so I'd be glad if you walked with me."

"Okay that's cool, you mustn't forget that a young, foreign girl like you is an easy target."

"True enough, Peter, we'd better get going. Hey I just thought of something, why don't we deliberately walk through the reception area holding hands? That would really freak that stuck up woman out," I grinned.

We arrived at the Shell Fish Hotel, to find Claudia and Doctor Farthing sunning beside the outdoor pool. "Where's Walker T?" I asked, approaching them.

"Oh, he probably went to the plaza, he wanted to pick up a few things," Claudia said, easing back in her deckchair, "he should be back shortly."

"No worries I'll take my shopping upstairs. Want to come with me Peter?"

"Thanks Kathleen I have to get back to work, so I guess I'll see you another time."

"Sure will, you should come to Santiago House one of these days, okay. Thanks for walking with me, and I guess I'll see you soon."

Claudia turned on her side, "Honey," she called out, and Doctor Farthing immediately came over, kissed her and lathered her with suntan oil.

"Hi Peter," he said, momentarily looking up from his task, "Too bad you can't stay and have soft drinks with us on the patio."

"Work calls," Peter smiled, as he backed away. "Guess I'll see you all, when I see you. Have a safe journey back to St. Thomas."

"Thanks. Take care."

I watched Peter disappear through the crowded hotel lobby, realizing that without him there for company I would feel like an odd man out. How was David doing I wondered.

With eyes only for each other, Claudia and the doctor hardly noticed when I left the poolside. I took the elevator up to our room, all the while thinking how nice it would have been if David was there. But when I entered the immaculately decorated hotel room. I found it sterile and eerily silent, as though echoing my loneliness. I was so overwrought; I sat at the edge of my bed thinking about home. I was sick with longing as I thought of my parents and even Mrs. Allen who had been so kind to me. I don't know how much time slipped by, while I was sitting there before I finally put away my shopping and headed downstairs.

The lobby was empty. I felt conspicuous as my sandals slip slapped across the tiled floors. I looked around self-consciously and met the eyes of a friendly looking East Indian woman at the reception desk. She smiled and beckoned to me. "Hi, you're Miss Dunkley, aren't you?" she said, "We've been trying to reach you, there's a telephone message for you that hasn't been picked up."

"Oh thanks I was out shopping, and my friends are out by the pool," I said nervously, "But how did you remember my name?"

"It's a talent I have."

"No way."

"Yes, once I hear a name it sticks. For instance, your companions are Mr. and Mrs. Farthing and Mr. Robinson. Anyway, you can pick up your message here; it would save you going all the way back upstairs."

"Wow! Wish I had a talent like that and thanks I'll take the message here."

I tried to sound confident, though it crossed my mind that something might have happened to Walker T I felt unsteady as I watched the receptionist press the phone to her ear to retrieve the message. From where I was standing, I could hear a cheerful recorded voice coming through.

"Any idea who left the message?" I asked nervously.

"No I haven't a clue, but here it comes now. It was marked urgent."

Urgent!! I hadn't expected that. I almost toppled over in

sheer panic. Something terrible must have happened, I told myself. But how did anyone even know where to find me? Perhaps it was Doctor Farthing who had informed others.

"The person left voice mail," the receptionist said, "here's the phone."

"Thanks." I said, as I pressed the phone to my ear and clung to it like a barnacle. It was a surprise when I heard David's mother's voice, suddenly I was a bag of nerves. I hoped that nothing bad had happened to David. His mother's voice sounded emotional and she might well have been holding back tears.

"Kathleen dear," she said, hesitantly, "I'm really hoping you will get this message. I'm calling about David...He's awake.... He's going to be alright. He's tired and hungry and wants pumpkin soup. His dad's gone to get some. Did I mention he's been asking for you? He'll be allowed to see you in the morning."

When I returned the phone to the receptionist, tears were streaming down my cheeks, and she kindly offered me a box of tissues. "So sorry it's bad news Miss Dunkley." She said sympathetically lowering her voice to a hush. "It wasn't bad news," I replied, drying my tears. "It was the best news I could ever have."

"If you'd like to call the person back I'll connect you."

"Thanks but that's okay I don't need to call back. My friend David Chang is in the hospital but he's doing much better now. That was his mother on the phone with the good news."

"I'm glad to hear that it is good news."

"Me too."

"Hope you won't mind my asking but would that be David Chang from the Historical Society?"

"Yes that's David. Do you know him?"

"Course I know him, the whole of Montego Bay knows him, or say they do, but he and I went to school together. Everybody's talking about what happened to him. By the way if you see him, tell him Chelsea Nathan sent best wishes and also, tell him that he's very lucky."

"He sure is."

The next morning I was pleased when Claudia offered to give me a ride to the hospital. She suggested that I could stay with David for as long as I would be allowed, and she assured me that she would pick me up when I was ready to return to the hotel.

Over breakfast down in the cozy dining room of the Shell Fish, Walker T told us that he had run into some old friends from his school days. He said he was so pleased to see them, and he arranged to have lunch with them and would be away for most of the day.

"I'd better go upstairs to get ready," he said and there was no hiding the smiles in his cheeks. I had to wonder if his friends were female. "Young lady," he said, "I hope your visit goes well at the hospital, be sure to give David my regards and I guess I'll see you at supper."

"Thanks," I replied, "and I hope you'll have a good time with your friends."

As Walker T excused himself from the table, Doctor Farthing folded his napkin and stood up. "I should go for a walk along the beach front. I need to stretch my legs. Honey I'll see you when you come back," he announced.

"But I thought you'd be coming with us," Claudia said, sounding disappointed.

"Oh no," Doctor Farthing chuckled, and he bent and kissed

her full on the lips, "I really need to be away from hospitals, when I'm relaxing with my wife. Why don't I meet you at the tennis courts in an hour or so? You really don't know how much I am enjoying being here with you."

"Oh I know," Claudia laughed seductively and he kissed her hand and walked away from the table already looking lonely and when I looked over at Claudia she seemed to be just as lonely, and I envied them.

"Kathleen," Claudia said solemnly, "if it wasn't for the thing with the White Witch I might at one time have considered living in Montego Bay. I can see that Cedric would enjoy it here. It is a faster pace and he'd have access to so much more than just relaxation. I think he seems extra attentive here too, but maybe that's because sometimes he and I get so caught up in work at home, that we are often too tired to pamper one another. Don't get me wrong though, things are fine between us. We are still very much in love. I bet you couldn't help but notice how affectionate he is, he kisses me every opportunity he gets?"

"You're right I've noticed."

"Well I'm sure that one day you'll find someone. How old are you anyway? I remember you had a birthday some months ago."

"I'm well over sixteen. Do you think I'm too young to fall in love Claudia?"

"Not at all Kathleen; love doesn't have boundaries like that, but to be honest I've never loved anyone the way I love Cedric, and look at me I'm no spring chicken."

"Well you aren't old either. I'm so glad for you, and it's clear Doctor Farthing thinks you're hot."

"It's not just that Kathleen," Claudia laughed, "the thing is, we're having a baby. Cedric is over the moon."

"Cool, that is so exciting," I said, though I could hardly believe my ears, no wonder Claudia seemed to have an extra glow and it wasn't just her hair and her skin.

I've been eating healthy," she smiled, following my glance.

"I'm so happy Claudia, congratulations. Let me give you a hug."

Chapter 66

Finally
a Visit with David

Half an hour after our conversation, Claudia and I drove to the hospital. The sky was cloudy and already there were a few drops of rain. "Doesn't look as though Cedric and I will be playing tennis today," she said, "perhaps this is the perfect day to indulge in some indoor games." We both laughed at her double meaning, as she parked the car in front of the hospital. "Let me know whether or not they'll let you see David. I'll wait here."

"Okay I will, thanks for everything."

Armed with a smile I entered the hospital heart pounding, not noticing anything or anyone as I headed for the information desk.

"I'm here to visit David Chang," I said hesitantly and the male attendant looked at me askance then immediately began tapping something out on his computer. His bushy brows were knitted so fiercely together that I thought perhaps he was bent on denying me the privilege. But when he briefly looked up and forced a smile I heard him say: "Room 306" though he continued to stare at the computer screen as he continued: "You might want to use the elevator, though there is another route."

"Thanks I'll take the elevator," I said, "But I have to go tell a friend what I'm doing before I go up."

Claudia was almost as happy as I was and she blew kisses at me as she drove away. What an amazing mother she will be I thought, as I retraced my steps. But I might as well have had wings on my feet, because I rushed back into the hospital, more excited than I dared admit. There were people everywhere, nurses, doctors, orderlies, visitors and patients but the only thing on my mind was David Chang.

"Going up?" a woman said as we both stepped into the elevator, "yes," I replied, barely looking at her and keeping my eyes on the door. "So am I," the woman said. We were alone on the elevator for less than a minute but it wasn't until she stepped out on to the floor below David's, that I noticed that she was wearing riding gear. I immediately peered out the elevator door to get a better look at her but there was no sign of her, and as far as I could see there were no doorways, along the empty corridor.

The elevator door closed slowly, my heart pounded, when I finally approached David's room, totally forgetting about the woman on the elevator.

I walked into the room and saw that David's parents were already there. He was sitting up having breakfast.

"Good morning Kathleen, how nice that you could come," Mrs. Chang said with a smile, as she rose from her chair to greet me. Mr. Chang came and hugged me, then offered me his chair. "Good to see you," he said huskily.

David immediately pushed his tray aside, his eyes bright as they met mine. "Come here," he said and I bent and hugged him, and he pecked my cheek. "I've missed you," he whispered, "can't wait to get out of here."

"Doctor Farthing says you'll need lots of rest, be prepared to be here for a while," I teased and David took my hand and held me fast. "Please sit here," he said pointing at the bed, "You don't know how glad I am to see you."

"Kathleen," his mother said, "David's doctor has told him the same thing you just said about needing rest, but he's determined to be up and about."

"Mama," David laughed, still holding tightly to my hand, "you should know how I hate being helpless, you know exactly where I got that trait."

"I sure do sweetheart," Mrs. Chang chuckled, "you didn't inherit it from your father, since you and I both adore looking out for him, we are at least even."

Mr. Chang drew her to him and looked at her adoringly. "David my son, you can see why your mother and I get on so well, we need each other. I think you are beginning to develop that trait, regarding a certain young miss"

"I realize that dad."

We all laughed, though I must have been blushing redder than a beet."

"Know what, let's go walk in the garden darling," David's mother said, taking her husband's hand and gently tugging him towards the door, "we need to give the young people space."

Mr. Chang caught my eye and he looked quite mischievous, "better still," he said, "why don't these young folks give us space darling. I'll take you shopping, even though I hate shopping, and then we can do lunch, and who knows what that might lead to afterwards."

"Dad!!" said David in mock horror, "don't talk like that in front of company!"

I immediately burst out laughing; it was a long time since I had laughed so hard.

"So now you can go shake up the bed," Mr. Chang said with a grin and it set me off laughing again.

The moment David's parents left the room, David hugged me, as close as he possibly could. He felt so warm, I wondered if he was feverish. "I've wanted to do that ever since you walked in." he said.

"I felt the same way," I murmured, as I buried my face in his hair. "Have you been alright Kathleen? You seem tired," he whispered, his eyes wide with sincerity.

"I'm fine. It's just that I missed you so much."

"I missed you too, and by the way I heard Gracie got married. I'm glad for her. Jonathan must be thrilled."

"They were both ecstatic, and when I was at the wedding I kept wishing you could be there."

"Is that so?"

'Yes, nothing's that great without you, you know that already don't you?"

"I feel the same way about you."

"Buddies for life?"

"Sure."

I was about to say something else, when a nurse burst through the door, looking all businesslike. "Time for your medication Mr. Chang," she said, "it will make you quite drowsy though."

"Should I leave then?" I asked, barely hiding my disappointment, and slowly easing myself from off the bed.

"You don't have to leave," the nurse said, "You're welcome to have a seat on one of the chairs beside Mr. Chang's bed. He should be awake in about an hour."

"Thank you'" I said and I couldn't bear to watch her administer David's antibiotic medication by needle. From the corner of my eye, I saw that she carefully took his temperature and his pulse, then plumped up his pillow. "There's still a bit of fever," she said, addressing him, "and your pulse is a bit worrisome but that might be because your girlfriend's here. So you'll need to take it easy, no fooling around okay."

I was about to say something in response when the nurse winked at me and smiled, "Just joking." she said, "Mr. Chang couldn't fool around even if he wanted to. Not with that leg anyway. But no doubt, we have to get that fever down." Then with a toss of her hair, she closed the door softly and stepped out into the corridor, leaving me alone with David.

Chapter 67

David's Story

David fell asleep almost immediately. At first, all I did was stare at him, mesmerized by his bone structure, the planes along his cheeks, his jaw, as well as his eyes. I longed to trace the lines formed by his lips as they curved ever so gently. His closed eyes appeared more oriental in sleep, than when awake, and it served to bring out the handsomeness I first found in him. My eyes wandered with delight to his brow, dark against his pale skin, then momentarily rested on his wayward locks that so often would have fought to cover part of his face. Reluctantly I averted my gaze; wondering what David would have thought of such scrutiny.

Left to my own devices I noticed a handful of magazines on his bedside stand, perhaps left there by his mother. I flipped through them without much interest. After a lonely while I heard a sound at the door, my heart was glad for company. I looked at the door expectantly, noticing that the doorknob was turning. Perhaps the nurse is coming to check on things I thought. I sat perfectly still, as the door slowly opened and almost jumped out of my skin, when I found myself face to face with the woman from the elevator!

"Need help?" I said, sounding calm and belying the bag of nerves I had become. Though her eyes never met mine I recognized her in an instant. She was the same woman I had seen at God's Waterway!

"Is he alright?" she said, her voice lilting, reminding me of an Irish accent. Her eyes were bright as though on fire, as her hand grasped the doorknob. Her pale face clouded over with a faraway expression. Never once did she remove her gaze from David.

"He's fine," I replied, trembling, hoping she wouldn't notice.

"It's your turn to take care of him," she said, her voice harsh and guttural chilled me to the bone. A salt-tinged scent like that of seaweeds wafted into the room. I quickly turned aside, to check on David. In that mere blink of an eye, the woman vanished from the room..

I was horrified and fearful of leaving David's side, two long hours passed before he finally stirred.

"Kathleen," he smiled as his eyes fluttered open, "you're still here."

"Yes."

I reached for his outstretched hand. "How are you feeling?"

"A bit thirsty I suppose, but there's juice in that bag over there by the table beside my backpack. Mum brought some."

"Are you sure you're allowed to have that?"

"Yes, I need lots of fluids. It's really just flavoured water anyway."

"David," I said, drawing my chair even closer to him, "There was a strange woman in here...I think it was Miss Palmer."

"Where'd she go I wanted to thank her."

"What do you mean thank her?"

"I'll tell you as soon as I get that drink. I'm parched"

"What bag is it in, your backpack or the shopping bag beside it?" I said nervously. My thoughts were in a state of confusion and alarm. Why would the White Witch come into David's room I wondered?

David sat up as best he could and almost drank the whole bottle of flavoured water. "Take it easy," I said, "you don't want to get sick or something."

"I'm already sick," he laughed, "please come sit near me. I need to tell you what happened that night."

I sat gingerly on the edge of his bed, hoping the nurse wouldn't return and assume that I had spent the last two hours sitting there.

"Don't worry Kathleen," David grinned they won't be coming to check on me for another hour or so. By the way, do you know that your hair looks amazing. I'd never get tired of looking at you."

I didn't know what to say. I looked into his eyes and saw sincerity.

"I'm listening," I said, feeling contented.

"Let me start at the beginning," he said in a low voice, "it was because of you that I went back into the tunnel."

"How's that, you can't be serious, can you?" I said, reaching for his hand.

"You mightn't have known it Kathleen but ever since I met you I've admired you. I was so afraid of my feelings for you that I once told you that I'm five years older than you or something like that." It was my way of distancing myself in order to put a barrier against getting involved. I have to now confess that I'm twenty, and finished college early."

"Really?"

"Yes." David replied, as he ruffled my hair playfully with his free hand, "Can you forgive my stupidity. You're actually going on seventeen Kathleen, that's not too much of a gap is it?"

"So is that why you seemed so oddly cold sometimes?"

"I suppose so, Kathleen, I had no choice; I hoped that you didn't find it too off-putting. Trust me; I never intended it to be like that. People could easily have said that I was 'robbing the cradle' but you are no baby."

"I did wonder about you David?"

"Bear with me Kathleen, the last thing I wanted was to alienate you. I thought people might gossip about our ages. I've been surprised that no one has mentioned it, perhaps it is because we were perceived as just friends."

"Well friend, you're not that much older than me," I fired back with a grin.

"You're right, I just didn't want to take any chances, not with someone I care about."

"Know what, you are a lot like your father. However, shouldn't you be telling me about what happened that night?"

"Did anyone ever tell you that you are a wonderful distraction?"

"No."

"I'll never forget that night Kathleen. I was so excited when I was coming back to the house with Peter. He was particularly proud of the shots he had taken of the artifacts underground and we briefly discussed the possibility of putting together a showing of his work. He mentioned that he had a friend who would enlarge his photos to make them more for visually appealing. I was pleased, since I had written reams of notes concerning those very artifacts and we agreed it would make a perfect script for a public viewing.

As I drew close to the house it occurred to me that I should have at least brought back something for you. I imagined that you would have been happy with whatever I brought. Then again, there was this certain something that nagged at me."

"Oh David, you should know that you don't need to give me things to make me happy. I remember Gracie saying that Jonathan is the best gift she could ever have, and as far as I'm concerned it holds true when it comes to you."

"Anyway, there I was, with you on my mind, when I told Peter to go on ahead, because I needed to get something from underground. I could see that he was reluctant to let me go back alone but I assured him that it was alright."

When I got back down into the tunnel I started to lose confidence I kept thinking about the creepy room with the slave bones. To be honest, it was a bit disconcerting but I didn't want to turn back. When I finally reached Santiago's room I went inside with my flashlight and I quickly found what I was looking for. I stuffed it into my backpack as carefully as I could and I was about to leave, when I heard a tremendous noise like a great rumbling roar. It really frightened me. So I ran towards the door, only to find that it was jammed. I couldn't open it no matter how hard I tried. Then out of nowhere I heard a voice. It sounded like a child's voice. At first it was just a whisper but it grew louder and suddenly the door burst open. I was taken off guard to see a small blond boy standing there. I looked down the tunnel in the direction I had come from. I saw a wall of fire. Kathleen. It was like being in some kind of hell. I tried to move but my feet wouldn't budge. It was as if I were glued to the ground and I started to panic. Suddenly the boy screamed, 'Help me!' and he grabbed my hand and looked into my eyes. He looked so trusting that my feet, that had been glued to the ground, began to move, though my heart told me that there was nowhere to run to. I even foolishly considered riding out the fire by staying in the room but the boy tugged at me so hard he pulled me right out into the tunnel. 'Run!' he shouted, 'Run!' and he never once let go of my hand, as together we barrelled down the tunnel in the opposite direction. My strides were much longer than his, so I swooped him up and carried him.

I had no idea who he was, though I thought perhaps he might be some tourist kid who had wandered into the shaft. Then again, there was something far too old-fashioned about him, something that seemed to suggest that he had wandered in from the past.

I was so concerned about him, that even as we ran I was careful with him, and jumped over objects in our path, holding him extra tightly against me. I remember reassuring him over and over and telling him not to be afraid, though he never once whimpered. I felt that despite the odds, he somehow knew that I would get him out of there.

"Oh my God David, what a nightmare I would have freaked out with the wall of fire chasing me and all that."

"Kathleen, that boy gave me purpose. I sensed that despite his size, he was bright and although he didn't say much, he seemed to know the underground passageways much better than I. I didn't even have time to panic; I just didn't want to admit defeat, not even with the fire at my shoulder and the boy believing in me.

He was light as a feather Kathleen and when he started speaking he kept urging me on, warning me against turns to avoid and doors that led nowhere. Yet something inside me would not be deceived even by the circumstances. What I'm trying to say is that even though I was swathed in fear and sweat I did not lose my reason, and in an epiphany I suddenly knew without doubt that the boy in my arms was Santiago!

"That's exactly what I thought David, I have seen him myself, and he's exactly as you describe. I was never afraid of him although I know he's been dead for many years. Strangely enough I always felt that there's something very wanting in him. The poor boy never had the love he deserved."

"Yes, Kathleen, you might be right, and I've come to realize that the legs that outran the fire were his, not mine. Sure I held him tight, but still, as he slumped against me as though exhausted I had no idea how to escape, yet the feet under me led me to all the right places, and I heard myself promising him blindly that we would escape. 'Don't worry little man,' I kept saying, trying to soothe him, though my eyes were filled with smoke and tears. I don't know how it was, but somehow, some hidden strength bore us both to the locked door at the other end of the tunnel. When I got there Kathleen I was so afraid that if I didn't make it out, the news of my passing would be painful for you. Then all of a sudden I heard your voice, telling me that you care about me and it gave me new determination to escape.

I even thought of Claudia and the nuns and because of their influence I said a prayer of hope, as the terrible roaring and rumbling and the burning heat drew closer. 'Kathleen!' I cried out in desperation, thinking that those words might be the last I would say on this earth. I was completely surrounded by thick clotty darkness, because in my flight I had lost my flash light and didn't realize it until that very moment. I was even more convinced that it was the boy that me and because of that revelation, I felt somewhat elated and somewhat blessed to be alive. despite my short-lived ecstasy. I stumbled over a large protruding jagged rock that jutted up through the dirt floor. I lost my balance, and fell into a heap, and I heard a loud resounding crack echo in my ears. I knew even then without doubt, that I had broken my leg. I couldn't move and I couldn't see, but worst of all, my arms were empty. I'd lost my grip on the boy. I flailed helplessly in the darkness and awaited death.

To my surprise I heard footsteps approaching and I saw a tiny light in the darkness. "Who's that?" I said, feeling sure it was the boy. There was no answer. I felt a pair of strong hands under my arms hoist me up and carry me. I tried to see the person's face but the darkness would not allow it. Then to my surprise the locked door that I had come upon opened slowly, and a rush of sweeter air hit my face, and I was whisked down a dimly lit corridor. Again I turned my head to see if I could see the face of the man that rescued me, but I was shocked beyond belief, because even in that dimness I could see that it was no man! The face belonged to a beautiful woman. Her face reminded me of your extraordinary Irish face, but then it morphed into Claudia's face. I knew it wasn't her either. It was the White Witch of Rose Hall!"

"Oh my God, that's too freaky"

"Yes Kathleen, it was freaky and she was as strong as a horse. She carried me as though I weighed no more than a matchstick. I knew I was at her mercy. My fear subsided under the weight of her gentleness, and I saw her smile as she easily pushed aside boulders, that gave way, as she opened up an exit to the fresh air outside.

"How wonderful that night air was, and how loud the insects were. The place where she placed me was the softest most comfortable spot in the world.

"I must have passed out though, because the next thing I remember is waking up to a blinding pain that threatened to knock me out again. Sunlight was bright on my face. It was a hot sticky day and my fingers, caked with dirt and dust were trying desperately to find a hold. You've never heard such loud birdcalls or such a scurrying in the bushes, and even the ants that came after crumbs in my pack, seemed to noisily navigate the gravel, the twigs and the grasses. My every breath seemed caught in the air as I wrestled with pain. I retreated into sleep, though I constantly awoke to face another threshold of agony. I have no idea how much time passed, while I was there. But when I opened my eyes in the bright lights of the hospital, I thanked the Lord, and the boy, and Annie Palmer for saving me. I couldn't wait to see you and my parents again. I am not the same person I was before this incident happened. Because now I want to make sure that my family and friends and you too Kathleen, know how much I love you all."

David closed his eyes and fell asleep again after telling me his story I remained steadfast at his side lovingly holding his hand. I did not let go of him, until there was a soft knock at the door.

It wasn't the woman in the riding gear, as I had feared. It was Walker T.

"I knew you'd still be here young lady. How's David?" he said thrusting a bunch of flowers into my hand. "These are from us, for David."

"He's asleep, thanks for getting flowers. I was so anxious to see him I forgot to bring anything."

"I'm sure he didn't mind one bit, seeing you is all that mattered, but did he have anything to say about that night? How's his leg?"

"We had a long conversation. I think he's improving and Walker T, he cares for me."

"That's good, I hope you told him how you feel about him. There's no better medicine young lady."

"Oh, he knows I'm sure he does, he was talking about his ordeal in the tunnel and how he managed to get out at the other end of it, at Rose Hall."

"Well, he and I have something in common. To be honest young lady I'm glad that tunnel has caved in and is no longer accessible."

"I'm glad of it too. I for one, will not be asking for it to be excavated. I've decided it would be best if Santiago House becomes a place to permanently house and display the artifacts we previously recovered, as well as the photographs Peter took down there."

"Good thinking young lady. Do you realize that Peter's photographs are one of a kind. are priceless. They are proof positive of a missing part of Jamaican history that can never be recovered."

"But Walker T, I have been wondering, what would happen if the Rose Hall foundation tries to reopen the tunnel entrance that is on their property?"

"Well, they don't know about it, and they won't know about it. David only has to say that he can't remember exactly how he got to Rose Hall. As far as I know, no one else knows about that entrance. It's merely a legend, wouldn't you say?."

"Walker T, David just told me that he thinks that both Santiago and the White Witch helped him to find that entrance."

"Well I'm positive that they helped him. But knowing the local people as much as I do, I hardly think they'll want to get involved with stirring up old ghosts and things like that, even though half of them claim not to believe in the supernatural. That is why I have a feeling that we can count on things being left well enough alone."

"I hope you're right," I said.

"Another thing is, we have to look at things realistically young lady, the government here doesn't have the kind of money to invest in such a venture and neither do we. Besides, there is no doubt that the fire destroyed everything. The whole place is nothing but soot and ash. I don't think anyone would be willing to invest in excavations. It would be a complete waste of money."

"By the way Walker T, weren't you supposed to be having lunch with friends?"

"I moved up the time, so that I could come see David. My friends and I are going to meet after two o'clock instead of noon. I just had to make sure David is alright, not just for your sake, although that is part of it but it's because I have great respect for the young man."

"I'm glad to hear that but aren't there ladies waiting for you Walker T?"

"How'd you know?"

"You look so spiffy?"

When I said that, Walker T threw back his head and laughed out loud, "You're starting to sound Jamaican, young lady. But anyway, the ladies are elderly, they sang in the church choir when I was at school, and did I mention that their husbands will be joining us. One of them referred to me as a youngster. Can you beat that?"

Chapter 68

The Morning's Light, the End or the Beginning

David awoke in about half an hour, when he opened his eyes and saw that I was still there, there was no mistaking his pleasure.

"Walker T's here too," I whispered, and he raised himself up on to his elbows. "Good to see you man," he said, "thanks for coming."

"Likewise," Walker T replied as he shook David's hand, his voice was almost a whisper, and there was a smile in his cheeks. "No more running around at night for you David. But seriously, you'll have to get well soon, you don't know how much this young lady has been missing your companionship."

"No more than I've missed her," he fired back, "You might want to take care of her, until I get out of here. I hope you're not going back to Canada anytime soon."

"It would be a pleasure to take care of her David. I'm sure you already know that our young lady has a mind of her own. She's independent, and very special. But as I said, you know that already. We're not going back to Canada yet. I'll stay here as long as she needs me to be here. You have to remember that now that

Gracie and Claudia are married, Kathleen and I would be alone out at Santiago House. I don't think either she or I, are keen on being out there anymore. We most likely will be occupied with finding a new place to call home right here in Montego Bay. Perhaps near you. But the most important thing now is, for you to get well.

I must have blushed beet red, though I enjoyed the attention, as well as the reassuring words. I watched with pleasure as David put two fingers on his lips, and affectionately blew me a kiss.

"That's enough of that," I said, with a laugh, somewhat embarrassed by Walker T's chuckling.

"No need to be embarrassed young lady," he said under his breath, "if it were me and my Marceline, I would have expressed myself in exactly the same manner as David. But anyway, I'd better be going along to meet my old friends. They'll be wondering if I fell off the edge of the earth. So young lady, I'll see you later at the hotel. Take good care David." Walker T smiled; winked, then edged towards the door.

"Don't go yet." David called out. "Before you go, I just want to say thank you. You've been kind and always generous with your time. I have a lot to learn from you. I have a feeling that Kathleen will agree with me, wouldn't you Kathleen?"

"I doubt any of you'll believe it," I said, "but as far as I'm concerned, you and Walker T, are at the top of the list of the finest men I've ever met, not to mention my dad of course."

Both of them laughed, and I couldn't help but wonder what kind of man my brother Gavin would have been, had he lived. I also wondered if Luke Whitefawn had loved my mother. It was clear that I was no longer the child I once was. I had come to realize that things are not always as clearly defined as black and white.

Blossoming into womanhood, I now saw the world through different eyes. Realizing that I could forgive, and understand mother's illicit passion, and yet still love father, a quiet man, not unlike David.

After Walker T left us, I sat on the edge of David's bed, contemplating the past, and perhaps looking more pensive than David had ever seen me.

"What's the matter Kathleen? he said, "cheer up, remember I said there was something I wanted to show you. Well this is a good time for you to see it."

David looked pleadingly at me, as he squeezed my hand affectionately, and I was thrilled.

"So what did you want to show me? Is it the messages your parents wrote on your cast?"

David didn't answer right away; he reached for me again, and gently stroked my hair. His eyes were tantalizingly mysterious. I could tell that perhaps he had something up his sleeve, but I couldn't even imagine what it could be. I was about to rephrase my question, when we both heard a soft knock at the door.

"Come in," I called out, half expecting that it was the nurse I had seen earlier. But it wasn't her, it was Peter."

"Hey man, come in and join us," David called out when he saw him, and Peter for some reason unknown to me, came stealthily into the room carrying a bunch of flowers, and a large plastic bag with something inside that emanated such a delicious aroma, that it made me realize that I was hungry.

"This is contraband," Peter whispered with a grin on his face, as he placed the bag on the side table. "How's it going man? You look good, but I shouldn't be surprised, not with Kathleen here and all."

"Thanks for coming man, did you take the afternoon off?"

"Yeah I took two hours off the moment I heard that you're allowed visitors, and by the way, this is for us."

"What's it man? It smells delicious, sort of like stew peas."

"No, it's red pea soup. I don't think we're allowed to bring food in, so maybe we'll have to drink it fast. I asked the cook to add extra salt beef and spinners, so it is stacked, and I brought paper bowls and plastic spoons, so we're all set"

"Thanks man, how'd you guess I was feeling for something just like that? You've saved me from having to eat the hospital's bland food. I bet it would have been milk, chicken breasts with mashed potatoes that taste like boiled newspapers."

We were all laughing ourselves silly when the nurse unexpectedly walked in on us. She wrinkled her nose and made a face. 'Boiled newspapers eh?' she said, "It just so happens that protein and calcium is good for you, especially now, but you know what? I'm going to pretend that I didn't smell, or hear anything about that soup, though it is against regulations. I didn't see it, and that's the truth isn't it? But first things first, let me just check your pressure, and take your pulse Mr. Chang. And since your girlfriend is still here, there's no doubt in my mind that your pulse will be racing. I'll be sure to cancel your chicken leg and mashed potato lunch as soon as I leave here."

"She's not a bad sort," David said, as he drank the last of his soup, and true to her word, the nurse left us to ourselves without further interruption.

"That soup was like unquestionably the best red pea soup I've had since coming to the island." I said, literally smacking my lips, wishing there was enough for seconds.

"Yes, that was really good," David said, leaning back on his pillow, "I wholeheartedly agree with Kathleen. Did you make it man?"

"Me! No, I couldn't even cook a fly. Debbie made it for us, because she couldn't come herself. She's a great cook eh?"

"She sure is, don't forget to thank her for us. I wasn't looking forward to the food here at all. But you already guessed that, didn't you?" David grinned. "By the way, I was just about to show Kathleen something before we all got carried away with the soup, and the nurse, and all that."

"Well, this is a good time to show her whatsoever it is; since there'll probably be more interruptions later. Should I leave the room or what?"

"It's nothing private Peter, you can stay. But do me a favour, could you pass me my back pack, it's over on that table near the closet."

"Sure, man."

I watched with bated breath as Peter passed the backpack. David carefully zipped it open. His eyes were fixed on mine, as he reached inside, and pulled out a long thin rolled up canvas. "Open it Kathleen," he said huskily, and though my hands were trembling, I took it from him hardly daring to breath, as I gently unfurled the canvas. I almost fainted with delight, seeing what I held in my hands.

My gasp of amazement was audible. I hugged David, and kissed his cheek. The painting I held in my hand was none other than the beautiful painting of a large mansion done by the boy Santiago, so very long ago. It was the very painting I had first admired in the dreary room underground.

"This is just exquisite," I said, reverently. "Are you sure I can have this? It is even more awesome in the daylight."

"Kathleen, this painting is what I went back for that night. It was on your property, so it is rightfully yours," David said. "I couldn't have thought of a better gift to give to someone I love."

I could hardly believe my ears, I wanted to say something, but was tongue-tied. 'David loves me', I kept repeating in my mind, and all at once, it was the very best day of my life.

"Look Kathleen," Peter said, bringing me back down to solid ground, "There's something written on the back of the painting!"

"Is it an inscription Peter?"

"Perhaps it is, but let me have a look," David said. I turned the painting around, and David and I read the words, though I didn't recognize a single word. "What does it say?" I asked eagerly. Is it Spanish?"

"Yes, it looks like Spanish," Peter said leaning closer. Our heads were together when David read the words out loud: 'El cielo morado en la luz del amanecer'

"What the heck is that?" Peter said knitting his brows, and when I searched David's face for answers, I saw that he was in deep concentration. "Let me try to translate," he said, squeezing my hand affectionately, "My high school Spanish is a bit rusty but I think it says: 'Purple skies at morning's light'."

End

Acknowledgements:

Thanks are due to Irish actor Brian Mac Gabhann aka
Brian Smith, who encouraged me to write this novel.

Thanks to talented Jamaican Fine Artist Barbara
Reynolds, who suggested my inclusion of the White
Witch in the story.

Thanks to the staff of the Annette Street Library for
their continued enthusiasm for my work.

And thanks to my three children with Irish roots,
David, Shannon and Rory.

A Short Author Bio:

Bernadette Gabay Dyer was born in Kingston, Jamaica, and has lived in Toronto, Canada for several years. She is a poet, a storyteller, an artist, a playwright and an author.

Her work has been anthologized widely and her short stories and poetry have been published in Canadian literary magazines, as well as the University of Miami's journal, and London England's St. Mary's University's *Wasafiri*. Her Short story collection is entitled: *Villa Fair*.

Recently, her poetry was included in the collection, *TAMARACKS Canadian Poetry for the 21ˢᵗ Century*, published by Lummox Press in the United States. Her science fiction short story: "Just A Single World", was published in Polar Borealis Press in Canada, and her historical fiction novel, *Chasing the Banyan Wind* was published by LMH Publishing in Kingston, Jamaica.

Bernadette works for Toronto Public Libraries, and is also the facilitator for an Open Mic Program, that gives an opportunity for writers of all genres to share their work with an audience.

Bernadette is the illustrator of the book covers for all three of her previous novels:

Waltzes I Have Not Forgotten (Historical fiction)
Abductors (Science fiction)
Chasing the Banyan Wind (Historical fiction)